BATTEN DOWN THE BELFRY

BATTEN DOWN THE BELFRY

DIANE
KELLY

St. Martin's Paperbacks

This is a work of fiction. All of the characters, organizations, and events portrayed in this novel are either products of the author's imagination or are used fictitiously.

First published in the United States by St. Martin's Paperbacks, an imprint of St. Martin's Publishing Group.

BATTEN DOWN THE BELFRY

Copyright © 2022 by Diane Kelly.

For information, address St. Martin's Publishing Group, 120 Broadway, New York, NY 10271.

www.stmartins.com

ISBN: 978-1-250-81603-0

Our books may be purchased in bulk for promotional, educational, or business use. Please contact your local bookseller or the Macmillan Corporate and Premium Sales Department at 1-800-221-7945, ext. 5442, or by email at MacmillanSpecialMarkets@macmillan.com.

Printed in the United States of America

St. Martin's Paperbacks edition / March 2022

10 9 8 7 6 5 4 3 2 1

To Kerrin Parris. Thanks for the friendship, laughs, and sharing ideas about creative home renovations.

ACKNOWLEDGMENTS

This book would not be in a reader's hands if not for the efforts, ideas, and encouragement of an entire team, both official and honorary.

As always, I owe many thanks to the fantastic folks at St. Martin's Press. Thanks to my insightful and industrious editor, Nettie Finn, for the helpful feedback on my stories, as well as all of your other author-wrangling duties. Working with you is a joy! Thanks also to Allison Ziegler, Kayla Janas, Sara Beth Haring, Sarah Haeckel, Talia Sherer, and the rest of the St. Martin's staff for the many things you do to get my books into the hands of readers, reviewers, bloggers, and librarians.

Thanks to Danielle Christopher and Mary Ann Lasher for creating such a unique and adorable cover for this book. I love the colors, and you captured Sawdust's cat curiosity perfectly.

Thanks to my agent, Helen Breitwieser, for all you do to keep my career on track and chugging along.

An ongoing debt of gratitude to my good friend Paula

Highfill, who suggested the house-flipping concept for this series.

Thanks to my nephew, Dylan W. Parsons, BSN, RN, for answering my questions regarding the emergency medical response process. Thanks to my son, Ross, who mentioned something in conversation that gave me the idea for the primary plot of this book. (It's a spoiler, so I won't repeat it here.) Thanks to my friend and former coworker Kerrin Parris for being a never-ending fount of fun story ideas and horrible but hilarious titles (you know what I'm talking about!).

And finally, thanks to all of you wonderful readers who chose this book. Enjoy your time with Whitney, Sawdust, and the gang!

CHAPTER I

THE WINDOWS OF THE SOUL

WHITNEY WHITAKER

On a sunny Monday morning in mid-September, my cousin Buck and I walked out of the real estate office with copies of our closing documents in hand, the most important of which was the deed to the ramshackle country church we'd just bought. The last property we'd flipped, an outdated motel we'd converted into condominiums, had netted us a pretty penny. With any luck, this new flip project would earn us a nice profit, too.

Treating my cousin to some of my sass, I tossed my long blond hair as we headed to Buck's van. "You're welcome."

Buck cocked his head, which bore hair the same pine-shaving shade of blond as mine, but he didn't break stride. "For what?"

"For me making you wealthy beyond your wildest dreams."

He stopped and harrumphed, rubbing his fingers over his bearded chin. "Number one, my dreams of wealth are far wilder than what we've accomplished so far. I have yet to sip my beer from a solid gold mug or have a personal masseuse on staff. Number two, you've got a lot of nerve claiming all the credit. As I recall, I invested most of my savings when you didn't have enough funds to get off the ground. I've worked my fingers to the bone, too." He turned his hand palm up. "Well, maybe not to the bone, but I do have these callouses to show for my work."

Indeed, each finger bore a thick callous, the rough skin a testimony to the hard labor he'd put into our projects. Of course, that wouldn't stop me from ribbing him. *What is family for if not to tease relentlessly?* "Flipping houses was *my* idea, remember?"

He snorted. "Just because it was your idea initially doesn't mean you get all the credit. Besides, our first flip was a bust. My money's still tied up in your place."

It was true. The first house we'd bought to flip was a quaint stone cottage in a well-established, upscale neighborhood of Nashville, Tennessee. Due to unforeseen circumstances involving a body in the flower bed, we'd been unable to sell the house at a reasonable price. Thus, I'd ended up moving into the place with two roommates, my best friend, Colette, and her coworker Emmalee. Fortunately, our second flip, a traditional colonial near the airport, had netted us a decent profit. But it was our third project, the conversion of the motel, that really paid off.

As much as I'd like to think it was my cleverness and determination that earned us the windfall, I had to admit that luck played a huge part in things, too. We'd been lucky to land a property in a prime location, and to buy it for next to nothing at a tax sale. Opportunities like that were rare. Still, I had a feeling this little country church would make a profitable flip, too. Seemed nobody wanted to live in a regular house these days. Everyone wanted to live in a converted school bus, airplane, boat, or shipping container. I'd heard of horse barns, fire stations, and even grain silos being repurposed into residences. Apparently, it was passé to live in something actually intended to be lived in.

Our administrative task complete, it was time to start working on our plans for the property. We swung by my house to pick up my SUV, cat, and roommate. Though Colette had been my best friend for years, she had also recently become Buck's girlfriend. The two had danced around each other for a while before Buck had made a grand romantic gesture by buying a food trailer for Colette, who was a professional chef. Though it might feel stifling to some to have their best friend and family intermingling, I was nothing but happy for the two of them. They both knew all of my secrets anyway. I had nothing to hide.

Colette gave me a grin and a wave as she climbed into Buck's van, and I slid Sawdust's carrier into my SUV. Sawdust lay down in his plastic cage but kept his head up and ears pricked, listening intently as I told him that he'd soon have a whole church to explore. He loved to see new places, so I often brought him along on my jobs to satisfy his cat's curiosity. "It's even got a bell tower," I told him. "Pretty cool, huh?"

My cat cocked his head and replied with a, *Mew?* His question, whatever it was, would likely be answered soon enough.

We headed up Interstate 65, my SUV following behind Buck and Colette. Fifteen minutes later, we exited the freeway and turned down a country road known as Lickton Pike, which ran alongside Walkers Creek. We slowed as we approached our destination. The five-acre property was far wider than it was deep, the parcel stretched along the frontage of the road.

Nestled back in the trees on the left side of the road sat the small, redbrick ranch-style home that had served as the church's parsonage. It might not be a large home, but it was quiet and peaceful. In fact, it was almost entirely obscured by the woods, the trees providing passersby only a glimpse of the front left corner. You'd hardly know it was there. We passed the narrow gravel road that led to the parsonage, drove another hundred yards past the rail-and-wire fencing, and pulled over to the side of the road so Buck could get out and open the gate. Once he had, we turned onto the paved road that led to the church. With so many cracks and potholes, the paved road jostled us as we went along. Sawdust stood in his carrier, his four legs splayed for better balance, a scared look on his usual sweet face. "Sorry, boy. Just a few more bumps." Once the work on the building was done, we'd get an asphalt company out to lay a fresh, flat surface.

The church was a typical country church, wood with faded white paint and a tall steeple that included the bell tower just above the roofline. The church had fallen into disrepair after sitting on the market for nine years without a buyer. The church's governing board had long ago decided it was no longer cost-effective to maintain the outdated building, and had built a modern church closer to the freeway with enough space to accommodate their growing flock. The trees had been cleared next to the church, providing an unobstructed view of the rolling hills that surrounded the city. Despite the pretty view, the property wasn't attractive to most rural buyers, as the acreage wasn't large enough for a farming or ranching operation. What's more, the same man owned all of the property that surrounded it, meaning there was no chance of expansion. The property had long since been paid for and wasn't costing the church anything just sitting there. It had become a long-ignored entry on their balance sheet until I came along.

The cost and hassle of razing the church turned off potential buyers, as well. But I saw potential in the existing buildings and thought the church could be reborn as a stately country home, or maybe a small winery. It could even be reconfigured to serve as a retreat center and spa. With all of the focus on self-care and wellness these days, a spa might be our best bet. The place had lots of potential and I had lots of ideas, though I had yet to settle on one.

I wasn't sure yet about the parsonage, either. Maybe we'd rehab it, or maybe we'd tear it down. Or maybe we could separate the lot it sat on from the remaining acreage and sell it as is for someone else to tackle. For the time being, it would make a good place for us to store our tools and building materials. Construction sites tended to draw thieves looking for equipment they could pawn. Hopefully, any would-be robbers who came out to the church wouldn't realize the house next door was part of the church property, if they even noticed it at all.

After parking my SUV, I donned my hard hat, which I'd decorated with daisy decals. Just because I'd be doing manual labor here didn't mean I had to look like a man. I handed another hard hat to Colette. The church building needed a lot of work, but it was unlikely to fall down on our heads. Still, it was best to take precautions. Better safe than sorry.

I retrieved Sawdust's carrier and carried him to the steps, taking care to avoid the horse droppings along the way. "Where did all this horse poop come from?"

Buck snorted. "From the backside of a horse, nitwit."

I rolled my eyes. "You know what I mean." I glanced around. Sure enough, a half-dozen horses were grazing on the church property. I pointed them out to Buck. "Someone must have a hole in their fence that the horses got through."

Buck grunted in annoyance. "That someone will probably come looking for them soon. I'd better go back and close the gate so they don't get out on the road." He turned and strode down the drive.

Colette's dark curls slid down her back as she turned her brown face up to look at the steeple. She'd grown up in New Orleans, and brought both her Cajun recipes and accent with her when she'd moved to Tennessee for college. "Is that an old-fashioned bell tower?"

"It is," I said. "This church is ninety-two years old. Back in the day, those bells would have been rung to let people know it was time to join in the service."

Colette and I climbed the three wide steps that led to the covered entrance. Thank goodness for the angled roof over the doorway. It had prevented rain from getting in through the two front doors, positioned on either side of the central bell tower. The right door hung cockeyed. The left door had fallen completely off its hinges and lay in the foyer.

We stepped inside. *Uh-oh.* Horse droppings decorated the floor of the high-ceilinged vestibule, too, which could only mean—

Neeeiiigh!

Colette and I looked through the second set of doors to

see a beautiful dark brown horse with a shiny coat and a black mane greeting us from the space between the pews and altar. Sawdust, who'd never seen a horse before, put his front paws on the metal grate of his carrier's door and eyed the enormous beast as she raised her head, seemingly surprised, and not all that happy, to see us.

I groaned. "How are we going to get that horse out of the church?"

"Don't ask me," Colette said. "The last time I was on a horse, it was a Shetland pony and I was all of five years old."

I carried Sawdust into the nave and set his carrier down in the center of the last pew, where he'd be safe should the horse buck or stampede. I patted my thigh and addressed the animal. "Here, horsey-horsey."

The horse didn't move. She just stared at me as if I were an idiot. She was probably right. I'd been treating her like a dog. Canines and equines were entirely different species. Fortunately, an idea came to me. "I've got an apple in my lunch box. Maybe that would work." I hustled back out to my van and grabbed my lunch box.

Buck returned from closing the gate. "Hungry already?"

"There's a horse inside."

"You're full of it."

"I'm not," I said. "But the church is."

Buck followed me in, his brows rising when he saw the horse. "I've heard of people worshiping a golden calf, but never a bay horse."

"Someone would bet on her, though." I whistled the intro to the classic song "Camptown Races."

Buck stepped back to open the remaining front door as

I placed my lunch box on the same pew as Sawdust and retrieved my apple.

"Careful now," Buck advised. "She might spook."

I approached the mare slowly and cautiously, murmuring soothing words. "Good horsey. Got a little something for you. Good horsey."

When I reached her, she eyed the apple I held up. Remembering that horses can accidentally bite fingers when being handfed, I placed the apple on my palm and held it out to her. She wiggled her gums as she tested it, then chomped down, taking it into her mouth and crunching noisily. When she finished, she looked at me expectantly. She hadn't moved an inch.

Buck snorted. "Think maybe you should've tried to lead her outside before giving it to her?"

I narrowed my eyes at him. "If you think you're so smart, you get her out of here."

"Okay," he said. "I will." He, too, approached carefully, reaching up to put a hand on her neck. "C'mon, girl. Let's go outside."

She didn't move for him, either. Colette made an attempt, too, clicking her tongue and motioning with her hand as she backed toward the door. Her efforts were met with equal success. None.

"What now?" I asked.

Footsteps sounded behind us, and we turned to see a man striding into the foyer. A black, pinch-front cowboy hat sat on his head. He wore boots, blue jeans, and an untucked denim shirt with the sleeves rolled up. But while his look might be casual, his clothing was designer. I recognized both the shirt and boots as the Tecovas brand, one that was popular with well-heeled southern folks. The boots were ostrich, too, which was an expensive option. I never understood why the bumpy ostrich leather was so popular. To me, it resembled prickly pear cactus, or a teen suffering the acne that often comes along with puberty. The nice tooling on the hat told me it was a higher-end model, probably one from Stetson's premium line. He carried a large hunting knife in a sheath on his belt and an electric cattle prod in his hand. The prod was bright red with two metal prongs at the end of the shaft. The man brandished it, looking like the devil with a pitchfork, and squeezed the button to activate the charge. *Bzzzt.*

The horse whinnied in fright and backed up a few steps. *If he uses that prod on the horse, I just might have to use my hammer on his head.*

The man had been trailed by another white guy with a scraggly brown beard and an oblong bulge of smokeless tobacco tucked in his cheek. While the men were equally weathered, they were not equally attired. This second man was dressed in more affordable, everyday ranch work attire. His worn Wrangler jeans were paired with heavy-duty work boots, a dusty padded protective vest over a faded T-shirt, and a riding helmet with a narrow, built-in visor. He wore thick, fitted gloves, too. Rather than follow the first man in, this one stopped in the doorway, casually leaned back on the jamb, and turned his head, expelling a gooey brown blob of tobacco and mucus onto the front stoop of the church. *Ew.* My nose crinkled involuntarily in disgust. No longer burdened by the moist mouthful, he issued a whistle and a, "C'mon now, girl!"

The man with the prod gave the button another squeeze. *Bzzt.* "You best git, Chessie."

Realizing her adventure in the church was over now, the horse issued a sigh and plodded past us, down the aisle, her hooves clopping on the wood floor. The man in the vest and gloves backed away from the door so the mare would have plenty of room to exit. The man with the prod walked out after her. We followed them at a safe distance.

As Buck and I went down the steps, I eyed the man who'd come inside more closely. My best guesstimate was that he was around fifty or so, but it was hard to pinpoint his age. He moved with ease, but his short hair was graying, and his once-white skin had been transformed by years of southern sun into a deeply wrinkled, reddish-tan hide resembling beef jerky or caked mud. A black Lab stood stiffly next to him, looking up at him with wary eyes as if waiting for orders, or a reprimand. The dog's body language said he respected the man's authority, but it didn't say he liked the guy. *Shame.* The friendly breed usually liked everyone.

"Chessie?" I repeated. "Is that what you call the horse?"

"It's short for *Chesapeake*, as in *Chesapeake Bay.*" The man slapped the horse's haunch much harder than necessary—*SLAP!*—and she trotted off.

The ranch hand cast his boss a look of disgust much like the one I'd just tossed him. "No call for that, Nolan. She was coming along."

The boss turned on him. "If you don't like the way I do things, you can go work for someone else."

The hand frowned, but said nothing more.

Buck gestured to the other horses grazing about, including a beautiful pure-white stallion with a long, thick mane. "All these horses yours, too?"

"Sure are," said the man we now knew as Nolan. "I breed 'em. Train 'em, too. Arabians are my specialty."

The horse farms dotting the Tennessee landscape played a large role in the state's history and culture. According to historians, Belle Meade Plantation, a Greek revival–style home that sat in southwest Nashville, was the site of the first thoroughbred stud business. The home's gaslights were originally lit with methane from the manure produced by animals on the plantation. Shortly after the Civil War, the Harding family purchased a stallion named Bonnie Scotland, who had been born in England. The stallion proved to be a solid stud horse, and went on to great renown as a sire. Many Kentucky Derby competitors descended from his line, including Seattle Slew, Sea Biscuit, and Secretariat.

For all the romance of horse racing, the industry had come under fire recently after a slew of horses died tragic and public deaths at racetracks. Moreover, due to lack of funding for proper governmental oversight, the illegal practice of soring had long been practiced by heartless horse trainers in the state. The famous Tennessee Walking Horses moved with an exaggerated gait, which was often the result not of training, but rather of various methods of inflicting pain on the animals so that they raised their feet higher. Barbaric trainers applied caustic chemicals, or engaged in "pressure shoeing," which involved cutting a horse's hooves down to the quick and tightly nailing on shoes. The performance horses were often not allowed to roam and graze with other horses, which was critical for a herd animal's sense of well-being and socialization. Rather, when not being trained or shown, these horses were confined to their stalls.

I hoped our neighbor wasn't engaging in any of these cruel practices. I vowed to keep an eye on the activities at his place. I addressed the men. "I suppose you two are here to round all of the horses up. We'd be happy to help you fix your fence if it's come down." I gave Nolan a pointed look. "That way, you won't have to use the prod."

He chuckled mirthlessly. "Don't you worry. Most of these horses learn quick. I only have to use it once on most of them, then they know to do what I ask. 'Course Pegasus was a different story. Took a dozen hits from the prod to get that stubborn SOB to behave."

He pointed the prod at the white horse, who raised his head, eyes wild, and nickered in either fear or fury. The horse reared up on his hind legs in a display of power before his hooves hit the dirt again, sending up small clouds of dust. Pegasus was the perfect name for the horse. Add a pair of feathery wings and he'd look just like the mythical creature.

Pegasus turned and plodded away, but not before casting a look over his strong shoulder that said he just might be biding his time until he could get revenge on his merciless trainer. The man with the bulge of tobacco in his cheek tossed a similar look of repugnance at the man with the prod, though he was more discreet about it than the horse had been.

Nolan slung the prod over his shoulder, like a soldier with a rifle. "I'm not here to round up my horses. Matter of fact, I'm here to tell you folks to get off my property."

If he'd come to deal with Buck, Colette, and me, that meant he'd brought the prod along to scare us, not the horses, didn't it? I exchanged glances with Buck and Colette before turning back to address the man. "What do you mean *your* property?"

He gestured at the building and land. "I own the church and the land it sits on."

Buck frowned and crossed his beefy arms over his chest. "Not trying to start a turf war here, but we've got legal documents that say otherwise."

I clarified. "We closed on the place this morning."

"Don't know anything about that," Nolan said, hooking the thumb of his free hand in the front pocket of his jeans. "But I got my own legal document. I own this place fair and square. Staked my claim through adverse possession."

Having once studied to become a real estate agent, a plan I later abandoned, I knew some things about property rights. Under Tennessee law, a person could obtain ownership of real property by using it openly for seven years after another party purported to convey or assure title, and without a party challenging the ownership claimed. *Adverse possession* was the technical term for what was commonly referred to as squatter's rights. However, the conveyance or assurance had to be recorded with the county clerk to be valid. Surely, whoever had run the title search at our title insurance company would have come across any such filing and advised us accordingly.

The man appeared ready to give us a slap on the haunches and send us on our way, just as he'd done with the horse. When we eyed each other again and made no move to leave, his friendly tone turned ornery. "Don't make me call the sheriff's department on y'all."

Buck straightened to every inch of his height. "Please do. They'll set things straight."

Nolan shook his head. "I didn't want it to be this way, but you've left me no choice." He turned and barked, "Luther! Otto! Let's go!"

Which of those two names belonged to the dog and which belonged to the ranch hand was anyone's guess. The dog trotted alongside Nolan and the hand followed a few paces behind as the horse breeder strode off in the direction of a sprawling Victorian-style farmhouse on the opposite side of the church as the parsonage. My subconscious seemed to be always scouting properties, and it crossed my mind that his place would make an adorable bed-and-breakfast. The porch would be a nice place to sit and read a good book while sipping a large, cold glass of lemonade or iced tea.

As soon as the guy and his ranch hand were out of earshot, Buck turned to me. "What the Sam Hill is he talking about, Whitney?"

I shrugged. "Heck if I know. I suppose we'll have to see what happens."

Colette's eyes flashed in alarm. "I don't like the sound of that. That prod was bad enough. Did you notice that big knife, too? What if he comes back with a rifle? Or a shotgun? Maybe you ought to call law enforcement yourselves."

Buck concurred. "She's got a point. Might be better if we're the first to call."

I agreed. We owned this land. The man and his horses, pretty as they were, were trespassers. Buck and I were the potential victims here. It was best we notify the authorities of the issue. I whipped out my phone and placed a call to the Metropolitan Nashville Police Department nonemergency line. They promised to send an officer out soon.

As I returned my phone to the pocket of my coveralls, I

said, "Time is money. No sense letting this dispute derail us. I'm sure it'll get sorted out. Let's take a look around and come up with some ideas for the place. But first, let's make sure we can defend ourselves."

I armed myself with my largest wrench, slipping it into the hip pocket of my coveralls in easy reach. I often carried the tool for self-defense, just in case. Buck did the same with a claw hammer, sliding it into a loop on his tool belt for easy access. As a chef, Colette was more comfortable handling a ladle, spatula, or whisk. After looking over our tools, she chose to arm herself with a cordless drill. "I like this thing. It feels like a hand mixer."

We walked back inside, again taking care to avoid the piles of horse droppings, some fresh, some dried. The first thing Buck and I did was wrangle the fallen door back into place. He managed to reattach the hinges to the frame, though it hung slightly askew. The door would definitely need to be refinished and rehung later. For now, though, it would allow me to release Sawdust from his cage without fear of him making an escape. I opened the door to his carrier and he gingerly stepped out onto the pew, raising his head to glance around.

While Sawdust set out to explore, Buck crooked his arm around Colette's. He took a step forward, singing the words that went with the wedding march. "Here comes the bride, all dressed in white."

When Colette giggled, I found myself wondering if either of them had considered taking that trip down the aisle. They hadn't openly talked about it yet. Although they'd been dating seriously for only a few weeks, the two had known each other for years, since I'd brought my new friend home with me from college and introduced her to my extended family. It's not like any of us were getting any younger, either. Still, marriage was a big step, not to be taken lightly.

I gazed about the interior of the church. The main room comprised approximately two thousand square feet, enough space for ten rows of pews on each side of a center aisle, with each pew wide enough to seat six adults. I turned around and looked up. The balcony contained six additional pews, three on either side of the aisle. All in all, there was seating for 130 people. But that count was irrelevant, wasn't it? After all, we planned to remove the seating when we rehabbed the place.

I ran a hand over one of the pews. As a trained carpenter, I appreciated nice wood. "These benches are solid oak. In decent shape, too."

Colette said, "Repurposing is all the rage. Maybe you can sell them to help finance the renovation."

We made our way down the aisle and up the two steps to the altar platform. The altar, too, was solid oak, and stood as high as a kitchen countertop.

Colette ran her hand over the smooth surface. "This altar would make a fabulous kitchen island."

Buck gave her a smile. "Then it's all yours."

"As much as I love it," she said, "it won't fit in our kitchen."

She was right. Buck and I had remodeled the small kitchen at the cottage, and it already had a breakfast bar. There was no space to add an island this big.

He shrugged. "We'll hang on to it, then. Until you have a kitchen of your very own."

Might that kitchen be one he'd share with her someday? It seemed possible. After all, she'd seen photos of me and my cousins when we were all at the awkward stage and she hadn't been scared off by the image of Buck with messy hair, a gap-toothed smile, and ears he had yet to grow into. If that hadn't made her think twice, I wasn't sure what would.

Each side of the church featured five windows. Two of the five windows were boarded up on each side, having been broken out by the settling of the building, vandals, or limbs fallen from the large oak that sat on the left side of the building. The late-morning sun filtered through the three stained-glass windows that remained on the east side of the building, creating soft colored patterns on the floors and walls as if we were inside a kaleidoscope. The effect was unique and charming.

I stepped over to one of the windows and admired the artistry that had gone into creating the piece. While some artists merely painted on clear glass to give the effect of stained glass, the practice was a cheap hack. These windows were the real deal, soldered by hand. The panes included bright diamond shapes in varying colors forming a line from top to bottom, with contrasting colors along the sides and a frame of narrow purple pieces around the perimeter. The colors were pretty and playful, uplifting. I sighed. "Would be a shame to replace these gorgeous windows with plain clear glass."

"I suppose," Buck said, "but people generally like to be able to see out of their windows."

He was right, of course, especially when they'd have a nice view of the trees and hills like they would here. Still, it felt like a sacrilege to think about removing the windows even though the place was no longer a house of worship. "We should save them," I suggested. "Maybe we could use them in another project."

We continued to look around. Unlike our earlier projects, where my mind easily came up with ideas for the properties, today my gray matter was giving me nothing. I supposed that was because I liked the space as it was. A happy, colorful gathering space. My brain gave me a nudge, reminding me about another former church, one built in downtown Nashville and originally called the Union Gospel Tabernacle. The church was later transformed into an entertainment venue and renamed the Ryman Auditorium, serving as the original home of the Grand Ole Opry. *Could this church, too, be reborn as an auditorium?*

It took me only a second to decide that it could. The classroom off the vestibule could be repurposed as a dressing room, with dividers set up to provide privacy. The church office could be reconfigured as a combination administrative space and ticket booth. All we'd have to do was refinish the floors, slap a new coat of paint on the walls and exterior, and update the restrooms. The intact stained-glass windows could remain, and we'd replace the broken ones with new windows in colorful patterns of our choosing. The instant the thought hit me, I knew it was the right thing to do. But to be sure, I had to test the acoustics. I opened my mouth and launched into the first verse of the Tennessee classic "Rocky Top."

Buck put his hands over his ears. "Why in the world are you caterwauling?"

Colette took my side. "I thought she sounded surprisingly in tune."

I could've done without the *surprisingly*, but I'd take it. "This place has excellent acoustics. We can't turn this church into a residence. We need to make it into an event venue, a live theater and music hall."

Buck cocked his head and glanced around, assessing the place a second time with my proposal in mind. "Turning it into an auditorium would be a lot less work than a house or spa. But the whole concept of flipping is to fix places up and sell them to someone else."

"True," I said. "But the bottom line is we're rehabbing old properties to make money, right? Just think how much money we could make on ticket sales for shows. There's no end of talent in this town, and not enough places for them to perform." It was true. Singers busked on street corners, in donut shops, at the airport, anywhere they could sing for an audience and earn some tips. "It's nearly impossible to get a seat at the Bluebird Café and some of the other venues. It's a bit of a drive out here, but it would make a unique venue."

"Maybe," Buck said, "but we don't have time to run a theater. Not on top of our carpentry and remodeling work."

"We wouldn't have to," I said. "We could be silent partners, just serve on the board of directors to keep an eye on our investment. We could hire someone to manage the place, get a lineup of acts." A name popped into my mind, as if divinely inspired. "We could lean into the fact that the place is a former church, and call it the Joyful Noise Playhouse."

Colette, who'd grown up in New Orleans, mused aloud. "You could put a statue of Saint Cecilia out front. She's the patron saint of musicians. One of Saint Genesius, too. He's the patron saint of actors, dancers, and comedians. Clowns, too."

Buck said, "Sounds like you ladies have made up your minds. I know better than to try to fight you on it."

Colette tossed him a smile. "Smart man."

"Then it's settled," I said. "We'll turn this place into Nashville's newest and hottest performance venue."

CHAPTER 2

FOR WHOM THE BELL TOLLS

WHITNEY

Sawdust trotted along with us as we returned to the vestibule.

Colette pointed to the closed door situated between the two exterior doors. A faded sign tacked to the door read AUTHORIZED PERSONNEL ONLY. "I'd love to go up in the bell tower."

Buck and I had ventured up the narrow, winding staircase when touring the property with the church's Realtor. The tower provided a bird's-eye view of the bucolic countryside surrounding the church.

Buck hunched over and dragged his leg along as he approached the belfry door, doing his best Quasimodo impression. "I must go ring the bell."

I pulled the ring of keys from my pocket, locating the one for the bell-tower door. I unlocked it and stepped back to let Colette lead the way. Naturally, Sawdust thought he should forge the trail, and he hopped up the wood steps ahead of us. The winding staircase was hardly more than a glorified ladder, but at least it had a railing on the lower flights. The steps made five sharp, ninety-degree turns as they took us up twenty feet to the tower, which was open on all sides to allow the sound of the bells to emanate. Fortunately, a decorative railing prevented people—and my precious cat—from falling out of the tower through the arched openings. We stopped and stood on the narrow platform at the top, gazing out through the open arches and over the treetops.

I pointed to the south. "Look," I told Colette. "You can see the tops of the skyscrapers downtown."

"Wow!" she said. "This view is amazing!"

It was, indeed. Besides the city skyline, we could see across the beautiful landscape in every direction, over the rolling wooded hills and the bucolic farms with their barns, ponds, and paddocks. We could see the entirety of our pushy neighbor's horse farm, too, all the way from the large, fancy barn near the front of his property to an older, smaller one at the far western end. The property was divided into a couple of large pastures, several smaller corrals, even smaller pens, and two riding arenas, one covered with a metal roof and the other open to the sun. Inside both arenas stood horse jumps of varying heights formed by black-and-white-striped poles resting on vertical supports. A cross-country course was spread about one of the pastures, with logs, narrow pools, trees, and other obstacles for the horse to navigate.

My gaze swept the perimeter of our property, noting the small flags our surveyor had placed here and there to note the boundary. Though it was not apparent simply from looking at our property, the parcel spanned two counties, Davidson and Sumner. The bulk of it sat within the Davidson County limits, with only a triangle-shaped sliver at the front edge lying within Sumner County. I wondered if our neighbor had somehow confused his property's boundary with that of Sumner County. He might have assumed his parcel ran all the way to the border rather than stopping just short of it.

A gentle breeze blew through the opening of the bell tower, causing the rope to sway. The movement caught Sawdust's eye. When he couldn't reach the thick rope with an outstretched paw from the platform, he retreated a few steps down and grabbed at it as it swung close, catching it with his claws. Problem was, when he tried to let go, he discovered the claws of his front right paw were stuck in the roughly textured surface. He backed down a step or two, the motion pulling down just enough on the rope to ring the bell softly. *Dong. Dong.*

"Don't worry, baby. Mommy's coming." I scuttled down the steps after him and sat down on a step to gently extricate his claws from the rope. Relieved, Sawdust sat back on his haunches.

Buck said, "My turn." He grabbed the rope and yanked it down, ringing the bell for all it was worth. *DING! DONG! DING! DONG!* The sound echoed at deafening decibels inside the tower. Colette and I cupped our hands over our ears to protect our eardrums.

"Cool it, Quasimodo!" I hollered.

Down below, we saw a Nashville police department cruiser pull up to the closed gate. I scooped Sawdust up in my arms while Buck dropped the rope and scrambled down the stairs to go let the officer through. Colette and I followed him down the steps. After I put Sawdust safely back into his carrier, we went outside to speak to the police officer.

Meanwhile, the interloper from next door was heading our way across our horse-doody-covered land with his cattle prod in hand, his obedient dog by his side, and a Sumner County deputy in tow. Technically, the deputy was out of his jurisdiction on this part of our property, which sat in Davidson County, but I figured I wouldn't earn points with either law enforcement officer by pointing that out. The ranch hand had stayed behind. I could see him in the distance, using a hoist and pulley system to lift bales of hay from the back of his dented, dusty blue pickup truck into the loft of the horse barn. His boss's much nicer extended-cab pickup sat in the paved driveway, both the black paint and chrome accents gleaming in the sun.

Once we were all gathered, the two officers greeted each other. The deputy turned to me and Buck and introduced himself, offering his hand. "I'm Deputy Atchison."

The police officer looked among the group. "What's up, folks?"

Before I could respond to the officer we'd summoned, our neighbor said, "They're trespassing on my property. Just waltzed right in like they own the place."

"We *do* own the place," I said, tempted to perform a little waltz just to get a dig in. With the police officers on-site, the hunting knife and cattle prod didn't scare me quite as much.

"Your claim's not legal." He waved a piece of paper. "See this? I filed an adverse possession notice at the courthouse, just like the law says to do. It's certified and everything."

I figured I might as well get the facts, at least as he claimed them to be. "When did you file the notice?"

"Eight years ago," he said. "Right after I talked to the

pastor of the church and he asked me to remove my horses. I told him there was no sense in this land just sitting idle. I said if he wanted me and my horses gone, he'd have to call the law or file charges against me. I figured he wouldn't do anything about it and I was right." He issued a nasty chuckle. "Guess he decided whoever bought the property could deal with me."

Apparently, that's where Buck and I came in. I sighed inwardly. "Our title company didn't find a cloud on the title," I told the officers. "They wouldn't have issued a policy if they had." In other words, the document had likely been filed improperly or was insufficient to transfer ownership to the man. Then again, on rare occasions, valid property filings were accidentally overlooked. *Could we have bought a property the church no longer legally owned?*

The police officer waggled his fingers, inviting the man to hand the notice to him. I eased up next to the officer and read it over his shoulder. The page was a copy of a "Notice of Adverse Possession" that had been typed up on a computer. The notice stated that Nolan Irvin Sibley thereby proclaimed adverse possession of the real property owned by the Walkers Creek Community Church. The notice provided the church's address, which was in Nashville, but it provided no parcel or lot number. As Nolan said, it had been filed more than eight years earlier. The Sumner County Clerk had applied the certification stamp, but all that proved was that the copy was an exact duplicate of the original paperwork filed with the county and the date the document was filed. It didn't prove the legal validity of the document. His misconception was a common one, much like many people who thought getting a document notarized made it legally binding. All notarization proved was that the people who signed the paperwork had provided proof of their identity. It was merely an assurance that the signatures were valid, not that the document was.

I attempted to explain this to Mr. Sibley. "Just because the document is certified doesn't mean it's lawfully binding." I pointed to the address on the page. "The address you show for the church here? It's in Nashville."

"That doesn't mean anything," he argued. "Lots of people have addresses that don't technically fall within the city limits. They just use the name of the closest city to make things easier on the post office."

He had a point. Mailing addresses didn't necessary correspond to legal jurisdictions and boundaries. Even so, his document still didn't seem valid to me. "Most of the church property is in Davidson County," I said. "Only a small part sits in Sumner County."

"That's where you're wrong," he snapped. "Guess you didn't see the county limits sign out there." He pointed to a sign just past the western end of our property.

"That sign marks only where the county line crosses the road," I said. "The line doesn't run straight back from the road. It angles across the front of our acreage toward yours." We'd paid a grand to a surveyor who'd told us as much, even given us a map to prove it. "Did you file a notice in Davidson County, too?"

"No," he said. "Even if the land sits in two counties as you claim, the land was all owned by the same party and treated as one combined estate. There'd be no need for me to file in Davidson County, too."

I have my doubts about that. "Did your attorney advise

you that filing in Sumner County was sufficient to claim the entire church property? Even the part outside Sumner County?"

He scoffed. "I didn't need an attorney. I run one of the largest and most successful horse-breeding operations in the area. I know what I'm doing. Real estate isn't rocket science. But I suppose you folks aren't sophisticated enough to understand these legal technicalities."

Buck, Colette, and I exchanged glances. The guy had essentially called us stupid. *What an arrogant boor.* To paraphrase Mark Twain, all that was needed for sure success was ignorance and confidence. This man seemed to have both in spades. But while he might run a profitable horse farm, he clearly wasn't a real estate expert.

Because the man didn't seem amenable to reason, I turned my attention back to the law enforcement officers. "My cousin and I bought the church property and parsonage this morning. I've got paperwork in my SUV that'll prove it."

The cop jerked his head to indicate our cars. "Go get it. Let's take a look."

I scurried over to my vehicle and retrieved the folder with the paperwork. I handed it to the cop, and he and the deputy huddled to read it over. I pointed out the survey we'd had done, which depicted a blueprint of the property, complete with outlines for the structures and a dotted line forming a triangle angling eastward across the front of the acreage, delineating the division between Sumner and Davidson County. The triangle was wide, but not tall, comprising only a nominal amount of land, about a fourth of an acre.

After flipping through the closing documents, the deputy turned to our neighbor. "This paperwork looks legit to me, Mr. Sibley."

"Me too," said the cop.

"Well, it's not, boys." His condescending tone and cocky grin said he thought he was much smarter than the law enforcement officers, too. "My claim has priority over theirs. This isn't my first rodeo. I've filed for adverse possession before. It's how I got the six acres east of my pond."

The deputy looked to the police officer and said, "Sounds like a civil issue to me."

"Me too," the cop agreed. "You folks will have to hash things out in court. But, for now, I've got to go with what I see here." He held the paperwork up before handing it back to me. "The documentation seems to prove that Mr. and Mrs. Whitaker own the church and acreage, so you'll need to remove your horses for now, Mr. Sibley."

He threw up his hands, raising the prod into the sky like the Greek god Poseidon with his trident, only Sibley's weapon had just two prongs rather than three. "This is an outrage!"

Seemed that trying to steal land, a building, and a house from a church group was the real outrage, but maybe that was just me. Even so, it would be best to make some effort to appease the man. We'd be neighbors, after all, and had to learn to get along. Besides, we'd have to get the property rezoned from a religious use property to a commercial theater. He could fight our plans in court, maybe even win. There would be more traffic, people, and noise here later at night after we finished the renovations and the venue was operating. What's more, I didn't trust the guy to control his temper. The knife might be merely for use around his property, but the prod proved he had a mean streak. "If you'll let me take a photo of your adverse possession notice," I said, "I'd be happy to run it by our title company and see what they tell us."

"You do that!" he spat. "They'll tell you I'm right." He held out the paper.

I snapped a pic with my phone, careful to keep one eye on the prod as I did so. "Thanks. I'll be in touch."

Nolan said nothing more, just cast me and Buck a glare and shook his head before storming off. The deputy went with him, helping Sibley round the horses up and get them all headed in the direction of his property. Fortunately, the prod was not needed. The horses went willingly if nervously, casting glances over their shoulders as Sibley walked behind them, brandishing the prod and hollering at them. *Sheesh.* Had he never heard of positive reinforcement?

Buck and I thanked the deputy and the police officer, and they headed on their way, too.

Once Buck, Colette, and I were alone again, my cousin exhaled sharply. "First thing I'm doing is putting up a pipe fence set in concrete. That'll send that man a message."

"I'm not sure that's a good idea," I said. "We've got to be careful not to antagonize him. He could make things miserable for us, set us back weeks or even months. He could even prevent us from getting the property rezoned."

Buck muttered a curse. "Why is it that every time we try one of these flips, something goes wrong?"

He had a point, but we'd mostly managed to overcome the problems, too. "No sense getting all worked up. Chances are everything will work out." Even as I said the words, I didn't entirely believe them. The man might not have a leg to stand on legally, but he could make things really difficult for us. Still, there was nothing wrong with trying to remain positive, forging ahead, and crossing the bridges as they came. "Let's go take a look at the parsonage."

The three of us headed across the church property, taking an overgrown dirt path that led into the trees and onto the wooded lot of the parsonage. We stopped in front of the house. The parsonage was a traditional redbrick ranch-style home, around fifteen hundred square feet, and had been built four decades after the church was erected. Though it was old now, too, I supposed it had replaced an older residence when it had been built. Many of the bricks were chipped or cracked, and the mortar was loose in a number of places, which meant it had let moisture seep into the structure. The house had a gravel driveway that led to a two-car garage. The metal doors bore the dings and dents that come from years of use. The gutters overflowed with leaves and debris, and the windows were covered in years of accumulated dust. The concrete walkway from the driveway to the door had settled unevenly, posing a tripping hazard.

Buck ran his fingers over his bearded chin, thinking. "What should we do with this parsonage? Tear it down? Sell it?"

"Neither." Colette wagged her finger. "You should turn it into a bistro and bar, one where the people can eat a pre-show meal, or enjoy dessert, cocktails, or coffee after the show."

I considered the possibility. "The place has a lot of cosmetic problems, but it's got good bones." Buck and I had carefully inspected it before making our offer. "It just might have potential as a restaurant." I eyed my best friend. "Especially if you were in charge."

Colette's brows rose and her mouth fell open. "Are you for real?"

I shrugged. "Why not? You're the best chef I know."

Her eyes gleamed as she considered the prospect. "It's always been my dream to run my own restaurant."

Buck asked, "Would you call it Voodoo Vittles and serve Cajun food, like you do with your food trailer?"

She shook her head. "The food trailer has been fun, and I still want to run the trailer at festivals and events. But it would be nice to build on that, take the next step, do something bigger and different." She looked up at the sky over the parsonage, as if willing divine inspiration to come her way. It did. She raised both hands as if envisioning a sign over the door. "We'll call it the Collection Plate Café."

The moniker was perfect, a fun nod to the property's former identity. "I love that name!"

Colette wasted no time coming up with design ideas. "We could remove the garage doors, paint the floor and walls, and turn the garage space into a covered patio for outdoor dining."

Buck nodded thoughtfully and built on her concepts, offering his expertise. "That could work. But instead of eliminating doors entirely, we should replace the garage doors with those clear glass type. That way, the space would be usable in winter, too. You'd just need a few of those portable heaters to keep the space warm."

Colette grinned. "Now you're talking. It would make a nice room for people who want to reserve a private space for small gatherings, too. Baby showers, graduations, anniversaries, birthdays. That kind of thing."

Buck had installed raised garden beds in our backyard at home so that Colette would have fresh vegetables to cook with. I asked whether she might want to do the same here.

"Definitely," she said. "Farm-to-table is very popular right now. Maybe we could even add some fruit trees and a greenhouse to extend the growing season." She continued to think out loud. "I'm sure I could find some sort of gold-colored dinnerware to go along with the collection plate theme. I could carry the theme into the menu, too. There's a candy-like dessert made of manna and nuts, and spiced with cardamom. One of the restaurant's kitchen staff did a tour of duty in Iraq and mentioned it to me. I could bake some specialty bread loaves. An olive sampler appetizer. Something with figs."

"Don't forget apples," Buck said. "That's the first food mentioned in the Bible."

"I could make apple popovers," Colette said, thinking aloud. "The bar could serve an Original Sin Sour Appletini."

"If the café will have a bar," I said, "we'll need to apply for a liquor license." While Tennessee was known for whiskey, and alcohol was a regular part of the state's culture, the fact that the café would serve alcoholic drinks could be another source of contention with the other property owners out here. But maybe we could offer concessions to appease them. We could put in noise abatement walls and use low, downward-facing outdoor lighting that wouldn't spill over onto their properties.

I led Buck and Colette to the door, unlocked it, and we went inside. The place was simple, with a square foyer bordered on the left by a living room with a brick fireplace, and on the right by an open kitchen with an L-shaped countertop. Ahead was a hallway that led to three bedrooms, a master with a full bath and two smaller secondary bedrooms with a full bath situated between them and the master. We quickly assessed which walls were load bearing, and which could come down to open up the space.

Buck pointed out that a bar could easily be installed along the back wall of the living room, with space for stools and tables in front of it. The fireplace could remain and be used in winter to add some ambiance. Though the wood paneling in the room might appear outdated in a residence, it would be at home in a bar setting, which was normally decorated in dark colors and dimly lit.

I imagined some décor ideas. "We could display a collection of colorful mismatched plates on shelves in the dining area. It would be a different take on the term *collection plate*."

Colette squealed and clutched her hands to her chest. "That would look so cute!"

We spent a few more minutes discussing flooring, paint, bathroom updates, and the kitchen redesign, which would necessitate ordering commercial appliances. Colette and I would spend some time on Pinterest later, looking at more design and décor options. I'd need to find a local stained-glass artist, too, who could make replacement windows for the church building. Despite the rocky start due to Mr. Sibley's specious land claim, I felt confident that once the title matter was sorted out, we'd have a moneymaking venture on our hands.

Monday evening, I ran a search online in the Sumner County property records. The tax notices helped me piece things together, and told me Sibley's history. He'd purchased the twelve-acre tract next to the church nearly two decades ago. He'd since bought out all the adjacent landowners—except the one whose land he'd acquired through adverse possession—thus expanding his holdings to forty-seven acres total. He appeared to be a man on a mission, amassing an empire in northeast Nashville. But just because he might have set his sights on the former church property didn't mean he was going to get it. It belonged to Buck and me, and I was going to fight for it.

On Tuesday morning, Sawdust and I arrived at the property before Buck. I climbed out of my SUV to open the gate. "What the—?" I muttered to myself. A heavy chain and padlock secured the gate. There was no doubt in my mind who'd attached it. *Nolan Sibley.*

I looked up to see Sibley's horses grazing on the dewy grasses around the church building. One noticed me and clopped over to the gate to greet me. She wasn't at fault here. Only her owner was. No sense treating her like the enemy.

"Hello, horsey." I reached out and scratched her behind the ears, same as I did for Sawdust when he came around, looking for love and attention. Just like my cat, the horse angled her head and leaned into the scratch. "You're a pretty, pretty girl."

She nickered as if to say she agreed with me.

I heard an engine start up and glanced over to see a white SUV in Sibley's driveway. A logo and black lettering on the driver's door told me it was a business vehicle, though it was too far off for me to make out the image or read the words. The driver made a three-point turn and headed down the driveway toward the road. The passenger side of the vehicle was plain white, bearing no lettering or logo. The driver turned out of Sibley's driveway and headed off in the opposite direction. There was no sign of the ranch hand's old blue pickup this morning. I supposed he either had the day off or was occupied elsewhere.

The sounds of another vehicle drew my attention to the roadway to the west. Buck approached in his van. When he pulled up, he unrolled his window to speak to me. "Shoo that horse away so we can get inside."

I took my hand from the horse and lifted the heavy chain, releasing it to let it clang back into place. "We can't get in with this lock and chain on the gate."

Buck scowled and cursed under his breath.

"Should we call the police out again?" I asked.

"No. I'm going to handle this myself." Buck shifted his van into park and turned it off. He climbed out, circled around to the back, and opened the door, reaching into the cargo bay to grab a tool. He emerged with a pair of bolt cutters in his hands. One quick snip later and the chain fell to the ground at our feet. *Clink.*

After picking up the lock and chain and stowing them in my SUV, I returned to the gate, put a hand on the horse's withers to direct her back, and swung it open, being careful not to let the horse escape. Buck drove through and climbed out so that the two of us could trade places. I drove my SUV through and we closed the gate behind us.

We were fastening tarps over the broken windows a few minutes later when my phone chimed in the pocket of my coveralls with an incoming call. I tugged off my right glove and retrieved my phone, checking the screen. "It's the title company."

Buck took a deep breath. "I hope it's good news."

To our relief, it was. The title company's attorney said they'd searched the records in both Davidson and Sumner counties a second time. They'd found nothing in the Davidson County records. Though they'd located Sibley's filing in Sumner County by the date on the copy I'd sent them, they'd concluded it wasn't legally binding. "It's no wonder we didn't uncover it earlier. His notice doesn't identify the property by address or parcel number. My opinion is that it's insufficient to give rise to a valid adverse possession claim." She went on to say that, even if it were somehow deemed valid, it would apply only to the quarter acre of the property that sat in Sumner County. That meant the church and parsonage were not at risk. *Phew.* We'd dodged a bullet.

"Where do we go from here?" I asked.

"I'll draft a cease-and-desist letter warning Mr. Sibley not to trespass on your property or harass you or legal action will be taken. I'll send it by overnight express."

"Can you tell him to keep his horses off the church grounds, too?" As pretty as the horses were, they left a lot of poop scattered about. I was also afraid they could get injured. Buck and I would be piling construction debris outside as we performed the demolition work, and it wouldn't be safe to have large animals milling about.

"Good point," the attorney agreed. "I'll insist he keep his horses away, too."

After ending the call and updating Buck, I drove to a country grocer and bought some carrots. Meanwhile, my cousin found the nearest hardware store.

We met back up at the property an hour later. After using Sibley's chain and our own new padlock to secure the front gate, we used the carrots to lure the horses back to Sibley's land. I gave the bay one last pat as she sauntered through the gate Sibley had installed in the fence separating our property from his. "Bye, sweetie."

Once her huge haunches had passed through, Buck closed the gate behind her. We used two spare wooden sawhorses to erect a simple barrier on our side of the gate, as well. The rudimentary fence would prevent the horses from coming through if Sibley opened the gate on his side. Once the makeshift fence was finished, Buck nailed a NO TRESPASSING sign to one of the sawhorses, facing Sibley's property. Our claim was thus laid.

We were wrangling tarps over the broken windows a half hour later when *HOOOOOOONK!*

Sibley had pulled his pickup truck up to our gate and was trying to get our attention. He climbed out to stand next to the open driver's door.

"Ignore him," Buck said, casting the man an irritated look before continuing to nail the tarp into place.

When we didn't respond, Sibley tried again. He reached

his hand into the truck and mashed on the steering wheel. *HONK! HONK-HONK-HONK! HOOOONK!*

I reached down to my toolbox and made a show of putting on my noise-canceling ear protectors. The puffy ear coverings made me look like a hardworking blue-collar Princess Leia. Buck did the same.

HOOOOOOOOOOOOOOOOOOOOOOOONK!

When the honking got him nowhere, Sibley reached down to the ground, picked up a rock, and hurled it in our direction. It hit the side of the church building with a thunk, missing me by only a few feet. I wasn't sure whether he'd intended to hit me and had bad aim or whether he had a good arm and only intended to get our attention but, either way, even Princess Leia couldn't ignore Sibley now. I yanked off my ear protectors. So did Buck. My cousin muttered a curse that would've gotten his mouth washed out with soap if we were two decades younger and his mother had overheard it.

"We're going to have to talk to him." I raised a hand to let Sibley know we were coming, and exchanged my ear protectors for the wrench, which I slipped into my pocket. Buck again armed himself with a hammer. Throwing rocks was bad enough. For all we knew, this guy could have a rifle or shotgun on him. Many rural residents owned guns, after all. Better safe than sorry. I hated to think it would come to violence, but this man seemed just mean, stubborn, and crazy enough to take it there.

Luckily for us, he didn't pick up another rock and he didn't pull a gun. Still, Buck and I stopped well back from the gate. No sense making ourselves an easy target.

Sibley had brought both his dog and his ranch hand with

him, probably as a show of force, but the hand's disinterested expression said he could not care less about his boss's problems. The dog just looked happy to be included in whatever was going on. He stood on the backseat, his tail wagging as he hung his head out of the window, eyeing us.

Sibley jabbed his finger over the gate, intruding on our airspace, and his eyes blazed with rage. "You two got a lot of nerve keeping a man from entering his own property!"

"That's the thing," I told Mr. Sibley. "It's *not* your property. Our attorney looked into things, and you didn't list a parcel number or address on your notice. Your claim is not legally valid. She's going to send you a letter to that effect. It'll be delivered tomorrow."

"Your lawyer's an idiot," he snapped. "I followed the law to the letter. I looked it all up online."

Buck groaned. "Google isn't a substitute for a law degree. I'm sure you did your best, but we're going to trust our counsel."

Putting the matter in our attorney's hands was a good idea. Sibley should do the same. "You should contact your own attorney," I suggested. "They could help you."

Sibley snorted. "I'm not giving my hard-earned money to some low-life ambulance chaser."

Buck snorted right back. "'Course not. You're not dumb enough to call a personal injury attorney to handle a real estate matter."

It was a veiled insult, but Sibley was too angry or dim to realize it. His ranch hand wasn't, though. A smirk tugged at the man's mouth, pulling his lower lip tight over the ever-present bulge of chewing tobacco. I wondered if he'd tried to talk some sense into his boss before they'd headed over here. I had a feeling that, even if he had, Sibley wouldn't have listened. I couldn't imagine having to work for such a hothead. It couldn't be pleasant. Why didn't the guy seek employment elsewhere?

Buck put the matter to rest, at least for the time being. "Look, Nolan. There's no point in you and us arguing about this. We'll never see eye to eye. This is in our attorney's hands now. You got a problem, you can talk to her after you get the cease-and-desist warning tomorrow. We won't be speaking with you again about it, no matter how many times you honk your horn or how many rocks you throw. In fact, if you throw another rock, we'll call the police out here to arrest you for assault. Hear me? You have a good day now."

With that, Buck and I turned and headed back to the church. I moved fast and cast glances back over my shoulder in case Sibley threw a rock after us or pulled a firearm. The man gave me the shivers.

CHAPTER 3

I DO DECLARE

WHITNEY

The next day, I drove to the Artistry in Glass studio in Franklin, a quaint town just south of Nashville with a trendy, artsy vibe. I'd discovered the artist, Laurel Cromwell, online. Those who'd bought her pieces had given her fantastic reviews, saying that she had made unique, quality pieces for a better price than many other glass artists in the area. Although I wanted to secure some nice pieces for the Joyful Noise Playhouse, I didn't want to bust our budget. A few splurges here and there could quickly eat up our available funds. While Buck handled most of the structural details on our projects, he left the design aspects up to me. With each of us staying mostly in our own lane, we managed to avoid butting heads too often, so the choice of stained glass would be entirely up to me.

On my way to Laurel's studio I drove past the Carter House, a significant site in the Civil War Battle of Franklin. Tennessee had initially remained with the United States, voting against separating. Those in the mountainous eastern part of the state owned few slaves and wanted to stay with the Union. Those in the more agricultural western part voted heavily in favor of separation. It was middle Tennessee that swung the second vote, some changing their minds after men became at risk of conscription into the federal army. Tennessee was thus the last state to secede. Battles later raged in the towns of Murfreesboro, Columbia, and Spring Hill, before the big battles in Franklin and Nashville.

Federal troops took over Carter House and the family was forced to take cover in their basement as the battle raged in their yard. The Carters' own son, who had joined the Confederate forces, was mortally wounded on the grounds of his childhood home and later died in the house. The structure bore holes showing where it had been struck by artillery.

Guided by the disembodied voice of the maps app, I turned into driveway of Laurel's studio on Hillsboro Pike. Her studio was in a small, older one-story strip center, between a florist and a bagel shop. Behind the regular clear glass in her front windows, her beautiful pieces were displayed. Large, long pieces in wooden frames, with glass cut and shaped into designs of flowers and birds. A square piece featured a flowering dogwood, a relatively small tree common to the region. Small suncatchers each featured a single flower or bird. Others featured geometric patterns. The Tiffany lampshades were even more impressive. Classic, classy, and gorgeous. I made a mental note to buy a Tiffany-style chandelier and lights for the playhouse. Light fixtures could be purchased cheaper machine-made from a home improvement outlet rather than having them custom-made by hand by an artist. But with the playhouse windows being visible from the seats, they were worth the splurge for artisan pieces.

The bells rang as I stepped inside. A woman's voice called through an open door at the back of the space, "Welcome! I'll be right with you!"

While I waited, I ventured up to the counter. Hanging on the wall behind the register were three five-by-seven photographs, school pictures of three blond children, a boy who appeared to be in his mid-teens and two younger girls who I guesstimated to be around eight and ten, give or take. All offered their best smiles, the youngest's displaying a mix of baby and permanent teeth. There was also a family portrait of the three children with a fortyish blond woman, presumably Laurel herself. Conspicuously absent was a husband to Laurel and father to the children. Looked like her marriage had fallen into the 50 percent that ended in divorce. At least she'd gotten three adorable kids out of the deal.

A few seconds later, a woman emerged from the back room. She was indeed the woman from the photo. She was short, only a hair over five feet tall, with the rounded physique that often comes with middle age and a slowing metabolism. She'd whisked her golden-blond hair into a messy knot on top of her head, the carefree coif looking cute with the ripped jeans, bright red ankle boots, and shapeless black blouse she wore. Her makeup and jewelry were as colorful as her artistic creations. She offered me a warm smile as she approached. "Hi, there. I'm Laurel. How can I help you?"

"My cousin and I just bought a former church property. We're looking to replace some stained-glass windows." I whipped out my phone to show her photos of the building and existing windows. "Four are broken out and need to be replaced. We'd like to put in something unique that goes along with our plan to turn the place into a playhouse for performances."

"What a fun idea!" She tapped a red nail against her chin as she thought. "Maybe a design with musical notes? A piano keyboard? A guitar and a banjo? Something like that?"

"Exactly," I said, glad to sense that she and I were on the same wavelength. "Maybe a window with drama masks, too?" After all, the venue would likely host some plays or musicals. Heck, maybe we could even hold an annual follies fundraiser for a local charity.

"What size do you need?" Laurel asked.

I gave her the dimensions.

"Custom windows that size will run around three grand depending on how intricate the design is," she said. "If that's not within your price range, we could look at some semi-custom or standard designs."

"We're on a budget," I said, "so I'd love to see the more affordable options, too."

"This way." She motioned for me to follow her over to the counter. She circled around the back and pulled a notebook from under the counter. She laid it on the countertop, facing me, and turned the pages to show me the possibilities. She pointed to a page that showed several windows with glass stripes along the bottom half and differing images above. An iris, which was the state flower of Tennessee. A mockingbird and zebra swallowtail butterfly, which were the state bird and butterfly, respectively. "I made those for a state senator," she said. "He wanted pieces that represented the state to hang in his office windows for privacy."

I leaned in to take a closer look. The soldering was smooth, the lines clean, and the glass shapes were precisely cut and ground. No irregular shapes filled in with solder here. "They're absolutely beautiful," I said. "Your workmanship is very high quality."

She beamed. "Thanks. I take a lot of pride in my pieces." She gestured to my coveralls. "What do you do, exactly?"

"Carpentry, mostly."

"Ah. A fellow artisan, a kindred spirit. You know the feeling of a job well done, then."

"I do." When I completed a carpentry project, turned raw wood into a functional work of art, I felt the same self-satisfaction at creating something beautiful. Not everyone understood this feeling. Laurel and I shared a smile at this connection.

Laurel flipped through a few more pages of the semi-custom pieces before showing me some standard windows. "These designs would run seventeen hundred. I can offer better pricing on these because I buy the glass in bulk and the shapes are less intricate and time-consuming. Also, I can work on more than one of them at a time, so it's more efficient." She also showed me some patterns that would cost only eight hundred dollars. The cheapest designs contained mostly straight edges.

I looked up from the notebooks. "I take it that circles and curves are harder to make than straight lines?"

"They are," she said. "There's much more grinding involved." She pulled out a charcoal pencil and sketch pad. "While you're looking through the book, I'll sketch a mock-up of some custom designs with the musical notes and instruments and drama masks. That might give you a better idea of which way you want to go."

"I appreciate that."

As she took a seat on a stool behind the desk to work on her sketches, I continued to look through the notebook. There were windows with shamrocks for an Irish pub. One with the name of the business, a bakery, spelled out in glass. Even a humorous window depicting a series of different-colored eyes that she'd made for the transom of an optometrist's office.

Laurel pulled out some colored pencils to do some quick shading on her sketches. When she finished her doodling, she set her sketchbook on the counter and turned it to face me. She'd nailed it. One of the windows had black and white piano keys along one side, with a guitar, fiddle, and banjo in a vertical line up the piece. Musical notes were interspersed between them at playful angles. The other design depicted the comedy and tragedy drama masks, one of the mouths open in anguish, the other open in laughter. A ribbon-like design connected them. Below, a pink pointe shoe met toe-to-toe with a high-heeled woman's tap shoe. She'd managed to combine both the theater and dance elements in one window.

"I love them!" I told her, clapping my hands in delight. "I'd like to order those two, as well as one each in these standard designs." I turned the book around to face her and turned to the first design, which she'd dubbed Cheerful Garden. The piece incorporated a variety of flowers in a rainbow of colors, from red roses and blue morning glories to yellow and white daisies, along with butterflies, bumble bees, and dragonflies. The other design, called Surprise in the Skies, had a bright yellow semicircular sunrise at the bottom, with white clouds and a blue sky above. The color of the sky grew darker near the top, a gorgeous midnight blue with a full moon, stars, distant planets, and even a whimsical flying saucer with two neon-green aliens in the cockpit. Though I liked the piece myself, another reason I chose it was for the astronomy theme. My boyfriend, a homicide detective named Collin Flynn, was an avid stargazer and often dragged me out to the middle of nowhere in the wee hours of the night to see one celestial event or another. Collin and I had met when he investigated the body found at our first flip house. He'd get a kick out of the piece, as well as the fact that I'd given him a small nod in our project.

She filled out the forms for my order and I paid her the 25 percent deposit.

"I'll have them ready in about a month," she said. "Delivery is included in the price."

"Great! Thanks." I could hardly wait to see them.

Over the next month, Sibley stayed off our property. The guy had filed a petition for something called a declaratory judgment. Our attorney explained that when only the law but not the facts is in dispute a party can ask a judge to rule on the law only. We all agreed on what paperwork had been filed with the county clerks. We simply disagreed on whether Sibley's notice was legally adequate to support his claim. A hearing would be held in a few weeks.

"Adverse possession is a relatively obscure and untested area of law," our attorney said. "There are very few decided cases addressing the issue. That said, the law doesn't favor dispossessing an owner of their property unfairly. I don't think Mr. Sibley has a leg to stand on, but the worst-case scenario is you lose the Sumner County portion of your property."

In the petition, Sibley argued that he had a right to the entire property, because anyone buying the piece of land should realize it sat in two counties, and that the buyer should have fully searched records in both jurisdictions. I was no legal expert, but it seemed a weak argument to me. There were good reasons why deeds, liens, and encumbrances had to be properly recorded to be enforceable. Even so, a little bit of worry wriggled in my gut. What if we put time and money into the remodel, only to lose the property in the court battle?

To relieve our anxiety and put the matter to rest, we offered Sibley $2,000 to waive any rights he might have. We hoped he'd bite and that we could resolve the matter quickly. He didn't. In fact, he interpreted our offer as a validation of his claim and only seemed to be emboldened by it, as if he'd smelled blood and wanted a better, bigger taste. He counteroffered to release his claim for half a million dollars. *Bloodsucker.* We'd paid only a little over $300,000 for the property when we'd bought it from the church. We were certainly not going to buy the property all over again, especially at a ridiculous price from someone who didn't even own it.

We continued our work on the property, doing our best to ignore both Sibley and his specious, though bothersome, claim. He went about his horse-breeding business, his hired hand coming and going, sometimes pulling a horse trailer behind his pickup truck, sometimes not. Meanwhile, we replaced the outdated bathroom fixtures with contemporary counterparts, repaired and refinished the wood floors and pews, and moved the altar table to the parsonage for Colette to use as a work island in her kitchen once the restaurant opened. After painstakingly comparing colorful paint samples to the existing stained glass and debating which colors seemed to coincide with the name Joyful Noise Playhouse, we chose a vibrant violet color for the interior walls and painted the exterior a darker shade in the same color family, a deep purple akin to grape jelly. The colors made a unique and unusual complement to the rich oak floors and pews. We decided to keep the steeple and trim white, though we gave them a fresh coat of paint to brighten them up.

As I painted the rails of the belfry, my eyes were drawn to a cloud of dust being kicked up by a pickup truck pulling a horse trailer on a dirt road that ran behind the northwestern part of Sibley's property. That particular section of Sibley's acreage lay behind a rise topped with a thick stand of trees, and would not be visible from the fancy horse barn that set to the southeast on his expansive spread. But from up here, I could see it all.

The truck stopped near a rear gate not far from an old barn. Sibley's hired hand rode up on a brown horse and slid off to unlock and open the gate. He held on to the horse he'd ridden while the driver of the truck backed a horse out of his trailer. The hand then guided the driver and his horse into the pasture, through a corral, and over to the old barn.

Leaving his horse tied to a fence post, the hand slid the barn door open. Pegasus stood in a pen inside. The driver led his horse into the barn, and the hand closed the door behind them from the inside.

I looked down to resume my painting, and realized the can I'd been using was empty. I climbed down the bell tower, rounded up another can from the stash of supplies in the foyer, and returned to the platform, turning my attention to the railings on the other sides. I'd forgotten all about the horses until an hour later, when movement at the barn caught my eye once again. The door opened and the driver led his horse out. After letting them out of the rear gate and locking it behind them, Sibley's hired hand released Pegasus into the pasture and climbed back onto the horse he'd ridden over on. He headed at a slow trot across the property in the direction of the main barn.

The following day, Buck and I finished the exterior painting. I could only hope that we hadn't just painted a building that we'd lose once we had our day in court. Surely this niggling worry was for naught, right? We wound a long strand of colored Christmas lights around the steeple and affixed more colored lights to the perimeter of the roof. The lights were an inexpensive and delightful way to add fun and color to the place. We had internet and phone service turned on at the building so that we could make sure the communication systems were functioning. We still had a few small items to take care of, such as replacing doorknobs, light switches, and outlet covers. We also needed to hang the curtains for the stage, and install the Tiffany light fixtures and the new stained-glass windows, all of which had yet to be delivered. While the curtain and lights weren't expected for another week or two, Laurel Cromwell should have the stained-glass windows ready any day now. I could hardly wait to see them!

CHAPTER 4

DING-DONG DEAD

SAWDUST

The cat had been stalking a spider in the foyer when he heard the sound of a vehicle approaching outside. Abandoning his pursuit of the insect, he stopped, turned his head toward the front doors of the church, and pricked his ears to listen. He heard a door slam shut, footsteps, and a screech of rusty hinges. More footsteps sounded, coming closer. He felt the vibrations in the floor as the person came up the steps.

Cats might be curious creatures, but they could be cautious at times, too. Sawdust didn't know who was coming to the door or why. He skittered over and crouched to hide behind Whitney's toolbox.

Rap-rap-rap. A man's voice called out.

Footsteps came from within the church now as Whitney walked to the front door to accept the delivery. Sawdust peeked from around the back of the toolbox as she opened the door.

The man stood on the stoop with a tall, narrow box standing beside him, his arm curled around it to hold it steady. Whitney pulled something from her pocket and handed it to the man before taking the box, bringing it inside, and leaning it against the interior wall. The man smiled, turned away, and went back down the steps. Sawdust noticed he walked funny, with a limp, as if he'd been hurt. He returned a moment later with another box. Again, Whitney took the box and leaned it against the inside wall. They repeated this process two more times until four boxes leaned against the front wall. The man turned to go a final time, but Whitney stopped him. She retrieved a bill from her wallet and handed it to the man, who gave her a smile and said, "Thanks," in return. He unzipped a bag belted at his waist, tucked the bill inside, and left. Whitney closed the door behind him.

Sawdust flexed his paws. He knew from experience that cardboard was wonderful for sharpening his claws. The points would dig right in. He eased out from behind the toolbox and padded toward the boxes. Whitney wagged a finger at him and said, "I know what you're thinking, and don't you dare!"

Sawdust sat on his haunches, doing his best to look innocent. He could tell Whitney didn't want him to scratch on the boxes and, so long as she was watching, he wouldn't. But if she only knew how good it felt to sink his claws into cardboard, surely she'd change her mind.

"Buck!" Whitney called. "Let's get these windows over to the parsonage."

Buck came to help Whitney carry the boxes away. Sawdust followed as they carried them into the church and out the emergency door near the raised stage at the back. He didn't try to follow them out the door, of course. Whitney didn't like him going outside unless he had his harness on. Not that he'd ever run away. Life with Whitney was comfortable and fun. But he might be tempted to take a few steps outside just to check things out, see what he might be missing.

The door latch slid home with a click. Looked like the excitement was over.

Or was it?

Sawdust's ears picked up the sound of another vehicle approaching out front. He returned to the vestibule and tried to peek between the two doors and the frame but he could see nothing. He tried peeking under the door but was unsuccessful there, too.

He heard men's voices. One sounded loud and angry. The other sounded weak and scared. The floor vibrated as footsteps pounded up the steps out front. Other footsteps followed, softer ones with an irregular rhythm, the gait uneven. Sawdust skittered back behind the toolbox to hide, pulling his limbs and head in tight to make himself as small as possible. He heard the front door open. The light spilling through told him they hadn't closed it behind them.

Judging from the sounds, one of the men was stomping about and opening doors, searching for something or someone. But what? Or who? The only people who had been here today were Buck and Whitney.

Footsteps pounded up the stairs to the balcony, then pounded back down. The cat couldn't see what happened, but he heard the sounds of a fist meeting flesh and a man crying out.

Scuffling sounds followed. Sawdust heard another door being yanked open and thrown back against the wall. *Bam!*

More pounding footsteps came from the stairwell that led to the belfry, but Sawdust didn't dare look. He only hoped nobody would see him cowering back here. He also hoped that the bad man wouldn't try to hurt Whitney. Good thing she and Buck had left the building. If Whitney came back while this man was still here, Sawdust would muster his courage and defend her with his sharp claws. He might be a fraidycat, but he loved Whitney more than life itself, and he'd defend her to the end.

A few seconds later, Sawdust heard more scuffling and banging, followed by the irregular ring of the church bell. *Ding-Dong! Ding-ding-dong! Diiinggg! Din-din-din-ding! Ding-dong!* A soft thud came through the open door, and the bell fell silent. Somehow, the silence scared him even more.

Footsteps came again, coming down the stairs of the bell tower, sounding like a stampede to the terrified feline. His heart beat so fast his chest shook, and his entire body trembled. *Please don't hurt me!*

Luckily for Sawdust, whoever had come inside left through the front door, leaving it ajar. Sawdust could feel the breeze come through the open door, smell the dust and the earthy odor of the horse manure on the parking lot. He heard a car engine start, heard the car drive away. But he didn't dare venture out. All he wanted right now was Whitney. *Where is she?!*

CHAPTER 5

DEATH KNELL

WHITNEY

I removed the boxes containing the heavy stained-glass windows from the dolly and leaned them against the wall in the master bedroom of the parsonage, where we'd been storing our equipment, tools, and materials for safekeeping. All of the boxes had the word FRAGILE stamped on them in bold red ink. The boxes looked to be about the size of the windows I'd ordered, plus an extra inch or two for Bubble Wrap or some other type of padding.

As I rolled the dolly to the corner where it wouldn't be in our way, a faint noise caught my attention. *Diiinggg! Din-din-din-ding! Ding-dong!* I strained my ears and turned to Buck. "Is the bell ringing in the tower?"

I was surprised I could hear it over Sibley's tractor, which he'd been driving up and down his property all morning. There was no tractor sound now, though. I checked my phone. It was just after one thirty. He must have taken a late lunch break.

Buck went to the window, cocked his head, and cupped

a hand around his ear. "I thought I heard it ringing a moment ago, but I don't hear anything now."

There was only one explanation. My cat had found the rope in the belfry again and had been playing with it. "Sawdust must've gotten into the bell tower somehow." *How?* was the pertinent question. I'd been very careful to ensure the door was securely closed. *But who else could have rung the bell?* Nolan Sibley hadn't been by since we'd filed our response to his petition for a declaratory judgment and the judge had issued a temporary injunction prohibiting him from entering the property until the hearing was held on his adverse possession claim this coming Tuesday. The only person besides me and Buck who'd been at the church today was the delivery guy, and as far as I knew he'd driven off after leaving the windows with me a few minutes earlier. After receiving notice from Laurel Cromwell this morning that the windows would be delivered today, I'd removed the lock from the gate and left the gate open so he could easily get inside. I hadn't yet had a chance to close and lock the gate after him.

"I'd better get back to the church before Sawdust tries to sneak out of the tower and onto the roof." The last thing I wanted was my furry little guy getting stuck on the roof or falling. I'd never forgive myself if he was hurt.

I hurried out of the parsonage. Buck rushed along behind me. He might act tough, but he'd taken in Sawdust's sibling when they were kittens. He loved my cat nearly as much as I did.

We hustled down the dirt path through the trees, unable to see much of anything through their branches. The autumn air was cool and the leaves had begun to turn their fall colors, vibrant oranges and reds, but they hadn't yet fallen. The bell was silent now. Had it been ringing? Or had we been mistaken? Maybe an ice-cream truck had gone by with its music playing and we mistook it for the church bells. But would an ice-cream truck come all the way out here in the country? In autumn? On a weekday? Maybe someone had driven by with their stereo blaring.

Movement on the road caught my eyes as we emerged from the woods around the parsonage and stepped out onto the more open church property. A white SUV drove by, heading in the direction of the interstate, but its windows were closed. Tinted, too. Between the dark film and the shade from the trees lining the county road, it was impossible to tell who might be inside. The only distinguishing thing about it was that it appeared to have two stick-on number decals under the back window, as if it was part of a commercial fleet. *Could it be the same white SUV I'd seen at Nolan Sibley's place a few days ago?*

Lest I trip over the uneven earth, I turned my attention back to the ground in front of me. As we drew near the church, I noticed that the deliveryman's car was stopped near the gate. He drove a pine-green Ford Bronco with fake wood side panels, an old one, manufactured before O. J. Simpson attempted to flee in his white Bronco, tainted the brand, and led to Ford shutting down production on the model for more than two decades. They'd only recently resurrected the Bronco. Inexpensive, bright yellow stickers had been applied to the faux wood on the driver's door, which hung open. The stickers spelled WOODY'S DELIVERY SERVICE.

I'd spotted the car through the door earlier as he'd handed over the stained glass. I'd even commented on it, noting the vehicle appeared to be a classic. The delivery-man had been a classic model himself, looking to be in his mid- to late sixties. He wore his thinning gray hair slicked back into a short ponytail and sported a spare roll of flesh around his middle. He'd informed me the Bronco was a '65 edition, the first year the model was made. When I'd said it must have a large cargo hold to be able to hold the long glass windows, he'd said the space was big enough to sleep in. I'd wondered if he was speaking from experience. Per-haps he'd camped in the vehicle, or maybe even lived in it at some point. While he'd been dressed in traditional navy chinos and a plain white polo, judging from the fit and the quality of the fabric they appeared to be cheap, off-brand pieces. But while the man's car was still here, he was no-where to be seen.

Buck ran alongside me. "Why is the deliveryman's car still here?"

"Don't know!" I called as I hurdled a pile of pony plop-pings.

"Think he's having car trouble?" Buck called. "Maybe he rang the bell to try to summon us back to the church."

Buck's question was clearly rhetorical, so I didn't bother to respond. Besides, by that point I couldn't catch my breath. My heart was somehow both pounding in my chest and clogging my throat as I noticed that the front door of the church stood open. *Did the deliveryman go inside?* Maybe he needed to use the facilities. Or maybe he had a question and went inside to search for me. I could only hope Saw-dust hadn't ventured out the open door. The mere thought that my sweet little boy could be lost gave me a renewed burst of energy and I sprinted the last fifty yards to the door in record time.

"Sawdust?" I glanced around as I ran up the steps, repeatedly calling my cat's name, but I didn't see Sawdust anywhere outside. *Where's my baby?!* I reached the door to find Sawdust standing in the foyer, gazing up through the open door of the bell tower. *Thank goodness!*

"Hey, boy!" I expelled a relieved breath as I rushed over to him. I reached down to pick him up, but before I could snatch him he bolted through the door to the belfry and ascended three steps. He looked back over his shoulder, as if to make sure I was following him.

"No, Sawdust." Still trying to catch my breath, I went after him, moving slowly so as not to spook him. He darted up a few more steps, glancing back over his shoulder again. "No-no, boy," I said. After the frantic sprint from the parsonage to the playhouse, I was in no shape to climb steep stairs. Sawdust didn't seem to care that I was out of breath. He continued up the steps.

I rounded the first tight corner, then the next. When I did, I found Sawdust stopped by a man's sneaker. My first thought was, *How did a man's sneaker end up on the stairs of the bell tower?* My next thought was, *Uh-oh, that shoe still has a foot in it, doesn't it?* It did indeed have a foot in it, and the foot was connected to leg clad in navy-blue chinos. The leg, of course, was connected to the rest of the deliveryman. He lay on his side, limp, facing the wall, his paunch pooled on the steps, testing the limits of his polo shirt. He wore a black nylon fanny pack. I'd noticed after

I'd handed him a tip earlier that he'd threaded the belt of the fanny pack through the loops on his pants to secure it. The fastener on the belt of his fanny pack was undone now, the ends lying unconnected at the small of his back. One of the straps had been pulled through a single belt loop, as if someone had tried to remove the pack but given up. The zippered pouch gaped open below his belly, empty. The tip I'd given him, as well as the other cash and contents, was gone.

My head went light as Buck came up the steps behind me. He did a quick intake of air when he spotted the man. "That can't be good." The staircase was narrow, but my cousin managed to squeeze past me.

I scooped up Sawdust and clutched him to my chest as Buck checked the man for a pulse. He tried the man's wrist first, then reached for his neck. At the last second, he jerked his hand back.

I bit my lip. "What is it?"

"His neck. It's got a bad rope burn around it."

We looked from the man to the thick rope dangling next to the stairs. The ringing we'd heard must have been him struggling against the bell's rope. Had he somehow gotten himself tangled up in it? Even as I had the thought, I realized how ludicrous it was. It would have been extremely unlikely that the man accidentally got the rope tangled around his neck. In fact, it was unlikely he'd have ventured up the steep, winding staircase on his own. He'd walked with a pronounced limp, even grimacing a time or two. Knee problems had been my guess. I'd felt bad for him. It couldn't be easy lugging heavy boxes and packages around with a bum leg. Someone had chased this man up the steps and attacked him. But who? And why?

While Buck performed CPR on the man, I pulled my cell phone from my pocket and dialed 911. "We need an ambulance!" I cried. "And police!" I told the dispatcher that it appeared the man had been assaulted. He said he'd get help en route right away.

While Buck continued his efforts to resuscitate the delivery driver, I rushed Sawdust down the steps and secured him in his carrier, placing his cage at the edge of the porch outside where he'd be out of the way of the first responders. My cat now safe, I scurried back inside and hollered up the staircase to Buck, "I'll go flag down the ambulance!"

I ran out the door and down the driveway to the front gate.

A few minutes later, an ambulance approached, the siren echoing off the barns and hills. I waved my arms over my head and directed them where to turn in to access the playhouse. The driver slowed and unrolled his window.

I pointed to the building. "He's on the stairs in the bell tower!"

The driver punched the gas and roared up to the church. I sprinted after the ambulance, sucking the exhaust into my lungs. In seconds, two EMTs had leapt from the bay of the ambulance, grabbed their medical bags, and entered the building. Sawdust stood in his carrier watching as they rushed past. By the time I reached the playhouse, the medics were rushing the deliveryman onto a gurney. Buck and I stepped outside the playhouse and stood beside the doorway, watching silently as the EMTs continued their attempts to resuscitate the man and loaded him into the back of the ambulance. The scene seemed especially macabre set against the playful backdrop of the colorful performance hall, especially given the building's past life as a house of worship.

The instant the bay doors were closed, the driver hit the gas and headed off to transport the deliveryman to the hospital. The wail of the siren reverberated once again off the nearby hills, and the flashing lights lit up the shady road as they went.

Buck and I stared after the ambulance in shock. After a few seconds, we turned to each other, both of us gaping.

Buck was the first to regain enough composure to speak. "What just happened?"

My words left my lips on my breath. "I have no idea."

A gentle breeze blew in through the door, and a rustle came from behind us. I turned to see a piece of lined paper on the floor of the foyer. It was folded in quarters and bore a ragged edge that said it had been ripped from a spiral notebook. I stepped inside, picked it up, and unfolded it to find a handwritten list of addresses alongside the names of people, restaurants, or other businesses. It appeared to be a list of the stops the deliveryman had made so far today. Judging from the notes he'd scrawled, I gathered he primarily worked freelance, picking up and delivering food orders. The page was completely full, an entry on every line. The last line read *Joyful Noise Playhouse*, along with our theater's address. All of the entries before the playhouse were crossed out. Looked like he'd made a delivery someplace identified as S.E.E. just prior to coming to our place.

It was the only entry for which no address was written. Presumably, the place was somewhere the man visited with enough frequency he could find the place without an address.

"What is it?" Buck asked.

"A list of places the delivery guy visited today."

"Better hang on to it," Buck said. "The police might need it."

When police came across a nonresponsive assault victim in crime dramas, the first thing they did was try to recreate the victim's day leading up to the attack. This piece of notebook paper detailed where the deliveryman had been before coming to the theater. It could prove helpful. Curious myself, I pulled out my phone and snapped a quick pic of the page.

A Metro Nashville Police Department cruiser arrived a few minutes later. The seasoned male officer climbed out of the car and walked our way, stopping ten feet or so away and eyeing us warily. "Someone reported an assault here?"

"That was me, Officer—" My eyes moved to his nametag, squinting to read it at this distance. "Tarver."

After Buck and I identified ourselves to Officer Tarver, he asked, "What happened?"

It was the same thing we'd asked ourselves moments before. *Only Sawdust can answer that question.*

I raised my palms. "We have no idea." I gave him the essential details. Bells ringing wildly. Body in the belfry. Rope burn around neck. Victim not breathing and currently on his way to the hospital via ambulance. I held out the list. "I found this in the foyer. The deliveryman must have dropped it." Or maybe it fell out of his pocket or fanny pack when he was struggling to free himself from the rope.

The cop's eyes narrowed as he stepped forward, took the paper, and assessed what we'd told him. "Show me where you found him. But don't touch anything else."

Buck and I led the officer into the foyer and pointed through the open bell-tower door. The cop ventured partway up the steps of the tower and took a look at the long, rough rope that hung all the way from the bell at the top down to where it ended about three feet above the floor at the bottom. He turned back to address Buck and me. "Fill me in, folks. Who was the victim?"

I raised my palms. "We don't know the deliveryman's name. He dropped off four stained-glass windows here about fifteen minutes ago." I hiked a thumb to indicate Buck. "My cousin and I carried them over to the parsonage next door to store them. We were inside the house when we heard the bell ringing in the belfry. I thought my cat was playing with the rope, but when we got back here we found the man collapsed on the steps. His fanny pack was unbuckled like someone tried to take it off him. The pouch was unzipped and all of the cash he'd had in it was gone. I know he had cash in it earlier because I gave him a tip and I saw several bills when he unzipped the pack to add my tip to them." I swallowed the lump of emotion clogging my throat. "Do you think it could have been an accident?"

Various teachers I'd had over the years had said there were no dumb questions, but the cop gave me a look that said I'd just proved otherwise. "From what you just told me, it doesn't sound at all like an accident." He rested his right hand on his belt, in quick reach of his gun, and looked Buck and me up and down, assessing us. "Mind if I pat you two down?"

The implication that we could pose a threat was insulting, but I couldn't blame him. He didn't know us. He was only being smart and cautious. After all, this was a crime scene. If I were in his tactical shoes, I'd want to pat me and Buck down, too. We both raised our hands, inviting him to pat us down and search our pockets. When he asked whether he could remove Buck's tool belt, which held a hammer, a long screwdriver, and a heavy wrench, Buck said, "Be my guest, Officer."

Once the cop had removed Buck's tool belt and placed it out of reach on the trunk of his cruiser, he pulled out a small notepad and pen to jot some notes. "Did the deliveryman come here alone?"

"As far as I know," I said. "He was the only one who came to the door of the church. I didn't notice anyone else in his car." Then again, I'd taken only a quick glance over his shoulder, noting that he drove the old wood-paneled Bronco but making no note of whether there was anyone else in the vehicle. He'd left the driver's and cargo doors open when he'd carried the glass to the doors of the playhouse. If someone had been sitting in the car, they would have likely caught my eye.

"Who hired him to make the delivery?"

"Laurel Cromwell," I said. "She's the artist who made the windows he delivered here." I whipped my phone from my pocket. "Do you need her phone number? She could help you identify him."

"Let me check his car first. I can probably get his name from his registration."

We followed Officer Tarver to the deliveryman's Bronco near the gate. He donned a pair of latex gloves and opened the passenger door. The deliveryman's cell phone rested in a holder mounted near the bottom center of his windshield. The screen was dark, probably having turned off automatically sometime between the deliveryman leaving the car and the deliveryman's last breath leaving his body. The phone was attached to a solar charger that lay upright on his dash where it could absorb the sun's rays.

Tarver fished a receipt off the dashboard and perused it. "Looks like he picked up lunch at a drive-thru before coming here." The wadded burger wrapper on the dash provided further evidence of the lunch stop.

The Bronco had been built in the era of eight-track tape players, well before cupholders, GPS systems, and USB ports became standard in vehicles. Manufacturers now made portable desktops designed for use in automobiles, a must-have for those who moved about on the job and used their car as a mobile office. Collin had such a desk in his unmarked cruiser, but the desks could be pricey. *Necessity is the mother of invention.* The deliveryman had been creative, using the seat belt to strap a cheap plastic lap tray to the passenger seat. A disposable cup sat in the tray's cupholder, a straw poking out of the plastic lid, the sides beaded with moisture. Atop the tray sat the man's spiral notebook, a ballpoint pen tucked into the metal loops so it wouldn't get lost. The spiral was open to a page with two lines filled. Looked like the deliveryman had places he'd intended to go after leaving the playhouse. I couldn't quite make out the entries from where I stood. *Is one of them a printing company?*

Tarver returned the fast-food receipt to the dash and opened the glove compartment. He pulled out an auto insurance card and the registration receipt, compared the two, and read the name aloud. "Gerard Michael Woodruff. Does that name mean anything to you?"

Buck and I both responded in the negative.

He placed the paperwork atop the makeshift desk. Keeping an eye on me and Buck all the while, he knelt down to feel about the floorboard. When he reached his hand under the passenger seat, his eyes sparked with curiosity. "What do we have here?" He pulled out a black plastic stick with a loop on the handle.

I craned my head for a better look. The stick looked like something a person might use to play fetch with their dog, or maybe to break their car window if they somehow ended up submerged in water. "What is it?"

"Fish bat," he said. "Fishermen use them to club fish after they reel them in. Some of those scaled suckers don't want to give up the fight."

Buck said, "You fish, I take it?"

"Sure do," the officer said. "I'll settle for fishing at a lake, but deep-sea fishing is my preference. My buddies and I spend a week each summer off the Outer Banks of North Carolina. Lots of shipwrecks along that part of the coast. They form natural reefs. You can catch all kinds of fish out there."

I wondered if Woodruff was a fisherman, too. There were a number of lakes and rivers in the area. Maybe he spent his personal time on the water with a rod and reel in his hand.

Tarver looked the fish bat over closely, inspecting it. "People sometimes use these bats as a weapon."

I could see why. The bat looked relatively lightweight and easy to carry. It looked hard, too, like a hockey puck. A blow from a bat like that could cause a world of hurt. "Do people use it as a defensive weapon or an offensive weapon?"

"Yes," the cop replied with a benign smirk. In other words, the bat could be used both to attack and defend, given the situation. I supposed the same could be said for nearly all weapons. He reached under the seat and felt around again. He must have felt something else under there, something that wasn't as easy to get to. He had apparently decided Buck and I weren't a risk, because he lowered his head to the floorboard and shined his flashlight up under the seat to get a better look. He reached under again and wrangled a black fanny pack out from under the seat. It was similar to the one that had been strapped to Woodruff's waist. This one looked newer, though. The nylon fabric was still shiny, having yet to be worn dull. The shape of the pack was better defined, too, not yet having been stretched by repeated use.

Tarver stood, laid the fanny pack atop the desk on the passenger seat, and was about to unzip it when a disembodied voice from Emergency Dispatch came over the radio clipped to his belt. "Got an update on the victim from Lickton Pike."

He pulled his radio from his belt, raised it to his mouth, and pushed the talk button. "Go ahead, Dispatch."

The operator came back. "The victim was pronounced dead on arrival."

DOA. The deliveryman hadn't made it. Though I'd worried that's where things were headed, on my hearing the formal announcement my heart sank and my gut churned. I closed my eyes and sent up a quick prayer that the deliveryman's soul would be safely shipped to the hereafter.

"Copy that." After returning the radio to his belt, Officer Tarver unzipped the fanny pack to reveal a canister of bear repellent and several plastic sandwich bags filled with dry, greenish-brown leaves. The cop tugged one of the clear bags from the fanny pack. While my mind immediately went to the cooking spices Colette used in our kitchen at home, I knew the bag must contain marijuana, not dried oregano, sage, or mint.

Buck asked, "Is that what I think it is?"

The cop cocked his head. "I take it he wasn't bringing this weed to you?"

"No, sir," Buck said. "I stick to beer."

I shook my head. "Marijuana isn't my thing, either." Though I knew that cannabis had become mainstream in many places and everyday people used it, the substance was still illegal in Tennessee. It wasn't worth an arrest. When I wanted to relax, I indulged in a long soak in the claw-foot tub at my house, along with a glass of wine.

Officer Tarver angled his head toward the shade of a nearby tree. "Why don't you two take a seat over there."

We did as he'd suggested . . . or maybe *ordered*? It wasn't exactly clear. Regardless, we'd do as he asked. No sense making his job more difficult. Besides, we were in no state of mind to continue working on the rehab at the moment, and the theater was now a crime scene, anyway. Once we'd taken seats on the sparse grass under the tree, the officer radioed for a homicide detective to come to the scene.

The sound of heavy equipment started up again and a breeze blew past, carrying dust and tiny bits of natural debris with it. Nolan Sibley rode his tractor across the front of his property, a tiller attachment hooked to the back, dragging along the soil and loosening it for planting alfalfa for his horses. As he made a turn at the end of a row and headed back in the other direction, he looked straight ahead, not once glancing our way. *That's a little odd, isn't it?* Seemed like he'd be curious what was going on over here. After all, it's not every day a police car was parked on the property next door, its lights flashing. But maybe Sibley was simply heeding the judge's order not to bother us until the matter of his adverse possession claim was litigated. Even so, a glance in our direction wouldn't be trespassing. His hired hand's pickup truck was gone now. It had been parked near the barn earlier.

We waited silently for the detective to arrive. Well, Buck, Officer Tarver, and I waited silently. Sawdust mewed vociferously from his carrier on the porch, calling out questions I had no answers for. *Mew? Meow? Mow-mow?*

Movement drew my eye to the road. A plain white sedan approached, a standard-issue vehicle for plain-clothes officers. It wasn't until the car turned into the driveway of the church that I could tell for certain it was my boyfriend, Collin. He stopped at the entry, unable to maneuver past the police cruiser and Woodruff's Bronco with the door standing open. He parked sideways and left the car, striding toward us.

"Wait here," Tarver said.

The two officials met up fifty feet away and ducked their heads together for a minute or so as the officer gave the detective an update. Their confab complete, Collin and the cop came over to talk to us.

"Hey," Collin asked softly, his gaze roaming my face, assessing, "you okay?"

Fighting back tears, I gave him a nod. Finding Woodruff had rattled my nerves and shaken my soul. Now that the initial rush of adrenaline was gone, the feelings became more acute. But breaking down into sobs wouldn't help anything, least of all help to solve this murder. *Who had killed Gerard Woodruff and why?*

Buck and I stood, and Collin gave me a few seconds to compose myself. At one point, he began to reach out a hand as if to give me a supporting touch on the shoulder, but seemed to think better of it. Best not to give any indication of bias. He had to treat me like any other witness, maybe even keep me more strictly at arm's length. "Tell me what happened here."

I ran through the facts again. The deliveryman handed over the stained-glass windows, Buck and I carried them over to the parsonage to store them, and, while we were there, we heard the bell ringing erratically. "I thought it was Sawdust playing with the rope again," I said. "But I had closed the door to the belfry and didn't know how he would have gotten back in there. Buck and I rushed over and found the deliveryman lying on the stairs with the rope burns on his neck." I angled my head to indicate the uniformed cop. "I gave Officer Tarver a list I found in the foyer. It showed the places where the guy made deliveries today."

When I finished speaking, Sawdust mewed again from afar, as if adding his own testimony.

Collin cast a glance at my distressed cat before turning back to me and Buck. "Did you see anyone leaving the theater or your property?"

"No," I said. "When we came out of the parsonage, I saw a white SUV driving down the road heading toward the interstate, but I can't say whether it came from here."

"Was it speeding?" he asked.

"It didn't seem to be."

"Any chance you got a make or model?"

"It was too far away for me to tell. It looked like there were a couple of numbered stickers on the back, like it was a fleet vehicle, but I couldn't read the numbers from here."

"What about the license plate?" he asked.

"I didn't get that, either. I didn't think it mattered. At that point, I just thought Sawdust had gotten in the bell tower and that I was rushing over to prevent my cat from climbing out onto the roof. I didn't realize someone had been killed here." I went on to tell him that I'd seen a white SUV at Sibley's place the day he'd put the lock on our gate. "I got the impression that it was a commercial vehicle, too. There was a logo of some sort on the driver's door, but it was too far away for me to get a good look at it."

"Did the SUV you saw today have the same logo?"

"I couldn't tell," I said. "The driver's door was on the opposite side of the vehicle." I explained that the SUV I'd seen at Sibley's didn't have a logo on the passenger side, either.

"Did the SUV you saw at Sibley's place have numbers on the back, like the one you saw today?"

I raised my palms. "I don't recall. Sorry."

Collin's head bobbed slightly as he processed these tidbits of information. He cast a glance at Woodruff's Bronco. The fanny pack was visible through the open door, sitting unzipped on the passenger seat. "Dealers sometimes get jumped by a customer who wants to steal their drug stash."

"Do you think that's what happened here?" I asked.

"Could be," Collin said. "But if they came for the stash, they didn't get it."

"Maybe they didn't spot the fanny pack in his car. It was shoved under the seat."

Collin asked Officer Tarver for Woodruff's list, perused it, and mused aloud, "This is a long list. He went from one end of the city to another, then all the way out here. Seems these stops would have taken up most of his day."

I offered my thoughts. "Maybe he made stops along the way to sell the drugs, too." With marijuana not only becoming more acceptable but also touted as a cure for pain and insomnia, he'd likely have an easy time cultivating a customer base.

"Could be," Collin said. "Or could be his murder had nothing to do with the drugs. Delivery drivers are common targets of crime. They carry cash to make change for customers, and robbers know that. Sometimes robbers lure delivery drivers to an out-of-the-way site by placing a food delivery order to an address that's not theirs, and then jump the driver when he arrives. Delivery work is a dangerous job."

Buck frowned. "But that would mean someone would have had to follow him all the way out here. Seems like a long way to come to rob someone."

"It is," Collin agreed. "But if the driver was followed for his cash, the thief wouldn't likely have known he was headed all the way out here when he started trailing him."

"Maybe they didn't have to follow him far," I said. "Maybe they started trailing him when he stopped for lunch on the way here. The deputy found a receipt on the dashboard."

"That's a possibility," Collin said. "Besides, this area is secluded. A robber would be thrilled to be able to jump the guy out here where there's less chance of witnesses."

It was true there seemed to be no human witnesses, and unfortunately there was no technological witness, either. We'd planned to install a security system in the theater, hiring a professional security company after the stained glass was installed, since setting up a large, commercial system was beyond our skill set.

Collin glanced about, his eyes lingering for a moment on Sibley as the man made another row with his tractor, throwing fresh dust and organic matter into the air. Collin knew about the claim Sibley had made on our property, how he'd attempted to lock us out of the place. "Has Nolan Sibley been out on that tractor all day?"

"Most of it," I said. "He was working on it all morning, and I heard the tractor running in the distance when I opened the door of the playhouse to accept the delivery."

"Has he been running it continuously since?"

"No," I said. "The tractor wasn't going when we heard the bells ringing. He didn't start it up again until after the ambulance had come and gone and we were being questioned by Officer Tarver."

Collin's brows lifted and he looked to Buck and the officer for confirmation. Tarver nodded in agreement.

Buck backed me up, too. "I'm not sure we'd have even heard the bells over the noise of the tractor. At least not if he was working this side of his acreage."

The implication of Collin's questions was that Sibley was unaccounted for while the murder was taking place, and that he could be a suspect. Though it seemed technically possible Sibley had killed Woodruff, I had a hard time believing it could actually be true. Would someone kill a stranger just to increase their chances of acquiring an adjacent property? To scare us off? While no reasonable person would murder someone for such flimsy reasons, killers weren't exactly reasonable, were they? Still, it seemed doubtful Sibley would go that far to try to get our land. And, though I shivered to think it, if he was planning to kill someone, wouldn't it have been Buck and me? A death here would have no effect on his adverse possession claim, though maybe he thought it would reduce the property's value and encourage us to offer him the land for cheap.

Because Collin had asked about Sibley, I figured it couldn't hurt to mention his ranch hand. "Sibley's assistant was around all morning. I saw him and his pickup by the barn."

"When did he leave?" Collin asked.

I raised my palms. "I didn't notice."

"Me neither," Buck said.

"Do you know his name?"

"It's either Luther or Otto." I told him that Sibley had called out both names when summoning his hand and his dog the first time we'd seen him at our property. Of course, I didn't know whether Luther or Otto was a first name or last name, either.

When we'd told Collin all we knew, which was precious little, he suggested we use our remaining time today to work on things at the parsonage. "It'll take us a few hours to process the crime scene." He turned to Tarver. "Mind holding down the fort for a bit? I want to go speak to the horse rancher."

The officer gave him a nod.

We left them to their police work and returned to the parsonage. There Buck and I ignored our rehab projects for the moment and instead played amateur investigators. It was impossible to focus on anything other than the violent death we'd just seen. *Poor Woodruff.* I wondered if he had a family. My heart broke afresh at the thought that he might have a spouse who was now widowed, children who would be mourning their father.

"What's your theory?" I asked Buck. "You think he got attacked for his cash, or you think someone followed him out here for the drugs?"

"My money's on it having something to do with the drugs," Buck said. "All those individual bags he had mean he's selling the stuff. He could have been jumped by a customer, like Collin said, or maybe he angered his supplier. Hard to say."

Unfortunately, drug-related crimes were common in the

state. Collin had once told me that around 80 percent of the crimes committed in Tennessee had some connection to drugs. Many assaults and murders were committed by people on drugs, and drug addicts often committed robberies or burglaries to obtain cash or property they could sell to buy drugs. He'd also told me that meth was a huge problem for law enforcement, with an estimated eight hundred meth labs operating in the state. But while meth had long been the drug of choice for Tennesseans inclined to partake in illegal substances, heroin was an up-and-comer, with more of the drug being found on the streets these days. The state's drug problems didn't stop at illegal drugs, either. The state ranked third in the country for prescription drug abuse. Not exactly a ranking we could be proud of. *Such is dinner conversation when you date a detective.*

I chewed my lip. "I know we'd planned to have a commercial security system installed at the theater once the windows were in, but I think we should put in some type of system today as soon as they're done collecting evidence." Presumably, whoever had come here had been targeting Woodruff and wouldn't return now that he was gone, but it couldn't hurt to be careful. If nothing else, cameras would deter the lookie-loos from snooping about. Murder scenes tended to draw people, like moths to a flame. People had a morbid curiosity about such things.

Buck agreed, though he lamented the fact that we'd have to spend unbudgeted funds on a system that would be only a stopgap measure. "I suppose we could use the system in another flip property later."

We drove to a local hardware store and bought the cheapest set of exterior cameras they had, a two-pack that would include one camera for the rear door and one we could situate between the front doors. We also bought an interior camera with a wide-angle lens that could capture the entire theater space. Along with the cameras, we purchased four red-and-white signs that read WARNING! SECURITY CAMERAS IN USE. We'd hang one on each door of the playhouse, and put one on the front gate, too.

We drove back to the property. With our work on the playhouse interrupted for the time being, we turned our efforts to the parsonage. We'd worked with Colette to devise a plan for the place. We'd decided to leave the walls in place around what was now the master bedroom. It would be less work and help to control noise in the café. It would also provide another private space that could be rented for celebrations. We'd replace the solid wood door with a glass-paneled option. We'd remove the walls between the secondary bedrooms to open up that space. The old carpet would be torn out and replaced with easy-to-clean wood floors painted white. The walls would be painted robin's-egg blue, a classic color that was nearly neutral. Colette planned to furnish the place with mismatched tables and chairs acquired at flea markets and garage sales, and she'd top the tables with tea candles in assorted vintage teacups for a fun splash of color. She'd also found adorable teacup chandeliers on Etsy that we would install for her. The place would look like something out of *Alice in Wonderland* when we were through with it.

With the master bedroom full of painting supplies, saw-horses, tools, and the stained-glass windows, we decided to focus our efforts on the other rooms. Before we began the demolition on the kitchen, Buck wrangled the refrigerator

onto a dolly and wheeled it out to the garage. The appli-
ance worked fine, but it wasn't suitable for a commercial
kitchen. We'd donate it to charity. I retrieved screwdrivers
and a hammer to start disassembling the cabinets. They'd
go into the rented dumpster. They were cheap, outdated, and
scratched, no longer of any use. Buck turned off the water
to the kitchen sink and removed it. We scored the old lino-
leum on the kitchen floor, and pulled it up, strip by strip.
It was backbreaking work. I hoped we were doing it for
our own benefit and not Nolan Sibley's. I couldn't shake
the nagging feeling that we were taking a risk by moving
ahead with the renovation. The court hearing on the adverse
possession claim couldn't come soon enough.

As I carried some of the flooring out to the dumpster
at the edge of the playhouse parking lot, I looked over at
Woodruff's Bronco. Members of the police department's
crime scene team were working on it. I could see only the
bottom half of one of them as he leaned into the car.

Collin came out of the playhouse, climbed into his car,
and headed down the drive. He turned left onto the county
road and drove down to the gated entrance to Sibley's farm.
Sibley was no longer on his tractor, but instead was moving about in front of the barn. Collin tapped the horn and
waved an arm out of the window to get Sibley's attention.
The man turned and stalked down his gravel drive to the
gate. I suspected Collin planned to question him about the
murder, to find out whether he'd seen anything unusual at
our place, noticed anyone fleeing the scene.

I could hardly wait to hear what the crime scene team
had found and what Sibley had shared, but I knew that things
never moved as fast in real life as they did in the movies

and on television shows. No doubt Collin would be busy the rest of today and tomorrow reviewing any evidence they found and piecing things together. Luckily, Collin and I already had plans for dinner and a movie at our house tomorrow night with Buck and Colette. He'd fill us in on the investigation then. With any luck, he'd tell us they'd identified the culprit, thrown him in jail, and obtained just a bit of justice for Gerard Woodruff.

CHAPTER 6

A MULTI-FACETED MIX-UP

WHITNEY

Once the head of the crime scene team cleared the way for us to reenter the theater, we installed and activated the security cameras. Good thing we'd already had internet service turned on at the place so the cameras could send us a notice and images if there was any activity.

Though the day's events had been emotionally exhausting, I barely slept Friday night. My mind repeatedly flashed to terrifying images of the dead delivery driver lying on the steps of the bell tower. I tried putting my pillow over my head, but while it might block the sound of crickets outside and the light of the moon coming through the window, it did nothing to block the horrific images in my head.

My mind went back to what Collin had said, that Woodruff might have been tailed by someone hoping to rob the driver. It seemed unlikely a robber would spend hours following someone. My presumption was that, if he'd been followed, the robber had followed him from a recent stop, probably his last stop before heading our way. Where was it he'd been right before visiting the playhouse? All I could remember was that the place was identified by some sort of acronym.

Sawdust stirred next to me as I reached over to my night table to pick up my phone. The screen seemed extra bright in the dark room, and both my cat and I blinked against the glare. Once my eyes had adjusted, I pulled up the pic I'd snapped of the handwritten list Woodruff had prepared. The last entry before our theater was somewhere identified as S.E.E. The initials rang no bell for me.

I typed the initials followed by the word *Nashville* into the browser on my phone. The first entry that popped up referenced a company called Specialty Export Experts, Inc., whose slogan was "S.E.E. THE WORLD." The international shipping company had an address in an industrial area in northwest Nashville, not far from where Interstates 65 and 24 converged. Until recently, I'd worked part-time as a property manager for Home & Hearth Realty, and had learned my way around the city taking care of the properties. After Buck and I had such success with the rehab of the motor lodge, I'd put in my resignation notice with the real estate company. Though I missed the owners, Marv and Wanda Hartley, my resignation had come at a good time. Their niece had been wanting to get into the real estate business, and was happy to take over my duties.

Could someone have followed Woodruff from the shipping company? Or had someone trailed him from the fast-food restaurant when he stopped to pick up lunch between leaving the shipping company and arriving at the theater? Could be. After all, with decals on his car spelling out WOODY'S DELIVERY SERVICE, it wasn't exactly a secret that he was a deliveryman. It was horrible enough that

Woodruff had been killed, but the idea that someone had taken his life in return for a relatively insignificant amount of cash was even worse. Robbing a delivery driver wasn't like robbing a bank. How much ready money would a delivery person even have on them? Maybe two or three hundred dollars? The man's life was worth far more than that.

I returned my phone to the night table and tried to sleep, but rest continued to elude me.

The first thing I did when I woke Saturday morning was to reach again for my cell phone. If an arrest had been made since last time we spoke, Collin would have texted me. Unfortunately, my screen showed no incoming texts from him. The only communication had come from my mother, asking how the renovations on the playhouse and parsonage were going. I decided not to tell her the bad news and cause her unnecessary worry. After all, it seemed that whoever had killed Gerard Woodruff had targeted him for one reason or another, not the theater. It was unlikely I was in any danger. I responded with the thumbs-up emoji and sent her some pics I'd snapped around the playhouse.

I picked Sawdust up in my arms and padded into the kitchen to find Emmalee and Colette sitting on stools at the breakfast bar, sipping coffee.

Colette cringed. "You look like hell."

I hadn't looked in the mirror when I left the bedroom, afraid of what I might see. "Is it that bad?"

"Not if you don't count the dark circles and bags under your eyes, the worry lines on your forehead, and the tangled mess of hair that says you tossed and turned all night." She slid off her stool. "I'll pour you a cup of coffee."

"Thanks." I set Sawdust down on the floor, fed him his breakfast, and took a seat on a stool, managing a smile when Colette set the steaming mug of coffee in front of me.

She said, "I've got some good news that might cheer you up a little."

"You do?" I took a sip of the brew. "What is it?"

"Emmalee is going to come work for me at the Collection Plate. She'll be my assistant manager."

I turned to our red-haired, freckle-faced roommate. "That's wonderful!" Though Emmalee was currently a server, she worked just as hard as Colette and was smart, to boot. I had no doubt the two would make the restaurant a thorough success.

Colette pushed a legal pad with some notes scrawled on it across the counter to me. "We've been brainstorming dessert ideas this morning."

I read over the desserts listed. "Fig and almond tart. Cherry angel food cake. Scripture cake." I looked up from the pad. "What's scripture cake?"

Emmalee told me that scripture cake included ingredients referenced in different Bible verses. "My granny used to make it. She stirred the batter with the same wooden spoon she threatened to smack our behinds with."

"Threatened?" Colette said. "So, she didn't follow through?"

"Not once," Emmalee said. "She didn't have to. Just her brandishing the spoon was enough to put the fear of God in us."

My roommate's story made me think of the biblical paraphrase "spare the rod, spoil the child." It also reminded me of Nolan Sibley's cattle prod and his poor horses. I read on down the list of proposed desserts. "Stained-glass cookies?"

"I'll show you." Colette reached for her electronic tablet, tapped a few keys, and showed me a photo of what appeared to be sugar cookies in various shapes with colorful glass-like centers. She explained that cookie cutters of the same shape in two varied sizes were used, such as large and small star-shaped cutters. Two large cookies would be cut. One of the larger cookies would form the base. The smaller cookie cutter would be used to cut a smaller shape out of the center of the second large cookie, forming a frame of dough that would be placed on top of the other large cookie. The clear, colored "glass" filled the frame on the finished cookie.

"How do you make edible glass?" I asked.

"Life Savers or another hard candy. You crush them up, sprinkle them in the center of the dough, and they melt while the cookies are baking to fill the frame."

"Clever." Speaking of stained glass, I'd better get moving. Buck and I had the four new windows to install today. They'd need custom framing, and it would be hours of backbreaking work. Even so, I was excited. I couldn't wait to get to work on them and see how they'd look once they were installed.

I tossed back the coffee, dressed, and grabbed a couple of Colette's biscuits for my own breakfast on the road. I'd decided to leave Sawdust home today. Between the murder yesterday and Nolan Sibley's claim hanging over us, I felt nervous and unsettled. Better not have my cat to worry about, too. Besides, Emmalee's calico, Cleopatra, had been thrilled when Sawdust had returned home last night. She'd missed her buddy and curled up on the couch side by side with him. That's where the two were now, too. I gave Cleo a scratch under the chin before giving my own little guy a kiss on his furry head. "Be good while Mommy's gone, okay?"

Sawdust gave me a soft mew that said he'd behave himself.

Buck and I carried the boxes containing the stained-glass windows from the parsonage to the playhouse, circling around horse manure along the way.

He looked up at the clouds gathering in the sky. "Looks like we're in for some rain."

With us hoping to install windows today, the timing couldn't be worse. Even so, the dreariness matched my mood. I couldn't shake the horror of finding Gerard Woodruff's body in our belfry.

We paused at the doors to the theater, exchanging a glance. The last time we'd been here, we'd found a man murdered inside. A pall had been cast over the place, one that needed to be cleared.

Though the place was no longer a house of worship, I nevertheless closed my eyes and sent up a prayer for Gerard Woodruff. "May his soul find rest, and may the Nashville PD find his killer."

Buck's voice came from next to me. "Amen."

I opened my eyes and, together, we stepped through the door and made our way across the foyer. Inside the theater, I leaned the long, narrow boxes back safely between two pews for support. Laurel Cromwell had slid a copy of our order for each window into a manila envelope with my name and the theater's address written on the outside, and affixed the envelope to the outside of the box with heavy-duty clear strapping tape. The paperwork for our two custom windows was correct. Oddly, although my name and the playhouse address were written on the envelope for the two mass-produced windows, the paperwork tucked inside listed the customer as someone named Antonia Szabo with Glassworks Gallery in Bucharest, Romania. The price for each window was $600 more than Laurel Cromwell had charged me. As I'd learned in my marketing class in college, charging customers different fees for the same product or service was common. Airlines and hotels did it all the time. The practice of trying to get the highest fee from each client or customer was known as price discrimination.

When I'd discussed the windows with Laurel at her studio, I'd made it clear that our project had a tight budget, and that cost would be a major factor in my decision-making. She'd likely offered me a lower price than she charged the gallery so that she wouldn't lose the deal. I'd also told her that Buck and I did a lot of rehabs. She might have discounted the price in the hope we'd become a repeat customer. Price discrimination wasn't really my favorite practice. I believed artists and craftsmen should be paid a fair price for their skills and work, but that they should be fair with their customers, too. I was glad that at least we'd gotten a good deal.

I carefully pulled the glass panels out of the boxes, removed the protective Bubble Wrap, and checked the windows. I was relieved to see that Laurel had sent us the designs we'd ordered, the ones she called Cheerful Garden and Surprise in the Skies. It appeared she'd erred only in switching up the paperwork. *No big deal, right?* Laurel Cromwell had given me a copy of my invoice the day I'd ordered the windows, so the other customer presumably had a copy of her original order, too. If not, Laurel could provide her another. We'd all gotten what we'd ordered and paid for, and that was the important thing.

Buck looked the windows over. "Nice. You picked some good designs."

"I did, didn't I?" I grinned, proud of my decorating talents. "If the glass looks this good now, just wait until we get the windows installed." They'd be even prettier with the sun shining through them, creating a rainbow of colors inside the auditorium. Still, a part of me was hesitant to install them just yet. "Do you think we should wait until after the court hearing Tuesday to install these windows? Just to be safe?" The thought that there was even the smallest chance the judge might award the church property to Nolan Sibley gave me pause. No doubt he'd refuse to let us back on the property to remove these valuable windows if they had already been installed.

Buck exhaled a sharp breath. "If the judge awards Sibley this place, I'll raise a ruckus about the windows, demand that we be given a chance to remove them. If that fails, I'll don a ski mask and sneak back here in the middle of the night to get them back."

"I'd keep watch from the bell tower." Hopefully, this plan would never have to be put into action.

Buck used an extension ladder outside the building while I stood on a step stool inside, facing him through the empty window space. My cousin looked up at the dark clouds gathering in the sky. "Storm's coming. We'd better get moving before the rain sets in."

Easier said than done. We had to make sure the glass was held securely in place so it wouldn't come crashing down on the audience of the playhouse. Installing the windows proved to be difficult work. The metal solder and thick glass made the windows especially heavy, and the sills sat high up on the walls. We had to be extra careful easing them into place. My arm and shoulder muscles strained with the effort, my wrists, too. No doubt I'd be sore later. Maybe I'd have time to soak in a hot bath before dinner and the movie tonight.

Once each glass panel was in place, we caulked around the edges to ensure moisture couldn't seep in around it. After we caulked, we finished the look with custom cut wood trim around the edges of the window, both inside and out. We cast repeated glances at the sky, hoping the storm would hold off a bit longer. Meanwhile, precautions were being taken next door. Either Luther followed Otto as he rounded up the horses and put them in their stalls in the barn or Otto followed Luther. I still didn't know which name belonged to whom.

Buck and I finished installing the two standard-order windows, as well as the custom one with the drama masks and dance shoes. We were heaving the final custom window with the musical instruments up to the sill when a car horn honked outside. Buck turned his head to look toward the gate.

I groaned. "It's not Sibley again, is it?"

"Nope."

Taking care so as not to fall out of the empty window

opening, I leaned out to take a look. A small silver sedan sat at the gate.

Buck asked, "You recognize that car?"

"No," I said.

"Me neither."

The driver must have realized our hesitation, because she climbed out of the car so we could see her better. She was short, round, and blond, and looked vaguely familiar. She cupped her hands around her mouth and hollered at the top of her lungs, "It's Laurel Cromwell! I need to talk to you!"

Ah. No wonder the woman looked familiar. "She's the glass artist," I told Buck.

As we carefully lowered the window to the floor inside the theater, he asked, "What's she doing all the way out here?"

"My guess is she heard what happened to the delivery driver and wants to talk about it." I didn't exactly relish the idea of having to revisit the horror of Gerard Woodruff's murder, but I couldn't very well ignore the woman. I climbed down from the stool, hurried out of the playhouse, and strode quickly down the drive to the gate.

As I approached, Laurel called, "I hate to bother you at work, but I couldn't reach you by phone. I've tried five times!"

My phone was in my purse in the playhouse foyer, which explained why I hadn't heard it go off. I stopped a few feet back from the locked gate. "I wasn't near my phone. We've been installing the windows. They look great, by the way. You did a wonderful job."

She cringed. "I'm so sorry, but I need those windows back. I gave you the wrong order."

Confusion brought my brows together. "But the windows that were delivered were exactly what I ordered."

"The custom ones are yours," she said. "It was the other two that I mixed up. Cheerful Garden and Surprise in the Skies." She offered a contrite cringe and apologized again.

"I don't understand," I said. "Those windows aren't custom designs." Hence the reason for their names, a shorthand to identify the standardized window models. "Don't you make them all the same?"

"Normally, yes," she explained, "but one of my customers ordered semi-custom versions that were upgraded with glass jewels."

"Jewels?"

"Mm-hm," she said. "They're the same types of faux gems used in costume jewelry. They add some extra sparkle to the windows. I accidentally sent the upgraded windows to you."

"The customer was Glassworks Gallery? In Romania?"

She nodded. "That's the one."

Ugh. I supposed I was partially at fault here. When I saw the gallery's name on the invoice, I shouldn't have assumed that only the paperwork had been switched. I should've checked with Laurel before we proceeded with the installation. "It's impressive that your work is sold overseas. It must be exciting to be a world-renowned artist."

Laurel chuckled softly. "As much as I'd like to think I'm world famous because I'm uniquely talented, I know that's not true. Don't get me wrong, I do phenomenal work, but there are talented glass artists all over Europe. Or so I hear. I haven't had an opportunity to travel there. But art is like other products. People think it's better if it comes from somewhere else. An import has more cachet. It's the same here. We'll pay more for French wine or perfume, Egyptian cotton, German beer, or Scandinavian furniture, excluding those do-it-yourself IKEA pieces, of course."

She had a point. People often didn't value things that were inexpensive, familiar, and easy to acquire. I glanced back at the church, thinking of the three hours Buck and I had spent installing the two windows she wanted back. A twinge in my back reminded me of the physical strain the installation had cost me, too. I turned back to Laurel. Maybe I could just pay her the additional charge and be done with it. "The upgraded windows were six hundred dollars more, right?"

She pressed her lips together before speaking. "Yes. Another six hundred. Per window."

Unfortunately, an unexpected twelve hundred dollars wasn't in our budget. We'd already exceeded the budget on the Tiffany light fixtures. But I had to wonder, why would someone pay an additional six hundred per window for a feature that was so easily overlooked? I hadn't even noticed the difference when we'd installed the glass. Then again, I supposed I might have noticed if it had been a brighter day. With the skies full of storm clouds, shutting out the sun, not much light had been shining through the windows. Without sufficient light, the glass gems wouldn't sparkle.

Before I could even tell Laurel that we wouldn't be willing to pay the difference and would return the windows instead, she said, "Unfortunately, paying the additional price isn't an option. This customer needs the windows right away. I don't have time to make another set."

A rush order from halfway across the globe? The

windows were being sent all the way to eastern Europe. They'd have to pass through customs at various ports, where they could be delayed. It seemed odd that the owner of Glassworks Gallery in Romania would expect a quick turnaround. Then again, seemed everything moved at warp speed these days. Overnight delivery used to be reserved for urgent matters, but now you could get everyday items dropped at your door in twenty-four hours or less. Maybe the gallery's owner—*Antonia Szabo, wasn't it?*—had already sold the pieces. Maybe she had a customer eagerly waiting on them.

As I looked back at the playhouse again, a pellet of cold rain pinged off my forehead. Dark gray clouds loomed overhead, pressing down on us. "Buck and I have to get the remaining custom window installed before the rain gets in the building. I can't remove the others while the rain is coming down or the floors could be damaged." We'd already spent hours replacing the water-damaged sections of the floor. We weren't about to risk the floors getting damaged again. Another cold rain pellet hit my cheek with surprising force. It seemed as if the gods were trying to get my attention, send me a message.

"What if I hold an umbrella over the hole?" Laurel offered.

When another drop of rain pelted my cheek, my patience ran out. "Look. I'll help you fix your mistake and get the upgraded windows back to you, but you've got to understand that Buck and I just spent three hours installing them. We sealed them, and then cut and installed trim around them, too. Our time and labor are valuable, and my back is already killing me." *Poor choice of words. Ugh.*

"You'll have to give us a little leeway here." I put my foot down. "I'll have them out by Monday morning. That's the best I can do." If she didn't like it, she could sue me, just like Nolan Sibley had. I was tired of people trying to boss me around on my property.

She bit her lip. "Do you have a security system?"

I moved closer to the gate and pointed at the sign affixed to it that warned visitors they were under camera surveillance.

She needed more assurance, apparently. "The sign's not a fake? I've heard people sometimes put up signs like this to scare off thieves, even when they don't actually have a security system."

I turned my pointer finger on the theater building now. "There's a camera between the front doors that will record anyone approaching the front of the building. There's one over the back door, too. We've also got an interior camera that will record any activity inside."

The tight expression on her face said she still wasn't entirely satisfied, but she acquiesced. "Okay. Thanks. And I am truly sorry. I know it's no excuse, but I was up late Thursday night with my fifteen-year-old son. He fell at his basketball game and broke his arm. It was a bad break and it took the doctors a while to determine the best way to treat it. I was exhausted yesterday morning when I was preparing the orders for delivery."

"Sorry to hear about your son." I felt guilty now for my impatience, especially given that I was experiencing a similar exhaustion today thanks to the murder keeping me up all night. "I hope he makes a full recovery."

"Thanks. Me too." Turning to the logistics of the window

exchange, Laurel said, "Your windows wouldn't fit in my car, so I couldn't bring them with me now. But I'll get in touch with my delivery guy. He can bring them when he comes here to pick up the others on Monday."

"Your delivery guy?" I said. "You don't mean Gerard Woodruff, do you?"

"That's him," she said. "He goes by *Woody*, though. Woody's Delivery Service."

She hasn't heard. My stomach sank. I hated to be the bearer of bad news, but Laurel had a right to know what happened to the man. Better she find out now, from me, and be able to make other arrangements for her glass deliveries. "You didn't hear what happened to him."

The color drained from her face, and she put a hand on the gate as if to steady herself. "What do you mean?"

Her reaction told me she assumed something awful. Still, she couldn't have foreseen that he'd be maliciously killed, could she? She probably assumed only that he'd been seriously hurt, or that he'd died from natural causes. It would be a logical supposition. He wasn't in great physical shape, and he was at the age when many men suffered heart attacks.

I tried to phrase things as gently as possible and ease her into the news, but there's really no way to soft-pedal murder, is there? "After Woody delivered the windows here, he was attacked in the bell tower." I let that soak in for a moment before adding, "His injuries were fatal."

Her jaw went slack, and her eyes widened and glistened. She gulped, hard. When she spoke again, her voice was weak and squeaked. "Someone hurt him? Who was it? Why?"

Her questions were the same ones we'd had, the ones Collin would try to find answers for. "We don't know," I said. "My cousin and I had carried the windows over to the parsonage, so we didn't see anything. The police are working on it." When an errant tear slid down her cheek, I asked, "Did you know him well?"

She shook her head and swiped at a second tear that had escaped her eye. "No. He just did deliveries for me, that's all. But he was always friendly."

With that, a bolt of lightning lit up the sky with a loud buzz and crack, the electrical charge from the sky reminiscent of Nolan Sibley's cruel cattle prod. A rumble of thunder followed. The heavens opened and cold rain pelted us like a shotgun spray of ice. I raised my bladed hand to my brows to shield my eyes and face from the heavy droplets. "I need to get back inside. I'll bring the windows to your shop Monday morning and pick up ours then, too. Okay? That'll give you more time to find a new delivery person."

"All right," she said. "See you then." She turned to rush back to her car, too, but it was too late. She was already drenched. So was I.

I sprinted through the pouring rain back to the playhouse. When I got there, I found Buck had already nailed a tarp over the remaining empty window opening to protect the floors.

He took one look at me and said, "You look like you've been baptized in the creek."

I shivered, the cold rain taking its toll. Buck tossed me a paint-spattered canvas drop cloth. A warm parka would have been better, but the drop cloth was all we had. I wrapped it around me and retrieved my phone from my purse. Sure enough, I had five voice-mail messages from

Laurel Cromwell, all left over the past three-hour period. Given the discussion I'd just had with her, I knew the content and didn't bother to listen to them.

Buck said, "What did the glass lady want?"

I pointed to the glass we'd just installed. "She wants the windows back."

"What?!" he snorted. "Every muscle in my back and arms is screaming. Did you tell her she's out of her ever-loving mind?"

I explained what she'd told me about the upgraded glass jewels. He walked over and looked up at the flowered window. I did, too.

His eyes narrowed as they searched the window. "What do glass jewels look like?"

"She said they're the same kind of fake gems used in costume jewelry." I used my phone to search for images of loose glass jewels so we could compare them to the window before us. The sites showed pieces of glass that resembled precious gems, with facets cut across their surface. According to the descriptions, most of the ones used in stained-glass art were around an inch in diameter or length, much larger than real gems, but some were smaller, closer to the size of real precious stones. The glass knock-offs weren't expensive, though, only a few dollars each. Laurel Cromwell had imposed a significant markup for the glass jewel upgrade.

I shifted my focus from my phone to the glass, and climbed up on my step stool for a better look. On close inspection, my eyes spotted one of the glass jewels in the center of a flower, a bright red one that resembled an oversized ruby. "There's one." I pointed it out to Buck.

Buck found another in a gorgeous deep green, like a faux emerald. "There's another."

We searched for more. It was a game, like those picture searches for kids in *Highlights* magazine. But here, up close, I spotted a few tiny glass jewels, too. Their size approximated that of Swarovski crystals, the popular jewels used in rings, bracelets, necklaces, and earrings, to adorn clothing and accessories, too. The smaller fakes were more opaque than the larger glass jewels, and looked remarkably like actual precious gems—not that an untrained eye like mine could tell the difference. I knew all about the different types of woods, but I was out of my element when it came to glass and gems.

I was soaked to the skin, and my teeth began to chatter. All I wanted to do was go home and stand under a hot shower. "Let's call it a day."

Buck tossed his hammer back into his toolbox. "You don't have to ask me twice."

We packed up our things and hustled out to our vehicles through sheets of pouring rain.

CHAPTER 7

DATE AND DATA

With the rain preventing us from finishing the installation of the custom window, Buck and I packed up and headed to my house. I indulged in a long, hot shower to warm my cold bones and relax my aching muscles. Afterward, I slathered my sore arms and shoulders with peppermint-scented pain cream. I smelled like a candy cane. Meanwhile, Buck helped Colette in the kitchen. She was trying out some recipes she might use in the restaurant, and Buck, Collin, and I would be her taste testers. She was a skilled chef, and we were more than happy to oblige.

An hour later, Collin had arrived and the four of us were seated around the dinette, sampling Colette's recipes. Collin updated us on the murder investigation as we tried the olive medley and the unleavened bread appetizer, to which she'd added a nice hint of garlic and rosemary. The bread served as a scrumptious scoop for the creamy hummus.

Collin swallowed a bite of bread and took a sip of beer. "In light of the weed and the weapon found in Woodruff's car, we suspect he was dealing drugs along with running his delivery service."

Buck and I had reached the same conclusion earlier. I held a large garlic-stuffed olive aloft. "His murder could be related to the drugs, then?"

"It's possible," Collin said. "He was on probation for an earlier drug offense. He was found with a small amount of marijuana last year. I've looked back through the police report detailing his arrest. He claimed he used the drug to help ease the pain of his arthritis."

Arthritis would explain his limp. I'd noticed it as he'd carried our windows into the theater. As sore as my back was, even after a warm and relaxing shower and the application of pain cream, I could understand his need to dull a disabling, chronic ache. "If he'd escalated to dealing, does that mean his delivery business was slow?"

"That's the thing," Collin said. "By all accounts, his delivery business kept him very busy. According to that list you found of his Friday deliveries, he took several orders of donuts and pastries to offices downtown early in the morning. In midmorning, he couriered some dental implants from the lab that fabricates them to the dental office that had ordered them. He then eased into lunchtime deliveries around eleven o'clock. In the early afternoon, he picked up the stained glass from Cromwell's studio and made a delivery to an export company before going out to the playhouse." Collin paused to take another sip of his beer before resuming. "We found several handwritten schedules in his car, just like the list you found, but for earlier days. Most of his business was making food deliveries for one of those app services. In between mealtimes, he'd do a few deliveries for small businesses, but he had a limited clientele. Judging from the times he jotted down on the lists, he worked very long days, from around six in the morning to nine at night."

My guess was that working for the food delivery app wasn't the most lucrative business and he'd had to work long hours to make ends meet.

Buck must have had the same thought. "Even if he was busy," he said, "was he making real bank? He'd have to do a lot of deliveries to cover the taxes, plus gas and upkeep on his Bronco."

"That's true," Collin said. "He might have been dealing drugs to supplement his delivery income. It would be easy to make stops to deliver drugs between his legitimate deliveries. Of course, he didn't document those deliveries. Not anywhere we could find them, anyway. But I did find something interesting on his phone when I went through it today."

"Oh, yeah?" I used a piece of bread to scoop up a big blob of hummus. "What was it?"

"Two phone calls to convicted dealers." Collin sipped his beer. "One was made two weeks ago. The other was made a month before that. It looks like he might have been working for them. I'm a little surprised his probation officer didn't catch these calls."

In light of the fact that my worst offense had been sneaking more Halloween candy after my parents explicitly told me no more for the day, I had no idea how probation worked. "Probation officers can check a person's phone?"

"They can if the probation agreement allows it," Collin explained. "Most do. Phones are a microcosm of a person's life. Their schedules, who they've been in contact with, what they've been up to. The PO can check e-mail, calendars, social media, map apps, whatever. When law enforcement wants information about someone, their phone is often the best place to look. Sometimes it answers all the questions—who, what, when, where, why, and how. In fact, Woodruff's phone is how we tracked down his family. He's got two sisters down in Murfreesboro, but they aren't close. I spoke with them, but they didn't have anything to offer. The last time they'd seen their brother was when they invited him down to spend Easter with them and their families, and that's been months ago."

I backtracked, returning to something he said earlier. "Woodruff had made calls to two *different* convicted drug dealers?" I asked. "Isn't that unusual?" Judging from television shows and movies involving the drug trade, loyalty to a particular gang or distribution network seemed to be expected and each drug lord had a specific area they claimed as their own.

"It's a little unusual." Collin shrugged. "But the dealers were small-time guys, not big fish. They might not have even realized he was working for both of them. One theory I'm working is that one of Woodruff's drug customers came after him. People who buy drugs pay cash, and they know dealers carry a lot of cash on them."

It was the same reason he'd put forth earlier about why delivery drivers were common targets of crime. They, too, carried a lot of currency. "Do you have any way of knowing who he sold to?"

Collin's expression soured. "No. The recent addresses he'd input in his maps app were all for legal deliveries that

appeared on his lists. But I'm planning to visit the two dealers tomorrow and see what I can find out."

Colette raised her wineglass. "They're not in jail?"

"No," he said. "They were both young, small-time law-
breakers with no priors and no violent offenses. The judge
went easy on them, gave them probation."

"What about Gerard Woodruff?" I asked. "You said he'd
been found with marijuana before. Did he spend time in
jail?"

"No," Collin said. "He got probation, too."

Collin went on to explain that, with society's view of recreational marijuana use changing, and with many states, including Tennessee, relaxing their laws, judges were hesitant to
impose harsh punishments for an offense that might not even
be illegal in the foreseeable future. In 2016, then-governor
Bill Haslam signed a law that reduced a third conviction
for marijuana possession from a felony to a misdemeanor.
More recent legislation expanded the list of qualifying medical conditions for the use of medical marijuana. But while
the list of approved medical conditions now included cancer,
epilepsy, Alzheimer's disease, multiple sclerosis, HIV/AIDS,
sickle cell disease, and Parkinson's, the expanded list did
not include arthritis.

"Tennessee law imposes mandatory minimum fines
for subsequent marijuana offenses, but jail time is at the
judge's discretion." Collin added that marijuana transac-
tions were also subject to a stamp tax, and that those who
bought, transported, or imported marijuana into the state
were required to pay $3.50 for each gram of marijuana or
$350 per plant. Because possession of the drug was illegal,

most people didn't pay the tax because it was an admission that they'd broken the law. Rather, the unpaid taxes were assessed upon their conviction. "When Woodruff was arrested before, the officers found five plants in his trailer."

"Oh, yeah?" Buck said. "He was growing his own stash. Kind of like Colette here." He gestured out the back window to the raised-bed garden he installed for her a while back. She'd harvested the last of her crops near the end of September. All that was left were a few straggly tomato and pepper plants.

Colette tossed Buck a look. "There's a slight difference between garden-to-table vegetables and garden-to-ganja weed."

I had to wonder why Woodruff would go from growing his own supply to buying marijuana from someone else. When I asked Collin, he said, "People on probation can have their residences searched at random without a warrant. He had to change his MO or risk getting busted again. My guess is he found a place where it was easier to hide the finished product than the plants."

As Colette served the next course, a delicious leek soup and falafel, I mulled over what Collin had told us, trying to make sense of it all. "You said the dealers in Woodruff's phone had no violent offenses before, right? Why would they suddenly turn violent now?"

Collin shrugged. "Everyone has a tipping point. Maybe more was at stake. Maybe Woodruff had stolen drugs or money from them. Or maybe they didn't even mean to kill him, only to scare him. Sometimes people take things too far and accidentally kill someone they only meant to rough

up. They might not have known how long it took to strangle a person to death."

That creepy thought put an end to my appetite. I set my
spoon down and sat back in my chair.

Colette frowned at Collin. "Thanks a lot, Detective. I
spent hours on this meal."

"Don't blame him," I said. "It's my fault for asking." I
forced myself to sit back up, pick up my utensil, and choke
down a spoonful of soup to show her that the meal hadn't
been ruined.

Buck asked about Collin's visit to our neighbor, the iras-
cible Mr. Sibley. "Did he see anything going on at the playhouse when Woodruff was murdered? Maybe that white
SUV Whitney saw go by?"

"He claims he didn't see anything," Collins said. "He
says the murder must have taken place while he was in his
barn, refilling the gas tank on his tractor."

"What about the SUV I saw at his place before? What
did he say about that?"

"He says he's got horse traders coming out to his property constantly and several of them drive white SUVs of one
type or another. He can't be sure which one you saw."

Hmm. "The SUV wasn't hauling a horse trailer behind
it."

Collin raised a shoulder. "Maybe it was someone just
coming out to take a look at the horses, someone who wasn't
yet ready to buy."

I was willing to accept that Sibley might not have seen
anything taking place on our property, but he must have
heard the bell ringing erratically. After all, his tractor hadn't

been running at the time, and the sound of the bell would carry quite far, probably half a mile or so. "What did he say about the bell? He had to wonder why it sounded so strange."

Collin's eyes narrowed slightly. "He claims he didn't hear it."

Buck snorted. "That's got to be a lie. We heard the bell at the parsonage, and that's farther away than his barn. We were inside, too. He would've had his barn door open if he was refilling his gas tanks."

"You're not wrong," Collin said. "Problem is, he hung wind chimes in his barn to scare the birds off. Three sets. He said he was tired of birds nesting in the rafters and making a racket and dive-bombing him when he went in to get his tools and equipment. He probably confused the sound of the bell with the wind chimes clanging."

Buck proposed an alternative, one that had crossed my mind, too. "Or maybe he's the one who killed the delivery guy and he's just saying he didn't see or hear anything."

Collin asked, "What reason would he have to kill the man?"

Buck shrugged. "Sibley still thinks he owns our property. Maybe the delivery guy did something to piss him off. Who knows?"

I didn't voice the thought that crossed my mind, that maybe Sibley had come over to the playhouse to give us grief somehow and Woodruff had gotten in his way or witnessed something he shouldn't. I wasn't sure the theory had legs.

"Sibley certainly acts arrogant and entitled." Collin lifted one shoulder, uncommitted. "But without more, I can't consider him a serious suspect or even a person of interest."

I took a sip of my wine. "If we can't solve the murder, at least you can solve the mystery of the names for us. Who's Luther and who's Otto?"

"Luther must be the dog's name," Collin said, "because Sibley told me his hand's name is Johnny Otto. Sibley said Otto left to deliver a horse to a buyer just as he went to the barn to refuel his tractor."

Buck said, "That means Otto wasn't around when the bell rang, then."

"Or he was," Collin said darkly, "but he left immediately thereafter."

Buck held his beer poised at his mouth. "Oh, yeah? Is he a suspect, then?"

Collin let out a long breath. "At this point," he said, "everyone's a suspect."

"Even Luther?" I asked, trying to lighten the mood.

Collin chuckled mirthlessly. "He's the only one we can eliminate. That is one friendly dog."

We seemed to have both exhausted the subject and thrown a pall over the dinner, so I changed the subject entirely. "Word has gotten out about the Joyful Noise Playhouse. I received three e-mails today from performers and band managers asking about pricing to rent the place for shows."

"That's great news," Collin said.

"I'd better find someone to manage the place," I said. "And soon."

Buck offered a great suggestion. "Why don't you call Presley Pearson? Maybe she'd be interested."

I'd met Presley Pearson a while back, when I was managing properties on behalf of Home & Hearth for a wealthy real estate developer. Presley had been the developer's executive assistant, and had aspirations to follow in her boss's footsteps. When we'd later needed additional funds to buy the motor lodge, she'd joined us as a silent partner. In fact, she lived in one of the refurbished motel units now. She was professional but approachable, personable yet assertive when necessary. She was also organized and could juggle a lot of things at once. She had the right skill set for the job, and she might enjoy being her own boss. "I'll give her a try." It crossed my mind that maybe I should wait until after the court hearing on Tuesday, but I quickly dismissed the thought. We'd win in court. Surely. Right?

The main course having been devoured during our conversation, Colette served the manna dessert she'd mentioned weeks earlier, when she'd been coming up with ideas for the Collection Plate's menu.

Buck wolfed down his piece and rested a hand on his full belly. "I can't eat another bite."

"Me neither," Collin said. "Everything was delicious."

"If I have to go a size up with my coveralls," I told her, "you're to blame."

Colette angled her head and eyed us. "Should I put all of the things I served tonight on the menu for the Collection Plate?"

Our answer was a unanimous and enthusiastic *yes!* Colette was radiant, proud of her culinary creations.

Dinner complete, we cleaned up the kitchen and made our way to the living room. Colette and Buck cuddled together on the couch, while Collin took a seat in the recliner and I curled up in Emmalee's comfy Papasan chair with Sawdust on my lap. Knowing Collin had some leads to pursue in the murder was reassuring. He was a smart guy, an astute investigator. He'd have the crime solved in no time. Even so, if there was anything I could do to help move things along, I would. While I abhorred murder, I found the search for clues and the quest for justice challenging and fulfilling.

The wine having dulled my back pain and the food and alcohol making me drowsy, I fell asleep in minutes, making up for the shut-eye I'd lost the night before. I wouldn't have been able to say what the movie was about if someone put a gun to my head. When the show was over, Collin woke me with a gentle shake of my shoulder. Colette and Buck were likewise asleep on the couch, Buck snoring softly, Colette's head leaning on his broad shoulder. Anxiety seemed to have kept Collin awake. His brow was furrowed and his jaw set. I'd seen this look before. I knew he'd look this way until the case was solved and the killer was behind bars.

I picked Sawdust up in my arms and, together, the two of us saw Collin to the door. "You'll let me know what you find out after you talk to the drug dealers tomorrow?"

"I will," he said, though it was with the mutual understanding there would be some things he couldn't share. Detective work required discretion. He'd tell me what he could, when he could. He gave me a soft kiss in good-bye.

Fortunately, there was no activity overnight at the theater. The cameras had sent no notifications or images to my cell phone. It was also fortunate that the rain cleared up by mid-day on Sunday and Buck and I were able to remove the windows that needed to be returned to Laurel Cromwell. We were none too happy about it, though. We both grunted, groaned, and grumbled about the time her mistake—and my failure to follow up with her before installing the win-dows—had cost us. Next time there was a discrepancy in paperwork, I'd confirm things with my supplier before uti-lizing the materials.

After we'd taken one of the windows down, a small blue glass gem caught my eye. I pointed it out to Buck. "These glass jewels are very well made. If this jewel wasn't part of the window, I might think it was a real sapphire."

Out of curiosity, I typed *How can you tell the difference between glass and precious gems?* into the browser on my phone and ran a quick internet search. Per the websites, glass and gems differed in their refractive index and pre-cious gems ranked higher on something called the Mohs Hardness Scale. Glass had a lower density, making it lighter than precious stones. Even if I'd seriously thought some of the gems could be real precious stones and wanted to compare their relative weights and hardness to the glass jewels, I couldn't remove any of them without damaging them or the window. I supposed I could test their refrac-tiveness while they were still in the window, though, just to satisfy my inquisitive nature. I activated the flashlight app on my phone and shined it about, performing a rudimen-tary examination. A few of the small jewels appeared more brilliant than the larger ones, but I chalked it up to the smaller ones having relatively more facets for their size.

My amateur experiment concluded, I tucked my phone back into my pocket.

The Bubble Wrap and cardboard were still sitting on the floor of the playhouse where I'd left the materials the day before. As I wrapped the windows in the Bubble Wrap, I eyed the jewels again, the same thought crossing my mind once more. *Some of them sure look real.* But it was a ridiculous thought, wasn't it? Who would put valuable gems in a stained-glass window? And why? It made no sense.

I riffled through the packing materials and located the manila envelopes for the two windows Laurel had asked us to return. Both had been ordered by Antonia Szabo of Glassworks Gallery, her customer in Romania. But if Laurel turned the glass over to a local courier, how did it get delivered to the gallery? I figured he must have taken them somewhere for shipping overseas, probably Specialty Export Experts, where he'd stopped before coming to the playhouse. I returned the paperwork to the envelopes in case Laurel needed it back. I'd take the documentation to her when I exchanged the windows tomorrow.

The upgraded windows now repackaged for their return to Laurel Cromwell, I helped Buck wrangle our other custom window into place, and apply the seal and trim. Once I'd exchanged the other two windows tomorrow, we'd get the glass installed and schedule a security company to come out and install a professional, commercial system.

I was soaking in a hot bubble bath in the claw-foot tub Sunday evening when a call came in on my cell phone. After drying my fingers on a towel, I reached for the phone. It was

Collin calling. I jabbed the icon to accept the call and put him on speaker so I could continue to soak while we had our conversation.

"How'd it go today?" I asked. "Did you make an arrest?"

"No. Both of the dealers claim they've never heard of Gerard Woodruff, and that they have no idea why their phone numbers were in Woodruff's phone or where he'd gotten their numbers. They say they've never spoken to him, in person or on the phone. They allowed me to check their devices. Their recent call data listed incoming calls from Woodruff's phone, but the information showed both were missed calls. They never spoke, at least not on the phones I know about."

"You think the dealers could have other phones?"

"Yeah. One of the guys even said that, if he were dealing again, he'd be smart enough to use a burner phone for his drug business and not give his legit number out."

"That makes sense, doesn't it?"

"It does," Collin said. "But maybe they screwed up and accidentally gave Woodruff the numbers for their legitimate phones rather than their burners."

Could be. People sometimes inadvertently mixed things up, just like Laurel Cromwell had mixed up our window order. *Except* . . . "But if the calls were made from Woodruff's legit phone, too, that would mean all three of them messed up, the dealers by giving Woodruff the numbers for their regular phones, and Woodruff by using his legit phone to call the dealers, right? That's a lot of mistakes. It would be awfully coincidental, wouldn't it?"

"Woodruff might not have a burner," Collin said. "Maybe

he planned to delete the calls from his outgoing calls list but forgot to do it. At any rate, both guys claim to have ironclad alibis for their whereabouts on Friday afternoon. One claims he was at a group drug therapy session. The other says he was at his job. He works at a call center scheduling maintenance and repair visits for a heating and air conditioning repair company."

"Those alibis would be easy to verify, right? Surely, they wouldn't lie about something that could be quickly disproved."

"You'd be surprised," Collin said. "People sometimes think if they say something that can be easily checked, they're more likely to be believed. They think law enforcement wouldn't expect them to be so bold, and that we won't spend the time to follow up. Besides, the one who claims to have been at work panicked when I started questioning him."

"He did? You think that means he's guilty?"

"Maybe. Merely consorting with another criminal is a probation violation. The call history could prove he's failed to comply with the terms. He's worried his probation could be revoked and he'd have to go to prison. I'll follow up with his employer tomorrow. If his alibi looks legit, I'll talk with Woodruff's PO, see if he might know anything that could help."

We ended the call, and I continued to soak in the bath. Sawdust, meanwhile, stood on his hind legs next to the tub, peered over the edge, and batted at the bubbles. He'd learned the hard way not to try to walk along the edge. He'd gotten away with it a few times, but the last time he'd tried it he slipped on a wet spot and ended up in the bath with me.

I closed my eyes and tried to enjoy the bubbles, but while the warm bath soothed my aching muscles, my nerves remained jangled. I wouldn't be able to completely relax until we solved the deliveryman's murder.

CHAPTER 8

PET PROBATION

SAWDUST

Sawdust trailed Whitney to the door of their cottage, hoping she'd open the door to his carrier, which sat next to the door, and take him with her to the big building with the long rope. He'd enjoyed playing with it. He'd been thinking maybe he'd even try to climb it next time he had the chance. She didn't put him in his carrier, though. She just gave him a good-bye pat on the head and went out the door, leaving him behind.

He skittered up to the top of his cat tree to watch her out the window. She climbed into her car and drove off, leaving him to wonder why he seemed to be in trouble here. Why was she punishing him by leaving him home? Didn't she realize how much he missed her while she was gone?

Mew?

Sawdust looked down to see his fluffy calico friend looking up at him, her expression concerned. She seemed to sense that he was upset and she wanted to console him. He'd allow her. He climbed down to stand next to her and angled his head. Cleopatra whipped out her pink tongue and licked him across the forehead. She then looked him in the eye as if to ask, *All better now?*

He gave her a lick back, a wet one across the cheek. She might not be Whitney, but Cleo was a good friend. *All better.*

CHAPTER 9

COLOR SCHEME

WHITNEY

—

A collision backed up morning traffic on Hillsboro Pike. *Ugh.* Not an auspicious way to start the week. What's more, I had a busy day ahead. Thanks to Laurel Cromwell switching our window order with the one for the Romanian gallery, we were behind on the schedule I'd made for the rehab. I knew that if I really needed to I could revise the schedule. I was in charge of this project after all, and only answered to myself. But if I started letting me and Buck off the hook so easily, it could be a slippery slope. I had high expectations of myself, and I didn't want to have to give myself a poor performance review.

To make matters worse, besides wrestling with the timeline for our flip and dealing with traffic, Sawdust had put me on a guilt trip this morning when I'd left the house. He'd clearly wanted to come with me. He'd skittered to the door after me, and looked up at me with his pleading eyes. But Buck and I would be doing demolition work at the parsonage today, and we'd be traipsing in and out with materials for the dumpster. It could be dangerous to have Sawdust underfoot, and trying to prevent him from sneaking out the door would be problematic.

As I inched along in traffic, I glanced over at the businesses along the way. A hair salon remained dark, Monday being the typical day off for most beauticians. On the other hand, an auto repair shop bustled with early-morning business, people eager to drop their cars off for service before going into their offices. My eyes also spotted a small mom-and-pop jewelry store.

Wait. A jewelry store? Before I could even consciously think about what I was doing, I'd turned into the parking lot. The sign in the window read CLOSED, and the posted hours said the store wouldn't open for another twenty minutes. But maybe I could convince them to open their shop a little early.

I parked in front of the store and wrangled the box containing the Cheerful Garden window out of the back of my SUV. I carried it to the glass door and knocked. A man looked up from behind a display case where he was setting out items for sale. I surmised they locked everything away in a safe overnight. He circled around and came to the door.

I gave him a smile and spoke loudly so he could hear me through the glass. "I realize you're not open yet, but could I pay you for a quick consultation?"

He looked me up and down, checked out my SUV, and glanced at the traffic behind me, seeming to realize that although the situation was odd, there were plenty of witnesses watching us from the road who could identify me and my vehicle if I pulled any shenanigans and tried to rob him. He unlocked the door. "How can I help you?"

I didn't want to give away that the window in my arms

came from Laurel Cromwell's studio a mile down the road, so instead I said, "I found this window at a secondhand store. I was looking it over after I brought it home, and I noticed some of the glass jewels look like real gems. I might be totally off base. In fact, I probably am. It would be silly for someone to put precious stones in a window. But I just want to know for sure what I've got here."

"You want a quick evaluation?" he asked. "Like *Antiques Roadshow*?"

"Exactly."

"I suppose I could take a peek at it." He waved me in and directed me toward one of the counters, where he spread a long piece of velvety cloth. I unwrapped the window, leaned it back against the display case, and gently tilted it backward until it lay across the counter. He ran his gaze over the piece and made a quick assessment of the larger faceted pieces. "The large 'jewels'"—he made air quotes with his fingers—"are clearly made of glass. Otherwise, they'd be worth a fortune."

"These smaller jewels were the ones I thought could be precious gems." I pointed out some of the relatively tiny pieces.

The man whipped out a loupe and bent over to examine the first one, a purple gem. "Glass, not amethyst." He moved on to another. "Glass, not emerald."

My cheeks heated. I felt like a fool. The glass jewels were exactly what Laurel Cromwell had said they were, just tiny sparkling baubles, nothing more. I was wasting this man's time and my own.

Before I could stop him, he moved on to a small, red pear-shaped flower petal and paused. He pulled his head back, blinked a few times as if to clear his vision, and bent over to take another look. "Well, I'll be damned. This one's a ruby. A high-quality one at that." He looked up at me, his expression a mix of awe and suspicion.

He moved on to another flower, one that hadn't caught my eye before. "This white piece is opal." He checked a few others, determining they were mere glass, before discovering a topaz, another ruby, an onyx, and a sapphire. He stood. "You're sitting on a veritable gold mine here."

"I am?" My head spun. The fact that this window was so valuable could explain Laurel Cromwell's anxiousness to get it back. It could also explain why she'd been so concerned about security at the playhouse. I wondered why she hadn't told me the window contained actual gems.

The jeweler's eyes narrowed. "Where'd you say you got this window?"

Uh-oh. What had I told him? "An antique shop," I said. *Or had I said secondhand shop?* I guessed the two were close enough.

"Local place?" he asked.

"No. It was up in the mountains. I visited a bunch of stores when I was on vacation in Gatlinburg last month." The small mountain towns in the Smokies in the eastern part of the state were known for their antique stores, most of which sold overpriced items to tourists on vacation.

"Which store was it?" he asked. "And do they have any more of them? I'll close up shop and drive out there today." He gave me a smile that said he was teasing, as least in part.

I chuckled softly. "I can't even remember exactly where I found it. I picked up several pieces that day at various shops in Pigeon Forge, Sevierville, Townsend, and Walland. But

I do know this window was the only one they had. I asked the owner. I'd have bought all they had if there were more of them. I restore old properties, and a window like this adds a unique element."

The man smelled an opportunity. "You'll need an appraisal for your insurance. I'd be happy to do one for you."

"What do you charge for an appraisal?"

"It's a one-hundred-dollar hourly rate. It would take me several hours to address all the gems in this window, but the appraisal report would include details about each gem and market research comparisons to support my valuation."

I had neither the time, the money, nor a good reason to spend on an appraisal, but I asked for his card all the same. "Let me check with my business partner and get back to you." I'd been in the shop for approximately ten minutes. I performed some quick math in my head and offered the man a twenty-dollar bill for his time. That should cover it. "Thanks for your help."

"My pleasure."

While he slid the cash into the register's till, I rewrapped and boxed the glass and carried it out to my SUV. By then, the accident that had been blocking the road had been cleared and traffic was moving again. I climbed into the driver's seat and debated what to do. *Could the glass have something to do with Gerard Woodruff's murder? Did he even know he'd been transporting glass worth, well, I didn't know precisely, but let's just say "a whole lot" of money?*

I debated calling Collin at that point, but I knew his time was as valuable as mine, if not more so. As a homicide detective, he always had two or three dead bodies on his plate, so to speak. Better for me to suss things out a bit more before possibly wasting his time with irrelevant information. Besides, I enjoyed the sussing process. Trying to wrangle facts out of people was like trying to pull a crooked nail from a piece of wood, wholly satisfying when it finally came out.

I turned out of the parking lot of the jewelry store and continued down the pike to Laurel Cromwell's studio. A ten-foot U-Haul truck was parked at the end of the strip center's parking lot, the smallest truck the rental company offered.

When I pulled to a stop directly in front of Laurel's studio and glass shop, she looked up from her workspace behind the counter and set down the small tool in her hand. She rounded up two tall, boxed pieces secured to a dolly and wheeled them out to my SUV, greeting me with a smile. "Good morning, Whitney."

While my curiosity about the gems was piqued, I knew she might clam up if I was too aggressive in my questions. The fact that she hadn't mentioned the gems when she came to the playhouse Saturday told me she didn't want me to know about them. I decided to try an indirect approach, attempt to wear her down as if with a fine-grain sandpaper. As I pulled the wrapped windows from my cargo bay, I said, "The glass jewels were an elegant touch on these windows."

"I think so, too," she said.

I leaned the bejeweled windows against the outside of my SUV and turned to her. "Why didn't you tell me that adding jewels was an option?"

She shrugged. "You made it clear you were looking for affordable windows, so I didn't think you'd be interested in the upgrade."

True. I had opted for only two fully customized windows. I eyed her closely. "They're very pretty. If I didn't know better, I'd think some of the small glass jewels were actually the real deal."

Her smile seemed to freeze on her face. "The real deal?"

"Precious stones," I said. "Rubies. Emeralds. Diamonds. Sapphires."

She barked a laugh. But was it a sincere one or a nervous one? "Credit goes to the glass companies for that. Like I said, I buy the jewels pre-made. I don't grind them myself like I do with the other glass. But I agree, they look amazingly real."

I'd suspected as much. "For knock-offs, they're remarkably hard, too."

She tilted her head, her expression puzzled. "Hard? What do you mean?"

I fabricated a story to see how she'd respond. "I leaned one of the jeweled glass panels up against a clear glass windowpane that we'd removed. A couple of the jewels scratched the clear glass."

She had a ready answer. "That doesn't necessarily mean the jewels are harder. It only means they're sharper. After all, you can scratch a smooth rock with a pointy one, or scratch a smooth piece of stainless steel with a sharp stainless-steel utensil. It's not just about hardness. It's about shape. The glass jewels that scratched your clear pane must have had a jagged edge. Maybe we were too quick to congratulate the glass companies on their workmanship." Her smile broadened and she exhaled a huff of air that approximated a laugh. "I wear gloves when I work. Keeps shards from imbedding in my skin. Otherwise, I might have noticed that the edges weren't smooth. Fortunately, such tiny imperfections aren't visible to the naked eye."

What she said made sense. I'd felt a kinship with her when we first met, too, a connection forged by both of us being craftsmen. I hated to think she wasn't telling me the truth. *Could it be possible she doesn't know she'd used precious gems in the window? Does she actually think the gems are mere glass?*

I debated whether to take things further. I didn't want to risk jeopardizing Collin's investigation, but I figured it couldn't hurt to try to get some real answers from her, determine whether the jewels might have anything to do with Woodruff's murder, whether she might be a suspect. If I could get some answers here, maybe I could save Collin some time. I decided not to pussyfoot around anymore. Instead, I'd hit her quickly with my questions. Catching her off guard might get me the truest response. Taking a deep breath, I dove in. "You're lying to me, Laurel. We both know it. I've verified that the jewels are precious stones. So, tell me. What's with all the gems inlaid in the glass? And why didn't you tell me about them when you came to the playhouse?"

Her head snapped back as if she'd been struck, but a second later she straightened and her mouth quirked in a feeble smile. "I couldn't very well tell you that the windows were worth tens of thousands of dollars," she said, her tone matter-of-fact. "Not once you told me you couldn't return them immediately, anyway. I had no idea who you might tell, and if word got out, someone might have tried to steal the windows right out of your theater. Or they might try to pry the gems out of the glass. The best I could do was try to make sure they were safe. That's why I asked about your security system." She offered a contrite cringe. "No offense, but I don't really know you well. How was I to know if I could trust you?"

She had a point. But while her explanation had some reason to it, I wasn't sure I bought it. "Did Gerard Woodruff know about the gems?"

"If he did," she said, "he didn't learn it from me. I didn't tell him for the same reasons I didn't tell you."

"But you trusted him to deliver the windows to the shipping company," I pointed out. "Why? Did you know him personally?"

"No, I didn't know him personally. I didn't arrange the courier service or the overseas shipping, either. My customer took care of all of that. I figured if the gallery owner trusted Woody with their valuable pieces, I could trust him with my regular stained-glass projects. His rates were very reasonable, so I hired him to make deliveries sometimes, too. Your delivery for instance. Since he was already coming to my studio to pick up the windows for the gallery, it made sense to have him take your windows and deliver them afterward."

I watched her closely as I asked the next question. "Do you think the gems were why he was killed?"

"I don't see how," she said. "The woman who owns the gallery made it clear she expects discretion. Even if Woody knew about the gems, I can't imagine he'd tell anyone."

"The shipping company would have to be informed, too." After all, they'd have to know to be extra careful with the valuable delivery. *There'd be customs taxes, too, right?*

"As far as the international shipping, that's on the gallery. They make their own arrangements. I didn't even know who they used until I got the orders mixed up. Normally, once Woody picked up the glass, it was out of my hands. Of course, I'll have to take the windows directly to the shipper today now that Woody's . . . gone." She inhaled a shaky breath. But who could blame her? Learning that someone you knew had been murdered would be upsetting, even if you had only a nominal business relationship.

"Did you find a new local delivery service?"

"Not yet," she said. "Got one you'd recommend?"

"Can't help you there," I said. "My cousin and I have a van and a trailer. We transport all of our own materials."

She hiked a thumb at the U-Haul. "I plan to do the same. At least for the time being. Woody's murder has me rattled. Do you know anything? Do the police have any suspects?"

I told her what Collin had told me. "The detective said that deliverymen are common victims of robberies. Thieves know delivery workers carry cash to make change, and that they receive cash tips, too. Plus, delivery people work alone. They're distracted and have their backs turned while they're unloading things from their vehicles. It makes them easy targets." I didn't tell her about the drugs that had been found in Woodruff's car. There seemed no point in disparaging his reputation unnecessarily. The marijuana might not have anything to do with his murder.

Her eyes glistened again, and her nose wriggled as she

seemed to fight a cry. "I wish that whoever attacked Woody had only taken his money and not his life."

"Me too," I said. "Nobody deserves to die like that." I was curious about the pricing of the windows and addressed this in my next question. "You charged the Romanian gallery only a few hundred dollars more for the windows than you charged me. Why didn't you charge them for the gems?"

Her vague smile disappeared entirely, replaced by a firm frown. "Look, Miss Whitaker. I've probably told you too much already. I can understand your curiosity, but it wouldn't be right for me to gossip about my clients. You're a businesswoman yourself. Surely, you can understand client confidentiality."

"I understand. I've known people who worked in the homes of local celebrities and they were asked to sign nondisclosure agreements." My uncle Roger, Buck, and my other cousin, Owen, had once signed an NDA when they'd built shelves in the home of a popular country-western star. The agreements were standard practice for people in the public eye who didn't want their secrets spilled. I raised apologetic palms. "Sorry I pushed." Actually, I wasn't sorry at all. Though it was risky to try to dig further, I decided a little subterfuge might get me some more information. If I accused her of wrongdoing, maybe she'd feel the need to defend herself and tell me more. "It's none of my business if you've got some kind of under-the-table operation going on here."

My ploy worked. Her eyes flashed in alarm. "Everything I do here is aboveboard. I run an honest business." She bit her lip, but after a few seconds she leaned in. "Can I trust you to keep a secret?"

I leaned toward her, too. "I'll take it to my grave."

"The customers provided the gems. That's why I didn't charge for them. The owner of the gallery told me the windows were a special order for a member of a European royal family. The client wanted their heirloom gems preserved in glass so that the entire family could enjoy them."

"I get it. I've worked on carpentry projects before where the customer provided special materials that they wanted incorporated into our projects, such as reclaimed wood from an old family homestead." Obviously, when a customer provided the materials, we only charged them for the labor.

Laurel straightened up, seemingly relieved that I understood her situation. "Can you imagine being so wealthy you can use precious stones in your windows?"

"Not at all," I said. "It's like something out of a fairy tale."

Moving on to the task at hand, I removed my standard replacement windows from her dolly and slid them into the cargo bay of my SUV. Once I was done, Laurel used a box cutter to slice the tape on the boxes I'd returned and peeked inside to verify that they were, in fact, the bejeweled windows. She removed the wrap and bent down to ensure that all of the jewels were intact.

"Everything okay?" I asked.

"Yes. I just wanted to make sure none of the jewels had come loose before I repackage the windows for shipping, especially since you mentioned the scratch. My reputation is at stake, after all." She released a long breath, and turned from the glass to me. "It's like they say. God is in the details."

"Some say that's where the devil is." I watched her closely, conflicted, unsure if I could trust her.

She chuckled softly. "I'll guess we'll never know, will we?"

Oh, we'll know all right. I'll make damn sure of it.

CHAPTER 10

HUSTLE AND RUSTLE

WHITNEY

I still felt slightly unsettled and unsatisfied as I drove away from Laurel's studio. Though her story was plausible and she'd come up with it quickly, an indicator that it was likely the truth, I wasn't entirely sure I could trust her. She seemed genuinely shocked and upset about Gerard Woodruff's death, so I didn't think she was involved directly in his murder. But was she otherwise involved in something shady? Something just felt a little . . . *off*. Then again, maybe it only seemed that way because the situation was unusual, to me at least. I flipped properties locally. What did I know about art and international business? Not much, that's for sure.

I mulled things over, trying desperately to reach conclusions. *Why would anyone put such valuable jewels in a window?* I'd barely noticed that the gems weren't mere glass. It seemed like a terrible waste. Then again, maybe I was being judgmental. Owning a cherished collection of precious jewels was so far out of my realm, I couldn't relate. Still, I decided it couldn't hurt to snoop just a wee bit more before heading back to the playhouse. It had yet to be determined whether the windows had something to do with Woodruff's murder.

Laurel hadn't mentioned the name of the shipping company the Romanian gallery had contracted with, but I knew which one it was. It had been noted on Woodruff's list of deliveries, right before the line for our theater. S.E.E. I still had the website pulled up on my phone. When I stopped at a red traffic light, I took a quick look to refresh my memory as to the address.

With so many black, silver, gray, or white cars on the roads these days, my red SUV wasn't exactly subtle. That's why I didn't try to follow Laurel to Specialty Export Experts. Rather, I put the pedal to the metal and beat her there. I had a hunch she'd want to divest herself of the bejeweled glass as quickly as possible—the windows were a liability, after all—and I wasn't wrong. *There she is now.* The orange U-Haul popped up over a rise and slowed as it approached the main gate.

I'd parked between two semis at the gas station and truck stop next door to the shipping company, but not before driving a circle around the company's expansive campus to get the lay of the land. A ten-foot-high aluminum fence enclosed the facility. Black mesh tarps had been affixed to most of the perimeter fencing. The fabric allowed wind to blow through and keep the facility cool, but it would prevent anyone from getting a good look inside. Just as delivery drivers were common targets for thieves, so, too, were truckers, who could have hundreds of thousands of dollars in valuable merchandise in a single trailer. I could understand why the company would want to keep prying eyes from seeing into the campus.

So instead of trying to see through the opaque fabric covering the fence, I focused on the things that stuck up over it. I could see the second floor of a contemporary two-story office building featuring floor-to-ceiling windows, the roof of an enormous prefab metal warehouse, and a truck-yard filled with tractor-trailers and stacks of large metal shipping containers that could be moved by truck, train, or boat. The colorful rectangular boxes were stacked like children's blocks. A tall crane and several forklifts maneuvered around the yard, moving the shipping containers.

The company had two wide gates—one in front along the main road and another at the back, allowing trucks to pull straight through the campus without having to make any turns. Both gates were adorned with the company's logo, a green-and-blue globe with Specialty Export Experts' slogan, S.E.E. THE WORLD, printed in block letters on a curved banner across the center. Both gates were flanked by enclosed booths manned by security personnel. My stomach clenched. This was one of the last places Gerard Woodruff had been alive before coming to the playhouse.

I couldn't see much from this distance, and I didn't have binoculars with me. I checked the app store on my phone and, sure enough, there was a binoculars app. *There truly is an app for everything.* I downloaded the app on my phone and was thrilled to see it provided up to forty-five times zoom, much better than the phone's built-in camera was capable of. Unfortunately, when I zoomed in on Laurel Cromwell unrolling the window of her rental truck to speak with the security guard at the front gate, all I got was a close-up of the man's shiny bald head and the irregularly shaped brownish mole on his forehead. *He should really get that looked at.*

I zoomed back out. The guy had no hair on his face, either, though he wore a warm smile. In an era when many men sported goatees if not full beards, his hairlessness gave him an appearance of innocence, like a young boy. He was average size and fit, his muscles well defined but not bulging under his polo shirt. The guy checked a clipboard and pushed a button inside his booth. The gate slid open, allowing Laurel to drive through. She disappeared behind the administrative building. Barely a minute later, she emerged from the back gate and circled around to the main road to access the southbound interstate entrance ramp. *The company sure runs an efficient operation.* Unfortunately, the company's efficiency was all I'd gleaned from my visit here. *What a waste of time.*

I lowered my phone and tapped the screen to close the binoculars app. After stowing my phone in my cupholder, I headed up the interstate to the playhouse.

My gut clenched again as I approached. A Sumner County Sheriff's Department cruiser was parked at the locked gate. Deputy Atchison had climbed out and stood before the gate. He was the same deputy who'd come out here before, when Sibley and I had first argued about the validity of his adverse possession notice. Nolan Sibley stood beside the officer. Sibley's Labrador retriever sat dutifully beside his master.

Buck's van was parked in front of the theater, but my cousin was nowhere to be seen. *He's okay, isn't he?* The mere thought that my cousin might have met the same fate as the delivery driver turned my blood to frozen slush.

I slowed and pulled over to the side of the road. Deputy Atchison raised a bullhorn to his lips and spoke through it, attempting to get the attention of anyone who might be in the theater. *Good luck with that.* Odds were Buck had country music playing at top volume through his earbuds. He wouldn't hear a meteor strike the earth. *He'd feel his phone vibrate, though.* I sent him a quick text: *Deputy at gate. Get your butt out here.*

A moment later, the door to the playhouse opened and Buck brought his butt, as well as all of the rest of him, to the driveway. I drove up, parked, and climbed down from my vehicle.

Ignoring Sibley, Buck addressed the deputy. "Hello, Deputy. What's going on?"

Despite the fact that Buck had addressed his question to the officer, Sibley responded. "What's going on is that you've stolen my best stud horse."

Buck didn't look at Sibley, again addressing Deputy Atchison. "What's this nonsense about us stealing a horse?"

The deputy pointed to an area to the left, behind the playhouse. Sure enough, there was Pegasus, happily rolling around on his back like an oversized dog. He looked thrilled to have escaped from Sibley's place. Who could blame him?

Buck shrugged. "I have no idea how that horse got here." He turned to Sibley. "But if this is your land, as you claim, then you've got no standing to accuse us of stealing your horse. He'd be rolling around on *your* property."

Sibley fumed. Buck's warped logic had pushed his

buttons. The way the man's chest was heaving, he just might bust the pearl buttons on his expensive Western shirt, too, if he didn't calm down.

Sibley pointed a finger at Buck. "Horse rustling is a felony. You're in big trouble here."

Buck snorted. "I didn't steal your horse. He probably hopped the fence because he was trying to get away from you and your electric prod."

A smirk tugged at the deputy's mouth, but he fought it back. "How 'bout you let Sibley round up the horse and get him back to his pasture?"

"Good idea." Buck unlocked the gate and cast a look of disdain at our neighbor. "Round up all of his poop while you're at it."

Sibley ignored Buck and stalked across our acreage with his rope and cattle prod at the ready. As he approached, Pegasus spotted the prod and reared up, letting out a loud whinny. If Sibley shocked the horse, I'd snag the deputy's Taser and give Sibley a taste of his own medicine, see how he liked it. Fortunately, Pegasus seemed to realize Sibley wanted him home. He galloped over to the gate between our properties. We could see that the gate was open and our sawhorses were knocked over. The horse must have figured out how to get the gate open. *Clever beast.*

The situation handled, Deputy Atchison bade us good day and drove off.

Once we were alone, Buck exhaled sharply. "That pony pimp is really chapping my hide. What time is the hearing on Sibley's claim tomorrow?"

"Ten A.M.," I said. One way or another, the matter would be put to rest then.

Buck muttered, "It can't come soon enough," and headed back to the theater.

I returned to my SUV, drove it through the gate, and re-attached the chain and padlock. As Buck and I installed the replacement windows, I told him about my trips to the jewelry store and Laurel Cromwell's studio. "The jeweler confirmed that the jewels were precious gems."

"Is that so? Huh." He pondered that fact for a second or two. "What did the glass lady say when you asked her about it?"

"She said the windows were a special order placed by the gallery for a royal family, and that the royals provided the gems to her. They wanted to display them in a prominent way in their home, and they thought stained-glass windows were the way to do it. Sounds over-the-top, doesn't it?"

"I don't know," Buck said. "Weren't there all kinds of stones built into the Taj Mahal?"

He had a point. Surely, the Indian palace wasn't the only structure to include precious gems. Probably some cathedrals and castles did, too. Maybe I'd been too quick to find the story fanciful. I went on to ask Buck whether I should bother Collin with the information.

"Might as well tell him," he said. "The jewels might have nothing to do with the case, but it's his call to make."

I felt inclined to share the news, as well. I texted Collin: *Got some info for you. Could be nothing. Could be something. Call when you can.*

He phoned an hour later as we were cutting trim for the windows.

I gave him the rundown and asked, "What do you think?"

He mulled it over for a moment. "The paperwork didn't

note that the window included precious stones. My guess is that only Laurel, the gallery owner, and the customer who ordered the windows knew that some of the jewels are real rather than glass. It seems unlikely the owner of the gallery would let her delivery guy know he was transporting something so valuable. He could up and disappear with them."

Even so, I felt a little disappointed. Here I thought I might be on to a critical piece of the mystery and Collin was easily explaining it all away. Maybe I wasn't as good at finding clues as I'd hoped. "You've got an answer for everything, don't you?"

"I'm not saying the gems couldn't be something," he said, possibly just to appease me. "Maybe I'm wrong. Maybe the gallery owner made sure Woodruff knew he was transporting valuable gems so he'd be extra careful with them. Maybe he spilled the beans to someone, and got himself killed for it. Once I've exhausted my other leads, I'll drive out and talk to Laurel Cromwell." He updated me on the leads he'd already pursued. "The alibis the dealers gave panned out. One was at work and the other was in group therapy, just as they'd claimed. Neither of them could have killed Woodruff. I talked to Woodruff's probation officer, a guy named Bill O'Brien. He said he routinely checked Woodruff's phone, but that he'd always start with the date *after* their last meeting. Woodruff apparently caught on, and realized he could make calls directly after his meetings with his PO, on the same day, and his PO would be none the wiser."

Something niggled at me. It was clear that, even if neither of the dealers had killed Woodruff, there was some sort of connection between him and the dealers. When trying to figure something out, it was wise to start at the beginning, right? Where had their relationship originated? "Where would Woodruff have met these guys?" I asked. "Were they in jail together? Maybe that therapy group?"

"No," Collin said. "I can't seem to determine how they crossed paths. They live in entirely different parts of the city, they aren't the same age, and they didn't perform their court-ordered community service together. I have no idea how they found each other."

"Online, maybe," I suggested. After all, a person could connect with anyone else across the globe via the World Wide Web, assuming both parties had internet access, of course.

"Could be," he said. "Odd thing is, both of the dealers are clean. They've passed their drug tests for months. We searched their houses and cars and found nothing. No drugs. No cash. There's no evidence that they're dealing again. But maybe they hooked Woodruff up with one of their contacts. I plan to check in with the guys they used to run with. I'm going to visit the trailer park where Woodruff lived and see what I can find out from his neighbors, too. They might have seen something. I'm also going to retrace all of his delivery stops on Friday, see if anyone he made a delivery to seems suspicious or saw anything out of the ordinary."

I didn't tell him I'd already made a stop at one of those places, the shipping company. He might not appreciate me snooping around. But I'd been careful and discreet. No one had even known I was there.

We ended the call so he could run down his leads. I had

an important matter to handle, too—convincing Presley Pearson that managing the Joyful Noise Playhouse would be the perfect opportunity for her.

I'd called Presley yesterday, and we'd arranged for her to come look at the playhouse today. She'd was due to arrive in just a few minutes. I walked out to the gate to unlock it for her.

Soon she arrived for her tour, turning through the gate in her bright blue Ford Fiesta. She climbed out of her car. Her short, dark hair angled over her forehead, ending in a stylish point above her left ear. She wore spike heels along with a sleek pumpkin-colored dress that skimmed her brown skin. She'd accessorized her attire with a chandelier necklace of champagne-colored beads, not unlike the precious stones in the Romanian gallery's window, along with matching earrings. As usual, Presley had dressed to the nines. I was dressed to the twos, as in two-by-fours. But our clothing accurately depicted the roles we'd chosen for ourselves. She was the sophisticated, up-and-coming real estate mogul, while I was the hands-on designer and contractor.

Presley had a natural nose for business. More importantly, she had a strong work ethic. We might not look or dress alike, but determination and tenacity were traits we shared. After getting off to a rocky start when we'd first met, I was glad the two of us had eventually found common ground, and that we could work together on these joint ventures.

After giving me a quick greeting, she looked up at the theater building and her mouth dropped in amazement. "Wow." She splayed her fingers and waved her hand in front of us to indicate the playhouse. "This place just screams 'good time.'"

"You don't think we overdid it with the purple paint and colored lights?" Okay, so I was fishing for another compliment on my design elements, but her opinion meant something to me.

"Not at all. It's unique and memorable. Now show me to the office."

I took her inside and showed her the space that would be her office if she chose to take on the role of theater manager. She glanced around the empty space as if envisioning how she would furnish and decorate it. Once she'd looked over the office space, I showed her the refurbished space that would serve as a dressing room for the performers, the storage area, and the stage. "We're still waiting on the curtain to be delivered, but it should only be a few more days." We'd ordered a thick purple velvet curtain with gold edging. Elegant, yet with a funky twist. We'd already installed the metal crossbeam it would hang from and the mechanized pulley that would open and close it.

When we were done at the playhouse, I took her over to see the parsonage. We weren't nearly as far along in the rehab of the old house, but we'd had to order many of the kitchen appliances and they'd only recently begun to arrive. We'd also had to work out how to install a grease trap and vents.

When we finished the tour, I said, "Buck, Colette, and I will offer you an equity interest in the business, as well as a salary and commission on ticket sales once things are up and running. What do you think?"

"I think I'll never get nearly as far as an executive assistant as I will working for myself." She dipped her head once in an emphatic nod. "I'll do it."

We quickly worked out the particulars. She'd keep her current job while spending time during her lunch breaks, on evenings, and weekends putting a lineup together. Once the playhouse was profitable enough, she'd turn in her resignation notice at her current job and focus on the theater full time, while pursuing real estate investments on the side.

I said, "Buck and I know nothing about outfitting a theater. We'll need to look into speaker systems, microphones, soundboards, spotlights, all kinds of show equipment."

She thought aloud, "We'll also need tables and display boards for performers who want to set up a merchandise booth."

"Let's host open-mic Mondays," I suggested. "We can let singer-songwriters sign up for ten-minute slots." Presley, Buck, and I had gotten our big break with the motel rehab. It would be nice to pay our luck forward, help launch someone else's career.

"That's a great idea," she agreed. "It'll help spread the word about this place and support emerging artists. I'll check with Gia Revello, too. She seems to know everyone in the music business. She can put me in touch with some up-and-coming singers and bands."

Gia Revello was a well-established, no-nonsense record label executive. I'd met her while rehabbing the Music City Motor Court motel. Gia and her husband had later bought one of the two-bedroom units. She and Presley were neighbors in the small complex.

I walked Presley out to her car and bade her good-bye. She raised a manicured hand out the open window and tooted her horn twice in good-bye. *Beep-beep!*

I felt a surge of excitement. Things were really moving along. But when a whinny sounded from Sibley's property next door, I had to wonder if we might be getting ahead of ourselves here. Could the man who'd accused us of horse rustling be legally allowed to steal our land tomorrow?

CHAPTER 11

SUITS ME JUST FINE

SAWDUST

The cat could tell something was up Tuesday morning. Whitney was distracted and anxious. He could smell the adrenaline on her. Cats had quite adept noses. She'd fed him his breakfast twice. Not that he was complaining. Who didn't like to indulge in a feast now and then? She hadn't dressed in her usual boots and coveralls, either. She'd set a pair of pumps on the floor and laid out a dress on the bed, shooing him away when he hopped up on the bed and tried to lie on it.

Sawdust wasn't sure what was going on, but he hoped whatever Whitney was worried about would work out in her favor. He didn't like to see her distraught. He did his best to help calm her, rubbing around her ankles just like she rubbed him to calm him down.

Finally, she grabbed her purse and headed to the door. He scurried up his cat tree to put his face in easy reach of hers. She gave him a quick kiss on top of the head and a scratch under the chin. "Wish us luck!"

CHAPTER 12

NOW HEAR THIS!

WHITNEY

Buck and I sat on a bench in the courtroom, speaking quietly with the attorney from the title company. Technically, our presence was not necessary. We wouldn't be called to the stand to provide testimony. The facts were not in dispute. The case involved an interpretation of law, not facts, and would be decided on the documents filed with the county clerks.

I'd arrived twenty minutes early and had been eyeing the clock every few seconds since. It was nine fifty now, and there was no sign of Nolan Sibley. Because he hadn't hired an attorney, he'd be representing himself today. They say a lawyer who represents himself has a fool for a client. Seems the same logic applied to nonlawyers, too. If he was as pompous and irritating in court as he'd been at the playhouse, he'd certainly win no brownie points with the judge.

As we waited, the judge called various parties up to her bench, and rendered quick decisions on procedural matters. Meanwhile, the minutes continued to tick away on the black-and-white wall clock mounted over the door.

Tick-tick-tick. Nine fifty-five came. Then nine fifty-six. Still no Sibley.

I leaned toward our attorney and whispered, "What happens if he doesn't show?"

Buck raised hopeful brows. "We'd automatically win, right?"

"Unfortunately, no," she said. "Because the judge will only be interpreting the applicable law, she can do that without the opposing party here."

Buck exhaled sharply. "Seems Sibley ought to have to show up for his own case. He's costing us time and money here. He should have to do the same."

Nine fifty-seven. Nine fifty-eight. Nine fifty-nine. The judge handled another matter that took several minutes before calling the matter of *Sibley versus Whitaker and Whitaker* at six minutes after ten.

Even though our presence was irrelevant, Buck and I figured it couldn't hurt to show the judge that we cared enough about the outcome of this hearing to be present today. We followed our attorney to the defendants' table and took seats there.

The judge greeted us with a nod and glanced over at the empty plaintiff's table. She looked out at the gallery with an expectant look on her face. When she saw nobody moving forward to claim the table, she called out, "*Sibley versus Whitaker and Whitaker*!" She looked down at the case file in front of her. "Mr. Nolan Sibley, *pro se*. Please come forward."

Buck leaned over to our attorney. "What's *pro se* mean?"

Our attorney whispered back to him, "It means he's representing himself."

As the judge scanned the room again, our attorney stood, "Mr. Sibley hasn't arrived yet, Your Honor."

"Have you heard from him?"

"No, ma'am."

She turned to her bailiff. "Has he called the court?"

He likewise said, "No, ma'am."

The judge's expression soured. Apparently she didn't like to have her time wasted, either. "We'll move ahead without him then." She ran her eyes quickly over the petition. "I see that Mr. Sibley asserts he owns the entirety of the property formerly owned by Walkers Creek Community Church, and which was recently purchased by Whitney and Buck Whitaker. He submitted a copy of his adverse possession notice filed in Sumner County with his petition."

Our attorney stood and presented the same arguments she'd set forth in our response, that his notice didn't adequately identify the portion of the property located in Sumner County, and that, having never been filed in Davidson County, it did not apply to the portion of the property within the Davidson County limits. The attorney's last word had barely left her lips when the judge said, "I find in favor of the defendants. Mr. Sibley's notice is legally insufficient. He has no interest in any portion of the property."

Buck and I threw our arms in the air as if performing the wave in a football stadium, then slapped them together in two high fives. A grin tugged at the judge's lips for a second or two, then she was back to business, banging her gavel and calling the next case. We thanked our attorney, left the table, and headed out of the courthouse.

The instant we passed out of the courthouse door, Buck shrugged out of his sport coat and yanked at the knot on his necktie. "Get me out of this monkey suit!"

I couldn't wait to get out of my demure black dress and pumps, either. The heels weren't high, but I still felt uncertain walking in them. They forced me into a tiptoe and offered no ankle support. I'd take my steel-toed work boots over kitten heels any day.

We made our way to the parking lot, where Buck climbed into his van and I climbed into my SUV. Less than a half hour later, we'd parked our vehicles side by side in the parking lot of the playhouse and stood shoulder to shoulder, looking over at Sibley's property. His fancy Ford F-150 Limited pickup sat in front of his Victorian farmhouse. His horses grazed nonchalantly in the pasture behind the house, while a trio of buzzards circled overhead. One of the barn doors stood open, but we didn't see Sibley anywhere. We didn't see Johnny Otto or his blue pickup, either. Maybe he was off delivering a horse or picking up supplies at the feed-store.

Buck's eyes narrowed. "Think Sibley forgot the hearing was today?"

"Who knows," I said. "Maybe he didn't show up because he knew he'd lose. He could be cowering in his barn, embarrassed to show his face."

After we stepped inside the playhouse, Buck stopped in front of the door of the bell tower, an evil grin on his face. "You know what Sibley can't hide from?" He opened the door and pointed up the steps. "Our victory bell."

"You're going to gloat?" Given Sibley's propensity to throw rocks and brandish his cattle prod, it could be dangerous to antagonize him. "I'm not sure that's a good idea. Sibley's got some screws loose. Who knows how he'll react."

"Just a couple yanks of the rope and I'll be done."

"You promise that'll be it?"

"I promise."

Given that I couldn't talk Buck out of it, I followed him into the belfry. With any luck, Sibley wouldn't put two and two together, wouldn't realize the bell ringing had anything to do with today's court hearing.

Buck pointed up to the bell above us. "Let's go up to the tower. Maybe we'll be able to see him from there."

In for a penny, in for a pound. I just hoped we weren't in for retribution.

We ascended the steps. I cringed involuntarily when we climbed the flight where Woodruff's body had lain. We took extra care as we climbed the last few extra-steep steps and ventured onto the platform. Buck reached over and grabbed the rope just a few inches below the bottom of the bell, pulling it down smooth yet hard. The bell swung to the side, and the clapper hit the metal with a resonant *DONG!* He pulled again. *DONG! DONG! DONG!*

I grabbed the rope and yanked it out of my cousin's hand. "That's enough. We won. It's over."

We edged to the railing and peeked out over Sibley's spread. We could see the top of his house with the rooster weather vane. His horses still grazing in the pasture. Walkers Creek cutting a meandering line across the acreage. The trio of buzzards continuing to circle in the air. But we saw something else, too. Something extremely concerning. There, fifty yards behind the barn, not visible from our earlier vantage point, lay Nolan Sibley, flat on his back, unmoving. His hat had fallen off, but he still gripped his cattle prod. Pegasus nuzzled a bale of hay nearby.

I pointed. "Buck! Look!"

Buck turned his head, spotted Sibley, and squinted. He cupped his hands around his mouth and hollered, "Hey, Sibley! You okay over there?"

We were too far away to get a good look at the man. I whipped my phone from my pocket and used the binoculars app I'd downloaded on my visit to the shipping company to get a better view. Buck stood next to me, eyeing my screen. As I zoomed in on Sibley's face, one thing became clear. He'd been hit. *Hard.* His nose was so purple and swollen it resembled a rutabaga, and his lips were split and bloody. His mouth hung partly open, revealing teeth as jagged as a monster's. They'd been broken. His eyes were at half-mast and not blinking, staring straight up into the cloudless autumn sky.

I gasped, my head going light and airy. "Oh, my gosh! Oh, my gosh! Oh, my gosh!"

Buck might have been gloating a moment ago, but he wasn't truly heartless. "I'm going over! Call for help!"

While I closed the binoculars app and dialed 911, my cousin bolted down the stairs of the bell tower and out of the theater, running for the fence like a man on fire. As I spoke to the dispatcher, I saw Buck reach the gate between our property and Sibley's. Finding it locked, he climbed over it, dropped to the ground on the other side, and sprinted in the direction of the barn. Sibley's Labrador bolted out from the barn door, barking, but when he realized his vocal warnings were ineffective, he gave up and instead fell in beside Buck, running along with him. The dispatcher kept me on the phone, but I carried it with me as I hurried out of the bell tower and out to the road. I'd wave down the ambulance, just as I'd done after we found Gerard Woodruff. Only this time, I'd do it from Nolan Sibley's driveway next door.

Three minutes passed, feeling like three eternities, before I finally heard the wail of the siren in the distance. The ambulance raced up Lickton Pike. I jumped up and down and waved my arms to get the driver's attention. The ambulance turned into the drive and the driver rolled down his window. I experienced a sick sense of déjà vu. It was the same man who'd driven the ambulance that had come to pick up Woodruff on Friday. I'd never dreamed I'd be giving this team of medics repeat business.

I pointed. "Behind the barn!"

The man drove the ambulance up Sibley's paved driveway and eased onto the dirt to head to the barn. I rushed after the vehicle. As I neared the sprawling Victorian, it dawned on me that someone might live here with Sibley. Though I'd seen people come and go with horse trailers, I'd assumed they were buying a horse from the man. I hadn't noticed anyone other than Nolan Sibley at the house regularly. Might someone be in the house? Someone who didn't yet realize that he'd been hurt?

I ran up the steps to the wraparound porch and knocked on the door. *Rap-rap-rap!* Spotting a doorbell, I tried that, too. *Ding-ding-ding-ding-ding!* But there was no response.

I darted back down the steps and ran around to the back of the horse barn. I found Buck and Luther standing there alongside the paramedics. While the EMTs had made efforts to revive Gerard Woodruff, they weren't attending to Nolan Sibley. One good look at him told me why. The guy had clearly gone to meet his maker. Beside the fact that his face was smashed nearly beyond recognition, his color was off and his limbs were rigid with rigor mortis. I turned my head away, grimacing in horror. *I hope I'll be able to get that image out of my head.*

Buck ran a hand over the dog's head to reassure him and cast me a glance. "The sheriff's department and someone from the medical examiner's office are on the way."

While we waited, the medics asked us questions we had no answers for. "What happened here?" "Did Mr. Sibley have any medical conditions?" "What medications did he take?" Other than calling in to report that he'd been injured, we were darn useless.

It seemed awfully coincidental that two men had been killed within the last five days on adjacent properties, only a couple hundred yards apart. Could Sibley's death have something to do with the murder of Gerard Woodruff in the bell tower? Had he been killed by the same person? Could the killer have thought Sibley might have seen them or have information that could implicate them, and come here to do away with him while Buck and I were at the courthouse? Had the killer known Buck and I would be tied up elsewhere this morning? But who would know besides Sibley, us, and our attorneys?

Johnny Otto. That's who.

But what reason would Johnny have to kill his employer? I could tell Johnny didn't care much for Sibley, but was the fact that his boss was a condescending jerk reason enough to kill him? If a person didn't like their boss, they could just up and quit, find a new place to work. Then again, maybe Sibley did something that made Johnny Otto snap. It had been clear Otto didn't like Sibley using the prod on the horses. Maybe Sibley had used it one time too many and Otto had confronted him. The two could have come to blows. I could see it happening, easy. Otto had expressed his disdain for his boss's aggressive tactics toward his horses the first time we'd met him. Heck, even if that's what happened, I'd bet Sibley would've thrown the first punch. I had a hard time seeing Otto as the bad guy.

A Sumner County Sheriff's Department cruiser arrived. Behind the wheel sat Deputy Atchison. I wasn't sure if that was good or bad. He knew we'd been engaged in petty squabbles with the man who was now lying dead in his barnyard. Deputy Atchison had been called out here the day we'd closed on the property, when Sibley first told us he'd filed the adverse possession notice. He'd come back again when Sibley had claimed we'd stolen his horse. Speaking of that horse, Pegasus stood only a short distance away, watching us intently, his back left leg cocked in a sassy stance like a can-can dancer.

Deputy Atchison's face tightened when he saw me and Buck and realized that the people who'd called in to report Sibley's injuries were the same ones involved in a property dispute with the man. "Hang tight," he ordered. He took the medics aside and questioned them for a brief moment before coming back our way. He looked from Buck to me. "Tell me what happened here."

"We don't know," I said. "We had our court hearing this morning on Mr. Sibley's adverse possession claim. He didn't show. When we came here afterward, we went up into the belfry." No point in telling him we planned to ring the bell and gloat. We'd look like a couple of obnoxious jerks. "When we looked down from the tower, we saw him lying here behind the barn. I called for help right away and Buck ran over here to check on Mr. Sibley."

The deputy glanced over at the bell tower. "Why were you in the belfry?"

So that we could ring the bell loud and proud, gloat over our win in court, and cause this dead man a little grief. Of course, we hadn't known Sibley was dead at the time or we'd never have done it. Buck and I exchanged a glance. Before we could come up with a good reason for being in the belfry that didn't make us sound juvenile and vindictive, the deputy said, "I saw that look you two just gave each other. Just shoot straight with me, okay?"

"Okay." Buck exhaled sharply. "We went up there to ring our bell, so Sibley would know we'd beat him in court."

"I see," the deputy said. "You wanted to throw some salt in the wound."

I cringed. Sibley's wounds had been bloody and horrific. The image of us throwing salt in them made my stomach churn.

"In our defense," Buck added, "he hasn't exactly been neighborly."

The deputy nodded. "He sure hasn't. It would be understandable if y'all found yourselves in a disagreement that accidentally got out of hand, led to something physical. I could see Nolan Sibley starting something, especially if he knew he'd lost the land to you two."

The deputy is trying to get us to admit to something, isn't he? "We rang our bell," I said sourly, "but we didn't ring his." What's more, the rigid state of Sibley's muscles said he'd been dead a matter of hours. He had never even known the judge had denied his claim.

Buck crossed his muscular arms over his chest. "We came over here to help the guy. If we'd been the ones to kill him, we wouldn't have called for an ambulance. We would've just left him for the buzzards to finish off."

My cousin probably could have chosen his words more carefully, but he was right. Out here, where there was little chance of witnesses, we could've easily offed Sibley, buried or dumped his body, and gotten away with it. After all, someone had as yet gotten away with killing Gerard Woodruff.

Deputy Atchison wasn't convinced of our innocence. "Seems awfully coincidental that someone died at your place just a few days ago and now there's a body here."

He'd heard about Woodruff, even though Metro Police had handled the matter, as it took place within the Nashville/Davidson County limits. It wasn't surprising. Bad news gets around, and law enforcement agencies regularly shared information. He gestured to Buck's crossed arms. "Let me see your hands."

Buck held both hands out in front of them, turning them over so the deputy could see both sides. His fingers and palms were calloused, and his knuckles were scraped.

The deputy angled his head. "Your knuckles look rough."

"Occupational hazard," Buck said. "I work in carpentry and construction."

I came to my cousin's defense. "None of those scrapes are fresh," I pointed out. "Besides, if he'd punched Sibley in the face, his knuckles would look far worse."

The officer wasn't yet satisfied. "Roll up your sleeves."

Buck's jaw flexed in irritation, but he did as he was told.

The deputy turned to me. "Your turn."

I held out my hands. I tended to wear gloves more consistently than Buck, so my hands weren't quite as hardened. Still, the short fingernails and scratches said I didn't work a cushy office job. I rolled up the sleeves on my coveralls and showed him my arms.

The fact that neither Buck nor I had defensive wounds didn't get us totally off the hook. "Once I get some backup out here, we'll want to take a look around your place if that's okay with you."

I knew he was asking permission merely as a formality. If we said no, the sheriff's department could get a search warrant and look around the theater and parsonage anyway. Or at least I assumed so. I didn't know how much basis was needed to constitute probable cause, but my assumption was that this situation would fit the bill. There'd been a person found dead on our premises only a few days before, and we had been in an ugly dispute with the man found dead today. What's more, Buck and I had been the ones to find both of the bodies. But we had nothing to hide. "You're welcome to take a look around," I said. "Does that mean we need to stay out of the buildings until you're done?"

"It does," he said.

Another construction delay caused by a dead body. What were the odds?

Fortunately for us, the deputy's backup arrived quickly, a pair of young male officers in a single cruiser. One of them stood guard over Sibley's body to make sure it wasn't disturbed before the medical examiner staff arrived. The other assisted in the search. They went through the theater in rather short order. With it being empty, there wasn't much to see. The parsonage was a different story. Tools, equipment, and materials lay all over the place. But the deputies found no blood spatter, nor any space that had been recently cleaned to get rid of evidence. The place was a mess, but it was the type of mess to be expected during a rehab. They found no bloody tools, either, nor any tools that had been recently wiped clean. I knew they wouldn't, but I still couldn't help breathing a very small sigh of relief.

Their search complete, we went back outside to see that two people from the Sumner County Medical Examiner's office had arrived. Several other horses had joined Pegasus, the group standing by silently, watching the people work. *Apparently, cats aren't the only animals with curiosity.* Luther lay in the shade of a tree nearby, panting softly and watching, too.

"What will happen to Sibley's horses and dog?" I asked.

"Don't worry," the deputy said. "We'll make sure someone looks after them until Sibley's next of kin has been notified."

The team loaded Sibley's body onto a gurney, covered it with a white sheet, and rolled him over to their vehicle to load him inside. After closing the doors, they climbed back inside and started the engine. As they drove away, Pegasus raised his head and issued a snicker-like nicker. My cousin, the deputies, and I looked from the horse to one another.

"If I didn't know better," Buck said, "I'd think that horse was laughing."

CHAPTER 13

THE ART OF INTERROGATION

WHITNEY

Collin stopped by my house around eight o'clock Tuesday evening. He sat at one end of the couch, rubbing the feet I'd been on all day, while I lounged at the other. Sawdust and Cleo lay side by side on my lap, each one draped over a thigh, and I paid Collin's foot massage forward by rubbing their ears. The two purred in complete contentment and gratitude. I would have purred for Collin, too, if I could.

As he worked the ball of my foot, he filled me in on the latest developments—at least where other potential suspects were concerned. In light of the fact that Woodruff's murder happened on our property and Sibley's unexplained death took place right next door, I knew that the authorities were still suspicious of Buck and me, excluding Collin, of course. He knew my cousin and I were totally innocent. Even so, he could only share so much evidence that might help us clear our names.

"No one at Woodruff's trailer park saw any unusual activity at his place. They said he was a nice guy, drove slow when kids were playing outside, kept his yard tidy. The manager said the same. Everyone I spoke to said they'd never seen any visitors at Woodruff's trailer, let alone people coming and going at all hours. If Woodruff was selling drugs, he wasn't doing it out of his home."

"*If?*" I said. "Why else would he have a fanny pack containing individual bags of marijuana if he wasn't dealing drugs?"

"Good question," Collin said.

"What about the burger place?" I asked. "Could someone have followed him from there?"

"I reviewed the security camera footage from the restaurant. If someone trailed Woodruff from the restaurant, it wasn't obvious. I ran the license plates on the vehicles in the parking lot. One of them belonged to a guy with a domestic violence charge, but his car remained there well after Woodruff was gone."

In other words, Collin had no new leads in Woodruff's homicide case. *Darn.* Of course, the deliveryman's death wasn't the only suspicious death under investigation. "What about Nolan Sibley?"

"His murder is in the hands of the Sumner County Sheriff's Department. They're keeping me in the loop, though, since his death could be related to Woodruff's. Last I heard, they're still trying to piece things together. He's married, but his wife up and left him years ago. She's living in Florida. According to the kids, she'd had enough of her selfish and greedy husband and couldn't take it anymore. He seemed to be expecting her to come to her senses and come back one day, couldn't imagine she'd give up a prize like him. She still had access to their bank accounts, so she didn't bother filing for divorce. His daughter and son live here in Nashville, but they only saw him on occasion. They both said he wasn't a pleasant person to be around, that all he seemed to care about was building his horse operation. Sibley's son said his father had mentioned a dispute with someone who'd bought a horse a few months ago for a large sum of money and later demanded the money back. The buyer said the horse had some type of tendon problem due to being overworked, but Sibley insisted the injury was the buyer's fault. There's a court case pending."

Sibley certainly seemed to keep the area's judges and bailiffs busy. "Was Sibley representing himself in that matter, too?"

"He was," Collin said. "The case hasn't gotten far. The sheriff's department plans to question the buyer."

I wondered if the buyer could be the person who drove the white SUV I'd seen at Sibley's place, the one that might or might not be the same one that had driven by the parsonage shortly after Woodruff's murder. Even so, it wouldn't necessarily show how, or if, Woodruff's and Sibley's murders were related. "Have they found any connection between Sibley and Woodruff?"

"None whatsoever," Collin said. He gave me a dark look. "Except that they both died in the same area, no one witnessed their deaths, and their bodies were found by the same two people."

I sighed. "Buck and me."

"Yeah. By all accounts the men were strangers. I've done some digging, too. Other than the fact that they'd both been at the playhouse property, I can't find a single thing that links them."

Though his hands remained on my feet, his fingers stopped moving. "Just so you know, the sheriff's department has you and Buck on their list of persons of interest."

I sighed. "I suspected as much."

"I told them that you and I are romantically involved." His jaw flexed, telling me the situation, which was rife with potential conflict, was causing him stress. "Disclosing our relationship was the professional thing to do. Of course, I vouched for you and Buck, too."

"Thanks, Collin." I hated to see them waste their time on us when there was a killer on the loose, maybe two killers. *Exactly how many bad guys are we dealing with here?* "I'm sorry that you've been put in the middle."

He lifted a tense shoulder. "It is what it is. For what it's worth, I'm sure they'll cross you off their list soon."

I placed the cats on the floor and circled my finger, directing him to switch places with me. Once we'd swapped spots, I began rubbing his tight shoulders. "Speaking of lists," I said, "have you visited the other stops on Sibley's delivery list?"

"That's my next step. The drug angle seemed more promising, so I pursued that avenue first. But since that lead has gotten me nowhere, it's time to try another approach."

"Will you go in order? Start with Woodruff's early-morning donut deliveries?"

"No," he said. "Those deliveries are likely routine. I'm going to start with Laurel Cromwell."

A-ha! Maybe I had been right to think she could have something to do with the murder. Or at least that the gemstones did. She'd fairly convinced me of her innocence after

I spoke with her the morning before, but I could have been wrong. "Does Laurel have a criminal history?"

"Let's find out."

I released Collin's shoulders so he could stand to round up his computer from his messenger bag. Sawdust and Cleo seized the opportunity to jump back into my lap. Collin sat back down on the couch next to me, plunked the computer on his knees, and booted it up. With only a single lamp turned on in the room, the screen lit up his face like a spotlight. After he logged into the criminal data base and entered Laurel's name, his brows rose. "What do you know. Laurel Cromwell has two misdemeanor theft charges. One from twenty-three years ago and the other from last year."

"Really?" I sat up straight, disturbing the cats, who'd reclaimed my lap the instant Collin had stood. Sawdust and Cleo gave me disappointed looks, hopped down to the floor, and sauntered over to curl up together on the rug. "What did she steal?" If it was gems or jewelry containing precious stones, we might be able to make a connection here.

Collin pulled up the police records and frowned. "Her first theft was a shoplifting case. She stole an eyeliner and a lipstick from a cosmetics store. She was only twenty at the time, still a student as Nōssi College of Art."

While I'd never visited the campus, I'd heard of the small arts college. It sat a few miles north of downtown and offered degrees in photography, graphic design, film and video, illustration, and even culinary arts. A couple of Colette's coworkers at the restaurant where she'd worked the last few years had studied there.

Collin tapped the keyboard to pull up the police report on her more recent theft charge. "Last August, Laurel stole an expensive calculator from an electronics store."

A calculator? What a boring thing to risk jail time for. "Did she spend any time in the clink?"

"No," Collin said. "Looks like she worked out a plea deal and got community service and probation."

"Is that normal for a second offense?"

"Eh. Depends on the circumstances."

Unfortunately, the online files were insufficient to tell us exactly what those circumstances were. Collin would find out tomorrow. Or maybe *we* would, if I could convince Collin to let me in on the interrogation. "Can I go with you to see Laurel?"

While there were times Collin couldn't let me in on his investigations, even when they involved deaths that happened on properties I owned, he'd realized early on that I could be a valuable asset. He'd studied criminal justice in college, and it served him well in his career. I'd studied business, and it had done the same for me. Fortunately, given my background, I sometimes looked at things from a different angle and had ideas he didn't.

He thought it over for a moment. "Laurel doesn't seem to be dangerous. Her criminal record doesn't include any violent offenses, at least. I suppose it can't hurt for you to be there. Maybe it'll even help to have a woman with me, a familiar face. You've already spoken with her about this case. You can tell me if she changes her story."

Woo-hoo! I resisted the urge to throw my hands in the air. I loved it when he let me in on his investigations, when I could help him figure things out. We made a good team.

The evening was growing late, and he packed his computer back up to go. We arranged to meet at Laurel's studio the following morning at ten o'clock. He left me with a kiss and a buzzing curiosity that wouldn't be satisfied until we spoke with Laurel Cromwell in the morning.

I arrived at Laurel's studio before Collin on Wednesday morning. Rather than go inside, I waited in the parking lot. As Laurel was helping a customer choose a piece of glass for a project, she glanced outside and spotted me. Was it my imagination, or had a cloud of concern skittered across her face when she caught my eye? *Hmm.*

Collin pulled up a few minutes later. I called his cell phone from my car. "She's got a customer inside."

"Let's wait, then."

The customer couldn't seem to make up her mind. Laurel showed her several pieces of blue glass in shades ranging from peacock to sky blue, then a few in bluish-green shades of teal and aquamarine. When the customer still didn't seem satisfied, Laurel showed her some glass in true greens. Finally, the woman settled on a piece of glass in a bright spring-green color. Laurel rang her up, wrapped the sheet of glass in padded paper wrap, and taped the wrap to keep it secure. The transaction complete, the woman came out of the shop, her purchase tucked under her arm.

Laurel had followed the woman to the door and stood there now, holding it open and looking out at me, a puzzled expression on her face. I raised a hand in greeting and slid out of my car. Collin did the same. Her gaze moved from me to him, and her face contorted further in confusion and concern.

Collin greeted her by extending one of his business cards. "Good morning, Ms. Cromwell. I'm Detective Collin Flynn with Metro Police. I'm hoping you can help me with the Gerard Woodruff murder case."

"I'd be happy to talk to you, but I'm not sure how much help I'll be." She pointed to me. "Mind if I take care of this customer first?"

It seemed she hadn't quite put it together that Collin and I were here on a joint mission.

Collin cleared things up. "Ms. Whitaker is here at my request. May we speak inside your shop?"

"Oh. Of course. Come on in."

We stepped inside the shop, but stopped just a few feet from the door. It swung closed behind us, shutting out the noise and smells of car exhaust from the traffic from Hillsboro Pike.

Collin wasted no time. He verified the information I'd given him from my earlier conversation with Laurel. Order placed by Antonia Szabo with the Romanian gallery. Gems supplied by her client. Szabo arranged for Woody's Delivery Service to pick up the windows and deliver them to the shipper. Being an ace detective, Collin knew which follow-up questions to ask to get the nitty-gritty details. "How were the gems delivered to you to be installed in the windows? Did Mr. Woodruff bring them to you?"

"No," she said. "Antonia Szabo brought them to me herself."

Collin's brows rose. "All the way from Romania?"

"That was my understanding," Laurel said. "She told me she was in the United States scouting pieces to purchase for her gallery, and brought the stones with her."

A slight frown claimed Collin's face. "It seems risky to travel with priceless gems. Any idea how much they were worth?"

She hesitated just an instant too long before answering. "No."

What is that about?

Collin said, "Could have been two grand, could have been two hundred grand, then?"

She raised her palms. "Your guess is as good as mine. There were quite a few stones, and some of them were surprisingly large. I know the value of gemstones can vary a lot depending on the four C's. Color, clarity, carat weight, and cut. But I'm no expert."

"Really?" I said. "Because it sounds like you know your stuff."

Her eyes flashed before she offered a nonchalant shrug. "It's common knowledge."

Common knowledge, I wondered, or *acquired* knowledge? Had she been curious about the stones, done some research to determine just how valuable they were? It would be the natural thing to do, wouldn't it? After all, I'd been curious, too, even when I'd thought the gems were only glass.

Collin asked, "You didn't question Ms. Szabo about their value?"

She didn't hesitate before responding this time. "No. I sensed she didn't want to discuss it, and it wasn't really any of my business."

Collin followed up with, "And you didn't get them appraised or looked at by a professional? Not even for insurance purposes while they were in your possession? It would have been a good idea since you could be liable if they disappeared from your shop. If I were in your shoes, I would've been very curious what they were actually worth."

She hesitated a second time. *Did she realize she'd backed herself into a corner by saying she didn't know their value? Had she actually had the gems appraised, or at least asked for a quick-and-dirty valuation, like I had?* She responded with, "I simply assumed the jewels were worth more money than I could fathom, and I did everything in my power to secure them while they were in my shop. My store and studio space came with a hardwired security system with an audible alarm, but the system was installed twenty years ago or more. The technology has gotten better and cheaper, so I added a second wireless system myself."

"Smart thinking," Collin said.

I suspected his compliment was an attempt to get on her good side. Flattery could also put a person off guard.

Laurel went on as if unaffected, though. "There was already a safe bolted to the concrete floor in the back room when I rented this space. Antonia asked to see it. She didn't feel entirely comfortable with it, so she brought me a second, smaller safe to put inside the larger one. The small safe weighs nearly a hundred pounds. We realized someone would still be able to cart it off if they were determined, but at least it wouldn't be easy on them and might slow them down long enough for law enforcement to arrive. I also added a roll-up security grill at the front of the store to stop anyone from getting in, even if they broke the windows." She pointed to a metal apparatus mounted above the windows and door at the front of her shop. It was the type often seen in the chain stores in shopping malls.

"Wow," Collin said. "You sure went to a lot of trouble."

"Antonia Szabo has given me a lot of business," Laurel said. "She's purchased nearly a hundred thousand dollars in stained glass since she became a customer. The least I could do was keep her client's gems safe."

"Did she say why they weren't using a European artist to make the window?"

"Privacy reasons," Laurel said. "She thought the European artists might be able to identify the client. She told me that royals tend to be extremely private and reserved. I supposed that maybe they didn't want people knowing the extent of their wealth. Plus, Antonia had ordered quite a few pieces from me before and was familiar with my work. I suppose she knew she could trust me." Laurel both beamed and blushed at that. The beam was pride, but what was the blush? Did she know Szabo's trust had been misplaced? Or did she realize that she'd breached that trust by telling me about the royal client when I'd visited her shop to return the bejeweled windows?

"Szabo knew she could trust you?" Collin said. "So, she'd given you gems before?"

He really knows how to wheedle information out of people, doesn't he?

"A few small, single stones," she said. "She gave them to me one at a time and asked me to incorporate the stones into suncatchers."

Collin cocked his head. "What's a suncatcher?"

She pointed to her window, where some of her smaller stained-glass pieces were displayed, hanging by small chains from suction cups adhered to the window glass. A butterfly in a delicate oval frame. A hummingbird in a square mount.

An iris in a rectangular fitting. "She planned to sell the sun-catchers in her gallery. My guess is that's how the royals got the idea to put gems in a window. They must have seen one of my smaller designs. Not to toot my own horn here, but they were especially beautiful. The perfect special occasion gift. She told me that many of them sold as wedding or anniversary presents."

"Did Woody pick up the suncatchers for shipping, too?"

"Most of them, yes," Laurel said. "Occasionally, Antonia would come by the shop and pick them up herself if she happened to be in the U.S. when they were ready."

Collin's head bobbed slightly as he pondered this information. "Can you tell me how you first learned that Ms. Whitaker's order had been switched with Ms. Szabo's?"

"Antonia called me Saturday morning and said the shipping company had opened the envelopes and noticed the discrepancy in the paperwork. They were concerned there might be a problem with the order, so they'd contacted her for further instructions. She asked them to unwrap the windows and send her pics. When they did, she noticed there were no glass jewels or gems in them, and she realized they weren't the right windows. She called me immediately after. She was angry and a little frantic. When I learned that I'd accidentally swapped the paperwork and caused the mix-up, I tried calling Whitney. Five times, as a matter of fact." She cast me an accusatory look.

I cringed. "Still sorry about that." I explained to Collin why I hadn't picked up the call. "Buck and I were in the middle of installing the windows and I'd left my phone in my purse."

He nodded in understanding.

"When I couldn't reach Whitney by phone," Laurel continued, "I drove out to the playhouse. That's when I found out that Whitney and her partner had already installed the jeweled windows. She told me they couldn't take them out right then, but she reassured me they had adequate security on the building and that she'd bring them to me on Monday. Naturally, I was a nervous wreck until she brought them back. Antonia was, too."

"As far as you know," Collin clarified, "neither the shipping company nor Antonia Szabo knew the windows had been switched until Saturday morning, the day after Woody's murder?"

She gave a nod. "That's right."

Did the fact that they hadn't noticed the error until Saturday mean that the windows had nothing to do with his death, then? Could be. But it could also mean that it was more likely that Laurel Cromwell might have been responsible for Woodruff's death. Maybe she'd swapped the windows on purpose and tried to frame him for stealing the jewels, no pun intended. If so, she'd know he'd be taking the valuable, bejeweled windows to the playhouse after dropping my standard-design windows at the shipping company. Maybe she'd hoped to intercept Woodruff before he transferred the windows to me, and take them back so she could keep the jewels to pawn or sell for cash. I wasn't quite sure if the scenario was true, but it seemed as if there could be some substance to the theory.

I ran my gaze over Laurel, assessing her. She looked innocent enough, but crooks and criminals often did. Would she be strong enough to choke Gerard Woodruff with the rope, though? Maybe. Maybe not. He couldn't move fast with the limp, and if she'd threatened him with a gun or other weapon she might have been able to get the upper hand. Then again, maybe I had an overactive imagination. After all, if she'd planned to pawn the jewels, wouldn't she have simply searched for the windows themselves after they'd been dropped at the playhouse rather than strangling the deliveryman?

Collin asked, "Did Ms. Szabo call your studio phone or your cell number?"

"They're one and the same," Laurel said. "The landline in my shop is only used for the old security system. All of my calls, both personal and business, come to my cell phone."

"May I see your phone?" he asked.

"Of course." She pulled her phone from her pocket and held it out to him.

He circled a finger over it. "Unlock it, please."

"Oh. Yeah." She typed her passcode on the screen to unlock the phone and handed it to him.

He pulled up her recent call list. I glanced over at the phone as he worked it. Sure enough, on Saturday morning, there was an incoming international call at 9:29. The number read *+40* before the remaining digits. I presumed 40 was the country code for Romania. The information showed that Laurel and Ms. Szabo spoke for just over two minutes. My guess was that Laurel spent most of those two minutes apologizing profusely and trying to reassure her client that she'd do everything in her power to set things straight. I felt a twinge of guilt that I hadn't returned the windows to her sooner so everyone could rest easy. Then again, if Laurel had been more forthcoming with me, told me the windows contained a wealth of precious stones, I would have removed them and given them back right away, weather and sore muscles notwithstanding. I wouldn't have wanted the liability. Any fault lay with her.

Collin pulled out a pen and notepad, and jotted down Szabo's number before handing the phone back to Laurel. "When did you first meet Ms. Szabo?"

She looked up in thought before returning her focus to Collin. "It was around four months ago. That was the first time she came here in person."

"What does she look like?" Collin asked.

"Pretty," Laurel said. "Thin. She has long black hair and wears glasses. She speaks with a thick accent. I had a hard time understanding her at first."

"Did she give you her business card?"

"Yes." Laurel went over her counter, circled around to the back, and pulled a small plastic box out from under it. She riffled through a stack of business cards and fished one out, holding it out across the counter.

I eyed the card. It was a fancy embossed one on a black background with raised gold lettering. It read *Antonia Szabo, Art Dealer & Gallerist, Glassworks Gallery*, along with a street address in Bucharest—*Strada Vasile Alecsandri 16*. The card also listed her phone number, including Romania's country code, which told me her business was indeed an international endeavor.

Collin snapped a photo of the card with his phone, returned it to Laurel, and turned to me. As if to justify my presence to Laurel, he said, "I trust that everything Ms. Cromwell has said today coincides with your conversation on Monday?"

"Yes," I said, "it does." I gave Laurel a small smile. I figured it couldn't hurt to try to salvage what little connection might remain between us.

"Thanks," Collin said. "I appreciate your assistance and cooperation. That will be all."

He'd clearly dismissed me and, just as clearly, planned to stay and ask Laurel some more questions. I hoped he'd fill me in later.

I left Laurel's shop feeling like a lousy crime solver. After speaking with her myself on Monday, I'd been fairly convinced she had nothing to do with Woodruff's death. But now she was my number-one suspect. It was very odd that she'd hesitated when Collin asked whether she knew the value of the gems. Had she truly planned on stealing them? It could very well be. After all, she was a convicted thief. While her earlier crimes had been petty theft, maybe she saw the gemstones as an opportunity to get her hands on a far more valuable take. I wondered what other information Collin might get out of her. *Might he even get a confession?*

CHAPTER 14

CRIMINAL INTENT

WHITNEY

I arrived at the parsonage to find Buck and Colette already hard at work. Colette had the day off from her current job. She, Presley, and I had appointments soon to meet with a business attorney and a CPA about setting up corporations and accounting systems for the restaurant and theater. Colette also wanted to be very hands-on with the rehab, not only so that she could ensure her café turned out the way she'd envisioned but also because she wanted to make this place her own by having a hand in bringing it to life.

I turned to my friend, who wore one of my extra hard hats with the daisy decals, as well as a spare pair of my coveralls. With me standing a few inches taller than her, she'd had to roll up the cuffs on the pant legs lest she trip over them. She'd rolled back the cuffs on the sleeves, too. "This must feel good," I said, "seeing your dream come to life."

"It does. I can hardly believe it's happening! It wouldn't be if not for you and Buck." She looked from one of us to the other, treating us to a grateful grin.

"Uh-oh," Buck teased. "Don't go getting mushy on us now."

While there was some truth to Colette's words, she'd been the first to suggest transforming the house into an eatery. We'd been at a loss concerning what to do with it. "This café was your idea. You get the credit."

"Let's just agree to call it a joint endeavor." She lifted her mask into place over her nose and mouth, and swung a sledgehammer at the wall, sending up a spray of drywall chunks and white powder. As the dust settled, she turned back to me. Though I couldn't see her mouth behind the mask, the crinkles around her eyes told me she was smiling. "I used to wonder what you loved so much about rehabbing old houses, but now I see now why you like it. Demolition work is oddly satisfying."

It was true. Nothing like knocking down a wall to relieve stress. Besides, demo work was the first big step on any project, a task that told us we were really moving forward.

We'd been working a few hours when a knock sounded at the front door. Buck, Colette, and I exchanged glances. After all the suspicious deaths that had occurred around the place lately, our nerves were on edge.

Buck handed Colette a hammer in case she needed to defend herself, then edged up to a front window to peek outside. His rigid muscles relaxed in relief. "It's Presley. She's got Gia Revello with her."

What would big-time record label executive Gia Revello be doing out here? Maybe she'd come to take a look at the theater, to get an idea of it so she could better know which acts might be best to suggest to Presley.

After I opened the door and we exchanged greetings, she

glanced around the parsonage. "Presley told me about this place and asked if I could put her in touch with some of my artists. I told her I wanted to see it for myself. Looks like you've got a long way to go in here."

"We do. We're still waiting on some of the kitchen appliances, but we've got the design elements nailed down." I rounded up my notebook to show her the mock-up drawings I'd made, as well as the paint samples and photos of the light fixtures we'd ordered. "Watch your step," I warned as I took them to one of the bedrooms to show them some of the mix-and-match tables Colette and Emmalee had found at flea markets, secondhand stores, and garage sales. Ditto for the dishware. The combination of styles and colors was cute, casual, and charming. We'd need a few more tables and dishes to fill out our collection, and Colette and I planned to scout for some this Saturday.

"You're going folksy," Gia said, her upbeat tone telling us she approved of the choice.

"Exactly," Colette replied. "We want people to feel welcome and comfortable." Colette went on to tell Gia about the plans to install an extensive garden out back to supply the kitchen with fresh fruits and vegetables in season. "I plan to feature local wines, too. I've been in touch with some of the area wineries. We're in the process of nailing down the particulars."

"In other words," Gia said, "you've been sampling a fair share of vino."

Colette giggled. "Busted!"

When we returned to the foyer, Gia glanced over at the kitchen. "What a nice, big island."

"It's the altar from the church." The table had once been

used to nourish spirits. Now it would be used to nourish bodies.

"What about the menu?" she asked. "Has that been finalized?"

Colette put down her tools and rounded up the folder containing the menu information. She showed Gia recipes and photos of the options that would be initially offered, as well as a sample laminated menu. "I'll refine the menu once I see which items the patrons like best. I'll serve a daily special, too. I want to be creative with the meals."

Gia perused the menu. "You've got a good variety here. Some unusual things that are sure to get attention. I'm impressed." She handed the menu back to Colette.

Having shown Gia all there was to see for now at the café, Presley asked if I'd like to accompany them to the theater.

"I'd be happy to."

We headed out from the parsonage on foot. Both Presley and Gia had a little trouble making their way across the field in their heels, which sank into the dirt. *Maybe I should have offered them a ride over in the wheelbarrow.* I assured them that Buck and I planned to install a walkway from the café to the playhouse so that patrons could make their way easily from one building to the other. "We'll install benches along the way so people can sit if they'd like, and we'll put in some festive string lights along the way, too."

As we neared the theater, activity by Sibley's barn caught my attention. Johnny Otto had a horse in the corral, and was working her on a lunge rope. The horse appeared to be the same bay mare that had been inside the theater building the day we'd first met Sibley. Chessie was her name, if I recalled correctly. Johnny wore his usual helmet and chest protector. He'd also put gray boots on the horse, padded protectors that wrapped around her legs just above her hooves so that she wouldn't inadvertently injure herself. He called out to her, giving her words of encouragement as he exercised her. She circled the corral at a trotting pace, her hooves plod-plod-plodding along. Johnny called out a command in a firm but nonthreatening tone, and she broke into a graceful canter. Meanwhile, Luther nosed around the fence outside the corral, his tail up in the air.

I was glad Johnny was looking out for the animals until long-term arrangements could be made for their care. He seemed to have a special way with them, to genuinely care about their welfare. I admired him for that. Now that Sibley was gone, I wondered who would take over his horse operation and whether they would keep Johnny on as a hand. I supposed it was too soon to know. I also still wondered where Johnny Otto had been the day before, when we'd found Sibley dead behind his barn. Maybe he'd had the day off, but maybe it was something more sinister.

I shook off my suspicious thoughts. I led Presley and Gia into the playhouse and repeated the tour I'd given to Presley weeks earlier. Ticket booth and office. Dressing room. Balcony. Back down to the foyer.

Gia glanced around. "You're planning to have a merchandise booth, right? You'd be amazed how much money there is in T-shirts, hats, pins, and posters. The markup is ridiculous, but fans will pay just about any price for a souvenir."

Presley let Gia know she'd already made arrangements for merchandise sales. "I've ordered a display table and a portable kiosk on wheels, the kind you see at trade shows.

When the weather is good, we can set it up outside so that the line won't crowd the foyer."

"That's a great idea." As we ventured onto the main seating floor, Gia gestured to the windows. "Smart move, keeping the stained glass. Adds character."

I pointed out the custom glass pieces Buck and I had requisitioned. "We found a local artist with reasonable rates."

Gia cut me a look of admiration and respect. "You're quite the designer, Whitney. You did a superb job with the motel's mid-century look, and you've turned this place into something fanciful."

"Thanks." I felt my chest swell. I was proud of my work, especially since most of what I'd learned was self-taught. Of course, it didn't hurt that I subscribed to every home and garden magazine published and spent untold hours poring over ideas on Pinterest. *That social media site is a rabbit hole if ever there was one.*

As we approached the raised platform that had once been a pulpit and would now serve as the theater's stage, Gia glanced left and right, then up.

I knew what she was looking for. "The curtain should arrive any day now. It was a special order." The curtain had cost a small fortune, but with it providing a focal point for the audience before the start of each show, we figured we should make sure it was a nice one that complemented the rest of the décor.

Gia took the steps up to the stage to look out onto the space. Presley and I followed her up.

"What's the seating capacity here?" she asked.

"One hundred and thirty, including the balcony."

Gia's head bobbed. "Small, but big enough to be profitable." She hummed a note to warm up her vocal cords and launched into a surprisingly skilled performance of the classic gospel song "In the Garden." After singing a few bars, she said, "Wow. This place has near-perfect acoustics."

"I didn't know you could sing," I said. "You've been holding out on us."

She laughed. "I sang in the church and school choirs growing up. I once thought of pursuing a career as a performer. When I was beating the bushes, trying to get gigs for myself, I ended up singing background for a female star in one of her recording sessions. The record label was hiring and I needed some steady money, so I applied for an administrative position working for one of the executives. I realized I had more talent at the negotiation table than on the stage. I have no regrets." Her gaze roamed the place once more before she turned to face me and Presley straight on. "I want in."

"In?" I repeated.

"On this." She circled her finger in the air to indicate the performance hall. "You've got some real moneymaking potential here. If you let me buy in, I can do much more than send some acts your way. I can help direct the theater business. You ladies know real estate, and you're smart enough to recognize an opportunity when you see it. But for this place to be all that it can, you'll need someone on your board with firsthand knowledge of the entertainment industry and the contacts to make things happen. My money will come in handy, too. Do you have any idea what professional sound equipment costs?"

Presley and I exchanged a look. We did, in fact, know how expensive the equipment could be. Presley had priced a sound system, and it was much more than any of us would have expected. An influx of cash from Gia would help make things happen here. Including her as an investor would also spread the risk around. As much as we hoped the place would be a success, there were no guarantees. We'd poured all of our profits on the motel into this property, and we stood to lose it all if the place didn't make it. Involving her would not only spread the risk; it would also help spread the word about the Joyful Noise Playhouse. Her association with the theater would give it greater legitimacy, street cred.

"What do you think?" I asked Presley.

Presley didn't pull any punches. "I think we'd be crazy not to bring Gia aboard."

Buck and Colette trusted me on the business decisions, so I knew neither of them would have a problem with Gia investing in the venture and joining us at the board table if I thought it was a good idea. Besides, with only Presley, Buck, Colette, and I on the board, we'd have an even number of directors. It was always good to have an odd number to avoid tie votes. Gina would expand the population of the board to five.

I extended my hand to Gia. "Welcome aboard." I gave her the information about our upcoming meetings with the corporate attorney and the CPA, and invited her to attend them with the rest of us.

Our business concluded for the time being, we exited the theater. Johnny Otto had finished exercising the horse, and was using a hose to fill a large metal water trough while she drank from it. The electric prod was nowhere to be seen. Johnny seemed to have no use for it. I hoped it was gone for good. He patted the horse's neck and, though I couldn't hear his words from here, it was evident by the way he put this face close to her ear that he was murmuring sweet nothings to her. I couldn't help but feel a little tug at my heart on seeing a man strong enough to be so gentle. Unlike Sibley, he didn't feel the need to dominate the horses and make them afraid in order to feel like a big man.

I was in bed that night, reading a new mystery release with Sawdust curled up beside me, when Collin phoned with an update on what happened after I left Laurel's studio.

"Did you notice she hesitated when I asked if she'd had the gems appraised?"

"I did," I said. "I got the feeling she was lying."

"She was," he said. "It took some doing, but I finally managed to wear her down and get the truth out of her. I asked about her theft charge from last year, the one that landed her on probation. She said her husband had abandoned her and the kids a few months earlier. He teaches history at a junior high, and he took up with one of his coworkers. Laurel hadn't seen it coming. He left her and the kids emotionally and financially devastated. She said the family had been stretched thin even before he walked out. They'd had a string of setbacks. Major car and home repairs. The husband had needed a couple of root canals and crowns. They didn't have dental insurance and had to pay out of pocket. One of their daughters has diabetes and they could barely afford the cost of her insulin. They'd maxed out their credit cards and were late on their payments."

I could only imagine the stress Laurel was under. I'd be a nervous wreck if I couldn't afford to take care of Sawdust's health needs.

Collin continued. "Their son is in high school, and he needed a graphing calculator for his math class. The calculators run over a hundred dollars. When she found out how expensive they were, Laurel suggested her son ask the teacher if the school could provide one for him to use. He told her he'd be humiliated to ask, and that he didn't want his friends to find out they were broke. She didn't want him to be embarrassed or to realize how bad things had gotten, so she went to the store and slid one into her purse. It set off the alarm when she went out the door and the security guard busted her. Luckily for her, the prosecutor and judge sympathized with her circumstances, and agreed to let her slide with just community service and probation."

I gathered Laurel might not have been so lucky if she'd stolen some type of luxury item for herself rather than a necessity for her child. "What did she do for her community service?"

"Walked dogs at the animal shelter."

Walking dogs was a good way to pay her debt to society and allow the dogs a little time out of their enclosures. Not all canines were as lucky as Luther, with acres upon acres of land on which to run and play freely. The mental vision of Laurel walking dogs made me feel conflicted again. Yes, she was a petty thief, but how bad was she, really? "How'd you get her to fess up?"

"I told her that I had noticed her hesitate earlier when I asked if she'd had the gems appraised, and that I had no doubt that stealing one or more of the gems had crossed her mind. I told her that I was going to speak with jewelers in the area, and that if I found out she'd lied to me I'd come back and arrest her on the spot. The judge wouldn't be so likely to go easy on her for lying to a detective in a murder investigation, so she was much better coming clean unless she wanted her kids to go live with their father and his new girlfriend or end up in the custody of child protective services."

"That must have been the last thing she wanted to hear."

"It was the last thing I wanted to say, too." Collin heaved a sigh. "But you gotta hit 'em where it hurts. Besides, none of it was a lie. She finally admitted that she'd taken three of the smaller stones to a jeweler. She got only a ballpark valuation and didn't pay for a full appraisal."

The irony of the situation struck me. Laurel had done the same thing I did, seek a professional estimate of the gems' value. I supposed it could make me look guilty, too, if I didn't have Collin on my side. "How much were the stones worth?"

"She was told that each of them was worth around two grand. She considered pawning some of them or trying to sell them online. She said she also thought about telling Antonia that she'd accidentally lost a stone when she was working with it, that it must have fallen to the floor and that she'd been unable to find it. She also considered faking a break-in so that she could then liquidate all the gems. But she realized that Antonia might get suspicious and would report the missing jewels to the police. Laurel figured she might get caught, and that she'd be unlikely to avoid jail time for a third theft offense, especially if this one was bigger and came so close on the heels of the calculator theft. Besides, Antonia was sending her a lot of work. With the extra income, Laurel was earning enough that she'd paid off some of her arrearages. Soon she'd be able to make ends meet and start chipping away at her debts. Laurel didn't want to jeopardize their business relationship. She also said she didn't want to be a thief. She'd stolen the lipstick as a young woman on a dare. She never would have stolen the calculator if her situation hadn't been so dire at the time."

I mulled the information over for a moment and proposed the scenario I'd considered earlier. "She admitted she had a compelling motive to steal the gems, and at least a temporary intent. Seems her biggest concern was getting caught. Do you think maybe she switched the shipping paperwork on purpose? She'd know Woodruff would go to the shipping company first with the regular windows, and then head to the playhouse with the gemstone windows. Maybe she hoped to steal the gemstone windows back from him before he delivered them to the playhouse, and to frame him for the theft. But maybe by the time she caught up with him, Buck and I had already carried them over to the parsonage. Maybe she got upset that her ploy hadn't worked and ending up killing him in the bell tower."

On the other hand, maybe she planned to steal the windows out of the playhouse after they were delivered but before we installed them. She might have arrived too soon and Woody could have spotted her, figured out what she was up to. She might have been afraid he'd rat her out to Antonia Szabo, and she killed him to keep him quiet. She might have had a change of heart after killing him, decided stealing the windows wasn't worth the risk, and then played out the accidental switcheroo story to throw suspicion off herself.

Even as I posed the theory, I realized it had holes. Collin was quick to point them out.

"If Laurel wanted to frame Woodruff for theft, why give him the windows at all, then? She could have simply told Antonia that she'd handed the windows over to Woodruff, and that if he said otherwise he was lying."

"You've got a point."

"Besides," he added, "Laurel has an ironclad alibi. She was at the orthodontist with her son getting his braces tightened last Friday afternoon." Collin let that sink in for a moment before he said, "Another theory I've considered is that she might have set Woodruff up to be robbed by switching the paperwork."

"Are you saying she might have hired someone else to do the dirty work, and that person killed Woodruff?"

"Exactly. Maybe she didn't intend for her partner in crime to kill him, but things spiraled out of control. They might have decided to abandon their plan to steal the windows after the murder. Remember how she asked about the security system at the playhouse?"

"Yeah?"

"Maybe that was her way of finding out if she or her cohort would be caught on camera if they tried to remove the windows from the theater, or if they tried to pry the gems out of them."

"Whoa. I hadn't even thought of that."

Collin's mouth quirked in an almost grin. "That's why I get paid the big bucks."

While this theory felt like more pieces were falling into place, I still had a hard time seeing Laurel Cromwell as a jewel thief and accessory to murder, despite the fact that she'd stolen the expensive calculator. I told Collin as much. "Stealing a hundred-dollar calculator for her son was small potatoes. Stealing tens of thousands of dollars in precious gems is a whole different ball game." I'd compared a vegetable to a sport, probably not the best example of metaphors, but my point was made. "Surely, she wouldn't risk serving serious jail time."

"You're naïve, Whitney," he said without malice. "Women turn into mother lions when their children's welfare is threatened. They'll do anything to protect their kids and make sure their needs are met. A woman in Michigan and another in California became serial bank robbers to make ends meet for their families. They'd been normal suburban mothers up until then. No one would have ever suspected them. Laurel admitted to me that their financial situation was dire. That would be motive enough for her to steal the jewels. She might have been so stressed out that she wasn't thinking clearly. Desperate people do desperate, even stupid, things when their back is against the wall."

Collin could very well be right. Still, something had been niggling at me, something that hadn't made sense to me all along. "Doesn't it seem odd that Antonia Szabo would hire Woody's Delivery Service to transport valuable gems? He was such a small operation, and his Bronco was ancient." His delivery vehicle wasn't one to instill a lot of confidence. It looked like it could break down at any second. "He could've easily disappeared with the gems, especially since he doesn't seem to have any family tying him down here. Why wouldn't she hire a better-known courier company? One that's bonded and insured?"

"I've wondered the same thing," Collin said. "I'm going to ask Szabo about it when she returns my call."

With that, we ended our conversation, and I set my

phone aside to return my attention to my cat and my mystery novel. We might not know yet who had killed Gerard Woodruff and why, but at least I knew the crime in the book would be solved and justice would be done.

CHAPTER 15

BOOKED FOR BELLY RUBS

SAWDUST

Sawdust rolled over onto his back alongside Whitney as they lounged on her bed. As expected, she reached over and scratched his belly. He liked it when she had a book in her hand. It meant she'd sit still for a while and that she'd use her other hand to pet him. She'd have to take her hand away occasionally to turn the pages, but she always returned the hand to him. All in all, he enjoyed her reading time as much as she did.

Cleo didn't like belly rubs for some reason. He'd noticed that when Emmalee, Colette, or Whitney tried to scratch her chest, she'd sink her teeth into their fingers and swat at their hands with her back feet. While he adored his feline friend, he had to admit she was prone to fits of feistiness.

He *purr-urr-urred* as Whitney scratched his belly. He could tell the sound of contentment and the soft vibration soothed her. The tension seemed to seep from her body, her rigid muscles slowly relaxing next to him. Though he was the one producing the sound, it soothed him, too, like a mantra. Before he knew it, he was drifting . . . off . . . to sleep. . . .

CHAPTER 16

IF THE SHOE FITS

WHITNEY

My cell phone rang midmorning on Thursday, while Buck and I were hauling demolition debris out of the parsonage and tossing it into the refuse dumpster in the driveway. The delivery person had arrived at the theater with the Tiffany light fixtures. I'd posted a note on the door of the playhouse asking them to call me when they arrived.

"I'm at the house next door," I told the man. "I'll be right over."

I stuffed the phone back into my pocket and hurried out the door. I raised a hand in greeting as I jogged toward the theater. The deliveryman waved back. The last person to deliver something to the playhouse had lost his life. I was determined to make sure that this man would leave with both his life and a nice tip.

As I came up the stairs, I noticed he had an enormous box on his dolly, nearly as big as the one that held the commercial refrigerator that had been delivered to the parsonage not long before. It must contain the Tiffany chandelier we planned to hang in the foyer. "Whoa," I said. "That's a big box."

"Heavy, too," he said. "Where do you want it?"

I unlocked the door and directed him into the foyer. "You can leave it here."

He wiggled the box back and forth until he'd walked it off the dolly. "I'll grab the others." He brought in four more boxes, all of these much smaller than the first. I assumed they contained the Tiffany sconces for the theater, restrooms, and the walls of the foyer.

Once he'd unloaded all of the boxes, I handed the guy a tip, as well as a card with a onetime promo code for two complimentary balcony seats to any performance. The free tickets had been one of my ideas to build buzz and fill seats until word spread about the venue. "Come back sometime when we're up and running. It won't be long now."

"Thanks," the man said. "My wife always complains I never take her anywhere. She'd enjoy coming out here to see a show."

As I walked him out, the breeze carried the murmur of voices our way. I looked east to see a Sumner County Sheriff's Department cruiser in the driveway at Sibley's place. Johnny Otto's pickup sat near the barn. A panel van sat nearby, the back open. From this distance and angle, I couldn't see the side of the van to tell if it had a business logo on it, but the equipment in the back told me there was some type of work being done over there. The deputy, Otto, and another man, presumably the one who'd driven the panel van, were gathered inside the corral with Pegasus. The beautiful white horse wore a bridle today, and Otto held tight to the rope under his chin.

As soon as the man who'd delivered the light fixtures had driven off, my curiosity carried me up into the bell tower, where I could get a better look at what was going on over at the horse ranch. I pulled out my phone and used my increasingly handy binoculars app to zoom in. As I watched, the unidentified man carried a long-handled tool over to the horse. He turned his back and stepped into place beside Pegasus's right haunch, lifting the horse's back right foot. He used a hoof pick to clean the compacted dirt, leaves, and what appeared to be several small pieces of white gravel from the bottom of the horse's foot, digging carefully around the triangular part of the hoof known as the frog. I'd learned the odd word at a riding stable when I was young, and it stuck with me. The man then used the pulling tool to pry the horse's shoe loose. *He's a farrier.* Once the shoe was off, the man whipped out an oversized file and used it to give Pegasus a pedicure, filing down the bottom and edges of the horse's hoof. Once the foot was properly prepared, he affixed a shiny new shoe to the hoof.

It was clear to me why the farrier was at the horse ranch: to shoe the horses. What wasn't clear to me was why the deputy seemed interested in the gunk the farrier had cleaned from the horse's foot, as well as his old metal shoe. He gathered up both and put them in a clear plastic bag. Horseshoes were supposed to bring good luck, but I doubted the deputy would be so superstitious. Could Pegasus have picked up something in his hoof that provided a clue as to who had killed Nolan Sibley? Maybe something that implicated Johnny Otto? I hoped it wasn't the latter. I'd been watching the guy. He might be a little on the scraggly side, but he seemed to have a big heart, at least where horses and dogs were concerned.

Still, with Otto working so closely with Sibley at the horse ranch, it seemed inevitable law enforcement would look to him as a possible suspect. I couldn't shake the feeling that maybe Otto had something to do with Gerard Woodruff's death, too. Had Woodruff seen something going on at the horse ranch that Otto hadn't wanted him to see? Had Otto been so afraid that Woodruff would spill the beans that he'd chased Woodruff up into the bell tower and choked him to death there?

It certainly seemed possible. Otto was adept at handling a rope. He used ropes in various ways when working the horses. I'd seen him toss a rope over a post from quite a distance. He tied a quick-release knot faster than I'd ever seen anyone do it, too. He'd have no problem working the rope in the bell tower. Maybe Woodruff hadn't even been choked with the rope hanging in the belfry. Maybe Otto had carried his own rope over with him to do the job.

As I returned my phone to my pocket, my elbow bumped the bell, and it gave off a soft clang. Though the noise didn't catch the attention of the farrier or the deputy, Johnny Otto's head turned upward. With his helmet shading his eyes, I couldn't be certain he'd seen me, but I wouldn't be hard to miss up here in my blue coveralls. My guts tied themselves into knots, but they weren't the quick-release type of knots used with livestock. In fact, my guts still felt tight and tangled when I returned to the parsonage.

I told Buck what I'd seen, and how I was fairly certain Johnny Otto had seen me watching them, too. "You think he might've killed Sibley? And maybe Woodruff, too? Maybe Woodruff saw Otto doing something he shouldn't have. But what could that be?"

Buck put a piece of wood in place to begin framing the cocktail bar in the living room. "I can think of something."

"What?" I pulled my mask into place and ran a piece of coarse sandpaper over the spot to smooth the rough edge where we'd taken the wall down.

My cousin picked up another two-by-four. "Remember when Sibley said that Pegasus was his best stud horse?"

"Yeah?"

"Stud fees for a good horse can run a grand or more. Maybe Otto was arranging a side piece for Pegasus, so to speak."

Could Otto have been studding out the stallion without Sibley's knowledge and pocketing the fees? "But he'd have to bring the mare to Sibley's place," I pointed out. "Or he'd have to take Pegasus to the mare."

Buck cocked his head. "Not necessarily."

It took a moment for me to put two and two together. "Ew. Do they really do that?"

"Artificially inseminate horses?" he said. "Sure."

"How do you know this?"

"Remember that barrel racer I dated a few years back?"

"Yeah."

"She told me."

I cringed. "How in the world does something like that come up in casual conversation?"

Buck shrugged. "The place where she boarded her horse had a prized stud. They shipped his horsey seeds to horse farms all over."

"Say no more," I begged, raising my palms in a stop gesture. But even though I didn't want to discuss the topic, my curiosity was piqued. Could Otto have procured seed from Pegasus to sell for stud purposes? Or could he have taken Pegasus elsewhere for stud purposes, and Sibley found out? Maybe the deputy was looking for soil samples in the horse's hoof, something that would prove he'd been taken to another property without permission. I recalled seeing Otto letting a man and his horse through a rear gate at the western end of Sibley's property when I'd been painting inside the bell tower. He'd let them into a barn where Pegasus had been enclosed in a pen. I'd assumed Otto had been working on behalf of his boss, but maybe he'd arranged that romantic equine interlude himself and pocketed the stud fee. After all, the remote barn wasn't visible from Sibley's house or the main horse barn.

I set the piece of sandpaper down and went over to my laptop. I kept it on hand at jobsites in case we needed to place orders for supplies, or so we could stream a show on Netflix or Hulu to keep us entertained while we worked. I ran an internet search for illegal horse stud operations. I found several links to cases in which a stallion was bred to a mare without the owner's knowledge or permission. There were also cases of accidental breeding, when a mare and stallion somehow ended up coming into contact with each other in a pasture or paddock, engaging in a whirlwind romance. One link led me to a story involving a horse named Jet Deck. He'd been a valuable stud horse and in his prime until he was found dead from a massive overdose of barbiturates. Someone had intentionally killed the stud horse, and rumors flew afterward. One theory was that Jet Deck was killed by someone who owned a stallion Jet Deck had sired. They realized they could charge greater stud fees for their horse if Jet Deck's seed was no longer available. They might have killed the competition. *Poor horse.* Seemed when there was money to be made from animals, they sometimes suffered for human greed.

While the facts and theories seemed to point to Johnny Otto, I still had a hard time seeing the softhearted guy as a cold-blooded killer. The horses loved him. So did Luther, who followed the ranch hand around like a puppy. But he couldn't be ruled out. *Ugh.* I felt so conflicted.

I e-mailed Collin the link to the article about the murdered horse, and added a note telling him that I'd seen the deputy with a farrier and Otto next door. Although first and foremost I wanted Woodruff's murder solved, I also wanted to see Collin get credit for it. He'd been working hard to dig to the bottom of things. But if Otto had killed Woodruff because the deliveryman had seen something untoward going on at Sibley's property, it seemed the Sumner County Sheriff's Department was already working that theory and would probably reach a conclusion before Collin could. They'd get the glory when the case was solved. I knew Collin would simply be happy to see justice done. He wasn't in the investigation game for the glory. Even so, I hoped he'd get some recognition for the time and effort he'd put into the case so far.

Collin picked up a pizza and brought it over to my place for dinner. Over soda and slices topped with tomatoes and green olive, we discussed the plausibility of the stolen stud fee scheme. He agreed it was a viable plot.

"Otto probably wasn't paid much as a hired hand," Collin said. "Sibley couldn't have been an easy guy to work for, either. Maybe Otto decided he deserved a bonus and he saw Pegasus as a way to pad his paycheck."

I supposed we'd find out soon enough. Turning to our other potential theory, I asked, "What did Antonia Szabo say when you talked to her?"

Collin's face clouded. "I didn't."

"She hasn't returned your call?"

"No," he said. "I've left her three messages. In all of them I stressed the urgency of the matter. There's another strange thing, too. I couldn't find any references to her gallery online."

I remembered the name listed on the mismatched paperwork. It was Glassworks Gallery, at least in English.

"Could something have been lost in translation?" I suggested. "Maybe the gallery's name is listed in Romanian online."

"Could be," he said. "I tried searching the address for Glassworks Gallery that was listed on her business card, and it's the same address as an art museum."

"Maybe her gallery shares space with the museum." It would be a smart business decision to position a gallery in or near an art museum. After all, the museum and the gallery would appeal to the same types of people. "Maybe the museum leases space to galleries or artists looking to sell their work."

"I suppose it's possible. I tried to call the museum this afternoon, but there's an eight-hour time difference between Nashville and Bucharest. I only got a recording. It was in Romanian so I had no idea what it said or how to leave a message. I've got my alarm set to wake me up at two o'clock this morning so I can call the museum as it opens for the day."

"*Two A.M.?* Ugh. You're a very dedicated detective."

"Just doing my job."

I reached across the table and gave his hand a supportive squeeze. His dedication to his work was one of the many things I admired about him. Even so, I knew his job took a toll. I looked forward to showing him a fun time at the café and theater once they opened. A delicious dinner at a charming restaurant followed by an entertaining show would be just the thing to take his mind off murder.

CHAPTER 17

AN EXISTENTIAL CRISIS

WHITNEY

On Saturday, Buck continued to work on transforming the ranch-style parsonage into a café. Owen, Buck's younger brother, joined him. Owen was a slightly thinner, clean-shaven version of Buck. He and his wife had three young girls. Like Laurel Cromwell, they lived on a fairly tight budget, and some extra funds could really come in handy. That's where Buck and I lucked out. We could count on him to help us out now and then, and to do solid, high-quality work.

While the guys rehabbed the parsonage, Colette and I went in search of more secondhand tables, chairs, and dishware to outfit the café. We scored an adorable set of bright, floral cake dishes at an antique store, and a walnut trestle table at Goodwill. We came across a picnic table, too, and realized it could be a fun addition in the covered patio area of the café. All the wobbly table needed was some new screws and supports, as well as a coat of paint, and it would be as good as new. Garage sales yielded a set of pretty blue glassware, a pair of salt-and-pepper shakers in the shapes of black-and-white cats, and an assortment of mismatched silverware. A thrift stop find added three ladder-back chairs to the mix. It was a good thing we'd borrowed Buck's flatbed trailer and hitched it behind my SUV. All of the furniture never would have fit inside my vehicle.

As we drove home, Colette confided in me, "I'm excited, but I'm nervous, too. What if the café flops?"

"That'll never happen," I said. "You're a talented chef and you've thought of every detail."

"A lot of good restaurants go under. I've been in charge of the kitchen before, but never the entire restaurant. What if I bit off more than I can chew? Maybe I got so excited about the thought of running my own restaurant that I got carried away." She bit her lip. "I don't want to let you and Buck down."

Colette normally brimmed with confidence, but I could understand her jitters. "Buck and I had the same worries with every flip we've done," I said. "The truth is, there are no guarantees. All we can do is work hard and hope for the best. But nothing ventured, nothing gained, right? Better to take a chance than to look back one day and wonder 'what if.' Besides, whatever happens, we're all in this together."

Though my words seemed to have made her feel somewhat reassured, they didn't calm her nerves entirely. "I'd feel better if we do a dry run before the restaurant opens. We can invite family and friends to play the role of customers, and make sure nothing goes wrong."

"That's a good idea," I said. "Presley's pulling the opening-night lineup together. We can hold a dress rehearsal that evening, too. It can't hurt to make sure everything at both the restaurant and the theater is in working order."

We drove our finds out to the parsonage, where Buck and Owen helped us unload them and carry them inside. My cousins had made quite a bit of progress today, too.

As they unloaded the picnic table, Owen said, "This thing is as wobbly as a newborn colt."

I gave him a smile. "It won't be after you tighten the screws."

He harrumphed. "Bossy."

He'd been calling me the same name for years, ever since we were kids, and just like always I ignored him and instead expressed my appreciation for his work. "Thanks for helping us out today, Owen."

"I was told to insist on front-row seats to every show as a bonus, plus babysitting services."

Buck chuckled. "The wife is bossing you around, too, huh?"

The two deserved some nights out, and I'd be happy to watch their three adorable girls. "You got it, Cuz."

By the end of the day, we were all tired but buoyed by the pace at which things were moving along. As we headed out to our vehicles, I gave the gang a big smile. "Opening night will be here before we know it!"

Sunday was a gorgeous fall day, sunny with just a hint of chill in the air. While Collin often worked weekends when he had a homicide to solve, he'd exhausted his leads for the time being and was thus free to enjoy the day. We decided to take a drive out to the Natchez Trace for a hike.

The trace was a historic trail that ran over four hundred miles from the Cumberland River in Nashville all the way to the Mississippi River in Natchez, Mississippi. It had been a trade route used by Native Americans and European settlers. Unfortunately, some of that trade had been in human slaves. Famous explorer Meriwether Lewis had also met his demise along the trace, the assumption being his death was at his own hand after the government refused to reimburse expenses he'd incurred exploring on its behalf.

I supposed these sad stories came to mind because I couldn't quite escape the shadow of Woodruff's and Sibley's murders, even out here. My thoughts kept returning to them, my mind trying to sort through the facts and reach some conclusions. But, despite the tragedies incurred along the trace, it was a beautiful natural area, especially today, with the autumn leaves turning from green to gorgeous shades of gold, orange, bronze, and brown. Collin and I hiked to one of the small waterfalls, early-fallen leaves crunching under our feet.

As we explored the woods, Collin updated me on his investigation. Apparently, he couldn't get his mind off the murders, either. "Antonia Szabo still hasn't gotten back to me. I spoke with the manager of the museum, though. He said he's never heard of anyone named Antonia Szabo. He said the museum has been in that location for years. He has no idea why the museum's address was printed on Antonia's business cards. I spoke with law enforcement in Bucharest. They gave me contact information for three women with that name, but it got me nowhere. One of them said they'd never been to America. The second had come to New York City once a decade ago, but hasn't been back in the states since. The third didn't speak English and, without a translator, I couldn't explain myself."

"How do you know if the two you spoke with are telling you the truth?" I asked.

"I don't," he said. "But short of flying to Romania to interrogate them in person, I have to take them at face value."

"Szabo has come here in person," I pointed out. "That means she must have a passport. Can you get some information from Homeland Security?"

"There would be a lot of legal hurdles to jump through," he said. "At this point, we don't know if she had anything to do with Woodruff's death. I don't even know if Antonia Szabo is her real name. Laurel Cromwell said she never saw the woman's ID. She just took her word for it."

"How did she pay Laurel for the windows?"

"Cash."

"Isn't that suspicious?" I asked. "I mean, who uses cash anymore?"

Collin lifted one shoulder. "International bank fees and credit card charges for foreign purchases can be steep. Cash would be a way for Szabo to avoid them."

I thought some more. "Someone with the name Antonia Szabo would have had to be in Bucharest to pick up the glass shipments from Specialty Export Experts, right? I can't imagine the company would hand over a shipment without proper identification, especially one that's so valuable."

"That crossed my mind, too," Collin said. "I plan to speak with the staff at the shipping company again. They're my best chance of finding Szabo. She's the only person who seems to link everyone together. She ordered the glass from Laurel Cromwell, she hired Woody's Delivery Service to transport the pieces from Laurel's studio to the shipping company, and she contracted with the shipping company to get the windows to Europe. She seems to be the person most likely to know something. Of course, that's assuming Woodruff's murder had something to do with the stained-glass windows and not the drugs that were found in his car or Sibley's horse operation."

"Still no word from Sumner County?"

"Not yet."

I found myself once again in the position of having to assure someone that they knew how to do their job and would succeed. If I had to do any more cheerleading, I might need to invest in a pair of pom-poms. "You'll figure it out," I said. "I know you will. You always do."

He slid me a soft smile. "Usually with your help."

"I am pretty clever, aren't I?"

"Clever, for sure," he agreed. "Maybe a little nosy and pushy, too."

I stopped walking and put my hands on my hips. "Hey!"

He raised his palms, fighting a grin. "I meant that in the most flattering way possible."

I scowled. "I'm not sure *nosy* and *pushy* can ever be considered flattering."

"How about *inquisitive* and *assertive*, then?"

"That's better."

Our hike proved to be a pleasant diversion, maybe even a romantic one. We stood side by side, our arms wrapped around each other's backs as we watched the sun set on the western horizon behind the double-arch bridge along the trace. Like the colorful stained-glass windows in the playhouse, the setting sun filled the sky with colors. Pinks.

Oranges. Blues. Plums. I could only hope that, very soon, things would become clear.

Things did not become clearer. In fact, after Collin spoke with the staff at Specialty Export Experts on Monday morning, things seemed even more convoluted.

He phoned me with an update. "The head of operations for the shipping company is a woman named Marie Vanderhagen. I spoke with her and the head of security, a guy named Christopher DuPont. Vanderhagen said that they ship a very wide variety of items for their customers. They can't be expected to be familiar with every one of them. When they value the merchandise for customs purposes, they go by the amounts the customer gives them. But they do require their customers to provide invoices or receipts to show what they paid for the products. If the shipping client is a manufacturing business, the manufacturer will provide documentation showing what their customer paid them for the products being shipped."

"Did they show you paperwork for Szabo's orders?"

"They did. She's moved quite a lot of art pieces. Not just the windows she ordered from Laurel, but from other artists, too. Painters. Sculptors. Fiber arts. Pottery."

"Were all of the artists based in Nashville?"

"No," he said, "but they're in this general region. Memphis. Knoxville. Louisville and Lexington, Kentucky. Huntsville, Alabama."

"Does she buy art elsewhere in the U.S.?"

"It's possible," Collin said. "But S.E.E. only has an office here. Szabo might use other shipping companies for her art purchases in other areas of the country."

"You've talked to the people here," I said, "but what about the people at the other end? In Europe?"

"The shipping company's staff said that someone with identification in the name of Antonia Szabo has been picking the items up from their warehouse in Bucharest."

Hmm. "I guess all of this means that Laurel Cromwell didn't just make the woman up, then."

"I'd wondered about that, too. I was starting to think Antonia Szabo doesn't even exist."

"What now?" I asked.

"The shipping company said they'll discuss the matter with their staff in Bucharest. Szabo's windows are currently still in transit, but they're expected to arrive in Bucharest late next week. When she goes to pick them up, the warehouse staff will put her in touch with the local staff here. Marie Vanderhagen will tell Szabo they can't release the windows until she speaks with me."

"Good," I said. "You'll finally get some answers."

CHAPTER 18

SMOKE AND MIRRORS

WHITNEY

The Sumner County Sheriff's Department got their answers before Collin got his. On Monday afternoon, the deputy drove up to the parsonage while Buck and I were working with two plumbers to install extra pipes in the café's kitchen for the commercial dishwasher and sinks. Converting an outdated private kitchen into a contemporary commercial one had proved to be quite an undertaking, but I was happy to do it for my best friend and Buck was thrilled that he could help make his girlfriend's dreams come true.

I saw the cruiser through the window. "Buck!" I called.

When my cousin turned my way, I angled my head toward the window. He looked outside, saw the deputy's cruiser, and told the two men we were assisting that we'd be right back.

We went out front and met the deputy as he climbed out of his cruiser. "You're off the hook," he said without preamble. "We've identified Nolan Sibley's killer."

"Hot damn!" Buck said. "It was Johnny Otto, wasn't it?"

I elbowed my cousin in the ribs. We certainly hadn't liked

being wrongfully accused. It wasn't nice to assume someone else was guilty, either, no matter how likely a suspect
he might be.

"No," the deputy said. "It wasn't Otto."

"Who, then?" I asked.

Rather than give me a name right away, he said, "Remember when you were spying on us? When we were
checking out that big white horse?"

No sense denying it. Otto had seen me after I'd accidentally bumped the bell and the resulting clang told them I
was up in the bell tower, looking down on them. "Yes?"

"We found tooth fragments encased in the mud in the
horse's hoof. There was dried blood, hair, and skin tissue
under his horseshoe, too. The medical examiner compared
the DNA and confirmed that the teeth, hair, and skin belonged to Mr. Sibley."

"What?!" It seemed like we were living through some
sort of warped Greek tragedy. I felt my jaw go slack.

Buck's did, too. His mouth gaped for a moment before
he said, "Pegasus killed Sibley?"

The deputy gave a nod. "Equine activities are inherently
dangerous. Johnny Otto took precautions, but Sibley didn't.
Of course, a helmet and a chest protector aren't going to help
if a horse is bound and determined to kick you square in
the teeth."

I remembered the snicker Pegasus had issued when Sibley's body had been hauled away. *Maybe he really had
been laughing.*

Buck shook his head. "Live by the sword, die by the
sword."

A more precise saying might have been *live by the*

prod, die by the shod. If Sibley hadn't been so harsh on his horses, maybe he'd still be alive today. As I'd been puttering around the playhouse, I'd surreptitiously watched both Nolan Sibley and Johnny Otto work with them. From everything I'd witnessed, Johnny seemed to be a horse whisperer type. The horses trotted off when Sibley walked into the barnyard, doing their best to avoid the blowhard and his electric stick. But when the horses saw Johnny coming, they'd often move toward him, knowing he'd treat them to a carrot or two, maybe a scratch behind the ears or a pat on the flank.

Otto had been continuing to care for both the horses and Luther since Sibley had died. I supposed Sibley's family had made arrangements to keep him on the payroll, at least until they figured out what they were going to do with the horse ranch long-term. I felt relieved to know that Sibley's death had nothing to do with Woodruff's, and that Otto was not responsible for his boss's demise. It had been disconcerting to have a murder suspect working right next door. I supposed he'd probably felt the same way about me and Buck. Of course, it was still possible Johnny Otto could have something to do with Woodruff's death. Seemed he had the opportunity, maybe even a motive.

We thanked the deputy for the information. Still, there was one question that had yet to be answered. Though it seemed irrelevant now, to satisfy my curiosity I went ahead and asked it. "Where was Johnny Otto on Tuesday? Seems like we see him over at the farm most days. We were surprised he wasn't there when we found Sibley."

"Sibley had sent him down to Shelbyville to check out a mare another breeder had for sale."

"I see." No doubt it was Otto who'd provided that bit of information. I wondered if the sheriff's department had verified whether it was true, or whether they'd deemed it immaterial now that the medical examiner had determined Sibley was a victim of horsey homicide.

Having completed the task he'd come to do, the deputy gestured around the parsonage. "When will y'all have this place up and running?"

It was nearing late October now, and we'd need at least another month to finish up our work on the parsonage. Then the holidays would hit, and everyone would be busy with shopping and celebrations. But Presley had been auditioning acts for opening night and given them a date in early January. The café would open the same night the playhouse held its first public performance. "We're looking to open just after the start of the new year," I said. I reached into my pocket, pulled out one of our promo cards, and handed it to him. "Details will be posted on our website as soon as we nail them down. The code on that card will get you a couple of free show tickets. Come on out."

"I'll do that. Thanks. You folks take care now." He tucked the card into his wallet, turned, and walked back to his cruiser.

As he drove off, I whipped out my phone to call Collin. Naturally, he'd heard from the deputy before we had.

"What do you think?" I ask. "Even if Johnny Otto didn't kill Sibley, do you think he might have killed Woodruff?" The theory still seemed plausible to me. From the activity I'd seen at Sibley's ranch, it seemed that the boss and his hired hand had worked independently most of the time. Of course, Sibley had Otto doing the bulk of the dirty work—mucking the stalls in the barn, carrying heavy buckets of feed, and otherwise caring for the horses. But with his boss often handling business matters from the comfort of his home office, Otto could very well have been running an unauthorized stud operation right under his boss's nose. It wasn't like Pegasus would kiss and tell.

"I'll come out to talk to him again," Collin said. "The fact that the sheriff's department solved Sibley's murder gives me a reason to stop by. I'll see if his story has changed from when I interviewed him before. I'll ask about the stud service, too, see how he reacts."

We ended our call and I got back to work. A half hour later, I saw Collin's plain sedan drive by on the country road in front of the parsonage. He was on his way to speak with Otto. I was a little concerned that he was going out to the ranch alone. After all, if Otto was the killer and if he'd killed Woodruff because Woodruff had seen him doing something related to a clandestine stud operation, he might get defensive when Collin questioned him about it. There was no end of things at the horse farm that Otto could use as a weapon. Sibley's electronic prod. A pitchfork. Even a loose horseshoe, which could be thrown or jabbed at someone. Otto could use one of those ropes he was so adept at handling. *Ugh.* The thought made my stomach sour. I reminded myself that Collin was well trained and armed, with a gun and pepper spray. He could take care of himself if he had to. Even so, I was tempted to climb up in the belfry and keep an eye on things. Collin wouldn't appreciate it, though, and I might be putting him in danger if Otto spotted me at the wrong moment, so I restrained myself.

A half hour later, he pulled up to the parsonage and my

tense muscles relaxed in relief. I went outside to speak with him. He tilted his head to indicate the passenger seat next to him. Looked like he wanted to talk privately.

I climbed in and closed the door. "What did you find out?"

"Nothing definitive," he said. "But when I asked Otto if he was offering unauthorized stud services, he didn't deny it outright. He wanted to know why I was asking."

In other words, he wanted to know whether Collin had amassed any evidence against him before deciding how he would respond. "What did you tell him? Did you say I'd seen him let someone in the back gate with a horse a while back?"

"No," Collin said, his eyes darkening. "I wasn't about to implicate you in any way. Even though it was a kick from Pegasus that killed Sibley, Johnny Otto could have played a part in it. He might have orchestrated things, choreographed that kick. He claims he was down in Shelbyville all day, and that he'd gone directly there from his home in Ridgetop. But Sibley's place is on the way. He might have stopped by early in the morning before heading down to see the mare."

Given the state of Sibley's body, the medical examiner had determined that Sibley had died early Tuesday morning. Collin could be on to something.

He continued to fill me in. "Otto told me he's been working horses since he was fourteen. That's three and a half decades of experience. Plus, he spends a lot of time around Sibley's horses, knows their personalities. He could've done something to spook Pegasus, or to irritate him when Sibley was standing behind the horse. I've done a little digging, some research on equine behavior. Evidently, horses sometimes kick if a saddle cinch irritates their belly."

Otto could have purposely pinched Pegasus with the cinch. "Getting the horse to do his dirty work would be a clever ploy."

"Definitely," Collin agreed. "It would make intent and premeditation much harder to prove. He could claim the horse decided to kick all on his own. There's no way he could be sure the kick would do the job, either. People get kicked by horses all the time. Some are severely injured, but live to tell about it."

Was it possible that the kick from Pegasus had only injured Sibley, but not killed him immediately? "Any chance Otto helped things along?"

"Hit Sibley when he was down, you mean?"

"Yeah. Maybe Pegasus got things started and Otto finished them. I don't know how much damage one kick from a horse can do, but Sibley's face was totally mangled."

"It's out of my realm, too," Collin admitted. "But the sheriff's department didn't find anything implicating Otto, and the medical examiner's office seems satisfied the injuries are the sole result of a single horse kick. I'm thinking that Sibley could have caught on somehow that Otto was stealing stud fees. Maybe someone who owned one of the breeding mares contacted Sibley for one reason or another and he found out. Or maybe Sibley caught Otto in the act and threatened to fire him and sue him. Letting Pegasus take the blame might have looked like an easy solution to Otto's problem." As if realizing he'd made a lot of assumptions, he backpedaled a bit. "Still, we don't know for certain there is a problem. I know squat about horses and horse breeding. I asked Otto what type of paperwork is involved. He said that registration is optional for Arabian horses, and that the Arabian Horse Association requires all horses be DNA tested to prove their lineage."

"Does that mean Pegasus has his DNA on file? Like a 23andMe kind of thing?"

"It does."

I wondered what the DNA might tell us. Maybe Pegasus had descended from a horse once ridden by an Arab sultan. "You could contact the registry then, right? They'd be able to tell you which horses Pegasus has sired, and you could compare that to Sibley's stud service records."

"Contacting the registry wouldn't help. At least not yet."

"Why not?"

"Because horses gestate for eleven months. Sometimes a little longer." He frowned. "Otto only started working for Sibley eight months ago."

I mulled the information over for a moment. "If Otto was up to no good at Sibley's place," I said, "he's probably done questionable things before. Do you know where he worked before he started at Sibley's horse farm?"

"He told me he worked for years at a recreational stable. They didn't do any breeding there. They bought their horses. He said he trained both horses and riders. He led trail rides, too. He met Nolan Sibley when he came to pick up a horse the stable had bought. He said Sibley's last hand had up and quit on him and Sibley offered him a job on the spot."

I wasn't surprised Sibley had run off his former hand. He'd run his wife off already, and the horses would likely have left his farm if they could. Pegasus had already proved that by escaping to the playhouse more than once. Sibley clearly wasn't an easy man to get along with. "So, Otto took the job right off?"

"He did. He'd become bored at the riding stable and he thought working for Sibley might offer more opportunities. He admitted he didn't like the way Sibley did things, that he thought the guy was too harsh with his horses. Otto said he did his best to keep Sibley away from the animals, encouraged him to handle just the business end of things while Otto took care of the training."

This information left me feeling conflicted once again. *Is Otto a hero or a homicidal hired hand?* It crossed my mind that he might even be both. "Is there any way to track down who he might have been in touch with about stud services?"

"No," Collin said. "I don't have probable cause to search Otto's phone, pickup truck, or home. I asked him if I could take a look and he refused. He claims he has nothing to hide, but that he doesn't believe in letting law enforcement run roughshod over him. No judge would give me a warrant based on speculation. Unless I find more evidence, I'll have to wait at least three more months and search the registry. Even then, I'd be stepping on toes. The Sumner County Sheriff's Department considers Sibley's death investigation closed. If I start poking around Otto as a suspect in Woodruff's murder and it then implicates him in Sibley's death, as well, I'd likely ruffle some feathers."

Despite what he'd said, I knew Collin was willing to ruffle feathers if necessary to fulfill his duties. He was a dedicated detective who wouldn't let politics get in the way of doing his job. I supposed only time would tell whether the feathers would remain unruffled, or whether the feathers would fly.

Three weeks later, it was mid-November and Woodruff's murder remained unsolved. Renovations on the playhouse, on the other hand, were coming along rapidly. Colette, Presley, Gia Revello, and I had met with the business attorney and CPA, who set up a corporation for our business and advised us on how to handle sales, employment, and income tax matters. Other than serving on the board and offering my two cents at the board meetings, I would be a silent partner in the business, leaving the day-to-day operations up to Colette and Presley, while happily accepting my share of the profits—assuming there were any. Despite our hard work, no new business came with a guarantee of success. All of the money Buck and I had invested in the place could be lost. It was a scary thought, given that we'd invested nearly every cent we had.

As all of the pieces started coming together, I grew more jittery. I couldn't wait for opening night, which would be a big test. Would we have a full house? Or would our venue prove to be too far off the beaten path to attract diners and an audience? And when would that darn curtain arrive? Every time I checked with the manufacturer, they told me it would be just a few more days. If the curtain didn't arrive by opening night, we might have to hang old painting tarps in the theater. Maybe the audience would be fooled into thinking the colorful paint splotches were a form of artistic expression rather than drips and drops falling from our brushes as we painted walls and ceilings.

Antonia Szabo proved to be as elusive as the theater's curtain. Szabo's windows had long since arrived in Bucharest and, according to the staff at the shipping company, the woman had made no attempts to pick them up. They'd attempted to inform her that her items had arrived, left her multiple voice mails, but the shipping company's calls had not been returned. Neither had Collin's. When Collin had tried her most recently, he discovered that her outgoing message had been changed to say that she had been forced to close her gallery and would be unable to take calls for the time being due to a sudden serious yet unspecified health issue. The situation was odd. It felt like smoke and mirrors. *Or should I say smoke and stained-glass windows?* At least with a mirror you got some sort of reflection of the truth. Our situation felt more like trying to look through thick, virtually opaque glass, where the results were shadowy and colored by illusion.

With no further leads, Collin's investigation ground to a standstill. When we met up for dinner or he took me out on a date, his frustration was palpable. Despite daily runs, his go-to method of stress reduction, every nerve in his body seemed to be on edge, every muscle tense.

He confided in me on the drive home from a movie on a Saturday night. "My boss knows I've busted my butt on this investigation. Nobody is pushing me to find Woodruff's killer. Not the public, not the media, not even Woodruff's sisters. It would be easy to just give up, call it a cold case, and move on. But it's investigations like this where I feel like I need to go that extra mile, to make especially sure I've done all I can, to make sure a killer doesn't go free because he picked the right victim."

In other words, he had to care because no one else seemed to. He had to be the victim's advocate, in addition to being an investigator. I reached out and took his hand in mine, giving it a squeeze. Collin had a sharp mind, but he also had a caring heart. A girl could do much worse.

The following evening, I found myself home alone. Emmalee and Colette were both at work, with plans to give their two-week notices in mid-December to their boss at the restaurant where they currently worked. Sawdust was curled up next to me on the sofa, and Cleo lounged in Emmalee's Papasan chair. At this point, it seemed Collin's only hope for a break in the case rested with Specialty Export Experts and their tenuous connection to their client Antonia Szabo. After all, it was their connection that would likely be critical to locating the woman.

While I'd perused the shipping company's website a while back, I hadn't dug deep. There hadn't seemed to be any reason to at the time. But now, with the fate of the case seemingly in the company's hands, I was much more curious. I also wondered why the royal family member who'd requisitioned the bejeweled windows hadn't made arrangements to pick them up from the shipping company themselves, once their agent fell ill. It was odd that they'd let such valuable gems sit in a warehouse for weeks on end, wasn't it? Then again, a royal family was probably dripping in diamonds, rubies, sapphires, and emeralds. Even though the stones were valuable, worth far more than the average person could fathom, they probably represented a mere pittance to a royal family. Why else embed them in stained glass?

I looked over the shipping company's website again. The main page prominently featured the company's logo, S.E.E. THE WORLD, across a globe. The logo appeared on the other pages as well, though it was much smaller and relegated to a narrow band across the top of the screen. Information about the founding family appeared on the "Company History" page, as well as then-and-now photos of the man who'd bought the first tractor-trailer and arranged for the first international shipment, which contained sugary American-made soft drinks going to Europe. His wife stood alongside him in both photos. The two had aged well and remained alive and kicking at ninety-two and eighty-nine, respectively, their longevity and preservation a testament to good genes, healthy living, and, I presumed, the best health and beauty treatments money could buy.

Though clearly prosperous, they were not as successful or well-known as the Vanderbilts, who'd made their fortune in shipping, too, and for whom Nashville's Vanderbilt University was named. Commodore Cornelius Vanderbilt had shipped primarily by steamboat and railroad. According to the website, however, S.E.E. moved goods primarily by semitruck and merchant vessels. The founders had decided to base their U.S. headquarters in Nashville in the late 1950s, just after Interstates 40 and 65 had been completed. I-40 connected the country from Wilmington, North Carolina, in the east, to Barstow, California, in the west, while I-65 ran from Mobile, Alabama, in the south to the Chicago, Illinois, area in the north. Easy access to these interstate highways, as well as the ports on the coasts, was instrumental in building the shipping business.

Another page, titled "Our People," featured short bios and photographs of the key personnel, both in its Nashville headquarters and at its facilities around the world. While some of the executives and upper management were second- and third-generation members of the founding family, others were not. Among the non-family members who worked at the company was the woman Collin had spoken to, the head of operations, Marie Vanderhagen. She looked to be in her early forties, and wore her platinum-blond hair in a short, sleek blunt cut that angled inward to frame her pointy chin. According to her bio, she spoke seven languages, many of them having been learned abroad when she was a child while her family moved about the world, following her father, who performed diplomatic work at various embassies. Even though I tended to be a homebody, I had to admit that a childhood moving from country to country every few years sounded quite exciting. Her foreign-language skills were likely a big reason she landed the job with an international shipping company. Her MBA from the University of Chicago, from which she'd graduated summa cum laude, couldn't hurt, either.

Also featured on the page was a photo of the man who ran the shipping yard. While the other key personnel wore business attire, he was dressed as one who worked outdoors in a bustling shipyard would be expected, in coveralls and a hard hat. Large metal shipping containers formed a colorful backdrop behind him. The head of security earned a smaller photo on the bottom row. His name was Christopher DuPont. He was the bald man I'd seen through the binoculars when I'd followed Laurel Cromwell to the shipping company a few weeks ago, the one with the suspicious-looking mole on his head. Collin had mentioned speaking with both DuPont and Vanderhagen, though he'd learned little from them.

Unfortunately, while looking over the company's website had introduced me to its people, it didn't tell me anything that could be helpful in locating Antonia Szabo. I decided to search the name of the company and see what other links might tell me.

Sawdust rolled over onto his back next to me, his movement an implicit request for a chest scratch. I accommodated him, running my nails through his soft, buff-colored fluff. He showed his appreciation with a loud purr. I could feel his happy vibes through my fingertips. Though my cat had been the one to witness Woodruff's murder and lead us to his body, he seemed to be the least affected by the event. He wasn't kept awake at night with flashbacks to the rope burn on Woodruff's neck, or sickened by any noise that remotely resembled the dong of a large bell. *Lucky cat.*

The first dozen links I came across after typing the shipping company's name into my browser included reviews of the company's services. The vast majority of the reviews were favorable, earning them 4.9 out of 5 stars. One of those stellar reviews was written by Antonia Szabo herself: *You can trust S.E.E. with your most precious cargo. I do.*

A few of the links led to articles written about the founding family and published in business and trade publications.

Other links detailed awards given to the staff by the local chamber of commerce and various charitable organizations that had benefited from the owners' philanthropy. Nothing seemed out of the ordinary. I was just about to close my computer and turn in early when a link at the bottom of the fourth page caught my eye. *S.E.E. Employee Pleads Guilty to Embezzlement.* Finally, something interesting.

I clicked the link, which took me to a short entry that had appeared on the *Nashville Business Journal* website six months ago. The piece comprised a mere two sentences. The first noted that a former company accountant named Kevin Pham had pleaded guilty to embezzling $50,000 from S.E.E. The second sentence stated that, under the terms of his negotiated plea, Pham would pay full restitution, a $1,000 fine, and serve one year of probation. Seemed everyone we'd come across lately was on probation. Laurel Cromwell. Gerard Woodruff. And, now, this Kevin Pham guy. *Hmm. What's Kevin up to now?*

I googled the guy's name along with the words *Nashville* and *accountant.* Another website popped up, this one for a freelance bookkeeper who called himself K. P. Pham. *Is this the same guy?* Maybe he was going by his initials rather than his first name in the hopes that people wouldn't make the connection and realize he was the same guy who'd stolen from his workplace. I couldn't be certain, though, at least not until I determined who owned the domain name he'd used.

Hmm. I ran a search for *how can I find out who owns a website?* The results led me to a search site where I could type in the domain and identify the owner. I typed K. P.

Pham's website domain into my browser, hit the enter key, and leaned in to read the results. Sure enough, the site was owned by a Kevin Pham. But was it the same Kevin Pham? How many Kevin Phams might there be in Nashville, especially ones who worked in the accounting arena? I decided it was highly likely the two were one and the same, especially when I noted that the domain had been created only a month after the article about Pham's plea bargain had been posted. He'd have been looking for new work at that time.

Pham marketed his services to small businesses and tradespeople who had insufficient activity to keep an in-house bookkeeper busy full-time but needed some help processing their paperwork and maintaining their financial records. His site included testimonials from clients, including a massage therapist, the manager of an auto repair shop, and the owner of a yarn store, who deemed him "reliable," "efficient," and "a cost-effective solution for small business owners who'd rather focus on their trade than record keeping." I wondered if these clients were aware of Pham's criminal record. Probably not. For better or worse, most people were not suspicious and took things at face value. Few people took the time to run a search like I had, or had the patience to scroll through pages and pages of links. They assumed someone was on the up-and-up until their own experience told them otherwise. Often, it was too late then.

I sat back and thought over what I'd found. By all accounts, Pham was a scam artist who'd stolen from his employer. But he was also someone who'd been on the inside at the shipping company. He might be privy to information anyone still with the company might be hesitant to share. *Is there anything to be gained by talking to him?* If nothing else, I decided, it might make Collin feel like he was doing something on the case other than spinning his wheels. I whipped out my phone and dialed Collin's number.

CHAPTER 19

A CALL TO COLLIN

SAWDUST

Sawdust didn't understand all of the words Whitney said. The term *bookkeeper* meant nothing to him. Neither did *embezzlement. What's a Kevin, anyway?*

He did recognize some of the things she said, though. He knew when she said *Collin* that she was referring to the nice guy she spent a lot of time with, the one who'd roll a jingly ball around for Sawdust to chase, or who would get out the fishpole toy and dangle the dancing mouse in front of Sawdust and Cleo so they could pounce on it. Collin's clothing often bore a trace of fur and smelled like cats, and sometimes his hands smelled of cats, too, ones he must have petted before coming over. Sawdust surmised Collin shared his home with two of his fellow felines.

But while Sawdust didn't quite understand all that had transpired during the phone call, he was glad when it ended, glad to sense that Whitney felt more excited than frustrated now. She scooped him up in her arms and carried him off to bed. *Purrrrrr.*

CHAPTER 20

SECRETS, SURPRISES, SYRUP, AND SHORT STACKS

WHITNEY

At ten o'clock Monday morning, Collin and I sat on one side of a red vinyl booth in the back corner of a diner, inhaling the aroma of the onions and hash browns frying on the grill and waiting for Kevin Pham. This meeting was my doing. After learning about the guy, I'd suggested to Collin that it might be worth contacting the disgraced former employee of S.E.E. and seeing if he might have something to offer about Antonia Szabo or the shipping company.

We'd ordered coffee and were sipping it when an Asian-American man of around thirty-five came in the door. He wore a nicely pressed white button-down shirt with a striped necktie, gray slacks, and a navy blazer. He carried a soft-sided computer briefcase in his hand. He'd clearly taken time to put himself together, to make a good impression, and was ready to get to work. I felt a twinge of guilt that we'd lured him here under false pretenses. He thought he'd come to meet potential new clients when, in reality, we planned to grill him just like those onions and hash browns.

He glanced around the diner. Collin raised a hand to signal him, and Pham headed our way. Collin rose from the booth to greet him. I was trapped on the seat between Collin and the wall, so I merely gave the man a smile and raised a hand in hello. He looked so hopeful of landing our business that the twinge I'd just felt in my gut turned into a full-fledged twist.

After the men had shaken hands, Collin sat back down next to me and Pham slid into the booth across from us. He unzipped his briefcase, whipped out a legal pad and pen, and placed them on the table. The server came over to take our order. Collin held out a hand, inviting Pham to go first.

"Just coffee for me," he said. "Thanks."

Collin and I each ordered a short stack of pancakes. I asked for sliced bananas, chocolate chips, and pecans on mine. *In for a penny, in for a pound.* Actually, with all those calories and all that sugar, I might gain more than a pound after eating the pancakes. At least my rehab work would burn some of those calories.

Once the server left the table, Pham turned back to me and Collin, looking from one of us to the other. "So, Mr. and Mrs. Flynn, how can I help you with your pet-grooming business?'

When Collin said we'd need a ruse for asking Pham to meet us, pet grooming was the first business that had popped into my mind, maybe because I'd had my hand buried in Sawdust's fluffy chest fur at the time.

Collin slid over slightly, poised on the edge of the bench in case Pham attempted to flee. Not that he had any right to stop the guy. The man wasn't under arrest, after all. But at least Collin would be ready to stand and impede his progress. We wanted this guy to talk to us, and we had no idea how receptive he'd be. A person on probation wasn't likely to be too keen on speaking with law enforcement. We hoped that the fact that he'd left S.E.E. in disgrace might encourage him to dish on the business, though. We needed information about their client Antonia Szabo.

Collin pulled out his business card and laid it on the table. "Sorry, Mr. Pham. The grooming business was something we made up to get you here. I'm actually a detective with Metro PD." Collin didn't identify me, probably for my safety. He'd let the guy make his own assumptions. Most likely, Pham would assume I was another detective who worked alongside Collin. *He wouldn't be too far off.* I'd left my coveralls in my SUV and wore more businesslike attire, green pants and a cream-colored sweater, something a person with an office job would wear.

Pham picked up Collin's business card, looked it over, and frowned. His gaze moved from the card to Collin. "Last time I spoke with a police officer, I was hauled out of my house in handcuffs, right in front of my wife and kids." His gaze and jaw hardened. *"For a crime I didn't commit."*

I knew it wasn't the first time someone with a record had claimed innocence, so I took this statement with a healthy portion of salt.

Rather than debate the merits of the guy's embezzlement charge, which was water under the bridge, Collin said, "That must have been humiliating."

"You know what else is humiliating?" Pham said. "The fact that my wife had to go back to work to support our family after I lost my job. I've been hustling to get work, but it's hard to build a freelance business from scratch. Do you have any idea what it's like not to be able to provide for the people you love?"

"No," Collin said. "But I can imagine it would be incredibly frustrating, screw with your sense of self-worth."

Although Pham's tone sounded beyond perturbed, he made no move to rise from his seat. Looked like Collin's attempts at empathy had won the guy over, or at least kept him in the booth. "What do you want?" he demanded.

"Information," Collin said, "if you've got it." He explained about the Woodruff case, how the man had been killed after delivering the wrong stained-glass windows to a theater.

"I don't understand." Pham was stiff with tension and his voice rose. "What does that man's murder have to do with me?"

"Absolutely nothing," Collin assured him, raising his palms. "You're not a person of interest. We're simply trying to get information about a client of Specialty Export Experts. Or maybe about the company itself. The woman who had ordered these particular windows was named Antonia Szabo."

Pham's expression didn't change. He continued to look at Collin expectantly, as if waiting to hear something he should respond to.

Collin added, "She's purportedly with Glassworks Gallery."

Still nothing.

"It's located in Romania."

That did it. Pham's gaze narrowed and his jaw flexed. "It was an art shipment to Romania that started this whole mess."

Collin and I exchanged a glance before he turned back to Pham. "What do you mean?"

"The day before I was arrested," Pham explained, "some paperwork crossed my desk. It was for a shipment of art. The piece was a painting by a local artist whose name I recognized. My wife is a nurse, but she minored in art. We go to nearly every exhibit at Cheekwood and the Frist Art Museum. We took the kids to the one by that artist that uses Legos."

Collin, Colette, Buck, and I had seen that exhibit, too. Buck and I had found it particularly fascinating. Art meets building blocks. We'd both loved playing with Legos as kids. In fact, we'd often planned the designs and built them together. I supposed it was no wonder we'd graduated from constructing things with plastic bricks to constructing things with actual bricks. "Sean Kenney," I said, noting the artist's name. "We saw it, too."

Collin chimed in. "His exhibit was really cool." He refocused the conversation. "But you'd said something about a painting by another artist?"

"Yeah," Pham said. "The value of the painting was listed as only one hundred and fifty dollars on the customs paperwork. I knew that couldn't be right. The discrepancy caught my attention because I recognized the artist's name. We'd attended his show at a gallery in Brentwood a week before, and none of his pieces were priced at less than ten grand. The valuation also caught my attention because my wife had recently shown me an article in one of her art magazines. The topic of the article was the use of art in money laundering."

Art? Money laundering? Huh? "How?" I asked.

"As a financial medium," Pham said, "art is flexible. The precise value of a work of art can be hard to pin down. Unless an artist has sold similar pieces, or the exact same piece changed hands recently between art collectors, the value can be very subjective. A lot of artwork changes hands at private sales rather than auctions, so the actual sales price isn't public knowledge. There's often very little paperwork to substantiate the amount that was paid for a piece, or even who bought it. People sometimes buy art anonymously. Art is easy to transport, too. Many pieces of art are lightweight compared to other valuable things, like gold bars."

I considered how what he'd said could pertain to Antonia Szabo's purchase of the stained-glass art and windows from Laurel Cromwell. The windows weren't nearly as lightweight as an oil painting, but they were still relatively portable. The smaller stained-glass suncatchers would be lightweight and easy to transport. Of course, the pieces would need to be properly wrapped and packaged to prevent breakage during shipping, but they'd still be relatively easy to move. And with actual jewels hidden in the glass designs, customs officers were likely to be none the wiser when the windows passed under their noses.

Pham said, "I showed the paperwork to my boss. I told her the value didn't look right, and that I didn't want the company getting in trouble if a client was trying to pull a fast one. I told her about the article my wife had shown me, how white-collar criminals were using art to move money around illegally. My boss ran the matter up the chain, talked to the customer, and found out that there'd just been an entry error. The clerk who'd accepted the shipment had forgotten to type in the two zeros after the decimal point, so it turned the fifteen thousand dollars they'd paid into the one hundred and fifty. My boss actually thanked me for my attention to detail and said she'd be sure to note my find in my next performance review." He beamed for just a second before his light seemed to go out. "The very next day, I arrived at work only to be escorted back to my car."

"By who?" Collin asked.

"Christopher DuPont," Pham clarified. "He's the head of S.E.E.'s security."

DuPont was the bald man I'd seen on the website and working at the shipping company's front gate security booth, the one with the mole on his forehead.

Pham dissed a bit of gossip. "Nobody at the company was supposed to know, but DuPont was dating the woman who heads up operations. Her name is Marie Vanderhagen. I don't know why they thought they had to keep their relationship under wraps. He didn't report to her. Maybe they just thought it would undermine their authority, or maybe they just didn't want everyone knowing their personal business. But one of the office workers saw them together having dinner at a restaurant and gossiped about it. The rumors flew from there."

Collin asked, "What did DuPont tell you when he escorted you out?"

"Nothing!" Pham said. "He said all he'd been told was to ensure I left the premises and didn't come back. He took my badge and followed me until I was out the gate. I was in shock. I had no idea what was going on or why. That evening, I get a knock on my door, right in the middle of dinner.

It was a couple of cops. They told me I was under arrest for embezzlement. They said that the afternoon before, just a few hours after I found the discrepancy with the artwork, someone had transferred fifty thousand dollars from the shipping company's operating account into my personal bank account. There was trumped-up paperwork that showed the payment was supposed to be for a new crane for the shipyard."

"Trumped-up?" Collin asked. "So, the paperwork was falsified?"

"It was, yeah. At least partly. Problem was, my initials were on the paperwork. I'd approved it for payment. Everything had looked to be in order when I reviewed the invoice. It had the crane company's logo printed on it, and I'd confirmed with the shipyard that they'd received a new crane with the model number that was noted on the form."

"Then what was the problem?" I asked. "How did the money end up in your account?"

Pham turned to me. "In the section of the paperwork that directed us where to send our payment, the invoice listed my personal checking account number rather than the crane company's bank account number. I didn't even notice that the payment account number was my own. After all, it was someone at the crane company who would have filled in the number—or so I'd thought. After I approved the paperwork, I sent it on to the accounts payable clerk, who issued the payment. The money went straight to my bank."

"Fifty grand isn't chump change," Collin said. "You didn't notice the extra funds were in your account?"

Pham shook his head. "The money was in my account for less than twenty-four hours. The company withdrew it before I even knew it had been deposited. I don't check my balance every day." As if to show that his actions were reasonable, he asked, "Do you?"

Both Collin and I said no, we didn't confirm our bank balances on a daily basis. Heck, once I'd gotten past the point of living paycheck-to-paycheck, I'd done well enough to take a look at my balance only once a week.

Pham went on. "I'm sure I would've noticed the error eventually, but my boss caught it before I did." He exhaled sharply. "My paychecks were direct deposited, so the shipping company had my bank account number. Someone in the company must have set me up."

Collin cocked his head. "Why would they do that?"

"I couldn't figure that out at first, either. The management at the company seemed to like me. I can speak English, Mandarin, and Cantonese. That's part of why they hired me. I often handled communications with the company's branches in Hong Kong, Taiwan, and Singapore. I'd worked there for five years with no problem. I got regular raises and promotions. I got along with all of my coworkers, too. The only thing unusual that happened prior to the transfer was my catching the discrepancy on the art shipment. That's why I thought it might have something to do with them framing me for embezzlement."

"'Them'?" Collin repeated. "Who is 'them'?"

"I have no idea!" Pham tossed his hands in the air. "That's what makes it all so crazy. I got e-mails and texts from my coworkers afterward saying they were sorry to see me go. DuPont was even pretty cool about tossing me off the property. He did what he had to, but he wasn't rude or insulting about it. It kind of seemed like he felt sorry for me. Everyone seemed as surprised as I was—at the time, anyway. I've tried to contact a few of them since, to see if they'd be references for me, but no one wants to get involved. It's like they're afraid I could drag them down with me." He let out a huff of frustration.

"The invoice you mentioned," Collin said. "You're sure it was for an art gallery in Romania?"

"Absolutely positive," Pham said. "I remember because I misspelled *Bucharest* on a geography test when I was in high school. I forgot the *h*, since it's silent. If not for that error, I would've had a perfect score on the exam. I think of that every time I see the name of the city."

Collin attempted to pin him down further. "Do you recall the name of the gallery? Or the name of the contact person at the gallery?"

"No. Sorry. All I remember is that the address was in Bucharest."

"Did anything else at the shipping company catch your attention?" Collin asked. "Anything else seem unusual?"

"No," Kevin said. "Until I got fired, it was a great place to work. They paid well and didn't work us to death. People were friendly. The company has an international staff, which made things interesting. They ship stuff all over. It was fun to feel like a cog in a big wheel that spanned the world." A scowl claimed his face and he gave us a pointed look. "Now I check in with a probation officer once a month and get excited about the chance of keeping books for a pet groomer. Pathetic, huh?"

The server brought our pancakes, and plunked plates down in front of me and Collin. Pham took that as his cue to go. He seemed to have told us all he knew.

Collin stood to give him a polite send-off. "I appreciate this information. If it leads anywhere, I'll let you know."

"Thanks. If you find out who framed me, give them a hit of your Taser for me."

The mere thought made me think of Nolan Sibley and his electric prod. Pham had turned and taken a few steps away before his "cog" comment seemed to process through my brain. We'd assumed Antonia Szabo was at the center of the case, that she was the cog who connected everyone and everything. But what if we were wrong? Better to explore all the possibilities. One thing Gerard Woodruff and Laurel Cromwell had in common, other than the stained glass and a connection to the shipping company, was that they were both on probation. Pham was, too.

"Wait!" I called after him, rising awkwardly from my seat with the booth's table in my way.

He turned back.

"Who's your PO?" I asked, hoping that by using the jargon I would keep those seated at the tables around us from realizing I was referencing Pham's probation officer.

"Bill O'Brien," he said.

Collin and I exchanged our third glance of the morning. *Bill O'Brien was the name Collin had given as Woodruff's PO, wasn't it?*

Collin dismissed Pham with a nod, then slid into the side of the booth the man had just vacated so that we could speak eye-to-eye.

I pushed his coffee mug and his stack of pancakes across the table to him. "What do you think of that coincidence?" I asked. "Woodruff and Pham share the same probation officer."

"It could be just that," Collin said. "Coincidence." Even so, he pulled out his cell phone.

I picked up the syrup dispenser and poured a generous stream of delicious maple goo over my pancakes. "Let me guess. You're calling Laurel Cromwell to find out who her PO is."

Collin input a number on his screen before looking up at me. "I'd tell you to stop doing my job if you weren't so damn good at it."

"Two minds are better than one," I said. I did have an undeniable knack for crime solving, but only because Collin usually got the cases on track first. I made a good sounding board for him and sometimes I came up with things on my own, but, in the end, we were in this together. We both had an interest in seeing the matter resolved, after all. For Collin, it was his duty. For me, it was personal. You can't come across a dead body without feeling like you owe the deceased a duty to avenge their death. Moreover, until Woodruff's murder was solved, I'd feel as if there were a pall over the playhouse. I wanted that pall lifted.

Collin tapped the button to place the call, put his phone to his ear, and jerked his chin to let me know Laurel had answered. After brief niceties, he asked, "Got a quick question for you. What's the name of your probation officer?"

He listened for a moment, staring expressionless at me, refusing to give up the goods. Though I'd strained to listen, I couldn't hear over the sizzling sounds coming from the grill, the murmur of the patrons' chatter, and the clinks of silverware. I raised my palms in question, but he gave me no indication.

"Okay, thanks," he said into his phone. "That's all I

needed for now." He ended the call and set his phone down on the table.

"Well?" I asked.

With a mischievous gleam in his eye, he cut into his stack of pancakes and shoved a huge bite into his mouth before raising his index finger in a *wait-a-minute* motion. I narrowed my eyes at my tormentor. I could tease him, too. I picked up the syrup dispenser. "Tell me now or you'll be wearing a pint of maple syrup." I picked up the sugar shaker in my other hand. "Topped with sugar."

He forced himself to swallow the half-chewed bite, banging a fist on his chest to help it go down. Once it did, he squeaked, "Bill O'Brien."

"Whoa." I lowered the syrup dispenser and the sugar shaker to the table. "That's too many people tied to O'Brien to be a coincidence, isn't it?" Three key people in the case shared a PO. He could be a cog for the group. *But in what way, exactly?* He was a probation officer, not a convicted criminal. In fact, his job was to ensure that convicted criminals behaved themselves, stayed out of trouble. "Could Laurel and Woodruff have been in cahoots with Pham somehow? Maybe they were laundering money using Laurel's art. Maybe they all met at O'Brien's office."

Collin looked skeptical. "Even if they all happened to be there at the same time, I have a hard time seeing people making small talk as they're waiting to meet with their PO."

He had a point. Nobody seemed to make small talk with each other at all anymore, really. Instead, everyone stared down at their phones, preferring the company of an electronic device to meaningless conversation with a stranger. I was guilty of the practice myself.

"In fact," Collin added, "they'd probably avoid conversation in the probation office reception area. Consorting with other criminals is a probation violation." His face took on a far-off look as he tried to process the information we'd learned this morning and make sense of it. "If the three were in cahoots, it seems that Pham would have had to be the one orchestrating it, at least as far as the customs paperwork being processed by the shipping company. I have to wonder why he'd mention the scheme if he was part of it. No one else seems to have narrowed in on that aspect yet. He's put himself at risk by drawing attention to it."

"He might have realized that you were on the trail when you asked about Szabo and the gallery. Maybe he thought if he claimed to be the good guy in all of this, that he was a victim himself, you'd look past him to someone else. Besides, you don't even know if his story is true, right? Maybe he was laundering money *and* embezzling from the shipping company."

Collin raised his coffee mug. "Maybe he killed Jimmy Hoffa, too."

I pointed my fork at him. "Watch the attitude, mister."

He took a slug of coffee. "You could be right. He might have been an opportunist. He mentioned that his bosses were friendly. He might have assumed that oversight would be lax, and that he could pilfer money without being caught. Maybe that magazine article his wife showed him gave him the idea for laundering money through the shipping company. But here's the thing. To launder money, there must first be money to launder. Pham didn't leave here in a Porsche or Mercedes. He left in an eight-year-old minivan."

"He did?"

Collin pointed out the window. "See where that blue Subaru is parked? That's the spot he was in."

I hadn't even noticed. Looked like my sleuthing skills could still use some honing. "He said he earned good money at the shipping company."

"He did," Collin agreed. "He also said that, until recently, his wife had been a stay-at-home mom. He's also got kids. They don't come cheap. I've heard it costs over two hundred thousand dollars to raise a kid to age eighteen. That doesn't even include college."

Looked like I owed my parents a long-overdue thank-you.

Collin stared at the parking spot, as if willing it to tell him more about the man who'd just been parked there. "I checked out Pham online last night. He and his wife own a modest home and still owe a hundred grand on their mortgage. By all accounts, he's where a typical man of his age and his profession should be financially."

In other words, he didn't appear to have a lot of money to launder, or to have come into an unexpected financial windfall. "Maybe he was just starting out when he got caught embezzling, and maybe Laurel Cromwell, Gerard Woodruff, and Antonia Szabo decided to carry on without him."

"It's possible, I guess," Collin said, setting his coffee mug back down. "Or he could have offshore accounts somewhere, or have been laundering money for someone else for a small percentage. He might not have been laundering money at all. The company, either. The discrepancy he noted might have simply been a clerical error, like his boss said it was. We could speculate all day. But I'd suggest we eat our pancakes before they get cold."

As we finished our late breakfast, I pulled out my phone, curious about the use of art in money laundering. I wanted to know more. I found some interesting links online. In 2016, a Panamanian law firm suffered a massive data leak, an event that later became known as the Panama Papers. The breach revealed that the wealthy owned hundreds of thousands of offshore shell companies, which they used to hide assets, including collectible items and valuable works of art. Holdings of collectibles and artwork were estimated to have a value of over $1.6 trillion, and that value was expected to grow to $2.7 trillion by 2026. *Trillions. Wow! That's a lot of zeros.* I wasn't even sure how many.

Evidently, Congress was aware of the illegal practice and had taken steps to hinder it. In early 2021, Congress had passed the Anti-Money Laundering Act of 2020, or AMLA, which expanded subpoena powers granted under the 2001 Patriot Act. The law enacted new record-keeping and reporting requirements. While people often hid behind the obscurity of limited liability companies, or LLCs, the law now mandated that owners of LLCs be identified and registered. The link further noted that art and antiquities dealers could be unwittingly sucked into tangled webs of fraud and deceit, and might soon be required to follow the same "Know Your Customer" guidelines that applied to financial institutions. These regulations required that customers produce positive identification when opening accounts, accessing safe-custody facilities, and conducting business. The regulations also required institutions to monitor unusual activities not commensurate with the client's purported type of business. Customer profiles were to be developed, which would help institutions know what to expect from the customers, and internal systems would be activated to catch aberrant activity.

I shared the information with Collin between bites of syrupy, sugary pancakes.

"If Woodruff's murder is linked to money laundering," Collin said, tilting his head to the left, "it will be the most intricate case I've worked so far. And it still doesn't tell us who killed him." He tilted his head to the right now, as if mentally weighing evidence. "The fact that Pham, Cromwell, and Woodruff have the same PO could be co-incidence. But there are dozens of probation officers. It's a correlation if not a causation, a common denominator." He downed the last of his coffee and wiped his mouth with his napkin. "That's a good enough reason for me to go see Bill O'Brien now."

CHAPTER 21

A NUMBERS GAME

WHITNEY

Collin and I parted ways in the diner's parking lot with a sticky, syrup-laced kiss. He headed off to speak with the probation officer Bill O'Brien. Meanwhile, every nerve in my body was buzzing. *Probably all the sugar and caffeine.*

I'd just climbed into my SUV when a call came in on my phone. The screen told me it was the curtain company trying to reach me. *If they tell me there's been another delay, I'm going to scream!*

Fortunately, no scream was necessary. "We've got your curtain ready," the woman on the phone said. "So sorry for the delays."

A frisson of fear twined up my spine, but I quicky realized it was baseless. What were the chances this delivery-man would meet the same fate as Woodruff? We'd had several deliveries at the playhouse and café since that awful day, and all of the other delivery persons had left with their lives. It was probably just the caffeine making me nervous and jittery. "Thanks. I'm not at the playhouse right now, but I'm heading that way. The delivery person can leave the curtain on the porch."

"Delivery?" the woman said. "I thought you were planning to pick it up."

Oh, for Pete's sake. I'd paid an extra thirty dollars for delivery, but at this point I just wanted the darn curtain. I bit back a curse. "Never mind. I'll come get it. Where are you located?"

She rattled off an address in northwest Nashville and I typed it into my phone. "I'll be there soon."

Hanging the curtain was bound to take several hours. We'd need to set up the scaffold, check the rollers to make sure they moved freely about the track, and attach the top to the dozens of small hooks to keep it hanging nice and taut. Once it was hung, we'd have to steam the fabric to get out the wrinkles, too. But even though we had a lot of work ahead of us, I was excited about it. Rehabbing the parsonage and transforming it into a café had been fun, but the concept and design ideas were primarily Colette's. The café was her baby, so to speak. The curtain would be the final touch on the playhouse, which had been my brainchild.

It wouldn't be long until opening night, and it was nice to see the place coming to fruition. It would be even nicer to see it filled with a sold-out crowd night after night. Not only would it be great to reap the financial rewards, but it also would feel good to play a part, not on the stage, but in providing people with a good time. Life was short, sometimes even shorter than we expected. Gerard Woodruff could attest to that. Actually, he couldn't, which was exactly my point. No one could know how long they had. Best to enjoy life to the fullest while you can.

I swung by my house to brush all the sticky sugar off my teeth before they started to rot, and to pick up Sawdust. He'd have fun exploring the theater while we hung the curtain. With construction complete, he wouldn't be in danger of traipsing through paint, being buried under a pile of demolition debris, or escaping through a loose door.

I gathered up the cat's go-bag, which contained a water dish, a package of snacks, a small bag of litter, and a plastic dishpan that served well as an improvised litter box and could easily be cleaned. I placed his carrier near the front door and opened the latch. "Come on, boy!" I called. "We've got work to do!"

Sawdust came running and trotted right into the cage, turning around to look out the front. We had our drill down. I carried him out the car, stashed him and his bag on the backseat, and climbed in. I typed the address the woman had given me into my maps app, and it generated two routes I could take. The curtain place was in the same general industrial area as Specialty Export Experts. Not surprising. Heck, although I'd ordered the curtain from a local company via their website, the curtain had probably been manufactured in China or Bangladesh, where most of the world's textile work was performed. For all I knew, the curtain had been shipped via S.E.E.'s network of ships and trucks, maybe alongside one of Szabo's art pieces.

Although I'd brushed the syrup and coffee off my teeth, the caffeine and sugar remained in my blood, and I all but bounced in my seat as I headed down the road. When I reached the fabric company, I was directed to drive around back to a loading dock where two men slid an enormous box into the cargo bay of my SUV. It just fit. If it had been a half inch bigger in any direction, I would've had to come back for it with Buck's van.

As I ventured back out onto the highway, a truck rolled past me, a shipping container on its trailer. I wondered if it might be headed to Specialty Export Experts. My buzzing brain said, *Why not swing by and take another sneak peek at the place?* It couldn't hurt anything, could it? It would probably be a waste of time given how little I could see on my last spy mission, but after meeting with Pham I was even more convinced that something going on at S.E.E., something the company might have unintentionally been a part of, was the reason behind Gerard Woodruff's murder.

I took the exit and did the same thing I did last time. I cruised the perimeter of the company's campus, noting that the bald man I now knew as DuPont was working security at the front gate. He greeted a trucker who'd stopped at the gate with a broad grin and a raised hand. After navigating the perimeter, I parked in the lot of the gas station next door and used the binoculars app on my phone to take a closer look at the place. Once again, I couldn't see much, only whatever stuck up above the tall fence. Cranes. Shipping containers. The roof of the warehouse. The second floor of the office building. *Wait. What is that?*

Movement at one of the wide, floor-to-ceiling windows in the office building caught my eye. When I zoomed in, I saw a woman in a black business suit with a fitted pencil skirt standing inside a window. She had platinum-blond hair and a pointy chin. She held a phone to her ear, the receiver attached to a cord that stretched back to the desk behind her. Her mouth moved as she spoke into it. None of that was unusual. But when she turned her head and looked directly at me, I simultaneously jerked my phone downward, shrank back against my seat, and gasped so loudly that Sawdust stood up in his cage.

In case the woman was still watching me, I turned my head and looked away, toward the freeway. Sawdust poked a paw through the metal bars of his carrier and inquired about my mental state with a concerned, *Mew?*

A few seconds later, I glanced back toward the building out of the corner of my eye, realized how ridiculous I was being, and exhaled in relief. The woman might have seemed to be looking my way, but without benefit of binoculars or some other zoom lens, there was no way she'd actually seen my face from this distance. I'd only seen hers because I'd been zoomed in on my phone. She had to be Marie Vanderhagen. She looked just like her photo on the company's website. It made sense that the head of operations would have an office with a window overlooking the shipyard. She'd probably left her seat to stretch her legs, and took her call standing at the window to enjoy some autumn sunshine. With days becoming shorter, you had to catch the sun while you could.

I lifted my phone and zoomed in on the window again. The woman had returned to her cushy swivel chair and returned the phone receiver to its cradle. She was focused on her computer now, looking at the screen and working her keyboard. *Phew.*

I wondered how things were going with Collin. He'd said that Probation Officer Bill O'Brien seemed to be a common denominator among the people involved in this investigation, but I wondered if he'd yet worked out the math, solved for X. I wondered if the equation would have to go through

more steps, be broken down and simplified before it could
be solved, like those tricky factors we'd learned in junior
high. I hoped not. I knew Collin had other cases he needed
to attend to and, after working Woodruff's murder case for
several weeks, he was ready to put it to rest and move on.
I was, too. Otherwise, it would feel as if Woodruff's ghost
were walking the aisles of the theater and haunting the bell
tower, seeking justice.

Another link among the parties was Antonia Szabo.
Unfortunately, she was a missing link, still proving to be
elusive and unreachable. A sick feeling slithered into my
stomach. *Could something have happened to her, too? Is
that why she hasn't returned Collin's calls or showed up to
claim the windows that Laurel had made, the ones waiting
for her at S.E.E.'s office in Bucharest?* Wherever she was,
I hoped the woman was safe.

I angled my phone slightly to the left to watch as a fork-
lift carried a shipping container up in the air and placed it
atop another as if playing a gigantic game of Jenga.

Rap-rap.

The sudden noise so close to my right ear caused me to
fling my phone in the air. It hit the ceiling of my SUV and
fell into the floorboard on the passenger side, where a smiling face with a suspicious mole on his forehead stared in
the window. *Christopher DuPont.*

Holy . . . "Hi!" I called, arcing my hand in an awkward
wave. Then, realizing I shouldn't know this man, I jabbed
the button to unroll the passenger window an inch or two
and pretended to think he'd come from inside the gas station. "I was about to come inside and buy something, I
promise."

"No worries," he said. "I'm not with the gas station." He hiked a thumb over his shoulder to indicate the shipping company campus. "I'm with Specialty Export Experts. We've got cameras on the place, and we couldn't help but notice you seemed to be recording a video. We're just wondering what's up." The guy seemed relaxed and casual, curious but not alarmed.

Collin had already spoken with DuPont when he'd gone to the shipping company to meet with Marie Vanderhagen, but I realized I had an opportunity to fish for more information here and I should seize it. "I was actually planning to come over to speak with someone at your company after I grabbed a snack here."

He cocked his head. "You were? Why?"

I'd heard that the best lies were the ones closest to the truth, so I devised a white lie on the spot. I pointed to the shipping container that was being moved by the crane. "I was checking things out through the zoom lens on my phone's camera. I flip houses, and I'm looking to buy some used shipping containers. Nobody wants to live in a house made of bricks or wood anymore. These days, everyone wants to live in a repurposed metal box."

The guy chuckled. "I've heard about people living in shipping containers, but I can't imagine why they'd want to. Seems awfully primitive. Nothing wrong with creature comforts."

"I agree. There's no accounting for taste, huh?" I chuckled. "But if someone's going to make a buck converting freight boxes, it might as well be me. If I could get my hands on some of the containers, I think I could transform them into tiny homes. Any chance your company sells old shipping containers? Maybe damaged ones?" I made a fist and flexed my shoulder muscle. "I could pound out a few dents."

He grinned at my lame flex. "Don't know what to tell you. Never been asked that question before. My guess is that the company sells them as scrap metal, but since that's not really my area I can't be sure. If you'll give me your business card, I can pass it along to the right folks and have someone call you back."

The last thing I wanted was to tell this guy who I was. After all, my name had been on the invoice in the envelope taped to Antonia Szabo's stained-glass windows. If someone recognized my name, they'd wonder why I was here, spying on the place. "I don't have a card," I said. "No real need for them since I work for myself."

"No problem." He pulled his cell phone from his pocket and held it up in front of him. "Just tell me your name and number and I'll type them into my notes." His thumb tapped the bottom of his screen.

Wait. Did he just snap a photo of me? There'd been no click sound, so I couldn't be certain. Still, I had an eerie feeling he might have captured my image.

I tried to think of a fake name on the spot. What name would be a good one for horsing around? *Horse. Pegasus. I could go by*—"Peggy Sussman," I said. I followed it up with my real phone number. The number wasn't listed in connection with my real name in any accessible database I was aware of, and I'd opted for the standardized voice-mail greeting that gave only my number, not my name, before asking callers to leave a message after the tone. If someone from S.E.E. called me, they wouldn't be clued in by my outgoing message that I wasn't really Peggy Sussman.

After entering the information into his phone, he said, "Got it," and slid the phone into his pocket. "Peggy was my mother's name, by the way. Don't hear of many young ladies named Peggy these days."

"I'm named after my great-aunt," I lied, venturing further from the truth.

He took a step back from my SUV, preparing to leave. "Next time you want to know anything about Specialty Export Experts, feel free to stop at the gate. We'd be glad to help you there. No need to spy."

Before turning to walk off, he gave me a wink and grin, seemingly the friendly guy Pham said he was. But if that was the case, why did I feel so creeped out?

As he stepped away, I felt my opportunity to get information walking away with him. "Wait!" I called after him. "Is there any chance I could talk to someone now? Maybe Marie Vanderhagen?" I figured dropping the boss's name might get me in the door and, if the rumors Kevin Pham heard were right, DuPont was dating the woman. If nothing else, my saying her name would get his attention.

As I'd expected, the man turned around, head cocked inquisitively. "You know Marie?"

"No," I said, "but I was given her name by a woman I met at a local gallery. I was looking for some art to decorate a flip house, and the woman was scouting some pieces herself for a gallery she runs. She suggested I contact your company about the shipping containers. She said she'd done business with y'all, used your company to ship artwork to Europe."

DuPont paused for moment and his eyes narrowed slightly, small crinkles forming at their outer edges. "What's this woman's name?"

"Antonia Szabo."

The eyes that had just narrowed flashed, much as the lightning flashed the day Laurel Cromwell had come to the playhouse hoping to reclaim the jeweled windows. Unfortunately, I didn't know why he'd reacted the way he did. I knew Collin had asked Marie Vanderhagen and DuPont about Szabo when he spoke with them earlier, so maybe my giving her name now raised an alarm. But was he concerned because he thought I might be in cahoots with the elusive Szabo, who had yet to claim her stained-glass windows in Romania? Or was he concerned for some other reason? If it was another reason, what was it?

I pretended I hadn't noticed his unconscious reaction. "Do you know her? Antonia?"

He angled his head to and fro. "The name rings a bell. But we handle a lot of freight, as you can see." He gestured back to the stacked containers before motioning with his hand. "Why don't you come with me? I'll take you to see Marie and you can ask her about the shipping containers."

Looked like dropping the boss's name had been a good idea, opened the doors for me. I hiked a thumb over the seat to indicate Sawdust. "Okay if I bring my cat with me? It's not safe to leave him in the car."

"Sure," the man said.

I rounded up Sawdust's carrier. When my cat spotted DuPont, he shrank back in the cage and hissed. *Hisssss!* Strange. *What's that all about?*

DuPont said, "I don't think he likes me."

"Don't take it personal," I said. "He was the runt of the litter. He's always been a fraidycat." I gestured to the gas station. "Let me check in with the guy working the counter. I want to make sure my car doesn't get towed while I'm gone." I also wanted to make sure I had a witness who could verify that I'd been here in case I disappeared. Probably not necessary, but Woodruff's unsolved murder had left me on edge.

I made a quick detour inside to assure the gas station's counter clerk that I would be back shortly to claim my car after I made a quick trip over to the shipping company. He jerked one shoulder, totally unconcerned. With customers constantly coming and going from the station, there were plenty of parking spots available and it wouldn't have made a difference if my car remained out front until the rapture.

While I was in the store, I bought a small packet of peanuts, paid for it, and carried it outside. I held the packet out to DuPont, offering to share. "Peanut?"

He raised a palm. "No thanks."

"Okeydoke." I slid the packet into the pocket of my coveralls for later.

Lugging Sawdust along in his plastic crate, I followed Du-Pont across the side street, along the sidewalk, and around the arm that controlled traffic at the security gate. The breeze carried a distinctive scent from the shipping yard, a mix of warm metal and petroleum. DuPont gave a nod to the guy now manning the front gate, and led me into the central administrative building. He bypassed the elevator and we took the stairs up to the executive offices. The suite was nicely appointed, with an intriguing and eclectic mix of art on the walls. An oil painting of a mountain landscape.

A mosaic in tiles of green and brown that formed a river and riverbank. An abstract piece of fabric art.

DuPont stopped before a desk to check in with Marie's assistant, a polished pewter-haired woman who kept a tidy workspace. She greeted him with a pleasant smile and a lift of her chin. He gestured to the door behind her. "Can you see if Miss Vanderhagen has a moment?"

"Of course." Marie's assistant picked up her telephone receiver, punched two digits, and listened for a response. "Mr. DuPont is here with—" She looked to me for a name.

My gut clenched in momentary panic. What name had I given DuPont? *It had something to do with Pegasus. . . .* Oh, yeah. "Peggy Sussman."

The woman repeated the name I'd given her, and listened for a few seconds. "I'll send them right in." She stood, walked the five steps to Marie Vanderhagen's door, and opened it for us, stepping back to let us pass and closing it behind us.

Through the window at the back of the room, where Marie had stood not long before, I could see my red SUV parked at the gas station in the distance. I turned my head to see Marie standing behind her desk, a professional, practiced smile on her face. She circled around to shake my hand. "Nice to meet you, Miss Sussman." She bent down to peer into the carrier in my hand. "And who is this fluffy little cutie?"

"That's Sawdust," I said. "Sweetest kitty in all the known world." I gestured to the S.E.E. company logo on the wall behind her, the one that featured the entire Earth.

She offered a small, breathy chuckle through her narrow

nose. Introductions now complete, she asked, "How can I help you?"

"I'm wondering if your company sells its old or damaged shipping containers," I said. "I do rehab work and I'm looking for some containers to convert to housing."

Like DuPont, she found the idea amusing. "People living in cargo boxes." She shook her head, her lips curved in a grin. "Who would've dreamed it?"

"I know, right?" I replied. "Maybe I should install a crank on the side that plays 'Pop Goes the Weasel' and make the top pop open when the song ends."

We shared a real laugh at the ridiculous idea. Marie even opened her mouth this time.

DuPont said, "Miss Sussman said she was sent here by an art dealer she met when looking for pieces to decorate her flip houses. The dealer is apparently a client of ours, a woman named Antonia Szabo."

Her smile faltered, but only for an instant. She angled her head. "You've met Antonia Szabo?"

"Yes," I said. "Just once, a while back."

"I see." She exchanged a glance with DuPont, as if trying to determine how much to tell me. Natural, I supposed, given that they'd been visited by a police detective who was trying to locate the woman. She seemed to decide that there was no harm in seeing what information I might have. "We seem to have lost contact with Miss Szabo," she said. "We have some art we've been trying to deliver to her. Any chance you have her current contact information?"

"Not on me," I said. "My art purchase was a onetime thing. But I believe I might still have her card back home.

It was a fancy one, if I remember right. Black with gold lettering."

Marie turned around and fished a card off her desk, holding it up. It was the same business card Szabo had given to Laurel Cromwell, the one I pretended to have at home.

I leaned in to read the address. Strada Vasile Alecsandri 16. "Yep, same address. That's the one."

Marie expelled a *hmph* of slight frustration. "I really need to get in touch with her. If you happen to run into her again, please ask her to call me, will you?"

"I'd be happy to," I said. "Now, about those boxes. Any chance you might have some available now?"

"We normally sell the containers we can no longer use for scrap." Marie told me the same thing DuPont had, that I was the first person to approach their company about buying used containers. "I'll need to check with the supervisor in the yard, see what we might have on hand, and work out a price. But I'd be happy to have someone get back to you."

"Wonderful!" I gestured to DuPont. "He's got my number."

Marie gave me a nod. "We'll be in touch."

DuPont saw me back out to the gate, where he bade me good-bye. Cat in hand, I walked back to my SUV at the gas station, still wondering all the while if Marie Vanderhagen had been looking my way earlier, if DuPont brought my presence to her attention before coming out to talk to me. I had no way of knowing, or what it might have meant.

I ate the peanuts on my drive to the playhouse. From the road, I could see Buck and Owen were busy assembling the greenhouse behind the parsonage, so I figured I'd take care of the curtain myself. Flying solo, it would take me longer to get it hung, but no sense interrupting their work, especially since they'd already unboxed all of the plexiglass panels. Besides, I'd have Sawdust to keep me company.

I pulled over to the side of the road, tooted my horn to get their attention, and unrolled my window. Cupping my hands around my mouth, I shouted at the top of my lungs. "I'll go hang the curtain!"

Buck acknowledged that he heard me by giving me a thumbs-up sign. I continued on to the playhouse, parked, and wrangled the big box out of my cargo bay and onto a dolly. After I'd wheeled it inside, I carried Sawdust into the foyer and released him from his carrier. I turned around and locked the front door behind me. That creepy feeling still hung over me and, after all, a man had lost his life here. Better safe than sorry.

After donning a pair of work gloves and assembling the scaffolding, I climbed the rungs carefully, pulling the heavy curtain up with me. My shoulders and arms strained with the effort. The darn thing had to weigh fifty pounds or more.

I stepped out onto the platform and draped the fabric over the rail. As I reached up to double-check that the rollers moved smoothly in the track, I heard Sawdust issue a little chirrup, the same noise he made when he got excited about a bird he saw flitting in the bushes outside our bedroom window. I looked down to see that he had hopped up onto the sill of the second stained-glass window from the foyer. His head bobbed as he attempted to watch something through the window. The colored glass seemed to be impeding his vision.

He jumped down to the floor, trotted over to the next

window, and hopped up on the sill to try again. *Is something out there?* The playhouse was surrounded by trees. Maybe he was following a bird who was moving from one limb to the next. He chirruped again and moved to the next window.

A rattling noise came from below me. Sawdust hopped down from the sill and skittered over to the back exit door, his ears pricked. *Had someone just tried to open the door?*

My head went light and my heart pounded as fast as my feet as I descended the scaffolding. *Ba-bum-ba-bum-ba-bum!* Movement behind the stained glass on the other side of the building caught my eye now. Something round and light colored had just passed behind the window. For the first time, I was having second thoughts about my decision to install stained-glass windows rather than clear ones. I couldn't see what was out there. *Could Sibley's horses have gotten onto our property again?* Maybe what I'd seen had been Pegasus's hindquarters. I wished I could know for sure.

There was only one way to see clearly what was going on outside of the locked building. *The belfry.*

I reached down to my toolbox, grabbed my largest wrench, and tucked it into my pocket. I sprinted down the middle aisle of the auditorium, out the double doors, and across the foyer. I whipped out my keys and unlocked the door to the bell tower as quickly as I could with my hands shaking. Sawdust had followed along behind me. "No, boy!" I said. "You stay here!" Thank goodness he was truly a fraidycat, like I'd told Marie Vanderhagen. If he sensed a threat, he'd run under a pew and hide.

I ascended the bell tower nearly as fast as I'd come down

the scaffold. I stepped out onto the platform and looked down on all sides. *Argh!* While the bell tower provided beautiful long-distance views, it wasn't nearly as easy to see things up close to the building. Looking straight down, I could see some of the area surrounding the structure, but I couldn't see the parts right up next to it, which were obscured by the overhang of the roof. I couldn't see behind the building, or the entrance doors below me, either, even though I leaned out as far as I dared.

I stood stock-still for a moment. If I couldn't *see* anything, maybe I could *hear* something. I closed my eyes to focus. All I heard was a far-off nicker of one of Sibley's Arabians, the sound of the wind rustling the dried autumn leaves that had accumulated on the theater's roof, and the soft clang of the bell next to me as the breeze caused it to sway.

When I raised my head and opened my eyes, something across the road caught my attention. A white SUV was parked behind trees on an unfenced stretch of land. If it had been summer and the trees had still retained their leaves, I never would have spotted the vehicle. I pulled out my phone and used the binoculars app to zoom in. Sure enough, it had two numbered stickers on the back, just like the one that had driven past the parsonage shortly after Gerard Woodruff had been murdered.

There was no doubt in my mind. *Someone has come for me.*

I closed the app and was about to dial 911 when a bam sounded from below. It was followed by two louder sounds. *BAM! BAM!* I heard the clinking sound of hardware coming loose and a door banging back against the interior wall of the foyer. *Bang!* Footsteps followed. Whoever had come for me had kicked in the door and was now inside the play-house.

I gulped. Law enforcement could never arrive in time to save me. Self-defense took precedence over summoning help. Frantic, I looked out over the railings of the bell tower. While I could venture out onto the sloped roof, I'd have a hell of a time not tumbling off the edge. It was at least a twenty-foot drop to the ground. If I didn't break my neck, I'd likely break a leg and be unable to run away. If the killer had a gun, they'd be able to pick me off easily as I tried to make a getaway. Even if they didn't have a gun, they'd be able to see which direction I ran off in and come after me. If I were injured, I'd have a hard time outrunning anyone.

I heard more footsteps below, someone scrambling around, throwing open the doors to the dressing room, ticket booth, and restrooms, looking for me. When I heard footsteps going up the stairs to the balcony, I dared an escape. I tramped frantically down the bell-tower steps only to come face-to-face with Christopher DuPont as he came down the stairwell from the balcony.

NO!

All my breath left me. I couldn't even gasp. His eyes were dark and icy, and an evil sneer quirked the corner of his mouth. Clearly, he got a perverse, powerful pleasure in frightening me.

Though I had yet to be able to breathe again, I had no choice but to turn around and run back up into the belfry. I heard his footsteps coming up behind me. *Oh, God! Oh, God! Oh, God! What am I going to do?!*

I reached the platform and looked down. The top of a

bald head rounded the staircase just below me. There wasn't time to call for help with my phone, but I could use the bell, couldn't I? My cousins weren't too far away. The cops couldn't get here in time to help me, but maybe Buck and Owen could. Buck would know that my ringing the bell meant I was in danger. He'd arm himself with a claw hammer and make sure Owen did, too.

I reached out for the rope and yanked it three times as hard as I could. *DONG! DONG! DONG!*

If my cousins were using a power tool, it could drown out the sound of the bell. Would Buck and Owen hear it all the way over at the parsonage? Could they get over here in time to help me? Oh, no! Had I just put them in danger, too?

CHAPTER 22

A GAME OF CAT AND MOUSE

SAWDUST

Sawdust liked to chase things. A spider occasionally found its way into their house. He'd chased a small mouse out of the parsonage a few days ago, too. It had squeezed out through a tiny hole before he could catch it. He even sometimes chased a mysterious bright red dot that appeared out of nowhere. He never could catch that darn dot, though.

He knew the hairless man was playing a similar game of chase with Whitney. She didn't look like she was enjoying the game. Sawdust could tell she was terrified. He was, too. But Whitney meant more to him than anything. He had to chase after the bad man and make him stop.

CHAPTER 23

PUPPET ON A STRING

WHITNEY

Two more steps and the man would be on the platform with me. He seemed to be taking his time, savoring the moment, seeming to know he could get to me before I could summon law enforcement with my cell phone.

I did the only thing I could do—yank the rope one more time. *DONG!* I was about to release it when an idea dawned on me. I'd seen Johnny Otto use a pulley and rope to lift heavy bales of hay up into the hayloft of Sibley's barn. Ropes worked in both directions, too. *I can slide down it!*

I reached out with my left hand and grasped the rope tight, just below my right hand. Holding the rope in both fists, I leapt off the platform and wrapped my legs around the rope as momentum swung me into the stairs and rail on the other side. *DONG!* I felt like a mad marionette on a string, one that had come to life and was attempting to escape the control of their sadistic puppet master. But holding on so tight wouldn't get me where I needed to go. *Down.*

I loosened my grip and down I slid, sailing down the rope much faster than expected. To my horror, I slid right past

Sawdust, who was scurrying up the stairs after me and Du-Pont. "No, boy!" I cried.

My cat stopped and turned sideways across the step, looking down at me with his head cocked in curiosity. With me descending to the ground floor at warp speed, DuPont realized he had to move quickly now. He turned back and stampeded around the curve in the staircase just as my feet hit the bottom of the bell tower. Good thing I'd had the innate sense to bend my knees to absorb the impact. Even so, it was no light landing. My ankles took the brunt of the force. *Ow!*

Grimacing in pain, I looked up. Above me, DuPont tripped over Sawdust and cried out in surprise. The man fell forward in a swan dive down the flight of stairs, while Sawdust rolled down sideways a few steps after him. Du-Pont slammed headfirst into the wall of the stairwell. *Bam!* Once Sawdust untwisted himself and got his footing, he leapt over DuPont as smoothly and gracefully as the horses Johnny Otto trained leapt over the jumps in their arena. Despite the head injury, DuPont got to his feet in an instant and bolted down the stairs after my cat and me. I turned to run out of the bell tower. Sawdust skittered past me and out the door. *Go, boy! Run!*

At the same time I felt hands reach out from behind to grab my shoulders, I heard a loud *crack* from above. DuPont and I looked up in unison to see the big bell come loose from its mooring. My ride down the rope must have pulled the fitting loose. It wasn't made to handle 150 pounds of extra weight. The bell plunged toward us, growing larger as it descended, as if we were zooming in on it.

I grabbed the door frame with both hands and yanked

myself out of DuPont's grasp and out the belfry. Just in time, too. The bell fell behind me with a sickening dong muted by flesh and bone, followed by a *clang-clang* as it hit the floor. A series of thuds followed as DuPont collapsed, his hip, limbs, and head hitting the floor in a sickening sequence. *Thud. Thud. THUD.*

"Whitney!" came Buck's cry from outside. "Whitney!"

I scooped Sawdust up in my arms and, not daring to look back, ran out onto the front stoop of the church.

Buck bolted up the steps. "We heard the bell! What happened?"

Though I tried to talk, no words came out, my mouth flapping soundlessly. Buck took one look at me and ran into the theater. Owen grabbed me by the shoulders, much as DuPont had just done, though Owen grabbed me from the front rather than the back. He leaned in to look me in the eyes. "Are you okay?"

All I could do was shake my head. *No. I wasn't okay.* But, eventually, I would be. I wasn't sure whether the same could be said for Christopher DuPont.

Owen lowered me onto a step, then rounded up Sawdust's carrier and stashed my cat safely inside. He went inside to assist Buck. I heard Owen use his phone to call for help, summoning both law enforcement and an ambulance. I also heard Buck say, "Looks like he's still breathing, for now. In case he comes to, we'd better tie his hands and feet with the rope." His words were followed by the *shlick* sound of a blade being opened.

My hand quivered as I pulled my phone from my pocket and dialed Collin. I was too frazzled to even think about easing him into the news. "Christopher DuPont just attacked me in the bell tower. The bell came down on him. If he's not dead soon, he'll probably wish he was."

There was a rustling sound that told me Collin was already in motion. "I'm on my way."

Metro Police had been handling another call in the area and arrived first. The officer grimaced when he peeked into the bell tower and took a look at DuPont. "That there is not a pretty sight."

I wouldn't know. I had yet to bring myself to take a look. Some things are better left to the imagination rather than forever imprinted in the memory banks.

The officer snapped several photos in case they'd later be needed. When the ambulance screamed up, lights flashing and siren wailing, he backed away to give the EMTs unfettered access to the bell tower. It was the same medics who'd come for both Woodruff and Sibley. With any luck, it would be the last time I'd ever see them.

The medical team worked their magic, carefully strapping DuPont to a board and loading him into the ambulance. Once Collin arrived and took control of the scene, the uniformed officer contacted Dispatch to let them know he was heading to the hospital to keep an eye on DuPont. Christopher DuPont would be promptly arrested—if and when he pulled through.

Collin ventured across the road to grab the license plate number of the white SUV secreted in the woods. He sat in the driver's seat of his sedan, the door open and one leg on the ground outside, as he ran the plate on his dash-mounted computer. "It's registered to Specialty Export Experts."

No surprise there. But while that question had been answered, dozens remained. Had DuPont also killed Woodruff? Why? Did it have something to do with using art for money laundering? Was DuPont in cahoots with Laurel Cromwell and Gerard Woodruff? Was Marie Vanderhagen involved? What role did Kevin Pham play in all of this? And what about Bill O'Brien?

The only question we could even attempt to answer at this point was the last. Collin filled me in on his visit to the probation officer. "He's definitely involved in some way. He got the deer-in-the-headlights look when I told him that, in addition to Gerard Woodruff, I'd also connected him to Laurel Cromwell and Kevin Pham. Pham was the one that really spooked him. I told him I was working a theory that they'd been committing crimes together. I asked if he knew how all three of his probationers might have met, but he claimed he didn't know. He didn't ask me what I thought they'd been doing. It's a sure sign someone is guilty when they don't ask questions. Innocent people tend to be curious about what's going on, why I'm poking around. He didn't want to know. That's especially damning in this instance because he's their PO. It's his job to keep tabs on what they're up to."

"You think O'Brien is directly involved then?"

"I'd bet on it. I'd also bet he phoned the shipping company right after I met with him, too. That's probably why they were on alert and spotted you spying." He glowered at me. "Which you never should have been doing, by the way."

"Sorry," I said. "I crossed a line. I know that now." I also knew that, other than the glower he'd just given me, there'd be no consequences for my doing so, at least not from him. He was a pretty forgiving guy. It was one of the many qualities I admired about him. Another was that he accepted me for who I was. He seemed to realize it was futile to try to stop me once I'd made up my mind to do something. "What about Pham?" I asked. "You think he's guilty, too?"

Collin frowned. "I don't know. Things seem to point his way, but I just wasn't feeling it when we met with him this morning. The guy didn't give off a bad vibe."

Although there was no doubt now that Bill O'Brien and Christopher DuPont were up to no good, there were many pieces of the puzzle that had yet to fall into place. At this point, though, I knew Collin would relentlessly pursue the missing pieces and form a complete picture.

A crime scene team arrived to process the aftermath of my attack in the bell tower. As I held out a hand to invite them inside, Collin gently took hold of my wrist. He looked down at my hand. I looked down, too. A thick red rope burn cut a slanted path across my palm and fingers. With the adrenaline finally starting to wane, I noticed my palms were throbbing, too.

Collin looked over at my younger cousin. "Owen! Can you take Whitney to get her hands looked at?"

Buck and Owen walked over and looked down at my hands.

Owen winced. "Ouch!"

Buck was more blunt. "That's a nasty rope burn. Looks like it took off most of your skin. That your finger bones I'm seeing?"

I cut him a look. "Hardee har-har."

He reached out and grabbed me in a one-armed, sideways

hug. "Glad you'll be okay, Cuz. It would stink to have to make all this money without you."

Despite his jovial tone, I knew Buck had been worried about me. He'd been panicked when he'd hollered my name as he and Owen ran up to the playhouse earlier. The two of us were closer than most siblings.

I left Sawdust in Buck's care. Collin drove off to pay a second visit to Bill O'Brien, one that would very likely end with the man being hauled away in handcuffs. I could only imagine who else might be rounded up along with him. Meanwhile, Owen drove me to my father's medical office. Though my dad was an otolaryngologist—more commonly known as an ear, nose, and throat doctor—he was qualified to treat routine medical matters. He was also the calmer and more reasonable of my two parents. My mother, who worked part-time at my dad's office, was another matter entirely. Unfortunately, she was sitting at the reception desk, processing bill payments, when we arrived.

She rose from her chair so quickly it rolled away behind her and crashed into the credenza. "Whitney!" she cried. "What's wrong?!"

"Nothing to get worked up about." I held up my hands. "Just a little rope burn."

"A *little* rope burn?" She reached over the counter and took my hands in hers, much like Collin had done only a short time before. "This isn't little! You've hardly got any skin left!"

"Don't worry," I said. "I can grow more skin. Besides, you should see the other guy. Heh-heh."

"What other guy?"

Uh-oh. I shouldn't have opened my big mouth. I'd have no choice but to give her the full details now. She'd been freaked out enough when Woodruff had died in the bell tower. She'd have a full-on conniption fit now.

After I filled her in, she shook her head. "Whitney, Whitney, Whitney."

When she said my name three times like that, she used to follow it with *What am I going to do about you?* Now that I was thirty, she no longer bothered asking that question. Like Collin, she'd long since realized that I was going to do what I was going to do, whether she approved or not. I supposed I shouldn't tell her that my ankles were sore now, too. The jolt of hitting the floor had taken a toll. Ankles didn't bend as far as knees did. No doubt I'd be hobbling around the next day or two.

While Owen took a seat in the waiting area, my mother followed me to the exam room. *So much for patient confidentiality.* She gave me a thorough scolding as my father cleaned my wounds, applied a topical ointment, and covered them in gauze.

She exhaled a loud breath. "You had no business insinuating yourself in this investigation. You could've broken your neck in that bell tower."

"But I didn't."

"I still think you should get your real estate license. You'd be good at it. You know houses."

Would she never give up? "We've been through this, Mom. I'm not having this discussion again."

When my dad finished with my hands, he pulled a sugar-free lollipop from the pocket of his white coat and held it out to me. "You've been a very good girl."

My mother disagreed. "No, she hasn't." She gave me a hug. "But we'll love her anyway."

I unwrapped the lollipop. "Thanks, you two. Love you right back."

CHAPTER 24

CURTAIN CALL

Christopher DuPont's skull was fractured and he'd suffered a major concussion, but he survived having his bell rung. Over the next few days, despite DuPont keeping his mouth firmly shut, the pieces of the puzzle fell into place.

Collin warned Bill O'Brien that he could face charges as an accessory to murder if he didn't spill the beans. The probation officer admitted that he was the spider who'd weaved the deadly web, though he'd never intended for anyone to lose their life. He'd only intended to pad his pockets. He said he was tired of the inequities, of seeing petty thieves serve time while white-collar criminals, who'd stolen much more but in a more sophisticated manner, skated by with a slap on the wrist, if even that. While O'Brien made a valid point about the injustices of the justice system, his actions had only added further to the problems.

He admitted that when he met with Kevin Pham the first time he believed the man to be innocent of the crimes he'd been accused of. Pham had complained that he'd felt forced to agree to a plea bargain after being framed by his employer. Like me, O'Brien had done some research and realized art was the perfect medium for moving large amounts of money right past the noses of unsuspecting customs agents. With pieces being unique and values often difficult to pinpoint, it was a perfect medium for obscuring wealth. He suspected the shipping company was engaging in money laundering using art.

O'Brien had contacted Pham's employer, Specialty Export Experts, and spoken with the chief of security, Christopher DuPont. He'd told DuPont that he could be of benefit to the company and suggested that, if DuPont was interested, he should meet O'Brien at a quiet bar the following night.

O'Brien wasn't sure DuPont would show, but he did. O'Brien told DuPont he believed Pham had been framed in a well-orchestrated scheme to discredit the man after he'd raised questions about art pieces being improperly valued on customs forms. He also suggested that, if the shipping company was laundering money in this manner, they might need people to help them do it, people who could take the fall if things went south. Rather than turning S.E.E. in, O'Brien offered to connect them with unwitting dupes from his bevy of probationers—for a cut of the action, of course.

He offered up Laurel Cromwell and Gerard Woodruff like sacrificial lambs. He knew Marie Vanderhagen—who turned out to be one and the same with the elusive Antonia Szabo—was looking for art pieces she could move under the radar. It was Vanderhagen who'd come up with the idea of embedding the gems in the glass. She bought them from another of O'Brien's unwitting probationers, a guy who robbed jewelers, pawnshops, and the homes of the wealthy.

The gems provided an easy way to move wealth for her money-laundering clients, whom she'd curated across continents and over the years.

O'Brien had also been the one to suggest that Woodruff use his only asset, the aged Bronco, to start a freelance delivery service. He'd convinced Woodruff that he'd have little chance of being hired as an employee with a drug conviction on his record, and that shuttling food and other items around town was his best chance of making a living. While there was some truth behind his statements, there were some employers who were willing to take a chance on workers whose worst crime was the use of recreational drugs that hardly raised an eyebrow anymore. Though helping probationers find honest work was one of his job duties, O'Brien never put Woodruff in contact with those employers.

What's more, to throw law enforcement off the scent in case things went awry, O'Brien planted evidence on Woodruff's phone to make it appear as if he were associating with drug dealers. He pulled their phone numbers from shared computer files in his office, and dialed them from Woodruff's phone at the end of their meetings. He'd made Woodruff wait over an hour before starting each of their meetings so that the calls would appear to have been made shortly after their scheduled meetings should have concluded.

When conducting earlier warrantless searches of probationers' vehicles, the probation officer had seized the fish bat and marijuana he'd later planted in Woodruff's car. He'd told the folks from whom he'd seized the illegal contraband that he wouldn't report the finds so long as he didn't find weapons or drugs in their possession again. Naturally, they were glad he didn't make a record of the seizures and revoke their probation, so they kept mum about it.

The dealers whose numbers he'd called from Woodruff's phone were livid, and rightfully so. Both had been doing their best to stay on the straight and narrow path, and O'Brien's scheme could have undermined their efforts and landed them in prison even though they'd done nothing wrong.

It wasn't clear exactly when Marie Vanderhagen had begun laundering money through Specialty Export Experts, using art as her preferred medium, but Collin suspected it had been going on at least ten years or more. Once he realized the breadth of the operation, and that we'd discovered only the tip of the iceberg, he turned the matter over to the FBI, which had the resources to further pursue the matter and the worldwide web of guilty parties.

Ironically, if Marie Vanderhagen had simply fired Kevin Pham, and not been so vindictive as to frame him, he never would have ended up on probation and we might not have made the connection that it was his probation officer who was at the center of the tangled web leading directly back to her. Prosecutors were working with Pham's defense attorney to have his guilty plea nullified and his record expunged.

Marie Vanderhagen attempted to sneak out of the country on a cruise ship. Fortunately, her plan was discovered before the ship made its first stop in San Juan, Puerto Rico. Though she remained as silent as her violent cohort, it was presumed she intended to disembark and not return before the ship set sail again. She'd likely have continued to run, possibly by booking passage on a private charter plane or boat leaving the island, where she could abscond under the radar.

The black wig and glasses she'd worn in her role as Antonia Szabo were found in the house she shared with Christopher DuPont in a neighborhood known as Brandy-wine Farms in the Nashville suburb of Old Hickory. Her five-bedroom, three-and-a-half-bath home backed up to an especially wide stretch of the Cumberland River, and offered both recreation and beautiful views. She'd be trading the thirty-six hundred square feet of living space for a mere seventy-square-foot jail cell.

DuPont was charged with the murder of Gerard Woodruff. Though neither would admit to it, Collin determined that Marie Vanderhagen and Christopher DuPont flew into a rage when my standard windows had been delivered to them by mistake. They'd assumed, wrongly, that Woodruff had switched the paperwork in an effort to steal the valuable bejeweled windows. They might have assumed, wrongly again, that he'd intended to frame Laurel Cromwell with the paperwork mix-up, though in actuality the switched documentation had been her error. The playhouse address had been in the paperwork attached to the windows Woodruff had delivered to S.E.E., so DuPont knew where to find the deliveryman after he'd left the shipping company. Presumably, a confrontation ensued in the foyer of the theater when DuPont discovered that Buck and I had already moved the valuable stained glass from the playhouse and the jewels could not be recouped. DuPont killed Woodruff, though the man had done nothing wrong.

With the killers in jail and the web of lies and deceit

untangled, Collin could add another successfully solved case to his record and I could sleep easy with my sweet boy, Sawdust, beside me.

Nolan Sibley's estranged wife, Sherry, returned from Florida. She came over to the theater to introduce herself when Buck and I were installing the statues of Saint Cecilia and Saint Genesius out front, as Colette had suggested when we'd first decided to turn the church into a playhouse. It seemed only right to immortalize the patron saints of musicians and performers in cement in the flower beds that flanked the theater steps. The statue of Cecilia depicted her holding a string instrument that resembled a harp. Genesius wore a robe adorned with drama masks like the ones in the stained glass in the theater.

Pegasus had trailed Sherry to the gate between our properties, and waited for her there while she walked through it. Sherry was tall and willowy, with champagne-blond hair she wore in a long braid. She was much more congenial than her husband, greeting us with a warm, genuine smile. After introductions were exchanged, she looked up at the theater. "Wow. What a transformation. I'd thought this old place was ready for the wrecking ball. Glad to see I was wrong."

I tucked the gloves I'd removed to shake her hand into the pocket of my coveralls. "Would you like a tour?" My offer was as much to appease her clear curiosity as to show off the results of our hard labor.

"I'd love one."

Buck and I took her inside and showed her the ticket booth, dressing rooms, and seating area. The light coming through the east windows turned the right side of the theater into a gorgeous kaleidoscope of color.

She clasped her hands together in front of her chest. "You kept the beautiful stained glass. I always thought it would be a shame to see the windows destroyed. Looks like you added some new panels, too. That must've cost a pretty penny."

Buck and I exchanged glances. The stained glass had cost one man his life, and nearly cost me mine, as well. But the glass was indeed beautiful. Laurel Cromwell might be an occasional petty thief, but she was a loving mother and an undeniably talented artist. *Maybe we could sell some of her suncatchers at the café, help her stay on her feet.*

As we turned to exit the playhouse, Sherry pointed to the door to the bell tower. "May I go up in the belfry?"

I held out a hand. "Be my guest."

While we'd originally considered making the bell tower off-limits to theatergoers, we realized that patrons might enjoy going up the belfry to enjoy the bucolic view of the countryside. We'd repaired the bell's mooring, rehung it, and even decided to let folks ring the bell to announce the approach of showtime. We'd have an usher stationed at the bell-tower door to facilitate the flow of traffic in and out of the tower, and limit the occupancy to no more than four patrons at a time. A local musical theater company had rented the space and planned to make the most of the belfry, incorporating it into their production of *The Hunchback of Notre Dame*. We'd agreed to cover the cost of the gargoyles they wanted to place on the playhouse roof. We figured we'd keep them afterward as another interesting design feature.

Buck and I followed Sherry up the stairs of the bell tower.

She stepped out onto the platform and looked to the east, over the horse farm. "Is this where you were when you saw my husband's body?"

Buck and I exchanged a glance, thinking back on that day. "It was," I said.

Sherry exhaled a long, soft sigh. "It's a shame he went the way he did, but he tempted fate with that darn cattle prod. I can't tell you how many times I told Nolan to get rid of that thing. He should have listened to me. He might be alive today if he had." She looked up at the sky for a long moment, her expression wistful. "I wish I could say I was going to miss him, but the kids and I learned to live without him a long time ago. He was always more interested in building his empire than spending time with us."

I wasn't sure how to respond to that, but I realized no response was necessary. Sherry seemed at peace with things, and she didn't need platitudes from me to console her.

Her head turned as she ran her eyes over the expansive acreage her husband had amassed, the barns and the horses grazing about. As her gaze landed on the beautiful Victorian farmhouse, her face brightened. "At least I'm back home now. I've missed that house. Luther and the horses, too. Especially Pegasus. He was always my favorite. I like to think he missed me, too."

As if he'd heard her, Pegasus lifted his head and whinnied from the pasture.

"You ride?" I asked.

"As often as I can," she said. "I used to give lessons. I think I'll start that up again, maybe turn the place into a boarding and riding facility rather than a breeding operation.

First thing I'll do is get the veterinarian out here and have Pegasus gelded."

While the horse might miss his reproductive organs, at least he would keep his life.

"What about Johnny Otto?" I asked. "Do you plan to keep him on?"

"Absolutely," she said without hesitation. "He's a fantastic hand and trainer. He understands horses better than anyone I've ever met. He must've been a wild bronc in a former life."

I felt she had a right to know how he'd reacted to Collin questioning him about the stud operation. "When Detective Flynn was trying to figure out whether the death over here was related to your husband's, he spoke with Johnny. I'd been up here one day and saw someone drive up to the back gate with a horse in a trailer. They unloaded her and Johnny took them to that barn back there." I pointed to the barn off in the distance. "Pegasus was inside."

Sherry said, "That's the breeding shed. It's fixed up specifically for that purpose."

I didn't ask for details about the equine brothel. I wasn't sure I wanted to hear more about the horse hanky-panky.

She added, "Of course, we'll just turn it back into a regular barn now."

"Johnny wasn't breeding Pegasus without permission?"

"Not to my knowledge," she said. "I can't imagine he'd be fool enough to try. Nolan wouldn't let Pegasus off the farm. If Nolan had found out that Pegasus sired a foal and he didn't have a record of it, there would've been hell to pay."

I didn't doubt that. Nolan Sibley wasn't the type of guy to back down from a fight.

We descended the bell tower and Buck and I walked Sherry over to the former parsonage, where I introduced her to Colette and showed her the Collection Plate Café. Colette had decorated each table with a lacy white cloth, and set a gold charger at each place setting to resemble a church collection plate.

Sherry glanced around at the colorful, kitschy décor. "This place is darling! I'm going to love having this right next door. You will serve Sunday brunch, won't you?"

"For sure," Colette said. "Your first mimosa is on me."

Not to be outdone, I offered Sherry two tickets to the opening-night show. "It's a variety show." Presley had arranged a lineup of varying types of performers to showcase the range of entertainment the venue could host. A stand-up comedian. A local tap-dance troupe. A sketch comedy group. A male a cappella trio. A female country vocalist. An emerging southern rock band. Gia Revello had recruited the singers. I'd dropped two opening-night tickets at the jeweler's, too. We'd never have solved the case if he hadn't clued me in that some of the jewels in the window were precious gems rather than mere glass.

Buck and I walked Sherry back to the gate. Pegasus had been munching on the grass nearby, and raised his head as we approached. He stepped closer to the fence and hung his head over it, clearly anticipating some affection. Sherry scratched him under the chin and gave him a kiss on the nose. I settled for running a hand over his withers. His big brown eyes met mine and I felt some type of silent, interspecies communication pass between us. The horse was happier than he'd been in a very long time.

The night before the debut show at the playhouse and the grand opening of the café, we performed a dry run to make sure we wouldn't encounter glitches. Colette flitted about the kitchen, the repurposed altar being ironically, or perhaps appropriately, used to break bread, the waitstaff using a long, serrated knife to cut the sourdough into thick slices on a cutting board atop it.

We'd invited friends and family to play the role of patrons and give us feedback on the service and operations. My parents shared a table with Buck's mother and father—my uncle Roger and aunt Nancy—as well as Colette's mom and dad, who'd driven all the way from New Orleans to see their daughter's dreams come true. Owen had brought his wife and their three young daughters, the youngest of whom sat at the table in an old-fashioned wooden high chair we'd scored at a secondhand shop and repainted white with green polka dots. My former bosses at the real estate company, Marv and Wanda Hartley, came out as well. Presley would be overseeing things at the playhouse later, but for now she could enjoy a nice dinner with her boyfriend. Gia Revello and her husband came to enjoy the trial run, as well. And, of course, Collin, Buck, and I shared a table with the woman of the hour, Colette.

Before dinner was served, Emmalee and the other waitstaff set a sparkling champagne flute down at each place, and poured us all a glass of bubbly so that we could toast one another. Colette went first, proposing a toast to me, "For her fantastic vision, creative design work, and especially for sharing her opportunities with others. This wouldn't be happening if Whitney couldn't see the value in old buildings and old friends."

Awwww. I wiped an emotional tear from my eye as I clinked glasses with her. After a sip of champagne, I raised my glass and returned a toast of my own. "To Colette, who is the best friend and business partner a woman could ask for. And to Buck, who is both a pain in my backside and the backbone of our rehab business. Thank you both."

We all clinked glasses and took another sip.

As Buck stood to make his toast, his left hand brushed against his silverware, knocking a small fork to the floor. We all watched as he knelt down to pick it up. But while we expected him to rise, he didn't. Instead, he remained on one knee and pulled a small velvet-covered box from his pocket. His clumsiness had been a mere ruse. He opened the box and held it up, the diamond sparkling in the candlelight emanating from the tea lights in the colorful mismatched teacups atop the tables. He looked up at Colette. She'd covered her mouth with her hands, her eyes wide and just as sparkly as the diamond he presented to her. "Colette, you not only fill my stomach, you fill my heart, too. Would you do me the honor of marrying me and making me the happiest man on earth?"

She burst into happy tears and nodded her head with so much vigor her chef's hat fell to the floor. Buck picked up her hat, slid the ring onto her finger and the hat onto her head, and sealed the deal with a big kiss. All around them, the group leapt to their feet, clapping their hands and exclaiming in delight.

When they broke their embrace, Buck turned to address

Presley. "We'll need to talk dates so we can book the play-house for our wedding."

Finally able to speak again, Colette said, "I've already got ideas for the dinner and cake." She turned to me and took my hands in hers. "You'll be my maid of honor?"

I gave her hands an affectionate squeeze and added a warm smile. "Was there ever any question?" Maybe some-day I'd ask her to return the favor.

As the waitstaff brought in the salad course, we retook our seats. Each course of the meal was delicious, and the dessert, a just-sweet-enough offering that Colette called her Easy as Sin Apple Rosettes, paired perfectly with the after-dinner coffee.

We finished the meal just in time. Presley had taken her dessert to go and headed over to the playhouse to check on things and ring the bell when it was fifteen minutes until showtime. We rose from the tables and headed over en masse to watch the dress rehearsal, making our way along the curved path Buck and I had laid with large concrete pavers to connect the café to the parking lot and play-house.

The variety show went off without a single hitch. Presley had seen to every detail. The performances were entertain-ing and perfectly executed. Everything had come together. Our hard work had paid off.

At the end of the night, Collin and I walked to his car and climbed in. We looked up at the playhouse, the steeple and bell tower wrapped in colorful lights.

"I can't believe we just finished this big project," I said, "and now I'll be helping Colette plan her wedding."

He cocked his head and gave me a mischievous smile. "Maybe I'll catch the garter and you'll catch the bouquet."

I returned the smile. "If we can catch a killer together, a strip of ruffled elastic and a bunch of flowers should be a cinch."

RECIPES

STAINED-GLASS COOKIES

Special tools: To make these cookies, you will need cookie cutters of the same shape in graduated sizes. Star, heart, and flower shapes make beautiful stained-glass cookies, but have fun experimenting with other shapes as well.

Ingredients:
1½ cups white or oat flour
¾ teaspoon baking soda
½ teaspoon baking powder
½ teaspoon salt
½ cup sugar, unrefined if desired
6 tablespoons oil
1½ tablespoons soy or almond milk
1 teaspoon pure vanilla extract
Life Savers or Jolly Rancher candies in various colors

Instructions:
Combine the flour, baking soda, baking powder, salt, and sugar in a bowl. Stir in the remaining ingredients except for

the candies and knead as needed to form a ball of dough. Refrigerate the dough until cold.

When you are ready to bake the cookies, preheat the oven to 325 degrees Fahrenheit. Roll out the dough with a rolling pin until it is approximately one quarter-inch thick. Using the larger cookie cutters, cut several cookies and place them on the baking sheet. Cut the same number of cookies with the large cookie cutter, but once they are cut, use the smaller cutter to cut the corresponding shape out of the center to form a "frame." Place these frames on top of the solid cookies on the baking sheet.

Place several of the candies in a plastic bag, lay the bag on a cutting board, and use your rolling pin to crush the candies into small pieces inside the bag. Fill each cookie frame three-quarters full with crushed candy evenly spread about inside the frame.

Bake the cookies until they are set and the candy centers have melted (about 12 minutes). Let the cookies cool for at least half an hour before eating, then wow your family and friends with your unique treat!

EASY AS SIN APPLE ROSETTES

Ingredients:

3 apples of your choice: Avoid types with a high water content. Honeycrisp, Gala, and Granny Smith are good choices.

Water

1 tablespoon lemon juice

2 sheets of thawed ready-made puff pastry: I recommend

Pepperidge Farm. It's tasty and also vegan. Another option you can use is refrigerated crescent roll dough.
3 tablespoons blackberry, strawberry, apricot, or raspberry jam
¼ cup coarse granulated sugar

Instructions:
Preheat oven to 375 degrees Fahrenheit. Spray or liberally grease a muffin pan.

Wash the apples. Core them and cut them in half. Cut the apples into thin slices, leaving the skin on. Place the apples in a microwaveable bowl, adding just enough water to cover the apples. Add the lemon juice to the bowl. Microwave the apples on high power until the apple slices are pliable and can bend without breaking (approximately 8 minutes). Drain the apples and pat them dry with a paper or dish towel.

Roll out one sheet of the puff pastry and cut it into six strips sideways along the shorter edge. A pizza cutter works great for this purpose. Place the jam and one tablespoon of water in a microwaveable bowl and heat for just a few seconds to make it easier to spread.

Spread the warm jam on the strip of puff pastry. Arrange the apple slices on the top half of each strip. Fold the lower half of the strip up over the apple slices, and roll it from one end to the other. Place the roll in the muffin pan.

Bake for approximately 40 minutes until golden and jam sauce is bubbling. Remove from oven, cool for 5 minutes, then carefully remove them from the muffin pan to finish cooling. Sprinkle with the coarse granulated sugar. Serve warm. Note that leftovers are best kept at room temperature.

Enjoy!

ORIGINAL SIN SOUR APPLETINI

Ingredients:

¼ ounce lemon juice

1 ounce apple juice or apple cider

1 ounce apple schnapps

1 ounce sour apple schnapps

1 ounce vodka

Green apple slices brushed with lemon or lime juice to preserve freshness

Instructions:

Put all of the ingredients except the apple slices into a cocktail shaker with ice. Shake vigorously. Strain the shaken contents into a martini glass. Dispose of the ice left behind in the shaker. (No shaker? No problem. Stir ingredients together in a tall water glass with ice. Using a strainer, pour the mixed ingredients into a martini glass, retaining the ice.) Garnish the martini glass with a slice of apple and enjoy!

"Problem?"

"No." She bit her lower lip. "Maybe."

"Tell me."

She opened her mouth and then shook her head. "My mom taught me to show not tell." And then her hands went to his chest, one of them right over the Band-Aid, which she touched gently, running her fingers over it as if she wished she could take away the pain. "I just . . . need to see . . ."

"See what?"

Her gaze dropped to his mouth and again she hesitated. Tenderness mixed with his sudden pervasive hunger and need, a dizzying combination for a guy who prided himself on not feeling much. "Pru—"

"Shh a second," she whispered. And then closing the gap, she brushed her lips over his.

By Jill Shalvis

Heartbreaker Bay Novels
SWEET LITTLE LIES

Coming Soon
THE TROUBLE WITH MISTLETOE

Lucky Harbor Novels
ONE IN A MILLION
HE'S SO FINE
IT'S IN HIS KISS
ONCE IN A LIFETIME
ALWAYS ON MY MIND
IT HAD TO BE YOU
FOREVER AND A DAY
AT LAST
LUCKY IN LOVE
HEAD OVER HEELS
THE SWEETEST THING
SIMPLY IRRESISTIBLE

Cedar Ridge Novels
NOBODY BUT YOU
MY KIND OF WONDERFUL
SECOND CHANCE SUMMER

JILL
SHALVIS

sweet
little
lies

A
Heartbreaker Bay
Novel

AVONBOOKS

An Imprint of HarperCollinsPublishers

AVON BOOKS
An Imprint of HarperCollins*Publishers*
195 Broadway
New York, New York 10007

Copyright © 2016 by Jill Shalvis
Excerpt from *The Trouble with Mistletoe* copyright © 2016 by Jill Shalvis
ISBN 978-0-06-244802-6
www.avonromance.com

First Avon Books mass market printing: July 2016
First Avon Books special mass market printing: December

Avon Trademark Reg. U.S. Pat. Off. and in Other Countries, Marca Registrada, Hecho en U.S.A.
Avon, Avon Books, and the Avon logo are trademarks of Harper-Collins Publishers.
HarperCollins® is a registered trademark of HarperCollins Publishers.

Printed in the U.S.A.

10 9 8 7 6 5 4 3 2 1

To HelenKay Dimon
for being a real friend (the very best kind!)
Also for introducing me to May Chen,
the new love of my life.
Thanks for sharing her.

And to May Chen, for bringing back
my love of writing.

sweet
little
lies

Chapter 1

#KeepCalmAndRideAUnicorn

Pru Harris's mom had taught her to make wishes on pink cars, falling leaves, and brass lamps, because wishing on something as ordinary as stars or wishing wells was a sign of no imagination.

Clearly the woman standing not three feet away in the light mist, searching her purse for change to toss into the courtyard fountain hadn't been raised by a hippie mom as Pru had been.

Not that it mattered, since her mom had been wrong. Wishes, along with things like winning the lotto or finding a unicorn, never happened in real life.

The woman, shielding her eyes from the light rain with one hand, holding a coin in her other, sent Pru a wry grimace. "I know it's silly, but it's a hit-rock-bottom thing."

Something Pru understood all too well. She set a wriggly Thor down and shook her arms to try and bring back some circulation. Twenty-five pounds of wet, tubby, afraid-of-his-own-shadow mutt had felt like seventy-five by the end of their thirty-minute walk home from work.

Thor objected to being on the wet ground with a sharp bark. Thor didn't like rain.

Or walking.

But he loved Pru more than life itself so he stuck close, his tail wagging slowly as he watched her face to determine what mood they were in.

The woman blinked and stared down at Thor. "Oh," she said, surprised. "I thought it was a really fat cat."

Thor's tail stopped wagging and he barked again, as if to prove that not only was he all dog, he was big, *badass* dog.

Because Thor—a rescue of undetermined breed— also believed he was a bullmastiff.

When the woman took a step back, Pru sighed and picked him back up again. His old man face was creased into a protective frown, his front paws dangling, his tail back to wagging now that he was suddenly tall. "Sorry," Pru said. "He can't see well and it makes him grumpy, but he's not a cat." She gave Thor a *behave* squeeze. "He only acts like one."

Thor volleyed back a look that said Pru might want to not leave her favorite shoes unattended tonight.

The woman's focus turned back to the fountain and she eyed the quarter in her hand. "They say it's never too late to wish on love, right?"

"Right," Pru said. Because they did say that. And just because in her own personal experience love had proven even rarer than unicorns didn't mean she'd step on someone else's hopes and dreams.

A sudden bolt of lightning lit up the San Francisco skyline like the Fourth of July. Except it was June, and cold as the Arctic. Thor squeaked and shoved his face into Pru's neck. Pru started to count but didn't even get to One-Mississippi before the thunder boomed loud enough to make them all jump.

"Yikes." The woman dropped the quarter back into her purse. "Not even love's worth getting electrocuted." And she ran off.

Pru and Thor did the same, heading across the cobblestone courtyard. Normally she took her time here, enjoying the glorious old architecture of the building, the corbeled brick and exposed iron trusses, the big windows, but the rain had begun to fall in earnest now, hitting so hard that the drops bounced back up to her knees. In less than ten seconds, she was drenched through, her clothes clinging to her skin, filling her ankle boots so that they squished with each step.

"Slow down, sweetness!" someone called out. It was the old homeless guy who was usually in the alley. With his skin tanned to the consistency of leather and his long, wispy white cotton-ball hair down to the collar of his loud pineapples-and-parrots Hawaiian shirt, he looked like Doc from *Back to the Future,* plus a few decades. A century tops. "You can't get much wetter," he said.

But Pru wasn't actually trying to dodge the weather, she loved the rain. She was trying to dodge her demons, something she was beginning to suspect couldn't be done.

"Gotta get to my apartment," she said, breathless from her mad dash. When she'd hit twenty-six, her spin class instructor had teasingly told her that it was all downhill from here on out, she hadn't believed him. Joke was on her.

"What's the big rush?"

Resigned to a chat, Pru stopped. Old Guy was sweet and kind, even if he had refused to tell her his name, claiming to have forgotten it way back in the seventies. True or not, she'd been feeding him since she'd moved into this building three weeks ago. "The cable company's finally coming today," she said. "They said five o'clock."

"That's what they told you yesterday. And last week," he said, trying to pet Thor, who wasn't having any of it.

Another thing on Thor's hate list—men.

"But this time they mean it," Pru said and set Thor down. At least that's what the cable company supervisor had promised Pru on the phone, and she needed cable TV. Bad. The finals of *So You Think You Can Dance* were on tomorrow night.

"'Scuse me," someone said as he came from the elevator well and started to brush past her. He wore a hat low over his eyes to keep the rain out of his face and the cable company's logo on his pec. He was carrying a toolbox and looking peeved by life in general.

Thor began a low growl deep in his throat while hiding behind Pru's legs. He sounded fierce, but he looked ridiculous, especially wet. He had the fur of a Yorkshire terrier—if that Yorkshire terrier was fat—even though he was really a complete Heinz 57. And hell, maybe he *was* part cat. Except that only one of his ears folded over. The other stood straight up, giving him a perpetually confused look.

No self-respecting cat would have allowed such a

thing. In fact, the cable guy took one look at him and snorted, and then kept moving.

"Wait!" Pru yelled after him. "Are you looking for 3C?"

He stopped, his gaze running over her, slowing at her torso. "Actually," he said. "I'm more a double D man myself."

Pru looked down at herself. Her shirt had suctioned itself to her breasts. Narrowing her eyes, she crossed her arms over her decidedly not DDs. "Let me be more clear," she said, tightening her grip on Thor's leash because he was still growling, although he was doing it very quietly because he only wanted to pretend to be a tough guy. "Are you looking for the person who lives in *apartment* 3C?"

"I was but no one's home." He eyed Thor. "Is that a dog?"

"Yes! And *I'm* 3C," Pru said. "I'm home!"

He shook his head. "You didn't answer your door."

"I will now, I promise." She pulled her keys from her bag. "We can just run up there right now and—"

"No can do, dude. It's five o'clock straight up." He waved his watch to prove it. "I'm off the clock."

"But—"

But nothing, he was gone, walking off into the downpour, vanishing into the fog like they were on the set of a horror flick.

Thor stopped growling.

"Great," Pru muttered. "Just great."

Old Guy slid his dentures around some. "I could hook up your cable for you. I've seen someone do it once or twice."

The old man, like the old Pacific Heights building around them, had seen better days, but both held a certain old-fashioned charm—which didn't mean she trusted him inside her apartment. "Thanks," she said. "But this is for the best. I don't really need cable TV all that bad."

"But the finals of *So You Think You Can Dance* are on tomorrow night."

She sighed. "I know."

Another bolt of lightning lit the sky, and again was immediately followed by a crack of thunder that echoed off the courtyard's stone walls and shook the ground beneath their feet.

"That's my exit," Old Guy said and disappeared into the alley.

Pru got Thor upstairs, rubbed him down with a towel and tucked him into his bed. She'd thought she wanted the same for herself, but she was hungry and there was nothing good in her refrigerator. So she quickly changed into dry clothes and went back downstairs.

Still raining.

One of these days she was going to buy an umbrella. For now, she made the mad dash toward the northeast corner of the building, past the Coffee Bar, the Waffle Shop, and the South Bark Mutt Shop—all closed, past The Canvas tattoo studio—open—and went straight for the Irish Pub.

Without the lure of cable to make her evening, she needed chicken wings.

And nobody made chicken wings like O'Riley's.

It's not the chicken wings you're wanting, a small voice inside her head said. And that was fact. Nope, what drew her into O'Riley's like a bee to honey was the six-foot, broad-shouldered, dark eyes, dark smile of Finn O'Riley himself.

From her three weeks in the building, she knew the people who lived and/or worked here were tight. And she knew that it was in a big part thanks to Finn because he was the glue, the steady one.

She knew more too. More than she should.

"Hey!" Old Guy stuck his head out of the alley. "If you're getting us wings, don't forget extra sauce!"

She waved at him, and once again dripping wet, entered O'Riley's where she stood for a second getting her bearings.

Okay, that was a total lie. She stood there *pretending* to get her bearings while her gaze sought out the bar and the guys behind it.

There were two of them working tonight. Twenty-two-year-old Sean was flipping bottles, juggling them to the catcalls and wild amusement of a group of women all belly up to the bar, wooing them with his wide smile and laughing eyes. But he wasn't the one Pru's gaze gravitated to like he was a rack of double-stuffed Oreo cookies.

Nope, that honor went to the guy who ran the place, Sean's older brother. All lean muscle and easy confidence, Finn O'Riley wasn't pandering to the crowd. He never did. He moved quickly and efficiently without show, quietly hustling to fill the orders, keeping an eye on the kitchen, as always steady as a rock under pressure, doing all the real work.

Pru could watch him all day. It was his hands, she'd decided, they were constantly moving with expert precision. He was busy, way too busy for her, of course, which was only one of the many reasons why she hadn't allowed herself to fantasize about him doing deliciously naughty, wicked things to her in her bed.

Whoops. That was another big fat lie.

She'd *totally* fantasized about him doing deliciously naughty, wicked things to her in bed. And also out of it.

He was her unicorn.

He bent low behind the bar for something and an entire row of women seated on the barstools leaned in unison for a better view. Meerkats on parade.

When he straightened a few seconds later, he was hoisting a huge crate of something, maybe clean glasses, and not looking like he was straining too much either. This was in no doubt thanks to all that lean, hard muscle visible beneath his black tee and faded jeans. His biceps bulged as he turned, allowing her to see that his Levi's fit him perfectly, front *and* back.

If he noticed his avid audience, he gave no hint of it. He merely set the crate down on the counter, and ignoring the women ogling him, nodded a silent hello in Pru's direction.

She stilled and then craned her neck, looking behind her.

No one there. Just herself, dripping all over his floor.

She turned back and found Finn looking quietly amused. Their gazes locked and held for a long beat, like maybe he was taking her pulse from across the room, absorbing the fact that she was drenched and breathless. The corners of his mouth twitched. She'd amused him again.

People shifted between them. The place was

crowded as always, but when the way was clear again, Finn was still looking at her, steady and unblinking, those dark green eyes flickering with something other than amusement now, something that began to warm her from the inside out.

Three weeks and it was the same every single time . . .

Pru considered herself fairly brave and maybe a little more than fairly adventurous—but not necessarily forward. It wasn't easy for her to connect with people.

Which was the only excuse she had for jerking her gaze away, pretending to eye the room.

The pub itself was small and cozy. One half bar, the other half pub designated for dining, the décor was dark woods reminiscent of an old thatched inn. The tables were made from whiskey barrels and the bar itself had been crafted out of repurposed longhouse-style doors. The hanging brass lantern lights and stained-glass fixtures along with the horse-chewed, old-fence baseboards finished the look that said antique charm and friendly warmth.

Music drifted out of invisible speakers, casting a jovial mood, but not too loud so as to make conversation difficult. There was a wall of windows and also a rack of accordion wood and glass doors that opened the pub on both sides, one to the courtyard, the other to the street, giving a view down the hill to the beautiful Fort Mason Park and Marina Green, and the Golden Gate Bridge behind that.

All of which was fascinating, but not nearly as fascinating as Finn himself, which meant that her eyes, the traitors, swiveled right back to him.

He pointed at her.

"Me?" she asked, even though he couldn't possibly hear her from across the place.

With a barely there smile, he gave her a finger crook.

Yep. Her.

Chapter 2

#TakeMeToYourLeader

Pru's brain wondered what her mom would've said about going to a man who crooked his finger at her. But Pru's feet didn't care, they simply took her right to him.

He handed her a clean towel to dry off. Their fingers brushed, sending a tingle straight through her. While she enjoyed that—hey, it was the most action she'd gotten in a very long time—he cleared her a seat.

"What can I get you?" His voice was low and gravelly, bringing to mind all sorts of inappropriate responses to his question.

"Your usual?" he asked. "Or the house special?"

"What would that be?" she asked.

"Tonight it's a watermelon mojito. I could make it virgin-style for you."

He saw God knew how many people day in and day out, and on top of that the two of them hadn't spoken much more than a few words to each other, but he remembered what she liked after a long day at work out on the water.

And what she didn't. He'd noticed that she didn't drink alcohol. Hard to believe that when he had a pub menu, a regular alcoholic beverage menu, and also a special menu dedicated solely to beer, he could keep it all straight. "You kept track of my usual?" she asked, warmed at the idea. Warmed and a little scared because she shouldn't be doing this, flirting with him.

"It's my job," he said.

"Oh." She laughed at herself. "Right. Of course."

His eyes never left her face. "And also because your usual is a hot chocolate, which matches your eyes."

Her stomach got warmer. So did some of her other parts. "The virgin special would be great, thanks."

The guy on the barstool next to her swiveled to look at her. He was in a suit, tie loosened. "Hi," he said with the cheerfulness of someone who was already two drinks into his night. "I'm Ted. How 'bout I buy you an Orgasm? Or maybe even"—wink, wink—"multiples?"

Finn's easy, relaxed stance didn't change but his eyes did as they cut to Ted, serious now and a little scary hard. "Behave," he warned, "or I'll cut you off."

"Aw, now that's no fun," Ted said with a toothy smile. "I'm trying to buy the pretty lady a drink, is all."

Finn just looked at him.

Ted lifted his hands in a sign of surrender and Finn went back to making drinks. Soon as he did, Ted leaned in close to Pru again. "Okay now that daddy's gone, how about Sex On The Beach?"

Finn reached in and took Ted's drink away. "Annnnd you're out."

Ted huffed out a sigh and stood up. "Fine, I gotta get home anyway." He flashed a remorseful smile at Pru. "Maybe next time we'll start with a Seduction."

"Maybe next time," she said, picking one of the sweet, noncommittal smiles from her wide repertoire of smiles that she used on the job captaining a day cruise ship in the bay. It took a lot of different smiles to handle all the people she dealt with daily and she had it down.

When Ted was gone, Finn met her gaze. "Maybe next time?" he repeated.

"Or, you know, never."

Finn smiled at that. "You let him down easy."

"Had to," she said. "Since you played bad cop."

"Just part of the service I offer," he said, not at all bothered by the bad cop comment. "Did you have to cancel your last tour today?"

So apparently he knew what she did for a living. "Nope. Just got back."

"You were out in this?" he asked in disbelief. "With the high winds and surf alerts?"

His hands were in constant motion, making drinks, chopping ingredients, keeping things moving. She was mesmerized by the way he moved, how he used those strong hands, the stubble on his jaw . . .

"Pru."

She jerked her gaze off his square jaw and found his locked on hers. "Hmm?"

A flash of humor and something else came and went in his eyes. "Did you have any problems with the high winds and surf out there today?"

"Not really. I mean, a little kid got sick on his

grandma, but that's because she gave him an entire bag of cotton candy and then two hot dogs, and he wolfed it all down in like two seconds, so I'm not taking the blame there."

He turned his head and looked out the open doors facing the courtyard. Dusk had fallen. The lights strung in pretty ribbons over and around the wrought iron fencing and fountain revealed sheets of rain falling from the sky.

She shrugged. "It didn't start raining until I was off the water. And anyway, bad weather's a part of the job."

"I'd think staying alive would be a bigger part of the job."

"Well yes," she said on a laugh. "Staying alive is definitely the goal." Truth was, she rarely had problems out on the water. Nope, it was mostly real life that gave her problems. "It's San Francisco. If we didn't go out in questionable weather, we'd never go out at all."

He took that in a moment as he simultaneously cleaned up a mess at the bar and served a group a few seats down a pitcher of margaritas, while still managing to make her feel like he was concentrating solely on her.

It's his job, her brain reminded her body. But it felt like more.

From the other side of the pub came a sound of a plate hitting the floor. Finn's eyes tracked over there.

One of his waitresses had dropped a dish, and the table she'd been serving—a rowdy group of young guys—were cheering, embarrassing her further.

Finn easily hopped over the bar and strode over there. Pru couldn't hear what he said but the guys at the table immediately straightened up, losing their frat boy antics mentality.

Finn then turned, crouched low next to his waitress, helped her clean up, and was back to the bar in less than sixty seconds.

"You've got an interesting job," he said, coming back to their conversation like nothing had happened.

"Yes," she said, watching as the waitress moved to the kitchen with a grateful glance in Finn's direction. "Interesting. And fun too." Which was incredibly important to her because . . . well, there'd been a very long stretch of time when her life hadn't been anything close to resembling a good time.

"Fun." Finn repeated the word like it didn't compute. "Now there's something I haven't had in a while."

Something else she already knew about him, and the thought caused a slash of regret to cut through her.

Sean came up alongside Finn. The brothers looked alike; same dark hair, same dark green eyes and smiles. Finn was taller, which didn't stop Sean from slinging an arm around his older brother's neck as he winked at Pru. "You'll have to excuse grandpa here. He doesn't do fun. You'd do better to go out with me."

Sean O'Riley, master flirt.

But Pru was a master too, by necessity. She'd had to become well versed in dealing with charming flirts at work. It didn't matter if it was vacationers, tourists, or college kids . . . they all got a kick out of having a female boat captain, and since she was passable in the looks department and a smartass to boot, she got hit on a lot. She always declined, even the marriage proposals. *Especially* the marriage proposals. "I'm flattered," she said with an easy smile. "But I couldn't possibly break the hearts of all the women waiting for their *cocktail* fantasies to come true."

"Damn." Sean mimed a dagger to the heart but laughed good-naturedly. "Do me a favor then, would ya? If you're going to take this one for a spin"—he elbowed Finn—"Show him how to live a little and maybe take him for a walk on the wild side while you're at it."

Pru slid her gaze to Finn, which was how she caught the quick flash of irritation as Sean sauntered off. "You need help living a little?" she asked him lightly. Not easy to do since her heart had started pounding, her pulse racing, because what was she doing? Was she really playing with him? It was a bad idea, the worst of all her bad ideas put together, and she'd had some real doozies over the years.

Don't be stupid. Back away from the cute hottie. You can't have him and you know why.

But the troubling train of thought stopped on a dime when Finn laughed all rumbly and sexy, like maybe he saved it for special occasions.

"Actually," he said, "I've lived plenty. And as for taking a walk on the wild side, I wrote the book on it." He leaned on the bar, which brought him up close and personal. Eyes locked on hers, he stroked a strand of wet hair from her temple.

She went still, like a puppy waiting for a belly rub, staring up at him, her heart still pounding, but for another reason entirely now. "What changed?" she asked, whispered really, because she was pretty sure she knew what the catalyst had been and it was going to kill her to hear him say it.

He shrugged. "Life."

Oh how she hated that for him. Hated it, and felt guilty for it. And not for the first time when she felt overwhelmed and out of her league, she opened her mouth and put her foot in it. "You know, in some circles I'm known as the Fun Whisperer."

He arched a brow. "Is that right?"

"Yep," she said, apparently no longer in control of her mouth. "The fun starts right here with me. I specialize in people not living their lives, the ones letting their life live them. It's about letting stuff go, you see." Seriously. Why wasn't her mouth attached to a shut-the-hell-up filter?

Finn smiled and blew half her brain cells. "You going to teach me how to have fun, Pru?" he asked in that low, husky voice.

Good God, the way her name rolled off his tongue had her knees wobbling. She could see now that his eyes weren't a solid dark green, but had swirls of gold and brown and even some blue in them in the mix as well. She was playing with fire and all her inner alarms were going off.

Stop.

Don't engage.

Go home.

But did she do any of those things? No, she did not. Instead she smiled back and said, "I could knock the ball out of the park teaching you how to have fun."

"I have no doubt," he murmured, and blew all her remaining brain cells.

Chapter 3

#GoBigOrGoHome

It wasn't until Finn shifted away to help one of his servers that Pru let out a shuddery breath. *I'm known as the Fun Whisperer?* She smacked her own forehead, which didn't knock any sense into her. Ordering her hormones to cool their jets, she turned away to take in the rest of the pub.

She was immediately waved over to the far end of the bar, which she'd missed when she'd first come in because hello, she'd honed in on Finn like a homing pigeon.

Informally reserved for those who lived and worked in the building, this end of the bar was instant camaraderie as someone you knew was always there to eat or drink with.

Tonight that someone was Willa, sole proprietor of the South Bark Mutt Shop, a one-stop pet store on the southwest ground-floor corner of the building.

Willa eyed a still very wet Pru and without a word pushed a plate of chicken wings her way.

"You're a mind reader," Pru said and slid onto the seat next to her.

Willa laughed at the squishy, watery sound Pru made when she sat. "When you live in a city that's all hills and rain and soggy rainbow flags you learn really fast what's valuable. An umbrella with all its spokes . . . and a man who believes in happily-ever-afters."

Pru laughed. "Aw. You believe in fairy tales."

Willa smiled, her bright green eyes dancing. If you took in her strawberry red hair cut in layers framing her pretty face and coupled it with her petite, curvy frame, she looked like she belonged in a fairy tale herself, waving her magic wand. "You don't believe the right guy's out there for you?"

Pru took a big bite of a mouth-watering chicken wing and moaned. Swallowing, she licked some sauce off her thumb. "I just think I'd have better luck searching for a unicorn."

"You could wish on the fountain," Willa said.

The fountain in their courtyard had quite the reputation, as the woman she'd seen earlier had clearly known. The 1928 four-story building had actually been built around the fountain, which had been here in the Cow Hollow district of San Francisco for fifty years before that, when the area still resembled the Wild West and was chock-full of dairies and roaming cattle.

Back then only the hearty had survived. And the desperate. Born of that, the fountain's myth went that a wish made here out of true desperation, with an equally true heart, would bring a first, true love in unexpected ways.

It'd happened just enough times over the past hundred plus years that the myth had long since become infamous legend.

A big hand set a mouth-watering looking watermelon mojito mocktail in front of her, the muscles in his forearm flexing as he moved. Pru stared at it for a beat before she managed to lift her gaze to Finn's. "Thanks."

"Try it."

She obediently did just that. "Oh my God," she murmured, pleasure infusing her veins. "What's in it?"

He smiled mysteriously, and something warm and wondrous happened deep inside her.

"Secret recipe," he said while she was still gaping up at him. He turned to Willa. "And your Irish coffee."

Willa squealed over the mountain of whipped cream topping the glass and jumped up to give Finn a tight squeeze.

Pru knew that they were very tight friends and it showed in their familiarity with each other. It didn't seem sexual at all so there was no need for jealousy but Finn definitely let down his guard with Willa. And it was *that*, Pru knew, that gave her the twinge of envy.

Finn waited until Willa sat and attacked her drink before he spoke again. "Your girl Cara tried to con Sean into a drink last night."

Willa, who'd just spooned in a huge bite of the cream, grimaced. She always had three or four employees on rotation at her shop, all of them some sort of rescue, many of them underage. "She have a fake ID?"

"Affirmative," Finn said. "He cut it up on my orders."

Willa sighed. "Bet that went over like a fart in church."

Finn lifted a shoulder. "We handled it."

Willa reached out and squeezed his hand. "Thanks."

Finn nodded and turned his attention back to Pru, who'd sucked down a third of her drink already. "You need your own order of chicken wings?"

What she needed didn't involve calories. It involved a lobotomy. "Yes, please."

"You warming up yet?"

Yes, but that might've had more to do with his warm gaze than the temperature in the room. "Getting there," she managed.

The barest of smiles curved his mouth.

Idle chitchat. That's all this was, she reminded herself. They were just like any other casual acquaintances who happened to be in the same place at the same time.

Except there was nothing casual about her being here. Finn just didn't know it.

Yet.

She'd have to tell him eventually, because this *wasn't* a fairy tale. And she absolutely would tell him. But as a rule, she tended to subscribe to the later-is-best theory.

She realized he was watching her and she squirmed in her seat, suddenly very busy looking anywhere and everywhere except right into his eyes because they made her think about things. Things that made her nipples hopeful and perky.

Things that couldn't happen.

As if maybe he knew what he could do to her with just one look—or hey, it wasn't like her wet white shirt was hiding much—the corners of his mouth quirked.

Which was when she realized that Willa had stopped eating and was staring at the two of them staring at each other. When Willa opened her mouth to say something, something Pru was quite certain she didn't want said in front of Finn, she rushed to beat her friend to it. "On second thought, can I double that order of chicken wings?"

"Sure," Finn's mouth said.

Stop looking at his mouth! She forced herself to look into his eyes instead, those deep, dark, mossy green eyes, which as suspected, was a lot like jumping from the frying pan into the fire. "Um, I think that's my phone—" She started digging through her purse. Wrapping her fingers around her cell, she pulled it out and stared at the screen.

Nothing. It was black.

Dammit.

Finn smiled and walked away, heading back to the kitchen.

"Smooth," Willa said and sipped her Irish coffee.

Pru covered her face, but peeked out between her fingers, watching Finn go, telling herself she was completely nonplussed by her crazy reaction to him, but the truth was she just wanted to watch his very fine ass go.

"Huh," Willa said.

"No," Pru said. "There's no *huh*."

"Oh, honey, there's a *huge* huh," Willa said. "I work with dogs and cats all day long, I'm fluent in eye-speak. And there's some serious eye-speak going on here. It's saying you two want to f—"

Pru pointed at her and snagged the last chicken wing, stuffing it into her mouth.

Willa just smirked. "You know, it's been a long time since I've seen Finn look at a woman like he just looked at you. A real long time."

Don't ask. *Don't ask*—"Why's that?" She covered her mouth. Then uncovered her mouth. Then covered it again.

Willa waited, eyes lit. "Not that *that* wasn't fun to watch, but are you finished arguing with yourself?"

Pru sighed. "Yeah."

"Finn's got a lot going on. Keeping the pub's head above water isn't easy in today's economy. Plus he's slowly renovating his grandparents' house so he can sell it and move out of the city—"

Pru's heart stopped and she swallowed a heavy bite of chicken wing. "He wants to leave San Francisco?"

"To live, yes. To work, no. He loves the pub, but he wants to live in a quieter place and get a big, lazy dog. And then there's his biggest time sink—keeping Sean on the straight and narrow. Add all of that up and it equals no time for—"

"Love?"

"Well, I was going to say getting lucky," Willa said. "But yeah, even less time for love."

Pru turned her head and watched Finn in action, taking care of his employees, his customers, his brother . . .

But who took care of him, she wondered as he worked his ass off, running this entire place and making it look easy while he was at it.

She knew it wasn't about making time. It was about what had happened eight years ago when he'd been just barely twenty-one. Her gut twisted, which didn't stop her from eating her entire plate of chicken wings when it came.

An hour later she left the bar warm, dry, and stuffed. Night had fallen. The rain had tapered off. With the clearing of most of the clouds, a sliver of a moon lit her way. The courtyard was mostly empty now, the air cool on her skin. Pots of flowers hung from hooks on the brick walls and also the wrought iron lining parts of the courtyard. During the day, the air was fragrant with the blooms but now all she could smell was the salty sea breeze.

A few people were coming and going, either from the pub or cutting through for a shortcut to the street and the nightlife the rest of the Cow Hollow and Marina area offered. But the sound of street traffic was muted here, partially thanks to the fountain's water cascading down to the wide, circular copper dome that had long ago become tarnished green and black. A stone bench provided a quick respite for those so inclined to stop and enjoy the view and the musical sound of the trickling water.

Pru stopped, staring at the coins shining brightly from the tiles at the bottom of the fountain. What was it the woman from earlier had said? *Never too late to wish for love . . .*

On a sudden whim, she went through her purse, looking for her laundry money. Pulling out a dime, she stared into the water. *A wish made here out of true desperation, with an equally true heart, will bring a first, true love in unexpected ways.*

Well, she had the desperation. Did she have the true heart? She put a hand to it because it did hurt, but that might've been the spicy chicken wings.

Not that it mattered because she wasn't going to wish for herself. She was going to wish for true love for someone else, for a guy who didn't know her, not really, and yet she owed him far more than he'd ever know.

Finn.

She closed her eyes, sending her wish to . . . well, whoever collected them. The fountain fairy?

The Karma Fairy?

The Tooth Fairy?

Please, she thought, *please bring Finn true love because he deserves so much more happy than he's been dealt.* And then she tossed in the dime.

"I hope you find him."

Pru gasped and whirled around to face . . . Old Guy.

"What's his name?" he asked.

"Oh," she said on a low laugh. "I didn't wish for me."

"Shame," he said. "Though it doesn't really work, you know that, right? It's just a propaganda thing the businesses here in the Pacific Pier building use to draw in foot traffic."

"I know," Pru said, and crossed her fingers. *Please let him be wrong . . .*

"I tried it once," he told her. "I wished for my first love to return to me. But Red's still dead as a doornail."

"Oh," Pru breathed. "I'm so sorry."

He shrugged. "She gave me twelve great years. Shared my food, my bed, and my heart for all of them. Slept with me every night and guarded my six like no other." He smiled. "She'd bring me game she'd hunted herself when we were hungry. She followed me everywhere. Hell, she didn't even mind when I'd bring another woman home."

Pru blinked. "That's . . . sweet?"

"Yeah. She was the best dog ever."

She reached out to smack him and he flashed a grin. "Don't be ashamed of wishing for love for yourself, sweetness," he said. "Everyone deserves that. Whoever he is, I hope he's worthy."

"No, really, it's not—"

"Or she," he said, lifting his hands. "No judging here. We all stick together, you know what I'm saying? Take Tim, the barista at the coffee shop. When he decided to become Tina a few years back, no one blinked an eye. Well, okay, I did at first," he admitted. "But that's only because she's hot as hell now. I mean, who knew?"

Pru nodded. Tina had made her coffee just about every morning for three weeks now, and on top of making the best muffins in all of San Francisco, she was indeed hot as hell. "I'm not wishing for me though. I'm wishing for someone else. Someone who deserves it more than me."

"Well, then," he said, and patted down his pockets, coming up with a quarter, which he tossed in after her dime. "Never hurts to double down a bet."

Chapter 4

#CarefulWhatYouWishFor

Two days later Finn was at his desk pounding the keys on his laptop, trying to find the source of the mess Sean had made of their books while simultaneously fantasizing about one sexy, adorable "fun whisperer," and how much he'd like her to fun whisper him. He was a most excellent multitasker.

He liked that sassy smile of hers. He liked her easygoing 'tude. And he really liked her mile-long legs . . .

He was in the middle of picturing them wrapped around him when he found the problem.

Sean had done something to the payroll that had caused everyone to get fifty percent more than they had coming to them. Finn rubbed his tired eyes and pushed back from his desk. "Done," he said. "Found the screwup. You somehow managed to set payroll to time and a half."

Sean didn't say anything and Finn blew out a breath.

He knew that sometimes he got caught up in being the boss and forgot to be the older brother. "Look," he said, "it could've happened to anyone, don't take it so hard—"

At the sound of a soft snore, Finn craned his neck and swore.

Sean lay sprawled on his back on the couch, one leg on the floor, his arms akimbo, mouth open, dead asleep.

Finn strode over there and exercised huge restraint by kicking his brother's foot and not his head.

Sean sat straight up, murmuring, "That's it, baby, that's perfect—" When he saw Finn standing over him, he sagged and swiped a hand down his face. "What the hell, man. You just interrupted me banging Anna Kendrick."

Anna Kendrick was hot, but she had nothing on Pru Harris. "You're not allowed to sleep through me kicking your ass."

Sean didn't try dispute the fact that Finn could, and had, kicked his ass on many occasions. "Anna Kendrick," he simply repeated in a devastated voice.

"Out of your league. And why the hell don't you sleep in your own office? Or better yet, at home."

Home being the Victorian row house they shared in the neighborhood of Pacific Heights, half a mile straight up one of San Francisco's famed hills.

"I've got better things to do in my bed than sleep," Sean muttered and yawned. "What do you want anyway? I've cleaned my room and scrubbed behind my ears, *Mom*."

"I'm not your damn mom."

This earned him a rude snort from Sean. Whether that was because Finn had indeed been Sean's 'damn mom' since the day she'd walked out on them when they'd been three and ten, or simply because Finn was the only one of them with a lick of sense, didn't matter.

"Focus," Finn said to his now twenty-two-going-on-sixteen-year-old brother. "I found the error you made in the payroll. You somehow set everyone to time and a half."

"Oh shit." Sean flopped back to the couch and closed his eyes again. "Rookie mistake."

"That's it?" Finn asked. "Just 'oh shit, rookie mistake'?" He felt an eye twitch coming on. "This is a damn partnership, Sean, and I need you to start acting like it. I can't do it alone."

"Hey, I told you, I don't belong behind a desk. My strength's in front of the customers and we both know it."

Finn stared at him. "There's more to running this place than making people smile."

"No shit." Sean cracked open an eye. "Without me out there hustling and busting my ass to charm everyone into a good time every night, there'd be no payroll to fuck up."

"You think that's all this pub is, a good time?" Finn asked.

"Well, yeah." Sean stretched his long, lanky body, lying back with his hands behind his head. "What else is there?"

Finn pressed his fingers against his twitching eye so that his brains couldn't leak out, but what did he expect? Back when he'd been twenty-one, he'd been as wild as they came. And then suddenly he'd found himself in charge of fourteen-year-old Sean when their dad had gotten himself killed in a car accident. It'd been hell, but eventually Finn had gotten his act together for both his own and Sean's sake. He'd had to.

When Sean had turned twenty-one last year, they'd opened the pub to give them both a viable future. And if Finn's other goal had been to keep Sean interested in something, *anything*, he couldn't very well now complain that Sean thought life was all fun and games.

"How about making a living?" Finn asked. "You know, that little thing about covering our rent and food and other expenses, like your college tuition? What are you now, a third-year sophomore?"

"Fourth I think." Sean smiled, though it faltered some when Finn didn't return it. "Hey, I'm still trying to find my calling. This year probably. Next year tops. And then the good times really start."

"As opposed to what you're doing now?"

"Hey, we work our asses off."

"You work part-time at a pub, Sean. By the very definition of that, you're having fun every single day."

Sean snorted. "Seriously, man, we need to redefine your definition of fun. You're here twenty-four seven and you know it. You should've let Trouble show you what you're missing. She's cute, and best yet, she was game."

"Trouble?"

"Yeah, man. The new chick. Don't tell me you weren't feeling her. You made her a virgin version of our special. You don't do that for anyone else ever."

True. Also true was that he'd been drawn in by Pru's

warm, shiny brown eyes. They matched her warm, shiny brown tumble of long hair, and then there was her laugh that always seemed to prove Pavlov's theory. Except Finn's reaction wasn't to drool when he heard it.

"Did you know she's a ship captain?" Sean asked. "I mean that's pretty badass."

Yeah, it was. She drove one of the fleet ships out of Pier 39 for SF Bay Tours, a tough job to say the least. Finn's favorite part was her uniform. Snug, fitted white Captain's button-down shirt, dark blue trousers that fit her sweet ass perfectly, and kickass work boots, all of which had fueled more than a few dirty-as-fuck daydreams over the past three weeks.

He'd never forget his first glimpse of her. She'd been moving in, striding across the courtyard with a heavy box, her long legs churning up the distance, that willowy body with those sweet curves making his mouth water. She had her mass of wavy hair piled on top of her head—not that this had tamed the beast because strands had fallen into her face.

Yeah, he'd felt her from day one, and though she often sat at the end of the bar he reserved for his close-knit friends, he hadn't spoken much to her until two nights ago.

"She offered to show you a good time and you turned her down," Sean said, shaking his head in mock sadness. "And you call yourself the older brother. But yeah, you were probably right to turn her down. Would've been a waste of her efforts, seeing as you have no interest in anything remotely resembling a good time."

"I didn't turn her down."

"Flat, dude."

Finn hoped like hell Pru hadn't taken it that way, because he sure hadn't meant it like that. "I was working."

"Always are," Sean said. "Whelp"—he stood and
stretched again—"this has been fun, but gotta run. The
gang's hiking Twin Peaks today. First to the top gets
number one draft pick in our fantasy football league.
You should come."

"I won the league last year," Finn said.

"Uh huh. Which means we'd totally try to push you
off the trail and sabotage your ascent. So you should
definitely come."

"Wow, sounds like a real good time," Finn said.
"But there's this . . ." He pointed to his desk and the
mountain of work waiting on him.

Sean rolled his eyes. "You know what all work and
no play makes you, right?"

"Not poor?"

"Ha-ha. I was going to say not laid."

This was unfortunately true but Finn turned back to
his desk. "Kick ass out there."

"Well, duh."

Chapter 5

#DidIDoThat?

Hours later, Finn was still at his desk when Sean sauntered back in, hot, sweaty, and grinning. He helped himself to Finn's iced soda, downing it in three gulps. "Asses have been kicked," he said.

"No way did you beat Archer," Finn said. No one beat Archer at anything physical. The man was a machine.

"Nah, but I got second draft pick."

Annie, one of the three servers coming on shift for the night, stuck her head in. "Already filling up out front," she told them both.

"Got your back, darlin'," Sean said and set Finn's now empty glass back onto his desk. "Always."

Annie smiled dreamily at him.

Sean winked at her and slid out of the office before Finn could remind him of their *no sleeping* with the hired help policy. Swearing to himself, Finn grabbed his iPad and followed. He intended to go over inventory, but was immediately waved to the far end of the bar.

Sitting at it were some of his closest friends, most of them having been linked together in one way or another for years.

Archer lifted his beer in a silent toast. The ex-cop worked on the second floor of the building running a private security and investigation firm. He and Finn went back as far as middle school. They'd gone to college together. It'd been Archer who'd been with him in their shared, tiny frat boy apartment the night the cops had come to the door—not because Finn had been caught doing something stupid, but because his dad had just died.

Next to Archer sat Willa. Bossy as hell, nosy as hell, and loyal as hell, Willa would give a perfect stranger the shirt off her back if Finn and Archer didn't watch her like a hawk.

Spencer was there too. The mechanical engineer didn't say much, but when he did it was often so profound the rest of them just stared at him in shock and awe. Quiet, although not particularly shy or introverted, he'd recently sold his start-up for an undisclosed sum and hadn't decided on his next step. All Finn knew was that he was clearly unhappy.

Since pushing Spence was like trying to push a twenty-foot-wide concrete wall over, they'd all unanimously decided to let it be for now. Finn knew he'd talk about it when he was good and ready and nothing could rush that. For now he seemed . . . well, if not miserable, at least better, and was currently stealing French fries on the sly from Elle's basket.

Elle was new to the group but had fit right in with the exception of Archer. Finn didn't know what was up, but the two of them studiously avoided each other whenever possible. Everyone but Elle was in shorts and tees, looking bedraggled, a little sweaty and a whole lot dusty. Elle hadn't gone on the hike. She didn't do dirt. Or excursion. Dressed to kill as always, she wore a royal blue sleeveless sheath and coolly slapped Spence's hand away from her fries.

He grinned in apology but the minute Elle's back was turned, he stole another. Only Spence could do that and live.

Haley was there too, an intern at the optometrist's shop on the ground floor of the building. But Finn's gaze went directly to the last person sitting there, just as dusty as everyone but Elle.

Pru.

"Got suckered into the hike up Twin Peaks, huh?" he asked.

She smiled the smile of someone who was very proud of herself.

He grinned back. "Number four?" he guessed.

Her smile widened. "Three."

Whoa. Finn turned to Spence, who shrugged. "On the way there, I calculated out who and what everyone's going to pick in the draft," Spence said. "All I needed was the fourth pick, so I didn't see any reason to go crazy out there."

"You did that on the way there," Finn repeated, a little awed.

"Actually, I worked it out in my head before we even left."

Elle looked at Spence. "Remember when you told me to tell you when you were acting like that kid that no one would want to be friends with?"

Spence just grinned and stole another fry.

"She looks so delicate," Willa said and jabbed a thumb in Pru's direction. "Totally thought I could take her." She shook her head. "She wiped the trail with me."

"You do a lot of hiking?" Finn asked Pru.

"Not lately." She lifted a shoulder and sipped at what looked like a plain soda. "I haven't had time," she said demurely. "I'm out of shape."

Archer laughed. "Don't believe that for a second. This girl can move when she's got inspiration, and apparently she takes her fantasy football seriously. You should've seen those long legs in action."

Oh, Finn had. In his sexual fantasies.

"Why didn't you go?" she asked. "Didn't want to show off *your* long legs?"

Archer choked on beer. "I like her," he announced.

Finn didn't take his eyes off Pru. Hers were lit with amusement, which went well with the streak of dirt across her jaw. There was another over her torso, specifically her left breast. "I have great legs," he said.

"Uh huh."

"I do. Tell her," he said to the room.

Spence shrugged noncommittally. "Archer's are better."

Archer grinned. "Damn straight."

Elle let out a rare smile. "I like her too," she said to Archer.

"It's not about my legs," Finn said to Pru. Shit, and now he sounded defensive.

"Maybe you should prove it," she said casually and Archer choked again.

Willa bounced up and down in her seat, clapping. "It's like Christmas!"

"We're keeping her, right?" Spence asked.

"Hey," Sean said, bringing them another pitcher of beer. "If a lady wanted to see my legs, I'd show her. Just sayin'."

Asshole.

Pru turned expectantly back to Finn and he had to laugh. "What, right here?" he asked in disbelief.

"Why not?" she asked.

"Because . . ." Jesus. How had he lost control of this conversation? "I am not dropping trou right here," he said stiffly, and great, because now he sounded like he had a stick up his ass.

"Maybe he hasn't shaved," Willa said. "That'd keep me from dropping trou. I only shaved from my knees down. My thighs are as hairy as a lumberjack's chest, which is why I'm wearing capris and not short shorts. You are all welcome."

Elle nodded like this made perfect sense.

"Gonna have to prove it to the lady," Archer said ever so helpfully to Finn. "Drop 'em."

He was an asshole too.

Willa grinned and tapped her hands on the bar in rhythm and began to chant. "Drop 'em, drop 'em . . ."

The others joined in. Shit. They were *all* assholes.

Pru leaned in over the bar and gave him a come here gesture. He shifted close and met her halfway, stilling when she put her mouth to his ear.

"No one but me can see behind the bar," she whispered.

It took a moment to compute her words because at first all he could concentrate on was the feel of her lips on his ear. When she exhaled, her warm breath caressed his skin and he had to remind himself that he was in a crowded bar, surrounded by his idiot friends.

She smiled enticingly.

"Not happening," he said on a laugh. At least not here, with an audience. He wondered if she'd still be playing with him if they were alone in his bed. Or if that was too far away, his office . . .

Her hair fell into his face and a stubborn silky strand stuck to the stubble on his jaw. He didn't care. She might be streaked with dirt but she smelled amazing.

He was mid-sniff when she whispered, "Fun Whisperer, remember?"

"Maybe I'm commando," he whispered back and was gratified by her quick intake of breath and the darkening of her eyes. "Either way," he said, "I don't drop trou on the first date."

She bit her lower lip and let her gaze drop over him, probably trying to figure out if he was telling the truth about going commando.

Then her phone buzzed and she flashed him a grin as she stepped aside to answer it.

Sean came close and nudged him as they both watched Pru talk into her cell. "That's the woman for you."

"No," Finn said. "She's not. You know I don't date women in the building."

"Which would be a great rule if you ever left the building."

"I leave the building." To get to and from work, but

still. He resented the implication that his life wasn't enough as is.

Elle shoved her glass under Sean's nose. She didn't like beer on tap. "Earn your keep, bar wench."

Sean rolled his eyes but took the glass. "What do you want, your highness? Something pink with an umbrella in it, I suppose?"

"Do I look like a college coed to you?" she asked. "I'll take a martini."

He grinned and shifted away to make it for her.

Willa came around to Finn's side of the bar. She was tiny, barely came up to his shoulder, but she was like a mother cat when riled. He knew better than to go toe to toe with her, especially when she was giving him The Look. But he wasn't in the mood. "No," he said.

"You don't even know what I'm going to say."

"You're going to say I'm being a stupid guy," Finn said. "But newsflash, I am a guy and sometimes we're stupid. Deal with it."

"I wasn't going to say that." She paused when he slid her a look and she sighed. "Okay, fine, I was. But you *are* being stupid."

"Shock," he said.

She put her hand on his arm until he blew out a breath and looked at her again.

"I'm worried about you," she said softly. "You've got yourself on lockdown. I know this place has taken off and you're so busy, but it's like Sean is the one having all the fun with it and you're just . . . letting him. What about you, Finn? When is it going to be about you?"

He turned and watched Sean work his magic charisma on a gaggle of young twenties at the other end of the bar. He'd never gotten to be just a kid. The least Finn could do was let him be twenty-two. "He deserves it."

"And you don't? You're working like crazy and just going through the motions."

True or not, he didn't want to hear it. "You want anything to eat?"

She sighed, getting the message, which was part of why he loved her so much. "No, thanks, I've gotta go. Gotta get up early tomorrow for a wedding. I've got a cake to make and flowers to arrange."

He found a smile. "Another dog wedding?"

In on the joke that she made more money off dog tiaras and elaborate animal weddings than grooming and pet supplies, she laughed. "Parrots."

Finn laughed too and gave her a hug goodnight. As she walked away, his gaze automatically searched for Pru. The gang was all moving to the back room and she was with them, heading for either the pool table or the dartboards. It was tourney night.

He took some orders and flagged down Sean to pass them off. "Fill these for Workaholic, Playboy, and Desperado at your four, five, and six o'clock." He turned and caught Pru staring at him. She'd come back for the bag of leftover chicken wings she'd forgotten.

"Workaholic, Playboy, and Desperado?" she asked.

"Customers," Sean explained.

"We all have nicknames?" she asked.

"No," Finn said.

"Yes," Sean said. And then the helpful bastard pointed out some more in the place. "Klutz, Pee-Dub, and Woodie."

"Pee-Dub?"

Sean grinned. "He's an old friend with a very new wife. He's Pussy-Whipped. PW, which cuts down to Pee-Dub. Get it?"

"I'm sorry to say I do," she said, laughing. "And Woodie?"

Sean smiled. "Would you like me to explain that one to you?"

Finn reached out, put his hand over Sean's face and shoved.

"Hey, she asked," he said, voice muffled.

"What's my nickname?" Pru asked.

Shit. This wasn't going to end well. "Not everyone has a nickname," he said.

She narrowed her eyes. "Spill it, Grandpa."

Sean snorted.

Even Finn had to laugh. "Well it *should* be Pushy."

"Uh huh," she said. "Tell me something I don't know. Come on, what do you two call me?"

"Your first day in the building, it was Daisy," Sean told her. "Because you were holding flowers."

"From my boss for my new place," she said. "What changed?"

"We saw you feeding our homeless guy, so we switched it to Sucker."

"Hey," she said, hands on hips. "He's a nice guy and he was hungry."

"He's hungry because he makes pot brownies," Finn said. "They give him the munchies. And just so you know, we all feed him too. He's got food, Pru. He's just got a good eye for the sweet cuties who are also suckers."

She blushed and he laughed.

"So I'm Sucker? Really?"

"Nope," Sean said. "You're Trouble with a capital T."

Finn shook his head at him. "Don't you have some orders to fill?"

Sean laughed and walked off, leaving him with Pru.

"I'm not a *lot* of trouble," she said.

His gaze slid to her mouth. "You sure about that?"

"Completely." And then she flashed him an indeed trouble-filled smile.

And that's when he knew. *He* was the one in trouble. Deep trouble. "What can I get you?" he asked, his voice unintentionally husky.

"I was sent over here to get a set of darts."

"You play?" he asked, digging some out of a drawer.

"No, but I'm a quick learner. I can do this."

He felt yet another laugh bubble up. "Good 'tude," he said. "Tell Spence to go easy on you, darts are his game. And don't bet against Archer. He grew up a bar rat, you can't beat him."

She bit her lip. "He said he was new at darts."

"Shit," Finn said. "He already conned you, didn't he?"

"No worries," she said. "I've got this."

He watched her go, shook his head, and then got busy making drinks because Sean was very busy flirting with Man-eater at one of the tables, even though she had already eaten him up and spit him out just last month.

When Finn looked up again after fulfilling a bunch of orders, half an hour had gone by and some serious chanting was coming out of the back room.

"Bull's-eye, bull's-eye, bull's-eye . . ."

He whistled for Sean. "Need two mojitos," he said

and dried off his hands before heading out from behind the bar.

"Hey, I'm busy," Sean complained. "Getting some digits over here. Where are you going—Hey, you can't just walk away, you—*Hell*," he muttered when Finn didn't slow.

He entered the back room hoping like hell Archer wasn't taking advantage of Pru. She had a sweet smile, and even though he knew she had a mischievous side and a unique ability to change the energy in a room for the better, she was no match against his friends.

And more had shown up, including some of Archer's coworkers, all of whom were either out of the military or ex-cops. He could see Will and Max up there, both skilled as hell in darts and women.

Shit.

Pru was at the front of the room, at the first of three dart boards. She was blindfolded, dart in hand, tongue between her teeth in concentration as Will spun her around.

Spun her around?

He had time to think *what the fuck* before Will let her go and Pru threw her dart.

And nailed Finn right in the chest.

Chapter 6

#DoNotTryThisAtHome

At the collective shocked gasp of the room, Pru ripped off her blindfold and blinked rapidly to focus her vision. And what she focused in on with horror was the dart stuck in Finn's pec, the quill still quivering from impact.

Archer and Spence had their phones out and were taking pics with big grins but Pru saw nothing funny about this. "Oh my God," she whispered as she ran to him. "*Oh my God.*" Panic blocked her throat as she gripped his arms and stared at the dart. "I hit you!"

"Bull's-eye," he said, looking down at it sticking out of his chest. "Not bad for a beginner."

He was joking. She'd hit him with a dart and he stood there joking. *Good God.* She wished for a big hole to swallow her up, but as already proven, she'd never had much luck with wishes. "I'm so sorry! Do we pull it out? Please, you've got to sit down." She was having trouble drawing air into her lungs. "You need to stay still. You could have a cracked rib or a pierced lung." Just the thought of which had her vision going cobweb-y. "Someone call 911!" she yelled.

Finn calmly pulled out the dart. "I'm fine."

But she wasn't, not even close. The tip of the dart was red. *His blood*, she thought as she felt her own drain from her face.

That's when the red stain began to spread through his shirt, blooming wide. She was living the worst scary movie she'd ever seen. "Oh, God, Finn—" She was freaking out, she could feel herself going cold with fear as she again tried to push him into a chair and put both hands over the blood spot to apply pressure at the same time.

He stood firm, not budging an inch as he captured her hands in his and bent a little to look into her eyes. "Breathe, Pru."

"But I—You—I'm so sorry," she heard herself say from what seemed like a long way off. "I wished for true love, not death, I swear!"

"Pru—"

She couldn't answer. There was a buzzing in her ears now, getting louder and louder, and then her vision faded to black.

Pru came to with voices floating around her head.

"Nice going, Finn. You finally got a good one on the line and you kill her." Archer, she thought.

"She's got a tat," someone else said—Spence?—making Pru realize her shirt had ridden up a little, exposing the compass on her hipbone, the tattoo she'd gotten after her parents' death, when she'd been missing them so much she hadn't known how to go on without them. The world had become a terrifying place, and all alone in the world she'd needed the symbol of knowing which direction to go.

"Finn's more of a piercing kind of guy," Spence said.

"I bet today he's more of a tat guy," Archer said.

"Hell, I'm sold," Spence said.

Pru shoved down her shirt and opened her eyes. She was prone on a couch with a bunch of disembodied faces hovering over her.

"She's pretty green," Spence's face said. "Think she's going to hurl?"

Willa's face was creased into a worried frown. "No, but I don't think she's moisturizing enough."

"Does she need mouth-to-mouth?" Sean.

"Out. All of you." The low but steely demand came from Finn and had all the faces vanishing.

Pru realized she was in an office. Finn's, by the look of things. There was a desk, a very comfortable couch beneath her, and on the other side of it, a large picture window that revealed a great view of the courtyard and the fountain.

She narrowed her eyes at the fountain, sending it *you're dead to me* vibes. Because really? She'd wished for love for Finn and instead she'd stabbed him with a damn dart.

Gah.

Finn was shoving people out the door. When they were gone, he leaned back against his desk to look at her, feet casually crossed, hands gripping the wood on either side of his hips. He was hot, even in a pose of subdued restraint as he watched her carefully while she sat up. "Easy, Tiger."

"What happened?" she asked. When she struggled to stand, he pushed off from the desk, coming to her.

Crouching at her side, he stopped her, setting his hands on her thighs to hold her still. "Not yet."

"How did I get here?"

"You fainted," he said.

"I most definitely did not!"

His lips twitched. "Okay, then you decided to take a nap. You weren't feeling the whole walking thing so I carried you."

She stared at him, horrified. "You carried me?"

"That bothers you more than the fainting in front of a crowded bar?" he asked. He shrugged. "Okay, sure, we can go with that. Yes, I picked you up off the floor and carried you. Not that I don't make sure the floors are clean mind you, but there's clean and then there's clean, so I brought you to my couch."

"Ohmigod," she gasped, "I hit you with a dart!"

He was still crouched at her feet. Close enough for her to push his hands from her and start tugging up his shirt, needing to see the damage. "Let me see. I'm a halfway decent medic—which I realize is hard to believe given I ended up on your floor—but I promise, I know what I'm doing." She couldn't shove his shirt up high enough. "Off," she demanded.

"Well usually I like to have a meal first," he said, "and get to know each other a little bit—"

"*Off!*"

"Okay, okay." He reached up and pulled the shirt over his head.

Pru nearly got light-headed again but this time it wasn't the blood. He had a body that . . . well, rocked hers. Sleek and hard-looking, he had broad shoulders, ripped abs, sinewy pecs—one of which had a hole in it an inch from his right nipple. A fact she knew because she'd leaned in so close her nose nearly brushed his skin.

"Feel free to kiss it better," he said.

"I'm checking to see if you're going to need a tetanus shot!" But good Lord, she'd done this to him. She'd put a hole in his perfect, delectable bod—

"Are you going to pass out again?" he asked.

"No!" Hopefully. But to be sure, she sat back. Just for a second she promised herself, and only because replaying the night's events in her mind was making her sweat. "First-aid kit," she said a little weakly.

"What do you need?" he asked, voice deep with concern.

"Not for me, for you!" She sat up again. "You could get an infection, we need a first-aid kit!"

He blew out a sigh, like maybe she was being a colossal pain in his ass. But he rose to his feet and walked toward a door behind his desk. The problem was now she could see his back, an acre of smooth, sleek skin, rippling muscles . . .

He vanished into a bathroom and came back with a first-aid kit, and then sat at her side on the couch. Before he could open it up, she took it from his hands and rummaged through. Finding what she needed, she poured some antiseptic onto a cotton pad and pressed it against the wound.

He sucked in a breath and she looked up at him.

"Getting hit with a dart didn't make you blink an eye," she said. "Neither did ripping it out like a He-man. But this hurts?"

"It's cold."

This got a low laugh out of her. She was trying not to notice that her fingers were pressed up against his warm skin as she held the cotton in place, or that her other hand had come up to grip his bicep. Or that his nipples had hardened.

Or that she was staring at his body, her eyes feeling like a kid in a candy shop, not quite knowing where to land. Those pecs. That washboard set of abs. The narrow happy trail that vanished into the waistband of his jeans, presumably leading straight to his—

"I think I'm all disinfected now," he said, sounding amused.

With a jerky nod, she set the cotton pad aside and reached for a Band-Aid. But her hands were shaking and she couldn't open the damn thing.

His fingers gently took it from hers. Quickly and efficiently, he opened it and put it on himself. "All better," he said and quirked a brow. "Unless . . ."

"Unless what?"

"You changed your mind about kissing it all better?"

That she wanted to do just that kept her from rolling her eyes again.

He laughed softly, which she assumed was because the bastard knew exactly what he did to her.

"So," he said. "You were right. You really do bring the fun. What's next?"

"Hitting you over your thick head with this first-aid kit," she said, closing the thing up.

"You're violent." He grinned at her. "I like it."

"You have a very odd sense of humor." She stood on legs that were still a little wobbly. "I really am sorry, Finn."

"No worries. I've had worse done to me."

"Like?"

"Well . . ." He appeared to give this some thought. "A woman once chucked a beer bottle at my face." He pointed to a scar above his right eyebrow. "Luckily I ducked."

She gaped at him. "Seriously?"

He shrugged. "She thought I was Sean."

"Well that explains it," she said and had the pleasure of making him laugh.

His laugh did things to her. So did the fact that he was still shirtless. "Do you have another shirt?" she asked.

"One without a hole in it, you mean?"

She groaned. "Yes! And without blood all over it." She bent and scooped up his fallen shirt. "I'm going to buy you a new one—" she started as she rose back up and . . . bumped into him.

And his bare chest.

"Stop," he said kindly but firmly as his hands came up to her shoulders. "I'm not all that hurt and you've already apologized. It wasn't even your fault. My idiot brother should never have allowed blindfolded darts. If our insurance company got a whiff of that, we'd be dumped."

But Pru had a long habit of taking on the blame. It was what she did, and she did it well. Besides, in this case, her guilt came from something else, something much, much worse than stabbing him with a dart and she didn't know how to handle it. Especially now that they were standing toe to toe with his hands on her.

Tell him, a voice deep inside her said.

But she was having trouble focusing. All she could think about was pressing her mouth to the Band-Aid. Above the Band-Aid. Below the Band-Aid. Wayyyyy below the Band-Aid . . .

She didn't understand it. He wasn't even her usual type. Okay, so she wasn't sure what her type was exactly. She hadn't been around the block all that many times but she'd always figured she'd know it when she saw it.

But she was having the terrible, no-good, frightening feeling that she'd seen it in the impenetrable, unshakeable, unflappable, decidedly sexy Finn O'Riley.

Which of course made everything, *everything*, far worse so she closed her eyes. "Oh God. I could have killed you."

Just as her parents had killed his dad . . .

And at *that* thought, the one she'd been trying like hell to keep at bay, the horror of it all reached up and choked her, making it impossible to breathe, impossible to do anything but panic.

"Hey. *Hey*," Finn said with devastating gentleness as he maneuvered her back to sitting on the couch. "It's all okay, Pru."

She could only shake her head and try to pull free. She didn't deserve his sympathy, didn't deserve—

"Pru. Babe, you've got to breathe for me."

She sucked in some air.

"Good," he said firmly. "Again."

She drew in another breath and the spots once again dancing in front of her eyes began to fade away, leaving her view of Finn, on his knees before her, steady as a rock. "I'm okay now," she said. And to prove it she stood on her own. To gain some desperately needed space, she walked away from him and walked around his office.

His big wood desk wasn't messy but wasn't exactly neat either, a wall lined with shelves on which sat everything from a crate of pub giveaways like beer cozies and mouse pads, to a big ball of Christmas lights.

Pictures covering one wall. His brother. His friends. A group shot of them on the roof of the building, where people went for star gazing, hot summer night picnicking, or just to be alone on top of the world.

There were a few pics of Finn too, although not many, she saw as she moved slowly along the wall, realizing the pics got progressively older.

There were several from many years ago. Finn in a high school baseball uniform. And then a college uniform. He'd played ball for a scholarship and had been destined for the pros—until he'd quit school abruptly at age twenty-one when he'd had to give everything up to care for his younger brother after the death of his father.

She sucked in a breath and kept looking at the pictures. There was one of Finn and a group of guys wearing no shirts and backpacks standing on a mountaintop, and if she wasn't mistaken, one of them was Archer.

Another of Finn sitting in a souped-up classic-looking Chevelle next to a GTO, a pretty girl standing between the cars waving a flag. Clearly a pre-street-race photo.

Once upon a time, he'd indeed been wild and adventurous. And she knew exactly what had changed him. The question was, could she really help bring some of that back to him, something she wanted, *needed*, to do with all her heart.

Chapter 7

#WafflesAreAlwaysTheAnswer

Finn watched Pru's shoulders tense as she looked at the pictures on the walls, and wished she'd turn his way so he could see her face. But she kept staring at the evidence of his life as if it was of the utmost importance to her. "You okay?" he asked.

She shook her head. Whether in answer to the question or because whatever was on her mind weighed too heavily to express, he had no idea. Turning her to him, he watched as her long lashes swept upward, her eyes pummeling him with a one-two gut punch.

And going off the pulse racing at the base of her throat, she was just as affected by him, which was flattering as hell but right now he was more concerned about the shadows clouding her eyes. "You're worried about something," he said.

She bit her lower lip.

"Let me guess. You forgot to put the plug in your boat and it might sink before your next shift."

As he'd intended, her mouth curved. "I never forget the plug."

"Okay . . . so you're worried you've maimed me for life and I'll have to give up my lucrative bartending career."

Her smile faded. "You joke," she said, "but I *could* have maimed you if I'd thrown higher."

"Or lower," he said and shuddered at the thought.

She closed her eyes and turned away again. "I'm really so very sorry, Finn."

"Pru, look at me."

She slowly turned to face him. There were secrets in her eyes that had nothing to do with the dart thing, and a hollowness as well, one that moved him because he recognized it. He'd seen it in the reflection of his own mirror. Moving in close, he reached for her hand, loosely entangling their fingers. He told himself it was so that he could catch her again if she went down but he knew the truth. He just wanted to touch her.

"I'm sure you have to get back out there—" she started.

"In a minute." He tugged her in a little so that they were toe to toe now. And thanks to her kickass boots, they were also nearly mouth to mouth. "What's going on, Pru?" he asked, holding her gaze.

She opened her mouth but then hesitated. And when she spoke, he knew she'd changed whatever she'd been about to say. "Looks like your life has changed a lot," she said, gesturing to the pictures that Sean had printed from various sources, stuffed into frames, and put out on the shelf in chronological order the day after they'd opened the pub.

When Finn had asked him what the hell, Sean had simply said "not everyone is as unsentimental as you. Just shut up and enjoy them—and you're welcome."

Over the past year new pictures just showed up. More of Sean's doing. Finn got it. Sean felt guilty for all Finn had given up to raise him, but Finn didn't want him to feel guilty. He wanted him to take life more seriously.

"It's changed some," he allowed cautiously to Pru. He didn't know how they'd gotten here, on this subject. A few minutes ago she'd been all sweetly, adorably worried about him, wanting to play doctor.

And he'd been game.

"It looks like it's changed more than some," she said. "The fun pics stopped."

"Once I bought the pub, yeah," he said.

He'd had different plans for himself. Without a maternal influence, and their dad either at work or mean as a skunk, he and Sean had been left to their own devices. A lot. Finn had used those years to grow up as fast and feral and wild as he could. Yeah, he'd been an ace athlete, but he'd also been a punk-ass idiot. He'd skated through on grades, which luckily had come easy for him so his coaches had been willing to put up with his crazy ass to have him on the team. His big plan had been to get drafted into the big leagues, tell his dad to go fuck himself, and retire with a big fat bank account.

It hadn't exactly gone down like that. Instead, his dad had gotten himself killed in a car accident that had nothing to do with his own road rage—he'd been hit by a drunk driver.

Barely twenty-one, Finn might've kept to his plan but Sean had been only fourteen. The kid would've been dumped into the system if Finn hadn't put a lock down on his wild side, grown up, and put them both on the straight and narrow.

It'd been the hardest thing he'd ever done, and there'd been lots of days he wasn't entirely sure he'd succeeded.

"Well I probably should . . ." Pru trailed off, gesturing vaguely to the door. But she didn't go. Instead she glanced at his mouth.

As far as signs went, it was a good one. She was thinking of his mouth on hers. Which seemed only fair since he'd given a lot of thought to the same thing.

"'Night," she whispered.

"Night," he whispered back.

And yet neither of them moved.

She was still staring at his mouth, and chewing on her lower lip while she was at it. He wanted to lean in and take over, nibbling first one corner of her mouth and then the other, and then maybe he'd take a nibble of her plump lower lip too, before soothing it with his tongue. Then he'd work his way down her body the same to every last square inch of her—

"Right?" she asked.

He blinked. So busy thinking about what he wanted to do to her, about the sounds she might make as he worked her over with his tongue, he'd not heard a word she'd said. "Right."

She nodded and . . . walked away.

Wait—what the hell? He grabbed her hand and just barely stopped her. "Where are you going?"

"I just said I really should go and you said right."

Not about to admit he hadn't listened to a word she'd said because he'd been too busy mentally fucking her, he just held onto her hand. "But you're the Fun Whisperer. You have to stay and save me, otherwise I'll go back to work."

"A real wild man," she said with a smile.

He gave another tug on her hand. She was already right there but she shifted in closer, right up against him.

She sighed, as if the feel of him was all she'd wanted, and then she froze. Her eyes were wide and just a little bit anxious now as she stared into his. "Uh oh."

Granted, it'd been awhile but that wasn't the usual reaction he got when he pulled a woman in close. "Problem?"

"No." She bit her lower lip. "Maybe."

"Tell me."

She hesitated and then said, "My mom taught me to show not tell." And then her hands went to his chest, one of them right over the Band-Aid, which she touched gently, running her fingers over it as if she wished she could take away the pain. "I just need to see something . . ."

"What?"

Her gaze dropped to his mouth and again she hesitated.

Tenderness mixed with his sudden pervasive hunger and need, a dizzying combination for a guy who prided himself on not feeling much. "Pru—"

"Shh a second," she whispered. And then closing the gap, she brushed her lips over his.

At the connection, he groaned, loving the way her hands tightened on him. She murmured his name, a soft plea and yet somehow also a demand, and he wanted to both smile and tug her down to the couch. Trying to cool his jets, trying to let her stay in charge, he attempted to hold back, but she let out this breathy little whimper like he was the best thing she'd ever tasted. Threading his fingers through her hair, he took over the kiss, slow, deeper now, until she let out another of those delicious little whimpers and practically climbed his body.

Yeah, she liked that, a whole hell of a lot, and he closed his arms hard around her, lifting her up against him for more. He'd known they had something but this . . . this rocked his world. Hers too because they both melted into it, tongues sliding, lips melding, bodies arching into each other in a slow rhythm.

The door to the office suddenly opened and Sean stood there, face tilted down to his iPad. "We've gotta problem with inventory—" he said, still reading. "Where the hell's the—*Oh*," he said, finally looking up. "Shit. Now I owe Spence twenty bucks."

Finn resisted smashing in his brother's smug smile, barely, mostly because he didn't want to take his eyes off Pru who'd brought her fingers up to her still wet lips, looking more than a little dazed.

Join my club, babe . . .

"Sorry if I interrupted the sexy times," Sean said, not looking sorry at all. He smiled at Pru. "Hey, Trouble."

"Hey," she said, blushing. "I've got to go." She turned in a slow circle, clearly looking for her purse, finding it where he'd dropped it on the couch. She slung it over her shoulder and without actually making eye contact with either of them, said a quick "'night" and headed to the door.

Finn caught her, brushing up against her back. "Let me walk you home—"

"I live only two flights up," she said, not looking at him. "Not necessary."

Right. But it was more than her safety he'd been worried about. She'd been with him during that kiss, very with him, but now there was a distance again and he wanted to breach it.

"If there's any complications from where I tried to kill you," she said to the door. "You need to—"

"I won't. I'm fine." He let his mouth brush her ear as he spoke and he could feel the shiver wrack her body.

"Okay then," she said shakily, and was gone.

Finn turned to Sean.

Who was grinning. "Look at you with all the moves. They grow up so fast."

"You ever hear of a thing called knocking?" Finn asked.

Sean shrugged. "Where's the fun in that?"

"Is everything about fun?"

"Yes!" Sean said, tossing up his hands. "Now you're getting it!"

Finn turned away and eyed the spot between the couch and the desk where he'd just about dragged Pru down to the floor and ended his long dry spell by sinking into her warm, sweet body. "What's the problem with the inventory?"

"It's down, the whole system's down."

Finn snatched the iPad and swiped the screen to access the data. "And you're just now telling me? Are you kidding me?"

"Yes," Sean said.

Finn lifted his head and stared at Sean. "What?"

His brother flashed a grin. "Yes I'm kidding. Funning around. Fucking with your head. I came back here because Archer and Spence sent me in here to spy on you and Trouble. We bet twenty bucks. They thought you might be making a rare move."

Jesus.

"Not me though," Sean said. "I figured you're so rusty you'd need some pointers. And here's your first one—lock the door, man. *Always.*"

Finn headed toward him but Sean danced away with a grin. "Oh and pointer number two—you got your shirt off and that's a good start, but it's the pants that are the important part." He was chortling, having a great ol' time.

Finn smiled at him, shoved him out the door, and slammed it on his smug-ass face.

Then he hit the lock.

"*Now* you lock it?" Sean asked through the wood, rattling the handle. "Hey. You do know I nap on that couch. Tell me you didn't do it on the couch."

Finn turned away and headed to his desk.

Sean pounded on the door once. "You didn't, right?"

Finn put on his earphones and cranked some music

on his phone. And then headed to his desk to wade through the mountain of work waiting on him.

Pru got to work extra early the next morning. It was month end and though Jake did his best to see that his boat captains didn't drown in paperwork, some of it was unavoidable. She wanted to catch up but she hadn't slept well and her eyes kept crossing. Finally, she caved and set her head down on her desk.

Just for a minute, she told herself . . .

Finn pressed his body to hers and she moaned as his hands stroked up her sides, his thumbs brushing over her nipples. She arched into him and he kissed her like it was an art form, like he had nothing more important to do than arouse her and he had all the time in the world to do it. She clutched at him and he ground his lower body into her, letting her feel how aggressively hard he was. Aching for him, she tangled her hands in his hair, kissing him deeper until he groaned into her mouth. "Please," she begged.

"Hell yeah, I'll please." His voice was sexy rough and she held tight, anchoring her hips against his as he slid a hand down her belly and into her panties.

He groaned again and she knew why. She was wet and on fire for him.

Breaking the kiss, he nibbled her ear. "Pru," he said in that deliciously gruff tone. "You have to wake up."

She jerked awake and sat straight up, realizing she'd fallen asleep at her desk doing the dreaded paperwork. "Wha . . . ?" she managed.

Finn was crouched at her side, fully dressed, and breathing a little ragged.

And that's when she realized something else—her hand was stroking what felt like a very impressive erection behind his jeans.

She snatched it back like she'd been burned and he dropped his head and gave a rough laugh. Ignoring how his laugh did funny things to her belly and parts south, she cleared her throat. "Sorry."

"Don't be. Best greeting ever."

"Okay, that was your fault," she muttered, her face heating. "That's what you get for waking me from a deep sleep."

"I'm not sure if you could call that sleep." He lifted his head. He was smiling, the smug jerk. "Jake let me in, pointed me in the direction of your office, which was unlocked. You were moaning and sweaty. I moved in to see if you were okay and you molested me."

She groaned and thunked her head to her desk a couple of times. "Why are you here?" she moaned. "Other than to rudely wake me up from the only action I've had in far too long?"

He laughed. *Laughed*. She gave some thought to killing him but then she realized he was holding a brown bag from which came the most delicious scent.

"Stopped by the waffle shop for breakfast," he said and lifted the bag. "Thought of you."

She went still. "Chocolate and raspberry syrup?" she asked hopefully, willing to let bygones be bygones for a sugar and carb load.

"Of course."

She didn't ask how he knew her kryptonite. Everyone she knew worshipped at the magical griddle inside the magical food cart outside their building that a woman named Rayna ran. Pru snatched the bag from Finn and decided to forgive him. "Do not think that this means we will be reenacting what I was dreaming about."

"Absolutely not," he said.

She paused, her gut sinking to her toes unexpectedly. "Because you don't think of me that way?"

He paused as if carefully considering his next words, and she braced herself. She was good at rejection, real good, she reminded herself.

Apparently deciding against speaking at all, Finn rose to his full height. Since she was still in her chair, this put her face right about level with the part of his anatomy she'd had a grip on only a moment before.

He was still hard.

"Does this look like disinterest to you?"

She swallowed hard. "No."

"Any further questions?"

"Nope," she managed. "No further questions."

Nodding, he leaned over her and brushed his mouth across hers. "Ball's in your court," he said and then he was gone.

Chapter 8

#AllTheCoolKidsAreDoingIt

Pru got up the next morning at the usual time even though it was her day off. She pulled on her tank top and yoga capris and shoved her feet into her running shoes. "I hate running," she said to the room.

The comforter on her bed shifted slightly and she pulled it back to reveal Thor, eyes closed.

"I know you're faking," she said.

His eyes squeezed tight.

"Sorry, buddy, you're coming with me. I ate that entire *huge* waffle Finn brought me yesterday. And I realize you don't care if you can fit into a pair of skinny jeans without your belly rolling over the waistband, and you don't even know who Finn is, but trust me, you wouldn't have been able to resist him or the waffle either."

Thor didn't budge.

"A doggie biscuit," she said cajolingly. "If you get up right now I'll give you a doggie biscuit."

Nothing. This was probably because he knew as well as she did that she was out of doggie biscuits. She would have just left him home alone but the last time she'd done that, he'd pooped in her favorite boots—which had most definitely taken some time and effort on his part.

"Fine." She tossed up her hands. "I'll buy biscuits today, okay? And we'll go see Jake too."

At the name, Thor perked up. He knew that Jake kept dog cookies in his desk so he lifted his head, panting happily, one ear up and the other flopped over and into his eye.

She had to smile. "You're the cutest boot pooper I've ever seen. Now let's hit it. We're going to run first if it kills us."

Thor hefted out a sigh that was bigger than he was but got up. She clipped his Big Dog leash on him, and off they went.

They ran through Fort Mason, along the trail above the water. Not that they could see the water today. The early morning fog had slid in so that Pru felt like she had a huge ball of cotton around her head. They came out at the eastern waterfront of the Port of San Francisco, constructed on top of an engineered seawall on reclaimed land that gave one of the most gorgeous views of the bay.

It was here that Thor refused to go another step. He sat and then plopped over and lay right in front of her feet.

A guy running the opposite way stopped short. "Did you just kill your dog?"

"No, he doesn't like to run," she said.

Clearly not believing her, he started to bend down to Thor, who suddenly found a reserve of energy—or at least enough to lift his head and bare his teeth at the strange man who'd dared to get too close.

The guy jumped back, tripped over his own feet, and fell on his ass.

"Oh my God. Are you all right?" she asked.

He leapt back up, shot her a dirty look, and ran off.

"Sorry," she called after him and then glared down at Thor. "You do know that one of these days some-one's going to call animal control on me and get you taken away, right?"

He closed his eyes.

"Come on, get up." She nudged him with her foot. "We've got a little bit more calorie annihilating to do."

Thor didn't budge an inch except to give *her* the low growl now.

"You know what? Fine. We'll risk not fitting into our bathing suits. I don't like swimming anyway," she said, happy enough for the excuse to stop. They walked the rest of the way to the Aquatic Park Pier, which curved out into the bay, giving the illusion of standing out on the water.

A wind kicked up and she was glad to not be out on the water. "Going to be choppy," she said. Which meant at least one person per tour would get seasick. Not that it was her problem. "No throw-up on my cal-endar today."

Thor, comfy in her lap, licked her chin. He didn't mind throw-up. Or poo. The grosser the better in his opinion. Setting the dog down, she craned her neck and took in the sight of Ghirardelli Square behind them.

It wasn't out of her way to walk over there, but if she did she'd buy chocolate and then she'd have to run tomorrow too. She was debating that when Thor was approached by a pigeon who was nearly bigger than he was.

Thor went utterly still, not moving a single muscle, the whites of his eyes showing.

The pigeon stopped, cocked its head, and then made a faux lunge at Thor.

Thor turned tail and ran behind Pru's legs.

"Hey," she said to the pigeon. "Don't be a bully."

The pigeon gave her a one-eyed stare and waddled off.

Pru scooped up Thor. "I need to get you glasses because you just frightened a full-grown man and then cowered from a bird."

Thor blinked his big eyes at her. "Wuff."

At the sound, the pigeon stopped and turned back. In her arms, all tough guy now, Thor growled.

Pru laughed. "I'm setting you down now, Mr. Badass. We're going to run into work real quick to pick up another box of my stuff—"

Thor cuddled into her, setting his head on her shoulder, giving her the big puppy eyes.

"Oh no you don't with that look," she said. "I'm not carrying you all the way there."

He licked her chin again.

She totally carried him all the way there.

"Jake!" she yelled as she and Thor entered the warehouse on Pier 39 from which SF Bay Tours was run. "Jake?"

Nothing. Besides being her boss, Jake was her

closest friend, and for one week awhile back, he'd also been her lover. They hadn't revisited that for many reasons, not the least of which was because Pru had a little problem. She tended to fall for the guys she slept with.

All two of them.

The first one, Paul, had been her boyfriend for two whole weeks when her parents had died. And since she'd fallen apart and he'd been eighteen and not equipped to deal with that, he'd bailed. Understandable.

Jake had been next. He'd loved her, still did in fact, but he wasn't, and never would be, *in* love with her. And the truth was, she hadn't fallen in love with him either. She actually wasn't sure she was made for that kind of love, receiving or giving. She wanted to be. She really did. But wanting and doing had proven to be two entirely different beasts. "*Jake!*"

"Don't need to yell, woman, I'm not deaf."

With a gasp, she whirled around and found him right there. She hadn't heard him come up behind her, but then again, she never did.

Jake had been in Special Forces, which had involved something with deep-sea diving and a whole lot of danger, and in spite of it nearly killing him, he hadn't lost much of his edge. He hadn't smiled when she'd nearly jumped out of her skin but he'd thought about it because his eyes were amused.

Thor was not. When Pru had jerked, he'd gone off, barking at a pitch that rivaled banshees in heat. "Thor, hush!" she said and turned to Jake, hand to her heart. "Seriously, you take five years off my life every time you do that. And you gave Thor epilepsy."

Jake didn't apologize, he never did. The man was a

complete tyrant. But a softie tyrant, who held out his arms for Thor.

The poor dog was still barking like he couldn't stop himself, eyes wide.

"You're such a pussy," Jake told him.

"Excuse me," Pru said. "You know he can't see very well and you scared him half to death. And hello, he's a *dude*. Which means you two share the same plumbing. So he's not a pussy, he's a big, *male* baby."

"He doesn't have *my* plumbing, chica," Jake said. "I might not have my legs but at least I still have my balls." And with that, he pushed off on his wheelchair, coming closer as he pulled something from his pocket.

A dog cookie.

He held it up for the gone-gonzo dog to see and Thor stopped barking and leapt to him without looking back.

Jake whirled his chair around, and man plus dog took off.

Pru rolled her eyes and followed them past the No One But Crew Past This Door sign, down a hall, then down another to a living area. "We're not staying," Pru said. "I'm just picking up one of the last boxes of my stuff."

"If you'd just use my truck, you could move all your stuff in one fell swoop instead of in a million stages," Jake said. "And I told you I'd help."

"I don't want your help."

He let out a rare sigh and rolled around to face her. "You're still mad that I kicked you out of the nest."

"No." *Yes.*

He caught her hand when she went to walk by him, looking up at her. "You remember why, right?"

"Because your sister's getting divorced and she needs the room you'd lent me here at the warehouse," she intoned.

"And . . . ?"

"And . . ." She blew out a breath. "You're tired of me."

"No," he said gently. "We agreed that I was a crutch for you. That you needed to get out and live your life."

"We?" she asked, her voice a little brittle. Because okay, she wasn't mad at him. She was . . . hurt.

Even as she knew he was right.

They'd been friends since her nineteenth birthday, when she'd applied for a job at SF Tours. He'd just recently left the military and had been through some painful recovery time, and was angry. She'd lost her parents and was equally angry. They'd bonded over that. He sent her for Maritime training and guided her way up the ranks. She couldn't have done it without him and was grateful, but she'd outgrown needing his help on every little thing. "Look," she said. "I'm doing what we both agreed needed to be done. I moved on, I'm getting back on the horse, blah blah."

Jake's mouth smiled but it didn't reach his eyes. "It's more than getting on the damn horse. I want you to want to get back into the game of life."

She sighed. "There's a reason no one plays Life anymore, Jake, the game's stupid. Important life decisions can't be made by a spin of a damn wheel. If it was that easy, I'd spin it right now and get my parents back. I'd make it so that they didn't kill someone else's dad and put all those others in the hospital, changing and ruining people's lives forever. I'd make it so that I could go back a few spaces on the damn board and stay home that night so that no one had to go out and pick me up at a party I should never have sneaked out to in the first place." She let out a rough breath, a little surprised to find out just how much she'd been holding in. Sneaky little things, emotions.

"Pru," Jake said softly, pained.

She pulled her hand free. "No. I don't want to talk about it." She really didn't. It took a lot of time and effort to bury the feelings. Dredging them up again only drove her mad. She moved to leave but Jake wheeled around to stop her exit.

"Then how about we talk about the fact that you've now helped everyone involved that night?" he said. "You sold the Santa Cruz house you grew up in—the only home you ever knew—to be able to put college scholarships in the hands of the two boys of that woman who was hit crossing the street—even though she survived. You even became friends with them. Hell, I now employ Nick in maintenance and Tim said you were helping him find a place to live now that he's out of the dorm—"

"Okay now wait a minute," she said. "I'm not some damn martyr. I sold the house, yes, but I did it because I couldn't handle the memories. I was eighteen, Jake, it was just too much for me." She shook her head. "I didn't give all of that money away. I went to school, I had expenses, I kept what I needed—"

"—Barely. And then there was Shelby, in one of the other cars, remember her? You gave her seed money she needed after her surgery to move to New York like she always wanted."

"I gave her some help, yes," she admitted. "Did you know she still limps?"

"You're still in touch with her?" he asked in disbelief.

She huffed out a breath. "Subject change, please."

"Sure. Let's move on to the O'Riley brothers. You made sure they got your parents' life insurance money, which they presumably used for education and to start their pub. So what now, Pru? It should finally be time to leave the past in the past, but it's not, so you tell me. What's really going on here?"

Yeah, Pru. What was going on? She drew in a breath of air, willing herself not to remember—and grieve—the home she'd sold, everything she'd given up. "He's not happy," she said.

"Who's not?"

"Finn. I want him to be happy."

Jake was shaking his head. "Not your deal."

"But it feels like my deal," she said. "Everyone else is happy, even his brother, Sean. I have to try and help him." Then she told him about the wish and he stared at her like she'd lost her marbles.

"He's going to fall for you," he said. "You know that, right? You have to tell him the truth before that happens, you have to tell him who you are first."

She snorted. "He's not going to fall for me."

Jake smiled, and this time it did reach his eyes. "Believe me, chica, you flash those eyes on him, that smile, some sass . . . he's as good as flat on the ground for you. And you know how I know?"

She shook her head.

"Because I've been there, done that."

"But you didn't stay flat on the ground."

Something flashed through his eyes at that. Regret. Remorse. "That's on me, Pru, not you. And you know it."

Jake didn't do love. He'd told her that going in and he'd never faltered, which wouldn't change the fact that he intended to keep her in his life. He'd proven that by being there for her through thick and thin, and there'd been a whole lot more thin than thick. She'd been there for him as well and always would be. But there were limits now, for both of them.

"Tell me about Finn," he said.

"You already know. He runs O'Riley's. He's loyal to his brother, he's protective and good to his friends, and . . ."

"And?" Jake asked.

And he kisses like sex on a stick . . . "And he works too hard."

"And you think what?" he asked dubiously. "That you're going to change that?"

"He needs a life," she said far more defensively than she'd meant to. "He was robbed of his."

"Not your fault, Pru," Jake said with firm gentleness.

"Well I know that."

"Do you?"

"Yes!" she said, *not* gently.

"Then why are you working your way into his life?"

A most excellent question.

"You didn't work your way into the life of any of the others," he said. "You did what you could and you stayed back, letting them move on without your presence. But not here, not with Finn. Which begs the question, chica—why?"

Again, a most excellent question. But she had the answer for this one, she just didn't want to say it out loud.

Finn was different.

And he was different because she *wanted* him in her life in a way she hadn't wanted anyone for a very long time.

Maybe ever.

"You know what I think?" Jake asked.

"No, but I'm pretty sure you're going to tell me."

"I think, Smartass," he went on undeterred by her sarcasm, "that he's different because you have feelings for him."

No kidding. And she could have added that she was thrown off balance by that very thing. Confused too, because she'd never felt this way about anyone and she didn't want to hurt him. She didn't, but that left her digging a pretty damn big hole for herself. "I said I don't want to discuss this with you."

"Fine. Then discuss it with *him*."

"I will. Soon. But I can't just spit it out, it's a lot to throw at someone. It's only been a few days, I'll get there."

Jake just looked at her for a long beat. "I was at the pub last night."

She froze. "What? I didn't see you."

"I don't see how you could have, since you didn't take your eyes off Finn."

Crap.

"I saw you with him. I saw the look on your face. And I saw the look on his. People are falling, Pru. Denying it is stupid, and one thing you aren't and never have been, is stupid."

"Okay, now you're just being ridiculous." But then she remembered Finn's unexpected kiss, that amazing, heart-stopping, gut-tightening, nipples-getting-happy kiss, and folded her arms over her chest. "*Seriously* ridiculous," she added and then paused. "You really think he could fall for me?"

Jake's eyes softened. "Any guy with a lick of sense would. But chica, you've got to—"

"—tell him, yeah, yeah, I know."

"Before it goes too far," he pressed. "Before you sleep with him."

"I'm not going to—"

Jake held up his hand. "Don't say something that you're going to have to take back, Pru. I was there." He gave her a grim smile. "Don't make me prove how much I love you by going behind your back to protect you by telling him myself."

She stared at him. "You wouldn't dare."

"Try me," he said. "And since I've got you all good and pissed off at me, you might as well remember something else as well. If you sleep with him before everything's square, I'll have to kill him for taking advantage of you when you're still messed up."

"I'm not messed up—" she started and then stopped. Because she was. She was *so* messed up. "Don't even think about interfering. This is my problem to handle." And with that, she strode into what had been her old room, grabbed one of her last boxes of stuff, and turned to go.

"Pru."

She stopped but didn't turn around. Instead she looked down at the box she held. It was labeled PICTURES, and she felt her heart clutch. She'd left this one for nearly last on purpose. Everything in it meant something to her and holding it all in her arms made her heart heavier than the box itself. It was almost more than she could bear, making her wish she'd grabbed one of the other few boxes left, like the one labeled KITCHEN CRAP I PRETEND TO USE BUT DON'T.

"You know I've got your back," Jake said.

She sighed and closed her eyes. "Even if I screw it all up?"

"*Especially* if."

Chapter 9

#RealWorldProblems

In the end, Pru and Thor and Pru's big box of stuff took a cab back to the Pacific Pier building. They had to get out a block early because of traffic, which meant dragging Thor on his leash and carrying the box, which got heavier with each step.

In the courtyard she stopped by the fountain and set the box down for a minute to catch her breath.

Thor plopped down at her feet, panting like he was dying even though he'd barely had to walk at all and he certainly hadn't had to carry a heavy box.

"Hey," she said, "this adulting thing isn't for the faint of heart."

Thor gave the dog version of an eyeroll and huffed out a heavy sigh.

She took pity. "Look, I'm just trying to keep us in shape. Some of us are supposed to be in our prime."

Thor was unimpressed.

She was about to coax him up to her apartment with another bribe when her phone rang. Tim.

She'd met him and his brother Nick after the accident, in the hospital. They'd spent a few days there with their mom, who'd needed surgery to repair her badly broken leg. Michelle had been unable to work for months afterward, a huge strain on the family. They'd lost their apartment and had lived in their car until Pru had been able to sell her parents' house and help.

Michelle had easily accepted her friendship but not the money. In the end, Pru had made an anonymous donation through her attorney. All Michelle knew was that someone in the community had come up with funds to help her and her boys out.

At the time the boys had been in middle school and Pru had been so worried about them. But Nick was working for Jake now and Tim was in college studying to be an engineer.

She was so happy for them.

"Tim," she said when she answered. "Everything okay?"

"That lead you gave me on the apartment near campus, it might pan out," he said excitedly. "They're going to call you as my reference. If we get it, me and my friends will live there together."

"That would be great, Tim," she said.

"You know how hard it is to get a place here," he said. "Almost impossible."

She did know. It'd taken a hell of a long time for her to get into the Pacific Pier building.

"Anyway," he said. "Thanks for the lead. It means a

lot." He laughed a little humorlessly. "We aren't looking forward to living in our cars. Been there, done that."

"No worries," Pru said, her stomach jangling unhappily at the memory. "How's school going?"

"Hard as fuck, but I'm in it," he said. "Gotta go. Talk to you soon."

Pru disconnected and looked at Thor. "We did good. They're going to be okay," she marveled. "All of them." And then she called her contact and put in a second good word for Tim, and was assured they were first in line for the place. It warmed her from the inside out to know it.

Now you need to get okay . . .

But she was working on that. "Come on, let's go."

Thor yawned.

"You know, I could have a cat. A big one who eats little dogs for snacks."

He blinked and she sighed. "Okay, I took that too far. I'm sorry." She crouched down and hugged him in, which he graciously allowed, even giving her a sweet little lick on her cheek. "Love you too," she murmured, kissing the top of his head. "I'm not going to get a cat." She could barely afford to feed the two of them.

She'd never even meant to get a dog at all, but about a year ago, she'd been walking home late one night when she'd heard a funny rumbling sound coming from behind a dumpster. She'd stopped to investigate, but the rumbling had stopped. It was only when she'd started walking again that the rumbling came back.

Pru had walked around the dumpster. Crouching low, using the flashlight on her phone, she'd fallen back on her ass when two glowing orbs had locked in on her.

Scrambling up to run, she realized the rumbling had stopped again and she slowly turned back. Channeling her inner Super Girl, she'd moved closer and had peered down at a scrap of fur surrounding those two huge eyes.

Thor, underfed, filthy, and trembling in terror. It'd taken a bribe to get him out, and another before he'd let her pick him up. All she'd had on her was a granola bar but he'd not been picky. Or dainty. He'd nearly bitten her finger off in his haste to eat.

And Pru, who'd been known to snarl herself when hungry, had fallen in love.

Straightening now with Thor in her arms, her gaze caught on the window across the way.

Finn's office.

The pub wasn't open. The accordion doors were shut and locked, but the morning sun slanted inside. She could see Finn behind his desk, head down. He was either dead, or fast asleep.

Both she and Thor stared at him. "I know," she whispered to her dog. "He's something. But you can't get attached to him, because once I tell him everything, it's over."

Thor set his head on her shoulder. He loved her no matter how stupid she was being.

Leaving her box and Thor—his leash wrapped around a bench—to guard it, she quickly crossed the courtyard to the coffee shop.

Tina stood behind the counter. Tall, curvy, and gorgeous, she had skin the color of the mocha latte she was serving. When it was Pru's turn, Tina smiled. "Your usual?" she asked, her voice low and deep and hypnotic.

"No, this one's not for me," Pru said. "It's for a friend. Um, you don't happen to know how Finn O'Riley likes it, do you?"

Tina smiled wide. "Sugar, he likes it hot and black."

"Oh. Okay, um . . . one of those then."

Tina laughed her contagious laugh and got it ready. When she handed it over, there was a dog biscuit wrapped neatly in a napkin to go. "For Thor," she said. "And how about some advice that you didn't ask for?"

Pru bit her lower lip. Was she that obvious? "Yes, please."

"Two things. First, don't even try to speak to him before he's caffeinated. That man is hot as hell and a great guy, but he's also a bear before his coffee."

"And the second thing?"

"There's no doubt, he's a serious catch," Tina said. "But he's barricaded himself off behind work. So if you want him, you're going to have to show him what he's missing."

"I'm think I'm working on that."

Tina grinned at her. "Because you're the Fun Whisperer?"

Oh, God. "You heard that, huh?"

"Sugar, I hear everything." Tina winked at her, making Pru wonder if that meant that she'd also heard about Pru nearly killing him. Or their first kiss . . .

"Good luck," Tina said. "My money's on you."

Pru took the coffee and dog cookie and headed back through the courtyard. Finn was still asleep. She gave

Thor his treat and put her finger to her lips. "Stay," she said and stepped into the planter that lined the building.

Thor ignored her and attacked his cookie.

Pru, draped on either side by two hydrangea bushes, knocked on Finn's window.

He shot straight up, a few papers stuck to his cheek. His hair was tousled, his eyes sleepy, although they quickly sharpened in on her. His five o'clock shadow was now twelve hours past civilized. And holy cow, he was a damn fine sight.

Before she even saw him coming, he'd crossed his office and opened the window, looking far more alert upon wakening than she'd ever managed.

"What the hell are you doing?" he asked, in the sexiest morning voice she'd ever heard.

"Got you something," she said. "It's not a waffle but . . ." She lifted the coffee and added a smile, trying to not look as if she hadn't just sweat her way through the courtyard with Thor and a heavy box of painful memories—impossible since her shirt was sticking to her and so was her hair. She didn't have to look in any mirror to know that she was beet red in the face, her usual after-exercise "glow."

Finn climbed out the window with easy agility. Pru backed up a step to give him room but he kept coming, stepping right into her space, reaching for the cup like a starved man might reach for a promised meal.

Clearly the man was serious about needing coffee. She stared up at him as he took the cup and drank deeply.

She might have also drooled a little bit.

"Thanks," he said after a long moment. "Most people won't come within two miles of me before I'm caffeinated."

Not wanting to tell him that Tina had already warned her because she didn't want to admit to soaking up info on him whenever and however she could, she just smiled. "How's the hole in your chest?"

He absently reached up and rubbed a hand over his pec, a completely unconscious but very male gesture. "Think I'm going to live," he said.

She eyeballed his hair and the crease on his cheek where papers had been stuck to him. "Living the wild life, huh?"

"The wildest." He looked past her. "So who's the fat cat?"

She turned and followed his line of sight to Thor, who'd curled up in a sunspot next to her box to doze. "I'll have you know that's my fierce, very protective guard dog."

"Dog?"

"Yes!"

He scratched his jaw while eyeing Thor speculatively. "If you say so."

"He protects me," she said. "In fact, he won't let anyone get near me. And don't even think about trying to touch him, he hates men."

"Not me," Finn said. "Dogs love me."

"No, really—" she started but Finn crossed the courtyard and crouched low, holding his hand out to Thor, who had opened his eyes and was watching Finn approach.

"Careful—" Pru warned. "He's like you without

caffeine, only he's like that all the time. He might nip—"

To her utter shock, Thor actually moved toward Finn in a flutter of bravery, his little paws taking him a step closer, his tail wagging in a hopeful gesture that, as always, made Pru's heart hurt.

Then, unbelievably, Thor licked Finn's fist.

"Atta boy," Finn said approvingly in an easy voice full of warmth and affection. "She says you're a dog, what do you think?"

Thor panted happily and rolled over, exposing his very soft, slightly enlarged belly.

"What's his name?" Finn asked, head bent, loving up on her dog.

She glared at Thor. "Benedict Arnold."

Benedict Arnold ignored her completely and she sighed. "Thor."

Finn snorted. "A real killer, huh?"

"Yes, actually, he—"

And that's when Thor strained to reach up and lick Finn's chin. Pru couldn't exactly blame him, she wanted to do the same.

And then . . . her poor-sighted, man-hater of a dog climbed right into Finn's arms and melted like butter on a hot roll. Except minus the hot roll and add a hot guy.

"I can't believe it," she said to herself, watching as Thor settled against Finn's chest like he belonged there, setting his head on Finn's broad shoulder.

"You were saying?" he asked on a soft laugh.

She stared at him, a little dazzled by the laugh. And then there was that stubble and she wondered . . . if he kissed her now and then nuzzled her throat like he had the other night, would it leave a whisker burn?

She wouldn't mind that . . . "Do you have a dog?" she asked.

"No, but someday," he said, reminding her of what Willa had told her, that he wanted a house outside the city and a big dog.

"So what are you doing today?" he asked.

She pointed to the box. "Unpacking some more."

"And you say *I* need a fun whisperer," he teased.

"You were asleep at your desk," she said. "My statement stands. You most definitely need a fun whisperer."

"I'll put fun on my calendar, how's that sound?"

She laughed. "Planning the fun kinda takes the fun out of fun. And anyway, maybe it's also about adventure. Spontaneous adventure."

"I don't know," he murmured, watching her as he still stroked Thor into a pleasure coma. "I can think of a few things that if planned right, would be the epitome of fun *and* adventurous."

She lifted her gaze from her dog's contented face to Finn's and found his eyes warm and lit with something. Amusement? Challenge? "Like?"

He set Thor down, back in the sunspot, and rising to his full height, shifted toward Pru.

She backed up a step, a purely instinctual move because while her body knew how badly it wanted him, her mind was all too well aware that it was a colossally stupid move of the highest order.

He merely stepped forward again, backing her flush to the brick wall lining the courtyard.

Her breathing had gone ragged. Even more so when

he leaned into her with his hands on either side of her head. "You're a contradiction," he murmured. "A push pull."

"Maybe it's because we're oil and water," she managed.

Hands still on her, blocking her escape—not that she wanted to escape those strong arms and that talented mouth—he flashed her a hot look. "Do you want this, Pru?"

She wasn't one hundred percent certain what "this" was, but she *was* one hundred percent certain that she wanted it. And God help her, she wanted it bad, too. When she gave a jerky nod, his hand came up and cupped her jaw, his fingers sliding into her hair, his thumb slowly, lazily, rasping over her lower lip. He watched the movement with a heat that made her legs wobble.

She swallowed hard. "We're in the center of the courtyard."

"What happened to adventurous?" he murmured, his thumb making another slow, intoxicating pass over her lip.

As always, her mouth worked independently of her brain and opened so she could sink her teeth lightly into the pad of his thumb.

He hissed in a breath. The sound egged her on and she sucked his thumb between her lips.

His eyes dilated to black.

Yeah. Suddenly she was feeling very . . . adventurous. Before she could stop herself, her arms encircled his broad shoulders, her fingers sinking into his hair.

This wrenched a low, sexy "mmmm" from him like he was a big, rumbling wildcat. A big, rumbly wildcat who clearly wanted more because he drew her up against him and lowered his lips to hers.

Meeting him halfway, she went up on her tiptoes. He slid a hand up her back to palm the back of her neck, holding her right where he wanted her. Then and only then did his mouth finally cover hers, his kiss slow and sweet.

After, he pulled back and looked into her eyes, smiling at whatever he saw—probably dazed lust. He kissed her again, *not* slow and most definitely *not* sweet this time. Again he ended it too soon but when he lifted his head, the rough pad of his thumb slid back and forth over her jaw while she struggled to turn her brain back on.

"Pru."

And oh, that deliciously rough morning voice. It slid over her like the morning sun, and made her eyes drift shut.

"You take the rugrat," he said. "I'll get your box."

Her eyes flew open. He was holding Thor again. "What?"

"I'll help you upstairs," he said.

Where her bed was. Oh God, had she made her bed? Wait—*was she wearing good panties*?

She mentally shook herself because none of that mattered. You're not going there with him, remember? She couldn't, wouldn't, because she hadn't yet told him who she was. She wasn't ready to do that. Because she knew that once she did, this would be over. He wouldn't want to be friends with the woman whose family had stolen his. He wouldn't want to make her fancy virgin cocktails or pet her silly dog.

Or kiss her stupid . . .

The truth was, he was the best thing to happen to her in a damn long time. And yes, it was selfish. And wrong.

And she hated herself for it.

But she couldn't tell him, not yet. "I've got it," she said. "Really. I'm good."

She just wished she meant it.

Chapter 10

#KarmaIsABitch

It was rare for Finn to find himself on unsure ground. Typically if he needed something, he handled it himself. If he wanted something, he went after it.

He both wanted and needed Pru. That was fact. The knowledge had been sitting in the frontal lobe of his brain and in the bottom of his gut, and also definitely decidedly south of both.

It'd been like that for him since the night she'd walked into his pub dripping wet and smiled that smile at him. And then she'd nailed him with that dart and he'd kissed her, and the problem had only compounded itself.

She drove him nuts, in the very best of ways.

And now she'd brought him a coffee and he'd kissed the daylights out of her again. But this time she didn't seem to want to climb him like a tree. She wanted to escape him.

Badly too, given the sudden panic in her eyes.

It should have been his clue to back off. Walk away. But he found himself unable to do that.

"How about I just get you upstairs with your stuff," he said, going for as nonthreatening as possible. He bent to put Thor down so he could pick up the box but the dog had other ideas and clung like a monkey. He glanced down. "You sure he's a dog?"

Some of the stress left Pru at that and she laughed a little. "Yes, but whatever you do, don't tell him." She covered Thor's ears. "I think that he thinks he's a grizzly."

Finn met Thor's wary gaze. The little guy really was the most ridiculous looking thing he'd ever seen. Bedraggled, patchy, mud brown fur, he had one ear up and one ear down, a long nose, a small mouth that lifted only on one side like he was half smiling, half smirking, and the biggest, brownest eyes he'd ever seen. Hell, his ears and eyes alone were bigger than the rest of him, and the rest of him didn't weigh as much as a pair of boots. "Little Man Syndrome, huh?" he asked the dog sympathetically.

"He just likes to be carried," Pru said. "He likes to be tall. And he can see better too. Once you pick him up, he won't let you put him down."

Finn tested this theory by once again starting to bend over.

Thor growled. Laughing, Finn tightened his grip on the little guy. "Don't worry, I've got ya," he said and reached to pick up Pru's box with his other hand.

Holy shit, it weighed a ton.

"What are you doing?" Pru asked, crouching at his side. Her voice was tight again. "I said I've got it."

"Pru, it weighs a ton. How far did you carry this thing?"

"Not far," she said, tug-o-warring with him. "Let go—"

"You're as stubborn as Thor, but I'm already here," he said. "Let me help—"

"*No*." She tried to wrench the box from him, her expression more than a little desperate now, which stopped him in his tracks. Whatever it was in the damn box, she didn't want him to see it, and he immediately backed off—just as she whirled from him. She lost her grip, and the box literally fell apart, the cardboard bottom giving way, the contents hitting the ground.

"Oh no," she breathed and hit her knees on the ground in front of a few old, beat-up photo albums, a few cheap plastic picture frames, and a glass one, which had shattered into a thousand pieces. "It broke," she whispered.

There was something in her voice, something as fragile as the now broken glass frame shattered in shards and pieces at their feet, and it made Finn's chest hurt. Even more so when he saw the picture free of its frame. A little girl standing between two adults, each holding one of her hands.

Pru, he thought, looking into those brown eyes. Pru . . . and her parents?

Her posture said it all as she reached right into the shards of glass for the picture, carefully brushing it clean to hug it against her chest like it meant the entire world to her.

Fuck. "Pru, here, let me—"

"No, it's fine. I'm fine," she protested, pushing his

hands away when he began to gather up the photo albums. "I told you I've got this!"

Thor, soaking up Pru's anxiety, lifted his head and began to howl.

Pru looked close to tears.

Eddie, a.k.a. Old Guy, came out of the alley, presumably to help, took one look at the mess that Finn had found himself in, and did an about-face.

Finn gently squeezed Thor to him. "Quiet," he said in a firm voice.

Thor went quiet.

Pru sucked in a breath, looking surprised right out of her impending tears, thank God. "Stop," he said as she reached into the glass for another picture with absolutely no regard for her own safety. Unable to put Thor down and risk him cutting his paws, he held the dog tight to his chest and reached for Pru's hand with his free one. Pulling her to her feet, he said, "Let's get Thor upstairs and then I'll come back and—"

"I'm not leaving it, any of it."

"Okay, babe, no worries." He whipped out his cell phone and called Archer. No way was Sean awake yet, much less up and moving, but Finn knew he could always count on Archer.

Archer answered with his customary wordy greeting. "Talk."

"Courtyard," Finn said and looked up. Sure enough Archer's face appeared in the second-story window of his office. "We need a box."

"Down in five," Archer said.

He made it in two. Archer set an empty box down

on the bench and reached for Thor, presumably so Finn could handle Pru, but Thor bared his tiny little teeth and growled fiercely.

"Whoa, little dude," Archer said and raised his hands. "I come in peace."

Satisfied he'd protected his woman, Thor went back to cuddling into Finn.

Finn grabbed the box in his free hand and crouched in front of Pru, who had an armful of stuff. "Set everything in here," he said.

She hesitated and he leaned in. "It'll be safer," he said quietly, and she nodded and unloaded her full arms into the box.

Archer had sent a text and Elle showed up with a broom and dust pan, which seemed incongruous to her lacy tee, pencil skirt, and some very serious heels.

"You could've sent someone," Archer said to her.

Elle gave him a don't-be-stupid look and smiled at Pru. "Pretty photo albums. Shame about the frame." She swept up the glass, the line of thin silver hoops clanging on her wrist. "I've got some spare frames I'm not using that would love a home. I'd be glad to give them to you. Is that you and your parents?"

Pru nodded and rose. "Thanks for helping."

"Don't give it another thought," Elle said. "Oh, and it's girls' night out tonight. Karaoke. Doll yourself up, Finn promised nineties glam rock band music." Elle flashed a smile. "My specialty, so just ring if you need something to wear, I've got a closet full."

Archer snorted.

"Okay," Elle said, "so I have two closets full. Eight-ish work for you?"

Pru, looking a little bit dazzled and probably also more than a little railroaded by Elle's gentle but firm take-charge 'tude, shook her head. "I can't sing," she said.

"Nonsense," Elle said. "Everyone can sing. We'll duet, it'll be fun."

Pru didn't look convinced but she did look distracted instead of anguished, and for that Finn was grateful. He brushed a quick kiss on Elle's cheek. "Thanks."

She kissed him back and gave him a look that said *take care of her*, and he knew better than to not do what Elle wanted.

Besides, he wanted the same thing.

A few minutes later he got Pru and Thor upstairs.

"Thanks," she said quietly. "But I'm good from here."

Oh, he got that message loud and clear, but he was still holding both her dog and her box so he stepped into her apartment behind her.

He could see her small kitchen and living room and the wall dividing them that had a square door right in the middle of it. It was a dumbwaiter, which cut through this whole side of the building, a long-ago leftover remnant from when the place had at one time been all one residence belonging to one of the wealthiest, most successful dairy families on the west coast.

Finn knew this only because he'd seen the dumbwaiter in Archer's office. Archer employed guys with major skills and they kept those skills sharp with company-wide training. Once a month that training came in the form of a serious scavenger hunt, and somehow Finn had once ended up one of the things on the list of items to gather.

Archer's idea of funny.

Team One had captured Finn in his sleep once. He'd escaped before they could win though, and he'd been lucky enough to use the dumbwaiter to make his hasty exit. He'd been unlucky enough to end up in the basement in nothing but his boxers, showing up at an illicit poker game between the building's janitor crew and maintenance crew.

He'd joined in and won two hundred bucks, which had kept him from trying to kill Archer.

Pru had the dumbwaiter door latched from her side. Smart girl. That didn't surprise him.

What *did* surprise him was that there was almost no furniture in the entire place.

"Where did you move from?" he asked.

"Not far. Fisherman's Wharf."

"You didn't move your furniture yet?"

"Uh . . ." She headed into her kitchen and was face first into her fridge now, leaving him a very nice view of her sweet ass in her snug yoga capris. "My place there was mostly furnished," she said. "But yeah I have a few things left to move over." Her tank gapped away from her front, affording him a quick flash of creamy, pale skin.

"You work out of Fisherman's Wharf too," he said. "At Jake's charter service, right?"

"Yes." She straightened and faced him. "He's got that huge old warehouse on Pier 39. I both work and lived there."

"With Jake." Wow, listen to him all casual, when his stomach had literally just hit his toes.

"He's got a lot of space. Not all of it is used for business. It's residential too."

Not, Finn couldn't help but notice, exactly an answer. He knew Jake. Knew too a little of the guy's reputation, which was that maybe his legs didn't work, but everything else most certainly did. That guy saw more action than Finn, Archer, Spence, and Sean all together.

Times ten.

"You and him . . . ?" he asked calmly, while feeling anything but.

"Not anymore."

Somehow this didn't make him feel better. He was still holding Thor and the box. Pru came back toward him and took Thor, setting him down, unhooking his leash. Then she turned back to Finn and reached for the new box.

Their hands brushed but he held firm, waiting until her eyes met his. He let his question stand. He had no idea why it mattered to him so much. Or maybe he did. In any case, he was usually good at letting things go, *real* good, but for some reason this wasn't going to be one of those things.

Finally, she blew out a sigh. "Did you think I'd kiss you if I was with someone else?"

"Do you always answer a question with a question?"

Making an annoyed sound, she tugged the box from his arms, her momentum taking her on a half spin from him but at the last minute she whirled back with something clearly on the tip of her tongue.

Problem was, he'd stepped in to follow right behind her. Which was how he ended up with the corner of the box slamming right into his crotch.

Chapter 11

#LoveBites

Pru felt the impact, took in where the box had hit Finn, and staggered back a step in horror. "Oh my God, I'm so sorry! Are you all right?"

He didn't answer. He did however let out a whoosh of air and bent over, hands on his knees, head down.

Good going, Pru. Since you didn't kill him the other night, you went for unmanning him and finishing the job. She quickly set the box down and hovered close, hands raised but not touching him, not sure *where* to touch him. Which was ridiculous. She'd had her tongue halfway down his throat. He'd seen her lose her collective shit over the photograph of her mom and dad . . . "Finn?" she asked tentatively. "Are you okay? *Say something.*"

Head still down, he lifted a finger, signaling he needed a moment.

Going gonzo with all the agitation in the air, Thor

was on a yipping spree, running in circles around them both, panting in exertion.

"Thor, hush!" she said, eyes on Finn.

Thor didn't hush, but she couldn't concentrate on the dog. "I'm so sorry," she said again, finally giving in to the urge to touch Finn, running her hand up and down his back, trying not to notice that under her fingers he was solid muscle. And thanks to his low-riding jeans having slid down his hips when he'd bent over, she could see an inch of smooth, sleek skin and it made her stupid. "I didn't mean to crush your . . . er, twig and berries."

He stilled and then lifted his head. He was pale. No, scratch that, he was green, and maybe sweating a little bit to boot. But he had a funny expression on his face.

Thor was still losing his mind, barking so hard that his upright ear bounced up and down and his floppy ear kept covering his eyes, freaking him out all the more.

"Shh," Finn said to him firmly but not unkindly.

Shockingly, Thor "shh'd."

Finn straightened up a little bit more, but not, Pru couldn't but notice, all the way.

"Twig and berries?" Finn repeated.

"Yeah, um . . ." Pru strained for another reference so that she didn't have to spell it out. "You know, your . . . kibbles and bits."

The corners of his mouth quirked but she wasn't sure if he was mad or amused. "Frank and beans?" she tried.

At that, he out-and-out smiled. "I'm torn between giving you a break and stopping you, or making you go on."

Oh for God's sake. She crossed her arms. "I suppose you have better words."

"Hell yes," he said. "And when you're ready, I'll teach them to you."

Breaking eye contact, she—completely inadvertently, she'd swear it on a stack of waffles!—slid her gaze to where she'd hit him. Did it seem . . . *swollen*? "I've got an icepack if you—"

He choked. "Not necessary."

"Are you sure?" she asked. "Because I really am a good medic, I promise, and—"

He choked off another laugh. "And you're offering to do what, exactly?"

Uh . . . She bit her lower lip.

"Kiss it better?" he suggested in a voice that made her get a little overheated.

Note to self: *not quite ready for prime time with Finn O'Riley.*

He gave her a knowing smirk and moved to the door. Definitely with a slight limp. "You should take Elle up on her offer for a new frame," he said. "That picture clearly means a lot to you and she's got some beautiful things in storage."

And then he was gone.

It was a matter of pride that Finn managed to walk across the courtyard without a limp. Or too much of one anyway. He'd thought about going up instead of down, heading to the roof, the only place in the building that he could go and probably be alone, but he didn't want or need alone time.

Or so he told himself.

"What's up with you, someone knee you in the 'nads?"

He turned his head and found Eddie in his usual place, sitting on a box in the alley. It was a good spot because from there the old man could see both the courtyard and the street.

"Isn't it early for you to be up?" Finn asked him.

"It's trash day."

Finn went through his pockets for extra change. Coming up with a five, he handed it over.

Eddie smiled his gratitude.

When a shadow joined theirs, Finn turned just as Archer appeared silently at his side.

Archer had some serious stealth skills, earned mostly the hard way. He'd lost none of his sharp edges, which considering what he did for a living and the danger he still occasionally faced, was a good thing.

"What happened to your boys?" Archer asked.

Finn resisted the urge to cup his "boys" because they still ached like a son of a bitch from his collision with the corner of Pru's box. "Nothing."

"Maybe he finally got laid," Eddie said to Archer.

Archer's gaze cut to Finn's face. "Nah," he said. "He'd be more dazed. And happy."

Spence joined them. "What's going on?"

"The debate is whether or not Finn got laid," Archer said.

Spence took his turn studying Finn's expression. "He's not happy enough."

"That's what I said." Archer gave a rare smile. "Given how long it's been, I'd assume he'd be doing cartwheels and shit."

Finn took a deep breath as they both laughed at his expression. "How about I *assume* my foot up your ass?"

This only made them crack up harder.

Eddie got himself together first. "Gotta go," he said and headed for the alley. Trash day was his favorite day of the week because he loved nothing more than to go dumpster diving for treasures.

Twice now, the entire building—all fond of Eddie and protective of him as well, had implemented a system where everyone bagged up anything that might be of interest to him separately so that he didn't have to go searching.

And then they discovered that Eddie was dumping out all the bags into the dumpster regardless.

Turns out, Eddie liked the thrill of the find.

"You smell like a skunk," Archer said to Eddie.

Eddie blinked. "Is that right? Well, I'm sure we have skunks around here somewhere."

"You think?" Archer asked casually. "Because I'm thinking it smells like weed."

"Huh," Eddie said. "Good thing you're not a cop these days, huh?"

Oh boy, Finn thought. Even Old Man Eddie knew better than to remind Archer of his cop days, which in turn would remind him why he wasn't one anymore.

Archer's eyes went flat. "You growing?"

"Only exactly what I'm allowed," Eddie said and pulled out a laminated card on a ribbon from beneath his shirt.

"You selling?" Archer asked.

"Sir, no sir," Eddie responded, adding a smartass salute.

Finn and Spence both grimaced. "Man," Spence said. "What have we told you? Archer has *zero* sense of humor."

Eddie grinned. For reasons that Finn had never figured out, Eddie liked to fuck with Archer.

Archer gave a slight head shake, like he was talking himself out of making Eddie disappear. "You know the rec center on Union?" he finally asked.

Eddie nodded. "Past the porn shop but before the COME TO JESUS sign?"

"Yeah," Archer said. "They're having a free meal tonight. Pot roast and potatoes."

"I love pot roast and potatoes," Eddie said.

"You want a ride, come by my office at six," Archer told him.

Eddie grinned at him. "See, I knew you liked me. Though not as much as Finn. Finn gave me five bucks." Eddie looked hopefully at Archer.

Well versed in this game, Archer snorted. "I'll pay you ten if you tell me why lover boy here's limping like he was rode hard and put away wet. I know you know more than you're telling."

"You think he got his knob polished," Eddie said.

Archer flashed another grin. "Yeah."

Finn flipped Archer off, which only made Archer's grin widen.

"I don't know everything," Eddie said. "But I guess I do know some things."

"Such as?" Archer asked.

Eddie held out his hand.

Archer rolled his eyes, fished through his pockets and came up with the promised ten.

"Okay," Eddie said. "I know he went inside Trouble's apartment with her, but only stayed a few minutes. He came back out in this condition. It wasn't long enough for him to get laid . . ." He slid Finn a sideways look. "At least I hope it wasn't. You ain't a quick trigger, are you, boy?"

Spence about busted a gut and handed Eddie another ten. "Totally worth every penny."

Finn shook his head and walked away from those assholes, and he wasn't going back to the pub either. He needed a few hours horizontal on his bed—where he would absolutely not think about how he'd rather be getting his knob polished.

Nineties Karaoke Night cheered Finn up considerably. First Archer bet the gang that Spence couldn't rap "Baby Got Back."

Spence rapped "Baby Got Back." Perfectly. He was in a suit too, evidently fresh from some business meeting.

The ladies went nuts.

In penance, Archer had to sing "I'm Too Sexy" by Right Said Fred.

Shirtless.

The crowd went wild. But even better was what happened when the girls showed up. They walked in together, Elle, Willa, Haley . . . and Pru, all dressed in vintage nineties.

It was a cornucopia of hotness but Finn's gaze went straight to Pru. His heart about stopped. She wore a tight, short, high-waisted denim miniskirt that showed off her mile-long legs to mouth-watering perfection, a cropped white tee with an equally cropped leather jacket that kept giving sneak, tantalizing peeks of smooth, flat belly, and some serious platforms that told him Elle had been in charge. Her hair had been teased to within an inch of its life and she appeared to be wearing glitter as makeup.

Everyone had fun ordering nineties-style cocktails, so he made Pru a special one—a Chocolate Mock-tini. She raved over it so much that everyone else wanted one as well, and it became the night's special.

Eventually the ladies all got up to sing "Kiss" by Prince and brought down the house. Not because they were good. But because they were so bad.

Pru had been right. She couldn't sing. Couldn't dance either. Or keep rhythm. Not that this stopped her or the glitter floating around her in a cloud everywhere she moved.

Finn loved every second of it.

That was until she dragged his ass up on stage and made him do a duet with her. "The Boy Is Mine."

He was pretty sure not a single one of the guys would ever let him forget it either.

Sean bailed shortly after that, a woman on his arm, a smile on his face. Finn was happy for him, but when the night ended and the girls went to leave, he realized he was screwed because he didn't have the option of taking Pru home.

Even if that was only up two flights of stairs.

He had to stay until closing, add up the till, make sure everything got closed and locked up.

Which means he got to watch Pru, his Fun Whisperer, walk out.

She hugged him good-bye, and the feel of her up against him almost had him saying fuck it to the pub. But he couldn't. He showered and hit his bed two hours later. Alone.

And when he woke up the next morning he had glitter all over his pillow.

Chapter 12

#BiteTheBullet

The next few days were busy at work, with Pru's shifts consisting of one cruise after another, but she still had plenty of time to think. A lot.

Karaoke night had been fun. Watching Finn laugh with Archer and Spence had been a highlight for her.

Fun looked good on him. It made her happy to see him happy, and she realized it'd been a good week for her, too. Willa, Elle, and Haley had been so welcoming, taking her in, adding her to their group without hesitation.

It meant a lot. It also meant that she wasn't entirely alone. She knew she had Jake, but he was like a brother at this point. An overprotective, obnoxious one.

You have Finn . . .

Even if she had no idea what to do with him. Although she'd had plenty of ideas the other night.

It turned out that dancing and singing karaoke in

front of a crowd with Finn's eyes on her had been shockingly arousing.

Which apparently had been obvious. Haley had given her a knowing glance at the bar. "You look hungry," she'd said.

"Oh, no," Pru had told her. "I'm fine, I had a plate of chicken wings."

Haley and Willa had laughed.

Even Elle had smiled.

"You're not hungry for food," Elle had informed her, with Curly and Mo nodding their heads in agreement. "You're hungry for a good time. With our boy Finn."

"Well that's just . . . a bad idea," she'd finished weakly. She looked at Willa and Haley for confirmation of that fact.

"Hey, sometimes bad ideas turn out to be the best ideas of all," Willa had said. "Just do it. Have some magical sex. And whatever happens, happens."

What would happen is that Pru would screw up one of the only good things she had going for her right now. "Just do it? That's your big advice?"

"Or in this case, him. Just do him."

Pru snorted.

Willa had turned to Elle and asked, "Think she'll follow my sage advice?"

Elle studied Pru's face carefully. "Hard to say. She's cute and sharp, but she's got some healthy survivor instincts. That might hold her up some."

"Stupid survivor instincts," Willa had said on a sigh.

And Pru agreed. She had some survivor instincts, and they often got in her own way.

"For days a cloud of glitter has been following you

around," Jake said, startling Pru back into the here and now.

"I went to Karaoke the other night," she said. "Rocked it too."

"But you can't sing," Jake said.

"I can totally sing."

He snorted. "And the glitter?"

"It was Nineties Night. This required copious amounts of glitter, which apparently is like the STD of the craft supplies. Once you use it without protection, you can't get rid of it." Pru looked down at herself. "Ever."

"Even Thor's wearing glitter," he said. "You're messing with his manhood."

"Real men aren't afraid of glitter," she said.

"Real men are terrified of glitter."

At the end of the day, Pru collected her dog from Jake's office, where she found him asleep sprawled on top of the desk.

"Seriously?" she asked.

"He likes to see what's going on," Jake said.

And Jake liked the company. She'd almost feel bad about taking Thor away when she'd moved but oh yeah, it'd been Jake's idea for her to go. "I hope he got glitter all over you."

"Hell no," Jake said. "Glitter doesn't dare stick to me. But you've got some on your face."

She couldn't get rid of it. She'd already sent Elle an I-hate-you text. Twice.

"We're going to have to forfeit tonight's game," Jake said. "We're short a player. Trev's out with mono."

She and a group of Jake's other friends and employees

played on a local rec center league softball team. Jake was their coach. Coach Tyrant. "Who gets mono at our age?" she asked.

Jake shrugged. "He's a ship captain, he sees a lot of action."

"I'm a ship captain," she said. "I see *no* action."

"And we both know why," Jake said.

Not going there. "Don't forfeit," she said. "I'll find us a player."

Jake raised a brow. "Who?"

"Hey, I have other people in my life besides you, you know."

"Since when?"

She rolled her eyes and ran out. Well, okay, she didn't run exactly. Thor refused to run. But they walked fast because she had an idea, one that would further her plan to bring Finn more fun.

Of course she'd deviated from the plan a couple of times now, starting with allowing her lips to fall onto his—not once but a holy-cow twice—but she'd decided to give herself a break because he was so . . . well, kissable.

And hey, now she knew that his mouth was a danger zone, she'd just steer clear. Her inner voice laughed hysterically at this, but whatever. She could do it.

Probably.

Hopefully.

In the courtyard, she tied Thor's leash to a bench, kissed him right between his adorable brown eyes and dashed through the open doors of the pub. Breathless, she scanned for Finn, but couldn't find him.

Sean flashed her a smile. "Hey, Trouble." He gestured to her face. "You've got some glitter—"

"I know!"

His smile widened. "Okay then, what can I get you?"

"Finn," she said, and then blushed when he just kept grinning. "I mean, I need to see him. Is he in his office?"

"Nope, boss man isn't in."

She'd never been here when Finn hadn't. "But he's always here."

Sean laughed. "Almost always," he agreed. "But right now, he's . . . well, let's just say he's pissed off at me, so we decided he'd work from the house office so I could live to see another day."

He didn't seem all too worried by this. "I need a favor," she said.

He leaned over the bar, eyes warm. "Name it."

"I need his address."

Sean went brows up. "His address."

"Yes, please."

"You going to show him a good time?" he asked. "Because darlin', he sure could use it."

"I'm on it," she said and then realized what he'd meant, which was not what *she'd* meant. "Wait, that's not—"

"Oh, it's *way* too late," Sean said, laughing his ass off.

"I just need to *talk* to him," she said, trying to regain some dignity.

"Whatever you say." Grabbing a cocktail napkin, he pulled a pen from behind his ear, scrawled an address down, and handed it over to her. "We share a house in Pacific Heights. Less than a mile from here. Go do your thing."

"Which is *talking*," she said.

"If that's what you kids are calling it these days," he said. "Good luck, Trouble."

Not sure why she'd need good luck, she grabbed Thor and headed back out.

Finn lived straight up Divisadero Street, a steep hill that had Thor sitting down and refusing to go another step about a hundred yards in.

Which was a hundred yards past when Pru had wanted to sit down as well. But she scooped the dog up and determinedly kept going, making a quick stop along the way for a spur-of-the-moment gag gift that she sincerely hoped Finn found funny.

By the time she arrived at his house near the top of the hill, she was huffing some serious air. She looked back at the view and was reminded of why she loved this city so much. She could see all of Cow Hollow and the marina, and beyond that, the gorgeous blue of the bay and the Golden Gate Bridge as well.

Worth every second of the walk. Almost. Finn's house was a Victorian-style, narrow row house. The garage was on the bottom floor, two stories above that, with steps leading up to the front door and down to a short driveway—on which sat a '66 Chevelle.

The sexy muscle car's hood was up and a very sexy jeans-covered tush was all Pru could see sticking out of it. She recognized the perfect glutes as Finn's—clearly a sign she'd been ogling said perfect glutes too much. Not that she was repentant in the slightest about this, mind you. In any case, his long denim-covered legs were spread for balance, his T-shirt stretching taut over his flexing shoulder and back muscles and riding up enough to expose a strip of navy boxers and a few inches of some skin.

She tried not to stare and failed. "Hi," she said.

Nothing. He just kept doing whatever it was he was doing under the hood, which involved some serious straining of those biceps.

She moved a little closer. "Finn?"

More nothing, but now she could hear the tinny sound of music and caught sight of the cord from his earbuds.

He was listening to something. Loudly. Classic rock by the sounds of it.

She stared at him, at the streaks of grease on his jeans and over one arm, at the damp spot at the small of his back making his shirt cling to him . . . It was the kind of thing that in the movies would be accompanied by a montage of him moving in slow motion to music, the camera moving in and focusing on that lean, hard body.

Giving herself a mental shake, Pru set Thor down, and holding his leash, shifted even closer to Finn before reaching out to tap him. But at the last minute she hesitated because once again she couldn't figure out where to touch him. Her first choice wasn't exactly appropriate. Neither was her second.

So she settled for his shoulder.

If he'd done the same to her, she probably would've jumped and banged her head on the hood. But Finn had better reflexes, and certainly better control over them. Still cranking on something with a wrench, he simply turned only his head to give her a level stare.

"Hi," she said again and bent over at the waist, hands

to her knees to try to catch her breath. "That's quite a hill."

He reached up and pulled out one earbud. "Hi yourself. Need an oxygen tank?"

"You kid, but I totally do."

"You're still wearing glitter," he said with a smile.

"Five showers since that night," she said, tossing up her hands. "I've taken five showers and it's still everywhere. And Thor has been pooping glitter for days . . ."

Still smiling, he crouched and held out his hand for Thor. "You were quite the show the other night."

She chewed on her lip, not sure if he was teasing or complimenting her or not.

"I could watch you do that every night," he admitted.

"What, make a fool of myself?"

His smile turned into a full-fledged grin. "Sing and dance like no one's watching. *Live* like no one's watching."

And just like that, she melted a little.

Thor was sniffing Finn's hand carefully, cautiously, wanting to make sure this was his Finn, and finally he wagged his tail.

"Atta boy. It's just me." Finn opened his arms and Thor moved in for a hug.

Pru stared at the big, sexy guy so easily loving up on her silly dog and felt her throat go a little tight.

"I know Archer didn't tell you where I live," Finn said, eyes still on Thor. "Or Spence. I mean, Spence would if he thought it was funny but they're both pretty hardcore about having my back."

The hardcore part was undoubtedly true. She'd seen the three guys with each other. There were bonds there that seemed stronger than any relationship she'd ever had, a fact that played into her deepest, most secret insecurity—that she might be unlovable.

"Elle values privacy above everything else," Finn said, "which leaves the busybodies." He was watching her now. "Willa or Haley?" he asked.

"Neither." She hesitated, not wanting to get Sean in trouble.

"Shit." Finn rose, Thor happily tucked under one arm like he was a football. "Eddie?"

"Eddie?" Pru asked, confused. "Who's Eddie?"

"The old guy who enjoys dumpster diving, eating dope brownies, and not minding his own business."

Pru gaped. "I've been feeding him for a month now and he's never told me his name. And I've asked a million times!"

"He likes to be mysterious. And also his brain might be fried from all those brownies. You going to tell me how you found me or not?"

She blew out a breath. "Sean. But he didn't tell me to mess with you or anything," she said hurriedly. "He did it because I have a favor to ask of you and needed to see you in person to do it."

"Sean was at the pub?"

"Yes," she said.

"Working?"

"I think so . . ."

"Huh," he said. "He must have fallen and bumped his head."

"He seemed to have all his faculties about him," she said. "Or at least as many as usual."

Finn snorted and set Thor down. The dog turned in a

circle at Pru's feet and then plopped over with an utter lack of grace.

"I brought you a present," Pru said.

"What?" Finn lifted his gaze from Thor to her face. "Why?"

The question threw her. "Well, partly to butter you up for the favor," she admitted. "I figured if I made you laugh, you'd—"

"I don't need a present to do you a favor," he said, his voice different now. Definitely wary, and something else she couldn't place.

She cocked her head. "You know, presents are supposed to be a good thing."

When he just looked at her, she wondered . . . didn't anyone ever give him anything? And suddenly she wished it was a real present and not a gag gift. But it was too late now so she slipped her backpack off and pulled the bag from inside. Seriously second-guessing herself, not entirely certain of this, not even close, she hesitated.

He took the bag from her and peered inside, face inscrutable.

Nothing. No reaction.

"It's a man's athletic cup," she finally said, stating the obvious.

"I can see that."

"I figured if we're going to hang out together, you might need it."

He stilled and then a low laugh escaped him. "What I need with you, Pru, is full body armor."

True statement.

He lifted his head. "And who says we're hanging out?" he asked, his gaze holding hers prisoner.

She hesitated briefly. "I do."

His eyes never left hers which was how she saw them warm. "Well, then," he said. "I guess it's true."

Their eyes stayed locked, holding for a long beat, and suddenly Pru had a hard time pulling in enough air for her lungs.

"So what's the favor?" he asked.

"I play on a coed softball league. We're short a player tonight and I was hoping—"

"No."

She blinked. "But I didn't even finish my sentence."

"You're short a player for tonight's game and you want me to fill in," he said.

"Well, yes, but—"

"Can't."

She took in his suddenly closed-off expression. "Because . . . you're against fun?"

He didn't react to her light teasing. He wasn't going to play. He clearly had a good reason, maybe many, but he didn't plan on sharing them.

"You should've called and saved yourself a trip," he said.

"I didn't want to make it easy for you to say no."

"I'm still saying no, Pru."

"What if I said I *need* you?" she asked softly.

He paused for the slightest of beats. "Then I'd say you have my full attention."

"I mean *we* need you. The team," she said. "We'll have to forfeit—"

"No."

She crossed her arms. "You said I had your attention."

"You have that and more," he said cryptically. "But I'm still not playing tonight. Or any night."

She knew he was living life carefully, always prepared for anything to go bad. But she knew that wasn't any way to live because the truth was that any minute life could be poof—gone. "Do you remember the other day when you caught me at my worst and saw a few of my demons?" she asked quietly.

"You mean when the picture frame broke."

"Yes," she said, not surprised he knew exactly what she was talking about, that she hadn't been even slightly effective in hiding her painful memories from him.

"You didn't want to talk about it," he said.

"No," she agreed. "And you let me get away with that." She dropped her gaze a little and stared at his torso rather than let him see what she was feeling now. "Whether it was because it doesn't matter to you, or because you have your own demons, I don't know, but—"

"Pru."

Oh thank God, he'd shut her up. Sometimes she really needed help with that. She stared at his neck now, unable to help noticing even in her growing distress and sudden discomfort that he had a very masculine throat, one that made her want to press her face to it and maybe her lips too. And her tongue . . .

"Pru, look at me."

He said this in his usual low timbre, but there was a gentle demand to the tone now that had her lifting her gaze to his.

"It matters," he said. "*You* matter."

This caused that now familiar squishy feeling in her belly, the one only he seemed to be able to evoke. But it also meant that it *was* his demons eating at him and this killed her. "Softball is a problem for you," she whispered.

"No." He closed his eyes for a beat. "Yeah. Maybe a little, by association." He blew out a sigh and turning his head, stared at the sweet car he'd been working on.

Which was when she remembered he'd had to quit playing baseball in college to raise Sean.

God, she was such an idiot.

"You'll have to forfeit?" he asked.

"Yes, but—"

"Shit." He shut the hood of the Chevelle and went hands on hips. "Tell me you guys are good."

She crossed her fingers. "You have to see us to believe it."

Chapter 13

#BadNewsBears

Not ten minutes into the game, Finn stood behind home plate wearing all of the catcher's gear, staring at the team in complete disbelief.

He'd been recruited by a con artist.

He slid his con artist a look. She was playing first base, looking pretty fucking adorable in tight, hip-hugging jeans and a siren red tee with a ragged penny jersey over the top of it, heckling the other team.

She was without a doubt, the hottest con artist he'd ever seen.

"You suck," she yelled to the batter, her hands curved around her mouth.

The batter yelled back, "How about you suck *me*?" And then he blew her a kiss.

Finn straightened to kick the guy's ass but the ref pointed to the batter and then gestured he was out.

"On what grounds?" the guy demanded.

"Being an idiot."

This came from the coach of Pru's team. Jake. He sat at the edge of the dugout, baseball cap on backward, dark lenses, fierce frown . . . a badass in a wheelchair.

With Thor in his lap.

Finn waited for the ump to give Jake a T and kick him out of the game but it didn't happen. Instead, the hitter took one look at Jake, kicked the dirt, and walked back to his dugout.

The next two batters got base hits and both made it all the way home thanks to the fumbling on the field.

Pru's team was the Bad News Bears.

In the dugout between innings, Pru tried to keep morale up, clapping people on the backs, telling them "good job" and "you're looking great out there."

Her rose-colored glasses must also be blinders. Because no one had done a good job and no one had looked great out there either.

At the bottom of the next inning, Finn watched his teammates blow through two strikes in two batters.

The third person up to bat was a twenty-something who had her dark hair up in a high ponytail that fell nearly to her ass. She was teeny tiny and had a sweet, shy smile.

Finn did not have high hopes for her. He might have muttered this under his breath. And Pru might have heard him.

She shot him a dark look. "Positive reinforcement only," she told him. "Or you'll have to go dark."

"Dark?"

"Yeah." She jabbed a thumb toward Jake, who was on the other side of her, watching the field, expression dialed to *irritated* as Thor snoozed on in his lap. "Like Coach Jake," Pru said and turned to her boss. "How are we doing tonight?"

Jake paused as if struggling with the right words. "Fuckin' great," he finally said.

He didn't look great, he looked like he was at stroke level, but Pru beamed at him and then patted his shoulder.

Jake blew out a heavy exhale. "I'll get you back, Prudence."

She gritted her teeth. "We talked about this. You only use my whole name if you want to die. Horribly and slowly."

"Prudence?" Finn repeated, amused by the death glare.

"I know, hard to believe, right?" Jake asked. "It's an oxymoron," Jake said. "She's anything *but* prudent."

Finn smiled. "And the 'they're doing great' part?" he asked *Prudence*. "Are we watching the same game?"

Jake did an impressive eyeroll, slid Pru a glare, and kept his silence, although it looked like it cost him.

"It's called encouragement," Pru said. "And Jake had to go dark, meaning he can't talk unless he's saying something positive, on account of how he used to lower our morale so badly we couldn't play worth anything."

Finn bit back the comment that they couldn't play worth anything now but as the girl at bat stood there letting two perfect strikes go by without swinging and Jake's expression got darker and darker, he nearly laughed.

Nearly.

Because he had no idea how Jake was doing it, keeping his mouth shut. Competition went to the bone with Finn and he was guessing Jake felt the same. "Is she going to swing?" he asked. "Or just keep the bat warm?"

A strangled snort came from Jake, which he turned into a cough when Pru glared at him.

"Abby is Jake's secretary," Pru said. "She's really great."

Finn looked at Jake.

Jake gave a slow head shake.

"What," Pru said, catching it. "She's wonderful! She handles your entire office and she's always sweet, even when you're a total asshole."

"Yes," Jake said. "She's a sweetheart. She's great. In my office and also at handling me, even when I'm a total asshole. What she isn't great at is softball."

"She's learning," Pru insisted.

Abby struck out.

The next batter was a lean and lanky kid, late teens, early twenties maybe.

"Nick," Pru told Finn. "He works in maintenance."

"Pru got him the job," Jake said and Pru shushed him.

Nick strolled out of the dugout, winked at Pru and got a second base hit.

The next batter was a young kid who couldn't have been more than eighteen. She wore thick-rimmed glasses and squeaked at every pitch. She also swung at every ball that came her way and several that didn't.

What she didn't do was connect with a single one. Probably because she kept her eyes closed, which meant that her glasses weren't doing jack shit for her.

Finn tried not to care. It was just a softball game, and a bad one at that, but come on. He looked over at Coach Jake and pointed to their batter. "Mind if I . . . ?"

Jake gestured for him to go ahead, his expression saying good luck.

"Kid," Finn called out.

The kid turned to face him.

"Finn," Pru said warningly but he didn't care. He didn't know how she'd gotten Jake to "go dark" but Finn hadn't made any such promise.

"What's your name?" Finn asked.

"Kasey," the girl said. "I work in accounts receivable."

"You know how to hit, Kasey?"

"Yeah." She paused. "No."

Shit. "Okay, it's easy," Finn said. "You just keep your eyes open, you got me?"

She bobbed her head.

"Make contact with the ball, Kasey. That's all you gotta do."

Kasey nodded again but failed to swing at the next pitch. She turned to nervously eye Finn.

"That's okay," Finn told her. "That was a sucky pitch, you didn't want a piece of that one anyway. The next one's yours." And he hoped that was true.

Pru watched Kasey swing at the next ball and connect.

Finn launched himself off the bench. "Yes!" he yelled, pumping his fist. "That's it, baby, that's it!"

He'd started off not wanting to be here, resenting the game, and yet now he was one hundred percent in it. Even, Pru suspected, having fun. Watching him gave her a whole bunch of feels, not the least of which was happy. She was really doing it, giving him something back.

After Kasey hit the ball, she dropped the bat like it was a hot potato and whipped around to flash a grin Finn's way, executing some sort of very white girl boogie while she was at it. "I did it! Did you see? I hit the ball!"

"Yeah, you did. Now *run*, Kasey!" Finn yelled, pointing to first base. "Run your little ass off!"

With a squeak, she turned and started running.

Finn laughed. He laughed and turned that laughing face Pru's way and she nearly threw herself at him.

"Having fun?" she asked, unable to keep her smile to herself.

"You tell me. *Prudence*."

She was going to have to kill Jake in his sleep.

He grinned at the look on her face and leaned in close so only she could hear him. "You owe me."

"What for?"

"For neglecting to mention that you guys are The Bad News Bears." He glanced at the field and leapt back to his feet, throwing himself at the half wall. "Go, Kasey, go! Go, go, go!"

Pru turned in surprise to see that the shortstop had missed the ball and Kasey was rounding second.

The ball was still bouncing in right field.

"Keep going!" Finn yelled, hands curved around his mouth. "Run!"

Kasey headed toward third.

Finn was nearly apoplectic and Pru couldn't tear her eyes off him.

"That's right!" he yelled. "You run, baby! You run like the wind!"

His joy was the best thing she'd seen all day.

All week.

Hell, all month.

Scratch that, *he* was the best thing she'd seen.

Unbelievably, Kasey made it all the way home and the crowd went wild. Okay, so just their team went wild. Everyone piled out of the dugout to jump on Kasey.

Except Pru.

She jumped on Finn.

She didn't mean to, certainly didn't plan it, her body just simply took over. She turned to him to say something, she has no idea what, but instead she literally took a few running steps and . . .

Threw herself at him.

Luckily he had quick reflexes, and just as luckily he chose to catch her instead of not. He caught her with a surprised grunt, and laughing, hauled her up into his arms. He slid one hand to her butt to hold her in place, the other fisting her ponytail to tug her face up to his.

"Did you see that?" she yelled, losing her ability to self-regulate her voice with the excitement. "It was beautiful, yeah?"

He looked right into her eyes and smiled back. "Yeah. Beautiful."

And then he kissed her, hard, hot, and quite thoroughly.

And far too short. She actually heard herself give a

little mewl of protest when he pulled back and let her slide down his body to stand on her own two feet.

"We're still down by ten runs," he said.

She nodded, but she'd never felt less like a loser in her entire life.

Chapter 14

#TheWholeNineYards

In the end, they lost by five, which Pru actually considered a total win. In the very last inning, she'd dove for a ground ball and slid along the ground for a good ten feet, bouncing her chin a few times while she was at it, but hey, she got the ball.

She also got some road rash.

She hadn't felt it at the time, but by the end of the game when they'd all packed up and were going their separate ways, Pru's aches and pains made themselves known. She slowly shouldered her bag and turned, coming face to face with both Jake and Finn.

Jake—with Thor in his lap—gave her a chin nod. Since their venue was a middle school field only two blocks from his building, they usually walked back together.

Finn didn't give her a chin nod. He just stood there, watching her in that way he had that made her . . . want things, things she wasn't supposed to want from him.

Clearly she needed to work on that.

Jake grimaced. "You're a mess. Let's go, I'll patch you up at the office."

"I'm fine." A big fat lie, of course. Her road rashes were stinging like a sonofabitch. "I'm just going to head home."

Jake slid a look at Finn before letting his gaze come back to her. "You sure that's a good idea?"

Of course it wasn't a good idea. But she wasn't exactly known for her good ideas now was she? "Yep," she said, popping the *P* sound.

"You shouldn't go alone, you might need help."

"I've got her," Finn said.

The two men looked at each other for a long beat. Pru might have tried to mediate the landmine-filled silence between them but her brain was locked on Finn's words.

I've got her . . .

She had long fantasies where that was true . . . She reached to take Thor but Jake shook his head.

"He's coming home with me tonight for dinner. I've got steak."

"Steak?" Pru repeated, realizing she was starving. "But after our games, you usually make hotdogs."

Jake shrugged. "It's steak tonight. I've got enough for you to join, if it's okay with Thor."

Thor tipped his head back like a coyote and gave one sharp "yip!"

Pru spent a few seconds weighing a steak dinner cooked for her versus watching Finn in those sexy butt-hugging, relaxed-fit Levi's of his for a little bit longer. It was a tough decision, but in the end, she took the jeans. "No, thanks."

Jake just gave her a knowing head shake and rolled off.

"Did you just almost trade me in for a steak dinner?" Finn asked.

Pretending she hadn't heard that question, she started walking, but he stopped her.

"You okay?"

"Yeah," she said. "We lose all the time."

"I meant because you used your face as a slip-n-slide on that last play." Earlier, when she'd convinced him to come play, he'd gone inside his house for a duffle bag, from which he'd pulled out his mitt earlier. Now he pulled out a towel and gingerly dabbed it against her chin.

"Ow!" she said.

"But you're fine, right?" he asked dryly.

She removed the towel from her chin, saw some blood and with a sigh put the towel back to her face.

Finn took her bag from her shoulder and transferred it to his, where it hung with his own. "I'll get an Uber."

"I don't need a ride." She started walking, and after a beat he kept pace with her. She worked on distracting herself. The temperature was a perfect seventy-five-ish. The sun had dipped low, leaving a golden glow tipped with orange flame in the west, the rest of the sky awash in mingled shades of blue.

"So what was that about?" Finn asked after a few minutes of silence.

"Nothing. Like I said, sometimes we lose, that's all." Or, you know, always.

"I mean the look Jake gave you."

"Nothing," she repeated.

"Didn't seem like nothing."

"He's got a condition," she said, huffing up the hill. Damn. Why had she said no to getting an Uber again? "You've got to ignore most of his looks."

"Uh huh," Finn said. "What kind of condition?"

"A can't-mind-his-own-business condition." Her aches and pains were burgeoning, blooming as they moved. It was taking most of her concentration to not whimper with each step.

"You sure you're okay?" he asked.

"One hundred percent."

He gave her a once-over, his dark gaze taking in the holes in her knees, and she amended. "Okay, ninety percent," she said and then paused. "Ten at the worst," she amended.

Finn stopped and pulled out his phone.

"We're over halfway there," she argued. "I'm not giving up now."

"Just out of curiosity—do you ever give up?"

She had to laugh. "No," she admitted.

He shook his head, but he didn't ask if she was sure, or try to tell her she wasn't fine. Clearly he was going off the assumption she was an adult.

Little did he know . . .

"Sean plays baseball too," Finn said out of the blue a few minutes later. "He sucks. Sucks bad."

"Yeah?" she asked. "As my team?"

"Well, let's not go overboard."

She took a mock swing at him and he ducked with

a laugh. "In high school, he made it onto his freshman team," he said. "But only because they didn't have enough guys to cut anyone. The painful part was making sure he kept his grades high enough."

Pru hadn't actually given a lot of thought to the day-to-day reality that a twenty-one-year-old Finn would have faced having to get a teenage Sean through high school. There would've been homework to do, dinners to prepare, food shopping needed, a million tiny things that parents would have handled.

But Finn had been left to handle all of it on his own.

Her stomach tightened painfully at all he'd been through, but he was over there smiling a little bit, remembering. "That year half of the JV and Varsity teams got the flu," he said, "and Sean got called up to the semifinals. He sat on the bench most of the game, but at the bottom of the eighth he had to play first base because our guy started puking his guts up."

"How did he do?"

Finn smiled, lost in the memory. "He allowed a hit to get by him with bases loaded."

Pru winced. "Ouch."

"Yeah. Coach went out there and told him if another hit got by him, he'd string him up by his balls from the flagpole."

Pru gasped. "He did not!"

"He did," Finn said. "So of course, the next hit came straight for Sean's knees, a low, fast hit."

"Did it get by him?"

"He dove for it, did a full body slide on his chin while he was at it." Finn gave her a sideways smile. "But he got the damn ball."

"Did he get road rash too?" Pru asked, starting to get the reason for story time.

"Left more skin on that field than you did." Finn grinned and shook his head. "He came through though. Somehow, he usually does."

She loved that the two of them had stuck together after all they'd been through. She didn't know anything of their mom, other than she'd not been in the picture for a long time. Whatever she knew about the O'Rileys was what she'd been able to piece together thanks to the Internet. She'd done her best to keep up by occasionally Googling everyone who'd been affected by her parents' accident— needing to make sure they were all doing okay. When she'd discovered that Finn had opened O'Riley's only a mile or so from where she was living and working, she hadn't been able to resist getting involved.

And now here he was, a part of her life. An important part, and at the thought she got a pain in her heart, an actual pain, because she knew this was all short-lived. She had to tell him the truth eventually. She also knew that as soon as she did, he wouldn't be a part of her life anymore.

"Tonight brought back a lot of memories," he said, something in his voice that had her looking at him.

Regret.

Grief.

"You miss baseball," she said softly.

He lifted a shoulder. "Didn't think so, but yeah, I do."

"Is that why you didn't want to come tonight?"

"I didn't think I was ready, even for softball." He shook his head. "I haven't played since my dad died."

"I'm so sorry." She sucked in a breath, knowing she couldn't let him tell her the story without her telling *him* some things first. "Finn—"

"At the time, Sean was still a minor. He'd have gone into the system, so I came home."

The familiar guilt stabbed at her, tearing off little chunks of her heart and soul. "What about your mom?"

He shrugged. "She took off when we were young. Haven't heard from her since."

Pru had to take a long beat to just breathe. "Sean was lucky to have you," she finally said. "So lucky. I hate that you had to give up college—"

"I actually hated school," he said on a low laugh. "But I really, *really* didn't want to go home. Home was full of shit memories."

Feeling land-locked by her misery, she had to run that through twice. "Finn, I—" She stopped. Stared at him. "What?"

He was eyeing a deli across the street. "You hungry?"

"I . . . a little."

"You ever eat anything from there? They make the most amazing steak sandwiches." He slid her a look. "Don't want you to miss out on steak on my account." He guided her inside where he ordered for them both.

Which was for the best because she couldn't think.

His memories of home were shit? What did that mean?

Finn paid and they continued walking. He was quiet, keeping an eye on her. But she didn't want quiet. "What do you mean home was full of shit memories?"

He took a moment to answer. "You grow up with siblings?" he asked. "Both parents?"

"No siblings but both parents," she said, and held her breath. "Until they died when I was nineteen."

He didn't make the connection, and why would he? Only a crazy person would guess that the two accidents—his dad's and her parents—were the same one.

"That sucks," he said. "Sucks bad."

It did, but she didn't deserve his sympathy. "Before that, it was a good life," she said. "Just the three of us."

"Well, trust me when I say, Sean and I didn't get the same experience."

His body language was loose and easy, relaxed as he walked. But though she couldn't see his eyes behind his dark sunglasses, she sensed there was nothing loose and easy in them. "Your dad wasn't a nice guy?"

"He was an asshole," he said. "I'm sorry he's dead, but neither I nor Sean was sorry to have to finish raising ourselves without him."

She stared at him in profile as she tried to put her thoughts together, but they'd just scattered like tumbleweeds in the wind. All this time she'd pictured his dad as . . . well, the perfect dad. The perfect dad who *her* dad had taken from him and Sean. She let out a shuddering breath of air, not sure how to feel.

"Hey." Finn stopped her with a hand to her arm and pulled her around to face him, pulling off his sunglasses, shoving them to the top of his head to get a better look at her. "You don't look so good. Your cuts and bruises, or too much sun?" he asked, gently pushing her hair from her face and pressing his palm to her forehead. "You're pale all of a sudden."

She shook her head and swallowed the lump of

emotion in her throat. He'd hate her sympathy so she managed a smile. "I'm okay."

He didn't look like he believed her, proven when he switched the deli bag to his other hand and with his free one, grabbed hers in a firm grip. They were only a block from their building at this point, but before they could take another step, Finn stilled and laughed.

Pru looked up to see Spence coming toward them.

Tall and leanly muscled, with sun-kissed wavy hair that matched his smiling light brown eyes, he was definitely eye candy. He wore cargo shorts and an untucked button-down, sleeves shoved up his forearms. He was a genuinely sexy guy, not that he seemed to realize it.

He was walking two golden retrievers and a cat, all three on leashes advertising South Bark Mutt Shop, striding calm-as-you-please at Spence's side.

Spence himself was calm as well, and completely oblivious to the two women craning their necks to stare at his ass as he passed them. He was too busy flipping Finn off for laughing at him.

"I didn't realize you worked for Willa," Pru said. *Or that one could actually walk a cat . . .*

"He doesn't exactly . . ." Finn said.

Spence didn't add anything to this as Finn looked at him. "You're walking a cat. They're going to take away your man card."

"Tell that to the owner of the cat," Spence said. "She asked me out for tonight."

"So now you're using these helpless animals to get laid?"

"Hell yes," Spence said. "And yuk it up now because later I'm going to let Professor PuddinPop here anoint your shoes. Fair warning, he had tuna for lunch and it's not agreeing with him."

"No cats allowed in the pub," Finn said.

"Professor PuddinPop is the smaller retriever," Spence said. "His brother Colonel Snazzypants is a specialist in evacuating his bowels over a wide area. Watch yourself. You've been warned."

"What's the cat's name?" Pru asked.

"Good King Snugglewumps," Spence said with a straight face. "He's actually an emotional support cat, which you look like you could use right now. What the hell happened to you?"

"I slid trying to catch a ball at my softball game," she said.

"With your pretty face?"

"No, that was collateral damage. But I did catch the ball."

"Nice job," he said with a smile and a high-five.

Finn had crouched down low to interact with the animals. The cat was perched on his bent leg, rubbing against him, and both dogs had slid to their backs so he could scratch their bellies.

"The Animal Whisperer," Spence said. "They always gravitate to him." He shook his head at Good King Snugglewumps. "Man 'ho."

Good King Snugglewumps pretended not to hear him.

Finn grinned. "I'm the Animal Whisperer, and Pru here is the Fun Whisperer."

Spence turned to Pru. "How's that going? He learning to have fun yet?"

"He's not much for cooperating."

"No shit." He looked at Finn. "Keep your shoes on, that's all I'm saying."

And then he strode off, two dogs and a cat in tow.

Finn pulled out his phone and snapped a pic of Spence from behind.

Spence, without looking back, flipped him off again.

Still grinning, Finn shoved his phone back into his pocket and reached for Pru's hand. "Let's get you home."

Good idea. In just the minute that they'd stopped to talk, she'd gone stiff, but did her best to hide it. They entered the courtyard and she glanced at the fountain, which, she couldn't help but notice, had not been very busy fulfilling her wish for love for Finn. She sagged behind him just enough that she could point at the fountain and then at her eyes, putting it on notice that she was watching it.

The fountain didn't respond.

But apparently Finn had eyes in the back of his head because he laughed. "Babe, you just gave that thing a look that said you'd like to barbeque it and feed it in pieces to your mortal enemy."

She would. She absolutely would. Hoping for a subject change, she waved at Old Guy, sitting on a bench.

"Eddie," Finn said with a male greeting of a chin jut. "You look better than the other night."

Eddie nodded. "Yeah, it was either a twenty-four-hour flu thing or food poisoning," he said.

"You could stop eating everything everyone gives you," Finn suggested.

"No way! I get good shit, man. Cutie Pie here gives really good doggy bags. Chicken wings, pizza . . ." He looked at Pru. "You know what we haven't had lately?

Sushi—" He broke off, narrowing his eyes. "What happened to you, darlin'? This guy get tough with you? If so, just say the word and I'll level him flat."

Eddie was maybe ninety-five pounds soaking wet and looked like a good wind could blow him over. Finn had at least six inches on him and God knew how many pounds of lean, tough muscle, not to mention a way of carrying all that lean, tough muscle that said he knew exactly what to do with it.

Pru caught him looking at her with a raised brow, like *are you really going to say the word*?

"I roughed myself up," she admitted. "Softball." She started to reach into her pocket for a few dollar bills to give Eddie but Finn put a hand on her arm to stop her. With his other hand he fished something out of his duffel bag.

The third sandwich he'd bought at the deli.

Eddie grinned and snatched it out of thin air. "See? I get good stuff. And you know your way to a man's heart, boy. Mayo?"

"Would I forget? And extra pickles."

"Chips?"

Almost before the word was out, Finn was tossing Eddie a bag of salt and vinegar chips.

Eddie clasped a hand to his own heart. "Bless you. And tell Bossy Lady that I got the bag of clothes."

"Elle?"

Eddie nodded. "She said I was going to catch my death in my wife beaters and shorts, and insisted I take these clothes from her." He indicated his trousers and long-sleeved sweater. It was the surfer dude goes mobster look.

"How do they fit?" Finn asked, smiling, enjoying the old man's discomfort.

Eddie rolled his eyes. "Like a cheap castle—no ballroom."

Finn laughed and reached for Pru's hand again, tugging her toward the elevator.

That's when a whole new set of worries hit Pru. Was he going to come in?

Had she shaved?

No, she told herself firmly. *It doesn't matter if your legs aren't hairy, you are not going there with him.*

At her door, he held onto her hand while rummaging through her bag for her keys, and then opened her door like he owned the place.

But before they could get inside, the door across the way opened and Mrs. Winslow stepped out.

Pru's neighbor was as old as time, and that time hadn't exactly been particularly kind. Still, she was sharp as a tack, her faculties honed by staying up on everything and everyone in the building.

"Hello, dear," she said to Pru. "You're bleeding."

This was getting old. "Skiing accident," she said, trying something new.

Finn flashed her an appreciative grin.

Mrs. Winslow chortled. "Even an old lady knows her seasons," she said. "It's high summer, which means it was softball."

Pru sighed. "Yeah."

"Did you at least win this time?"

"No."

"I think the idea is to win at least sometimes," Mrs. Winslow said.

Pru sighed again. "Yeah. We're working on that." She gestured to Finn at her side, steady as a rock, but looking a little hot and dusty. "I recruited a new player," she said.

"Good choice," Mrs. Winslow said. "He's put together right nice, isn't he."

Pru's gaze went on a tour of Finn from head to toe and back again. Nice wasn't exactly the description she would use. Hot as hell, maybe. Devastatingly, disarmingly perfect . . .

At her close scrutiny, his mouth curved and something else came into his eyes.

Hunger.

"I got a little something delivered today," Mrs. Winslow said. "That's why I've been waiting for you."

"Me?" Pru asked.

"Yes, my package came via your dumbwaiter."

"Why?"

"Because, dear, the dumbwaiter is only on your side of the building."

Okaaay. Pru gestured to her open door. Mrs. Winslow let herself in, unlatched the dumbwaiter door and removed a . . . platter of brownies?

Pru's mouth watered as Mrs. Winslow smiled, gave a quick "thanks" and exited the apartment, heading for her own.

"Those look amazing," Pru said, hoping for an invite to take one.

Or two.

Or as many as she could stuff into her mouth.

"Oh, I'm sorry," Mrs. Winslow said with a negative head shake. "These are . . . special brownies."

Pru blinked and then looked at Finn, who appeared to be fighting a smile. "Special brownies?" she repeated, unable to believe that Mrs. Winslow really meant what she thought she meant.

"Yes," the older woman said. "And you're not of age, or I'd share."

"Mrs. Winslow, I'm twenty-six."

Mrs. Winslow smiled. "I meant over sixty-five."

And then she vanished into her own apartment.

Finn gently nudged Pru into hers, which answered the unspoken question. He was coming in. Into her apartment.

And, if her heart had any say at all, into her life.

Chapter 15

#Doh

Finn dropped both duffel bags and the deli bag on Pru's kitchen counter and then turned to her. "Okay, time to play doctor."

Her entire body quivered, sending "yes please" vibes to her brain. Luckily her mouth intercepted them. "Sure, if I can be the doctor."

His mouth curved. "I'm willing to take turns, but me first."

Oh boy. "Really, I'm fine. I think I just need a shower."

"Do you want something to drink? I could call down to the pub and—"

"No, thanks."

"I wasn't talking about alcohol," he said. "I already know you don't drink."

There weren't many who would so easily accept such a thing without some sort of question. People wanted and expected others to drink socially when they did. Usually whenever she politely declined, the interrogation inevitably started. *Not even one little drink?* Or *what's up with that, are you an alcoholic*?

Pru couldn't imagine actually being an alcoholic and facing that kind of inquisition with class and grace, but the truth was that she didn't drink because her parents had. A lot. They'd been heavy social drinkers. She didn't know if they'd had an actual problem or had just loved to party, but she did know it had killed them.

And that had quenched her thirst for alcohol at an early age.

But Finn didn't push. "How about something warm?" he asked. "Like a hot chocolate?"

She felt her heart squeeze in her chest for his easy acceptance. "Maybe after my shower."

He nodded and leaned back against the counter like he planned on waiting for her. Not knowing how to deal with that, she nodded back and headed for the bathroom. She shut and locked the door and then stared at that lock for a good sixty seconds, because did she really want to lock him out? No. She wanted him to join her, the steam drifting across their wet bodies as he picked her up, pressed her against the shower wall and buried himself deep.

Ignoring her wobbly knees, she left the lock in place, shaking her head at herself. Apparently it'd been too long since her last social orgasm and while she handled her own business just fine, her business was clearly getting bored with herself.

Stripping out of her clothes involved peeling her shirt from the torn skin of her elbows, not a super pleasurable experience. Same for her knees and her jeans. Naked, she took inventory. Two bloody knees, one bloody elbow and a bloody chin.

When she was little and got hurt, her mom would hug her tight and then blow on her cuts and bruises and whisper "see, not so bad . . ."

It'd been a long time, but there were moments like right now where she would've traded her entire world away for a hug like that again. She looked at her bruised, bloody self in the mirror and took a deep breath. "See, not so bad," she whispered and got into the shower.

She made it quick, partly because as she ran soap all over her body, she only ramped herself up, but mostly because her various road rashes burned like hell. But also because as she soaped up, she couldn't help but think of Finn standing in her kitchen, arms casually crossed, pose casual, his mood anything but.

Waiting for her.

Her good parts quivered so she turned the water off, going from overheated to chilled in a single heartbeat. With her bad parts stinging and her good parts throbbing, she stepped out of the shower.

At the knock at the door, she nearly had a stroke.

"How bad is it?" Finn asked through the wood.

She yanked her towel off the rack and wrapped it around herself, her hair dripping along her shoulders and down her back. "Not bad." Her voice sounded low and husky, and damn . . . inviting. She cleared her throat. "Not bad at all."

"I want to see." He tried the handle. "Let me in, Pru."

Her hand mutinied and unlocked the door, but didn't go as far as to actually open it for him. She couldn't because dammit, he was already in. In her head, her veins, *all* of her secret happy places, and, she suspected, her heart.

Finn pushed the door open and stood there, eyes scanning her slowly, his body stilling as he realized she was in just a towel.

He took what looked like a deep breath and stepped the rest of the way in, a first-aid kit in his hand. "Had this in my bag," he said and set it on the countertop to the left of the sink. Turning to her, he put his hands to her waist and lifted her, setting her on the right side of the sink.

Ignoring her squeak of surprise, he opened up his kit, fingered his way through, and came up with gauze and antiseptic. Turning toward her, he sprayed and then bandaged up her elbows, his brow furrowed in concentration as he worked. When he'd finished there, he crouched low.

With another surprised squeak, Pru pressed her legs together and tugged at the bottom of her towel, trying to make sure it covered the goods.

This got her an almost smile as he went about doctoring up both knees, using the spray again, keeping his eyes on his work, his big, strong, capable hands moving with quick, clinical efficiency.

Pru occupied herself and her nerves by watching the way his shirt stretched taut across his shoulders and back, every muscle rippling as he moved. His head was bent to her, his eyes narrowed in concentration, his long, dark lashes hiding his thoughts.

Fine with her, as she was having enough thoughts for the both of them, the number one being—if she relaxed her very tense thighs even a fraction, he'd be able to see straight up to the promised land.

The thought made her dizzy but she told herself it was the spray giving her a head rush.

Because actually, there was something incredibly erotic about that, her being nude beneath the towel and him being fully dressed. But she was all too aware that not only was she a wreck on the inside, she was looking the part.

His concentration shifted from what he was doing, his gaze cutting to hers. Reaching out he brushed his fingers over her cheek. "Why are you blushing?"

"I'm not."

He arched a brow.

"I'm a mess," she blurted out.

He rose at that, brushing his hands from her ankles up the backs of her calves, resting just behind her knees for a beat before giving a little tug, sliding her forward on the counter toward him.

Her legs parted of their own volition and he stepped between them, leaning in close at the same time, his body heat warming her up. His arms slid around her hips, snugging her closer as his lips gently brushed hers. Then those lips made their way along her jawline to just beneath her ear, trailing tiny kisses as he then worked his way down her throat.

"You're beautiful," he whispered. "A beautiful mess."

She choked out a laugh.

"You are," he said against her shoulder now. "So beautiful you take my breath away." Then he lifted his head to look into her eyes letting her see he meant it, entirely.

It'd been a long time since she'd felt beautiful, but she realized that she did. Very much so. She wanted to close her eyes and get lost in that, lost in him, but with one last nip at the sensitive spot where her neck met her shoulder, he shifted his attention to her chin.

She hissed in a breath when he pressed a gauze to it and then held her next breath as well when he leaned forward and kissed her there.

He'd shifted slightly to reach and the rough slide of denim brushed the skin of her bare thighs, making them tremble for more. "What are you doing?" she asked, sounding a little like Minnie Mouse on helium as his mouth and stubbled jaw gently abraded over her skin.

"Kissing your owies," he said innocently, his voice anything but as he continued with his ministrations.

Her traitorous body responded by arching and pressing closer, oscillating her hips to his for the sheer erotic pleasure of hearing him groan.

His mouth brushed her jaw one more time before he met her gaze. "Where else?"

Completely dazed, she shook her head. "Huh?"

"Where else do you hurt?"

She stared up at him. Where else did she hurt? Nowhere, because with his hands and mouth on her, all her pleasure receptors had overcome the pain. But not about to look a gift horse in the mouth, she pointed to her shoulder.

Finn gave it his utmost attention, running his finger over a growing bruise. Then he bent and kissed her there, letting his lips linger a little.

She looked at his mouth on her, those amazing lips pressed to her skin, and shivered.

With a wordless murmur, Finn shifted even closer, his warm, strong arms encircling her so that she could absorb some of the heat coming off him in waves. His long, dark lashes brushed his cheeks when his eyes were closed, like now. He hadn't shaved that morning and maybe not the morning before either. She could feel the prickles of his beard when he turned his head slightly and opened his eyes.

"Where else?" he asked, his voice pure sex.

And here's where she made her mistake. She needed to stay strong, that was all she had to do. But the problem was that she was tired of being strong. And she was having a hard time remembering why she needed to.

"Pru?"

She swallowed hard and pointed to her mouth.

He pulled back, gave her a hot look that melted her bones, and slowly worked his way up her throat with hot, wet kisses. When he got to her jaw, he fisted his hands in her hair and tilted her head right where he wanted her. She felt him open his mouth on her jawline, and with just the tip of his tongue made his way back to her mouth.

Wrapping her arms around his broad shoulders, she moaned and held on tight as he kissed her like maybe she was the best thing he'd ever tasted. And God, the feel of him against her, steady and solid. She didn't know how he did it but even after a long ball game he still smelled amazing. Something woodsy and pure male . . .

Then he pulled back.

Staring up at him, she ached. "Finn?"

"Yeah?"

"Remember how you said the ball was in my court?"

He pressed his forehead to hers for a beat, like he was working on control. She knew she should be as well but she didn't want him to leave, didn't want to be alone in this. "Don't go," she whispered softly.

He opened his eyes, the heat in them nearly sending her up in flames. Nope, she wasn't alone, thank God, because that would really suck. Out of words, she arched into him a little.

He groaned. "Pru."

Afraid the next words out of his mouth would be good-bye, she snuggled in and pressed her mouth to the underside of his jaw in a soft kiss. When he opened his mouth to say something, she took a nibble. At the feel of her teeth on him, he stilled and shuddered, and then his arms tightened on her.

Yes. *This*. It was just what she needed, because here, held by him like this, her guilt, her regret, her fears . . . all of it gave way to this heady, languid sensation of being desired and she didn't want it to stop.

Any of it.

His eyes were deep and intense as he shifted, nudging against the apex of her thighs. Keeping his gaze on hers, he kissed her again, sending licks of fiery desire right through her. Then those hands drifted down to her thighs, his fingers over the terry cloth, his thumbs beneath.

"Is this what you want?" he asked.

She gasped at the sensation of his callused thumbs grazing over her inner thighs, and he caught her mouth with his in a deep, hot, wet kiss as he slipped beneath her towel now, cupping her bare ass in his big hands.

When she was too breathless to hold the kiss, she

broke it off, her head falling back as his mouth skimmed hot and wet down her throat, across her collarbone. Her entire body felt strung too tight, like her skin didn't fit. Impatient, she arched into him again, dragging a rough groan from him.

"Pru." His voice was thrillingly rough, but there was a warning there too. He wasn't going to let this get away from her. She was going to have to say how far they took things.

"I want this," she whispered, clutching at him. "I want . . ."

His mouth was at her ear, bringing her a delicious spine shiver. "Name it."

"You. Please, Finn, I want you."

Raising his head, he stared at her before kissing her again, stroking his tongue to hers in a rhythm that made her hips grind to his. The soft denim of his jeans rasped over the tender skin of her inner thighs and thrilling to it, she wrapped her legs even tighter around him, drawing him closer, the hottest, neediest part of her desperately seeking attention.

Finn said something low and inaudible, and then let out a quiet laugh as he nipped her lower lip, her throat, and then . . . her towel slipped from her breasts.

He'd loosened it with his teeth.

When he put his hot mouth to her nipple, she nearly went over the edge right then and there. He cupped her breasts in his big warm hands, shifting his attention from one to the other, his stubbled jaw gently scraping over her in the most bone-melting of ways, his movements sensual, so slow and erotic she could hardly stand it. "*Finn.*"

He lifted his head and held her gaze while he spread the towel from her, letting it fall to her sides before he worked his way south, lazily exploring every inch of her like he had all the time in the world, humming in pleasure when he found the little compass on her hip. He spent a long moment there, learning her tattoo— with his tongue.

And all she could do was grip the counter on either side of her, head tipped back because it was too much effort to hold it up, her nerve endings sending high bolts of desire through her at his every touch.

She was completely naked to his fully dressed body now. Open, exposed . . . vulnerable in more ways than one. Certainly more than she'd allowed in far too long, although she didn't feel a single ounce of self-consciousness or anxiety about it.

She felt nothing but the sharp lick of hunger and need barreling down on her like a freight train in tune to his clever mouth and greedy hands. She was afraid if he so much as breathed on her special happy place, she'd go off like a bottle rocket.

And then he dropped to his knees.

His hands glided up her inner thighs, holding her open so his lips could make their way homeward bound. About thirty minutes ago she'd thought she needed steak more than anything but it turned out that wasn't true. She needed this, with Finn.

One of their phones buzzed, either hers on the floor in her pants pocket, or his from wherever he had it tucked away. She started to straighten but then his fingers stroked her wet flesh and she forgot about the phone. Hell, she forgot her own name. "Oh God, don't stop. Please, Finn, don't stop . . ."

"I've got you." And then he replaced his teasing fingers with his tongue, giving her a slow, purposeful lick. She whimpered as he continued to nuzzle her, luring her into relaxing again—and then his lips formed a hot suction.

And that was it, she'd become the bottle rocket and was gone, launched out of orbit. Hell, out of the stratosphere. When she came back to planet Earth, she realized she had Finn by the hair, her fingers curled tight against his head, her thighs squeezing his head like he was a walnut to be cracked. "I'm so sorry!" she gasped, forcing herself to let go of him. "I nearly ripped out your hair."

The words backed up in her throat when he turned his head and pressed a soft kiss to her inner thigh, sending her up a very male, very protective, possessive, smug smile. "Worth it," he said, and licked his lips.

She nearly came again. "Please come here."

He rose to his feet and her hands went to his stomach, sliding beneath his shirt to feel the heat of his hard abs. So much to touch, and the question became up or down . . .

His eyes were dark and heated, flickering with amusement as he read the indecision on her face.

"I'm not exactly sure what to do with you," she whispered.

"I could make a few suggestions."

She laughed a little nervously but let her hands glide up his torso, shoving his shirt up as she went. He was so beautifully made . . . "Off," she said softly.

He had the shirt gone in less than a heartbeat and she soaked up the sight of his broad shoulders and chest while her fingers played at the waistband of his jeans. They were loose enough that she could dip in and—

"Oh," she breathed, sucking in a breath as she encountered *much* more than she'd bargained for.

His hot—and amused—gaze held hers. On the surface, he was calm and steady and unflappable as always, but there was an underlying erotic tension in every line of his body, a sense that he was holding back, keeping his latent sexuality in check.

She popped the top button of his Levi's.

And then the second.

And then she'd freed him entirely, pushing his knit boxers aside and all his glory sprung into her hand—and there was a lot of glory. "Finn?"

His voice was rough and husky. "Yeah?"

"I think I figured out what I want to do with you."

It involved the condom that he luckily had in his wallet and her leaning back on the cold tile of her bathroom countertop, but they managed.

And when he slid deep and then grasped her ass in his two big hands and roughly pulled her closer so that he went even deeper, she arched her spine and let her head fall back and felt more alive than she'd felt in far too long. She got chills all over her body and with a wordless murmur, Finn brought her upright so that she was pressed tight to his warm chest. He wrapped his arms around her and she could feel her toes curl. She clenched tight, eliciting a groan from him, and held on. She knew she was digging her nails into his back but she couldn't stop, couldn't breathe . . . "Finn—"

"I know." His hands slid south, cupping her ass, protecting her from the tile. When he did something diabolically clever with those long fingers, she came in a giant, unexpected burst.

From somewhere outside of herself she felt Finn lose control as well. They ended up smashed up against one another, gripping each other hard, faces pressed together, breathing like lunatics.

They stayed like that for a few minutes and then slowly separated. She flopped back against the mirror, not caring that it was chilly against her overheated skin.

Finn sagged against the counter like he wasn't all that sturdy himself. He made quite the sight, shirtless, his jeans opened and dangerously low.

Sexy as hell. She'd do something about it but she felt like a boneless rag doll.

A very sated one. "I'm hoping it was the antiseptic spray," she managed.

"I'm hoping not," Finn said.

She needed to move but couldn't find her limbs to save her life. Finn didn't seem to have the same problem, he used his arms to lean over her and kiss her, eyes open like maybe he was taking her vitals.

She quivered for more. Good God. Since when was she addicted to sex?

Finn caught the look in her eyes and he laughed low in his throat. Sexy as hell. "Give me a minute," he said, voice husky.

She arched a brow, impressed. "Just one?"

"Maybe one and a half," he said, his gaze dropping to her mouth. "Tops."

Her good parts actually fluttered. *Seriously, what was wrong with her?*

"How's the road rash?" he asked, helping her down off the counter and rewrapping her up in the towel.

It took her a moment to get her brain organized enough to even remember what he was talking about. "Good."

"Liar." His voice was quiet and very, very sexy. She wondered if he'd ever considered a side job as a phone sex operator. He'd be fantastic at it. Or maybe he could just read her a book, any book at all . . .

His phone buzzed once more and he blew out a sigh. "That's twice. I'm sorry, I have to look." He pulled his phone from his pocket and glanced at the screen.

A frown creased his brow as he accessed a text.

And then his easy demeanor vanished. He rose to his feet.

"What's the matter?" she asked.

He pulled her towel back around her, tucking it in between her breasts, stopping to brush a sweet kiss to her lips. "I'm sorry. I have to go. Sean's in trouble."

Her heart stopped. "Do you need help?"

"No, I've got it. We've been around this block before, more times than I can count."

"But . . ." She ran her gaze down his body, letting it catch on the unmistakable bulge behind his button fly. "Now?"

"Yeah." He ran the pad of his thumb along her jaw and kissed her again. "Thanks for giving me a taste of you," he murmured against her mouth. "I already want another."

And then he was gone, leaving her sitting there,

mouth open, blinking like a land-locked fish at the open doorway he'd just vanished through.

"I want a taste of you too," she said to the empty void he'd left behind. She looked around her at the steamy bathroom. "I don't even know what just happened," she told it.

But she totally did—she'd just complicated things even more. And in an irreversible way, too.

Dammit, she was supposed to be fun whispering him. Instead, she'd fun whispered herself!

Chapter 16

#MyBad

Finn took the stairs rather than wait for the elevator, and then jogged across the courtyard to the pub, his body practically vibrating with adrenaline.

He could still hear Pru's soft, breathy, whimpery pants in his ear. She'd stilled for his touch like she'd been afraid it would all stop too soon.

She'd even begged him. *Please, Finn, don't stop . . .*

If Sean hadn't called, they'd have moved to her bed by now and be in the throes of round two.

Not once in the past eight years since his life had changed so drastically had he'd had such a wildly hot, crazy sex-capade, but Pru brought it out in him. There was no denying that he felt more alive when he was with her than he'd felt in . . . well, shit.

A fucking long time.

There'd been few opportunities when he was busy

working 24/7 and trying to keep Sean on the straight and narrow.

But Pru had gotten under his skin, and like her, he wanted more. So much more. He wanted to know her secrets, the ones that sometimes put those shadows in her eyes. He wanted to know why she wanted to bring him fun and adventure, but didn't seem to feel like she deserved it as well. He wanted to know what made her tick. And more than anything, he wanted to taste her again.

Every inch of her.

He wanted to see more of her and he had no idea how she felt about that. For the first time in he had no idea how long, he was thinking about more than the bottom line of the pub.

He was thinking about a future, with an adventurous, frustrating, warm, sexy woman he couldn't seem to get enough of.

Skipping the crowded pub, he entered directly into his office, while thumbing through his email on his phone. "So what the hell's so important that—" He broke off as a sound permeated through his thick skull—the soft sigh of a woman experiencing pleasure.

Sexual pleasure.

Jerking his head up, he took in the sight on his couch and whipped back to the door, which he slammed behind him. Grinding his back teeth into powder, he strode around the courtyard to the pub door and went directly to the bar.

Scott, the night's bartender, started toward him but Finn waved him off and grabbed a shot glass to serve himself.

He was trying to lose himself in the happy sounds of the crowd around him, pouring a double when Sean appeared, shirtless, shoeless, buttoning his Levi's.

Behind him was a tall, curvy blonde in a little sundress, her hair tousled, her high-heeled sandals dangling from her hand. Shooting Finn a wry smile, she turned to Sean, ran a hand up his chest and around his neck and leaned in to give him a lingering kiss. "Thanks for a good time, baby." With a last lingering look in Finn's direction, she padded out.

"Fuck," Finn said.

"Exactly," Sean said with a sated grin.

Finn shook his head and headed down the interior hallway to his office.

Sean followed.

"What the hell's the matter with you?" Finn asked.

"Absolutely nothing."

"I'm working real hard here at not chucking this shot glass at your head," Finn said. "You want to come up with better than that and you want to do it quick."

Sean blinked. "What the hell's your problem? Why are you raining on my parade?"

"What the hell's *my* problem?" Finn sucked in a breath for calm. It didn't work. "You texted me that you had an emergency. I dropped everything and race over here to find you fucking some girl on the couch in *my* office."

"I told you, you have the better office."

Finn stared at him, and some of his genuine temper and absolutely zero humor of the situation must have finally gotten through to Sean because he lifted his hands. "Look, you got back here faster than I thought you would, all right? And Ashley just happened to stop by and . . . well, one thing led to another."

Finn tossed back the smoothest Scotch in the place and barely felt the burn. "You told me there was an emergency. That you needed me. Exactly how long did you expect me to take getting here?"

"Longer than sixty seconds," Sean said. "I mean I'm good, but even I need at least five minutes." He flashed a grin.

Finn resisted the urge to strangle him. Barely. "Emergency implies death and destruction and mayhem," he said. "Like, say, our *last* emergency. When dad died."

The easy smile fell from Sean's face, replaced by surprise and then guilt, followed by shame. "Oh shit," he said. "Shit, I didn't think—"

"And there's our problem, Sean," Finn said. "You never do."

Sean's mouth tightened. "No, actually, that's not the real problem. Let's hear it again, shall we? You're the grown-up. I'm just the stupid problem child."

"You're hardly a child."

"But I'm still a problem," Sean said. "Always have been to you."

"Bullshit," Finn said. "Get your head out of your own ass and stop feeling sorry for yourself. Now what the hell's the emergency?"

Sean paused. "It was more of a pub thing," he said vaguely, no longer meeting Finn's gaze.

And a very bad feeling crept into Finn's gut. "What did you do?"

"It's more what I didn't do . . ."

"Spit it out, Sean."

"Okay, okay. But before you blow a gasket, you should know. It's not as bad as the time I nearly burnt the place down by accident. Let's keep it in perspective, all right?"

"Accident?" Finn asked. "You opened the place after hours to have a party with your idiot friends and were lighting Jell-O shots when you managed to catch the kitchen on fire. How exactly is that an *accident*?"

"Well, who knew that Jell-O was so flammable?"

Finn stared at him, at an utter loss. "This is a fucking joke to you, all of it."

"No, it's not."

"Yes, it is. You think I'm just the asshole making you toe the line. I'm trying to give you a life here, Sean, a way to make a living and take care of yourself in case something happens to me."

Sean laughed. *Laughed*. The sound harsh in the quiet room. "You're not dad, Finn. I don't need you to give me a life. I can do that for myself. Contrary to popular belief, I can take care of myself."

"Because you've done a great job of it so far?" Finn asked.

"Fuck you," Sean said and walked out.

"What's the damn emergency?" Finn yelled after him.

But Sean was gone.

This left Finn in charge of the place for the night instead of getting to go back up to 3B where he'd left his mind, and maybe a good chunk of his heart as well.

The next morning was Sunday and despite it being a weekend, Finn was back at the pub. He was working his way through some of the never-ending paperwork that seemed to multiply daily when Sean appeared.

"Where have you been?" Finn asked, hating himself for sounding like a nagging grandma.

Sean ran his hand over his bedhead hair. "Slept on the roof."

Finn shook his head. "Bet you froze your nuts off."

"Just about." Sean paused. "I shouldn't have walked away last night. I'm sorry for that."

"Just tell me the damn emergency already," Finn said.

Sean's jaw went tight, a muscle ticking. A very unusual sight, and a tell that he was actually feeling stressed, something Finn hadn't known his brother could even feel.

Sean pulled two envelopes from his back pocket. "You know how I said I wanted to help you with the business side of things and you said I had to start at the bottom, and I said like the mail room? And you said we don't have a mail room, but yes a little bit like that?"

"It was a joke," Finn said. "Because you think you just jump in but there's a learning curve. So I suggested you start by handling our mail and our accounts payable. And you agreed as long as I didn't come along behind you to check up on you."

"Didn't need dad in the house looking over my shoulder," Sean said.

"Actually, if I'd been dad, I'd have used my fists, or whatever else was handy and just beat the shit out of you," Finn said. "Or have you forgotten?"

Temper flashed in Sean's eyes. Temper, and something else that he got a hold of before Finn could. He didn't speak for a moment, which was rare for Sean. He just stood there, fists clenched at his side, working his jaw muscles. "Fuck it. Fuck this," he finally said and started to turn away but stopped. "No, you know what? Fuck you. Sideways."

"Mature."

But Sean wasn't playing. He shoved a finger in Finn's face. "You think I've forgotten which one of us dad got off on beating up? You think I don't remember at night when I close my eyes that you took it for me, every single time? That I don't know you made sure you were between him and me so I'd be *safe*? That I survived only because of you? That I'm *still* surviving because of you? You think I don't know that I'm a fuckup who's only here with a semblance of a normal life because you gave it to me?"

Okay, so the something else in Sean's gaze had been grief and remembered horror. And Finn shouldn't have tried to be glib about it, there was nothing glib about how they'd grown up. "I didn't mean to take this there," he said quietly. "You're not a—"

"I forgot to pay our liquor license." Sean's face was hard. Blank. "I forgot and it was due today."

Finn stared at him. "That was the one thing I reminded you of two months ago when you took on the bills."

"The envelope fell behind my desk and got lost. And it wasn't alone. The property tax on the house was back there too and that one's now past due."

"Are you kidding me?"

"Do I look like I'm kidding?" Sean inhaled a deep breath, spread out his arms and shook his head. "See?

You were right. I really am just a fuckup. You should demote me back to—"

"What? Sweep boy?" Finn found his own temper. And hell if he was going to let Sean default to his favorite thing—self-destruction, just because it was easier than growing up. "You wanted to do this, Sean. You wanted in. And now you're telling me what, things are too hard, you're too busy having fun that you can't get your head out of your ass and grow up?"

Sean's eyes narrowed. "Guess so."

Finn stared at him waiting for regret, for an apology, for any-fucking-thing, but nothing came. Just Sean's hooded gaze, body braced for a fight, all sullen 'tude. Finn shook his head. "Fine. You win."

"What does that mean?"

"It means I need some air," Finn said and walked out the door to the courtyard.

It was late morning and unusually warm. Summer was in full swing, which in San Francisco usually meant a sweatshirt sixty-five-ish and fingers crossed for a hope to get into the seventies.

But now, in direct opposition to his mood, it was sunny and warm, and it didn't suit him in the least.

He had no idea where he'd intended to go, only knowing he was going somewhere, needing to vent the ugly inside him, the ugly his dad had bequeathed him.

The gym maybe. He'd go punch the shit out of a bag at the gym.

But to do that, he'd have to walk past Pru standing there watching him, a look on her face that told him she'd heard everything.

Chapter 17

#ThereAren'tEnoughCookiesForThis

Pru stared into Finn's face, wishing like hell she could go back and vanish before he caught sight of her, or barring that, at least do something to ease the pain and anger in his eyes.

"Did you get all of that or do you need me to repeat some of it?" he asked.

"I didn't mean to get any of it," she said. "It was an accidental eavesdrop."

He blew out a sigh, shook his head, and stared over her head at the fountain.

Regret slashed through her. She'd been caught eavesdropping many times, all of them accidental. Once when she'd been young, she'd caught her parents going at it on the dining room table with gusto. It'd been ten o'clock at night and she'd been fast asleep only to wake up thirsty. Not wanting to disturb her parents, she'd made her own way to the kitchen.

At first glance she'd smiled because she'd thought that her dad was tickling her mom. Her mom had loved it when he'd done that, and they'd touched often.

But she'd never seen naked tickling before . . .

Later when Pru had been a teenager, she'd come home from school to find her parents at the table with their neighbor, Mr. Snyder, who was also their accountant, talking about something called bankruptcy. Her mom had been crying, her dad looking shell-shocked.

And then there'd been the night her grandpa had shown up where she'd been spending the night at a friend's. Weird, since she'd called her mom and dad for a ride, not her grandpa. She'd wanted to go home because her friends had decided to sneak in some boys and she hadn't felt comfortable with the attention she'd been getting from one of them. He'd been in her math class, and was always leaning over her shoulder pretending to stare at her work when he was really just staring at her breasts.

The other reason it'd been weird for her grandpa to show up was because she hadn't seen him in years. Not since he and her dad had been estranged for reasons she'd never known. And her dad and her grandpa being estranged meant that Pru was estranged by default.

So why was he at her friend's house?

The night had gone on to become a real-life nightmare, the kind you never woke up from because she'd listened to her grandpa explain to her friend's mom that he'd come to tell his granddaughter that her parents were dead, that her father had been past the legal drinking limit. He'd crossed the center median in the road and had hit another car head on, clipping a second along with the people on the sidewalk.

Pru did her best not to think about that moment, but it crept in at the most unexpected times. Like when she was in the mall and passed by a department store in front of the perfume aisle and caught a whiff of the scent her mom had always worn. Or when sometimes late at night if there was a storm and she got unnerved, she'd wish for her dad to come into her room like he always had, sit on the bed and pull her into his arms and sing silly made-up songs at the top of his lungs to drown out the wind.

Nope . . . eavesdropping had never worked out for her. And when she'd heard Sean and Finn yelling at each other through Finn's open office window, she honestly hadn't meant to listen in. Now she couldn't un-hear what she'd heard. What she *could* do was be there for them. Because this whole thing, their fight, their being parentless, Finn having to raise Sean, all of it, was *her* family's doing. She swallowed hard. "I'm sorry, Finn."

He just shook his head, clearly still pissed off. "Not your fault."

Maybe not directly but she felt guilty all the same. But telling him the truth now when he was already lit up with temper wouldn't help him. It would hurt him.

And that's the last thing she'd ever do.

At her silence, he focused in on her. "How are you doing, are you—"

"Totally fine," she said. "The road rash is healing up already."

Something in his eyes lit with amusement. "Good, but this time I actually meant from when we—"

"That's fine too," she said quickly and huffed out a sigh when he laughed. She looked around for a distraction and saw a couple of women talking about throwing some coins into the fountain. Pru nodded her head over there. "You know about the legend?"

"Of course. That myth brings us more foot traffic than our daily specials."

"You ever . . . ?"

"Hell no," he said emphatically.

She managed a smile. "What's the matter, you don't believe in true love?"

His gaze held hers for a beat. "I try not to mess with stuff that isn't for me."

She couldn't imagine what his growing-up years had been like or the hell he'd been through but she managed a small smile. "Maybe you shouldn't knock something unless you've tried it."

"And you've tried it?" he challenged.

"Oh . . ." She let out a little laugh. "Not exactly. I'm pretty sure that stuff isn't for me either."

His gaze went serious again and before he began a conversation she didn't want to have, she spoke quickly. "I really didn't mean to overhear your fight with Sean. I was just wondering if I could help with whatever was wrong before I went to work."

"What's wrong is that he's an idiot."

"If it helps, I think he feels really bad," she said.

"He always does."

Her heart ached for him as she took in the tension in every line of his body. "You guys do that a lot?" she asked. "Fight like that?"

He slid his hands into his pockets. "Sometimes. We're not all that good with holding back. We sure as hell never did master the art of the silent treatment."

"My family never did either," she said. "Silence in my house meant someone had stopped breathing—thanks to a pillow being held over their face."

Finn gave her a barely there smile, definitely devoid of its usual wattage. "Was there a lot of fighting?" he asked.

"My parents were high school sweethearts. They were together twenty years, most of them spent in a very tiny but homey Santa Cruz bungalow house, where we were practically on top of each other all the time." She sighed wistfully, missing that house so much. "Great house. But seriously, half the time my mom and dad were like siblings, at each other over every little thing. And the other half of the time, they were more in love with each other every day." The ache of losing them had faded but it still could stab at her with a white hot poker of pain out of the blue when she least expected it, like now.

"Sounds pretty good, he said.

"It was." *He'd beaten the shit out of you* . . . The words were haunting her and her gaze ran over Finn's tough, rugged features. It hurt to picture him as a help-less kid standing between a grown man and his little brother, taking whatever punishment had been meant for Sean to spare him the pain of it, and she had to close her eyes against the images that brought.

A hand closed around hers. She opened her eyes as Finn tugged her into him. He stroked the hair from her face and looked down into her eyes. "You sure you're okay?"

He'd just had a huge blowout with Sean and he was

asking about her. She swallowed hard and nodded. It's you—"

He set a finger to her lips. "I'm fine."

The two women at the fountain were laughing and chatting. "Think it's really true?" one of them asked. "If we wish for true love, it'll happen?"

"Well, not with a penny," the other one said, eyeing the change her friend was about to toss in. "How many times have I told you, you can't be cheap about the important stuff."

Her friend rolled her eyes and fished through her purse. "I've got a quarter. Is that better?"

"This is for love, Izzy. Love! Would you buy a guy on the clearance rack? No, you would not."

"Um, I wouldn't buy a guy at all."

"It's a metaphor! You want him new and shiny and *expensive*."

Izzy went back into her purse. "A buck fifty in change," she muttered. "That's all I've got. It's going to have to be enough." She closed her eyes, her brow furrowed in concentration, then she opened her eyes and tossed in the money.

Both women held still a beat.

"Nothing," Izzy said in disappointment. "Told you." She turned away from her friend to stalk off and ran smack into Sean, who'd come out of the pub.

His hands went to her arms to catch from falling to her ass. He looked down into her face with concern. "You all right, darlin'?"

Izzy blinked up at him looking dazed. "Um . . ."

Her friend stuck her head in between them. "Yes,"

she told Sean. "She's okay. She just can't talk in the presence of a hot guy. Especially one she wished for."

He smiled, though it was muted. "You work at the flower shop, right?" he asked Izzy.

She nodded emphatically.

"Well come into the pub and have a drink any time," he said.

Izzy gave another emphatic nod.

"That means yes. And thank you," her friend translated and dragged Izzy away. "Oh-em-gee, the fountain totally works!"

Pru watched them go and had to laugh. Luck was where you made it for yourself and she knew that. She'd wished for love for Finn, and she still wanted that for him but she was realizing that would mean letting him go.

She had to let him go.

Sean looked at Finn. "Need to talk to you," he said.

Finn, face blank, nodded.

"I'll meet you inside," Sean said.

Finn nodded again.

When Sean walked way, Finn turned to Pru.

"Work calls," she said with a small smile.

"Story of my life," he said. "About last night."

Her heart skipped a beat.

"We were onto something."

Her nipples went hard. "Were we?"

"Yeah. And you liked it too."

She felt herself blush a little. "Maybe a little."

"Just a little, huh? Because I still have your finger-nail imprints in my scalp." He was out-and-out smil-ing now, a naughty sort of smile that made her thighs quiver. "I wasn't finished with you, Pru," he said softly. "I had plans."

Oh boy. "Maybe I had plans, too."

"Yeah?" Closing the gap between them, one of his hands went to her hip, the other slid up her back to anchor her to him. "Tell me. Tell me slowly and in great detail."

She laughed and fisted her hands in his shirt, but just before her lips touched his, someone cleared their throat behind them.

"Dammit," she whispered, her lips ghosting against Finn's. "Why do we keep getting interrupted?"

"That is the question," he murmured.

With a sigh she pulled free and turned. "Jake," she said in surprise. "What are you doing here?"

In Jake's lap was a box and on top of that box sat Thor, one ear up, one ear down, his scruffy hair looking even more thin and scruffy than usual, sticking up in tufts on his head.

"Brought you the last box," Jake said. "Never seen anyone stretch a move out so long."

"Yes, well, hiring movers was cut from the budget." Pru scooped up her Thor, kissing him right on the snout. He panted happily, wriggling to get closer, bicycling his front paws in the air, making her laugh and hug him.

"I'm taking him for a grooming at South Bark," Jake said. "He's past due."

"Also cut from the budget," Pru said. But she traded Thor for the box. "Thanks."

"I'll bring him to work when he's finished," Jake said.

And then he didn't roll away.

Pru gave him a long look, but Jake's picture was in the dictionary under *pig-headed* so he didn't budge. "You're going to be late," he told Pru in his boss voice.

With a sigh, she turned to Finn. "I picked up an extra Sunday shift today. I've got to go. Hope you have a good day."

"In case it's our last you mean?"

"You don't think Sean will get the license paid tomorrow?" she asked.

"If he wants to live, he will." But Finn's attention was on Jake.

Pru forced a smile. "Okay, so we're all going off to our own corners now, yes?"

"Go to work, Pru," Jake said.

"Um—"

"It's okay." Finn gave her hand a squeeze. "Knock 'em dead today," he said.

Right. Dammit. With nothing else she could do, she lifted the box of her stuff and walked away from the only two men to have ever earned a spot in her heart. She just hoped they didn't kill one another.

Chapter 18

#BeamMeUpScotty

Finn watched Pru make her way toward the elevator with her box before he turned back to Jake.

Both he and Thor were watching him watch Pru.

Jake was brows up, the picture of nonchalance. "What's going on?"

"Nothing much," Finn said.

Jake took that in and nodded. "You've got an arm on you. The other night at the game you nearly saved our asses—not that anyone could've actually saved our asses."

Finn shrugged. "I played some in college."

"You going to keep playing for us?"

"Depends."

"On what?" Jake asked.

"On if this sudden interest in my ball-playing abilities is in any way related to the woman we both just watched walk away," he said.

"About ninety-nine percent of it, yeah," Jake said.

Okay, so the guy got brownie points for honesty. "Why don't you tell me what you really want to know," Finn suggested.

"I don't want to know anything," Jake said. "I want *you* to know that if you make her so much as shed a single tear, I'll break every bone in your body and then feed your organs to the pigeons. I mean, sure, I'd have to hire it out to do it, but I'm connected so don't think I won't."

Finn stared at him. "You forget your meds or something?"

"Nope."

"Okay, then, thanks for letting me know," he said and turned to go.

Jake rolled into his path. "I'm not shittin' you."

"Also good to know." Finn cocked his head. "I'm going to go out on a limb here and guess that you already had a shot at her and you blew it."

"Why would you think that?"

"Because you just threatened me with death and dismemberment. Only one reason to do that—you fucked up somehow."

Jake stared him down for a minute. He might be in a chair but Finn got the sense he could more than handle himself.

"That might be partially true," the guy finally said.

Finn wrestled with his conscience a moment. "I'd say something helpful here, like it's 'never too late' or 'you can fix any mistake,' because truthfully, I like you. But—"

"—But you like *her* too," Jake said.

"But I like her too," Finn agreed firmly, not willing to back down, feeling a little bit like Thor did about his prized dog cookies. "Much more than I like you."

"It's a bad idea," Jake said. "You and her."

"That's for me and Pru to decide."

Thor jumped down from Jake's lap, walked over to Finn and put his paws on his shins to be picked up—which Finn did.

Then it was apparently Jake's turn to wrestle with his conscience. "What the hell. The damn dog likes you?"

Finn shrugged and gave Thor a quick cuddle before setting him back down on Jake's lap.

Jake muttered something to himself that sounded like "she bit off more than she can chew this time" and turned his chair to roll off.

"Yeah," Finn said to his back.

"Yeah what?"

"Yeah I'm going to keep playing on your team. But I want to buy new jerseys."

Jake rolled back around to face him. "Why?"

Because it would make Pru happy. "You got a problem with SF Tours splashed across everyone's backs in bold letters?"

"Not in the least." Jake paused. "I suppose you also want O'Riley's on there somewhere."

"It'd be nice."

Jake stared at Finn for a beat before nodding. "Our next game's tomorrow night," he said and again he made to leave but didn't. "About Pru and me. We didn't work out for one simple reason."

"What's that?"

Jake looked behind him to make sure Pru wasn't standing there, which normally would've made Finn smile but he wanted to know the answer to this question shockingly bad.

"I made a mistake with her," Jake said, and then grimaced. "Okay, more than one, but the only one you need to know is that she's strong and resilient and smart, so much so that I believed she didn't need anyone, and certainly not me. It must have showed since she called me out on it. She said we couldn't be intimate anymore because I wasn't in love with her and she didn't love me either, at least not in that way. To my shame, I didn't realize that I hurt her by so readily agreeing, by not giving much thought to how she felt about splitting." He paused. "Pru doesn't do casual. She can't. Her heart's too damn big."

"Are you trying to scare me off?"

"Yes," Jake said bluntly. "I hurt her," he said again. "Don't you do the same, don't you even fucking think about it."

"Or the aforementioned death and dismemberment?" Finn asked, only half kidding.

Jake didn't even crack a smile.

Monday morning Pru was waiting outside the county courthouse building, hoping she was in the right place at the right time. When she saw Sean heading for the steps, she pushed away from the wall with relief.

He stopped in surprise at the sight of her. "Hey, Trouble," he said. "What are you doing here?"

"Helping you fix your mess." She smiled at his

confusion. "You here to get the liquor license all square, right?" she asked.

He blew out a sigh, looking disgusted. "Finn told you I screwed up."

"No," Pru said quietly. "He wouldn't. I . . . overheard you arguing."

"Yeah." Sean grimaced and scrubbed a hand down his face. "Sorry. I just hate disappointing him."

"If that's the case, why do you give him such a hard time?"

Sean shrugged. "It's how we show affection."

Pru shook her head with a low laugh. "Boys are weird."

"Hey, at least we don't kick and scratch and pull hair when we fight."

"If that's how you think girls fight, you're with the wrong girls."

He grinned. "You know, I like you, Pru. I like you for Finn. You've got his back. He'd say he doesn't need that but he's wrong. We all need that. He know you're here?"

"No, and he doesn't have to know," she said. "Especially since I'm going to save your ass."

"What do you mean?"

"Follow me." She led him inside the offices, by-passed the public sign-in area and waved through the glass partition to a guy at a desk.

The guy was Kyle, Jake's brother.

Kyle gave her a chin nod and hit a button that had the door buzzing open to them.

"Hey, cutie," he said and took a look at Sean. "What's up?"

"I've got a friend who didn't pay their liquor license bill in time," she said. "What can you do for me?"

"First, tell your friend he's an idiot."

She looked into Sean's tight face. "I think he's aware," she said with a small smile.

"Second, have a seat. You're going to owe me," he told Pru. "Caramel chocolates from Ghirardelli. You know the ones."

"Consider it done," she said and ten minutes later they were back on the front steps of the building.

"You're a lifesaver," Sean marveled. "And a super hero."

"I'll add both to my résumé. Maybe it'll get me a raise."

Sean laughed and hugged her. "Dump my brother and marry me."

She laughed because they both knew he wasn't the marrying type, at least not yet.

There'd been a time where she would've said the same thing about herself, but she knew now that she was changing. A part of her *did* want to let love into her life again. Maybe even have a family someday.

How terrifying was that?

Finn made sure to get to the softball field well before the start of their game.

He had no idea why he was looking forward to it, there were a million things he should be doing instead. But he lowered his sunglasses and scanned the area for Pru.

"She's not here yet," Jake said, rolling up to his side.

"Who?" Finn asked casually.

But not casually enough because Jake snorted.

Giving up on pride, Finn asked, "Is she coming?"

"I'm not privy to her schedule."

"Bullshit."

Jake smiled. "Jealous of me, O'Riley?"

"Do I need to be?"

Jake's smile spread.

Shit.

"Got the new jerseys," Jake said. "You work fast."

Finn shrugged like no big deal. It'd only cost an arm and a leg and a huge favor to get them done in one day.

"I like the SF Tours across the backs," Jake said.

"Good."

"Could've done without the O'Rileys on the breast."

Finn smiled and didn't respond. He was looking forward to seeing his name on Pru's breast.

"What's going on with you two?" Jake wanted to know.

"You ask her?"

"Hell no. I like living."

This gave Finn some satisfaction—that she'd kept what was between them to herself. But then again, that could be because she didn't think there was anything between them.

"I meant what I said yesterday," Jake said.

"About the death and dismemberment?"

"About you and her not becoming a thing."

That's when Finn felt it, a low level of electro-current hummed through him. Turning, he leveled his eyes on Pru and watched as she found him from across the field and tripped over her own feet.

He read her lips and smiled because she was swearing to herself as she picked up speed.

"Sorry I'm late!" she exclaimed breathlessly, like maybe once she'd seen them talking, she'd run over as fast as she could. Hand to her chest, the other holding onto Thor's leash, she divided a look between them. "So . . . what's going on?"

Finn opened his mouth but Jake beat him to the punch. "Game's about to start. Head or tails for home advantage."

Pru slid him a long look and then leveled that same look on Finn, who tried his best to look innocent. And he was actually pretty sure he *was* innocent since he had no idea what was going on any more than she did.

"Tails," she finally said. "It's always tails."

It was heads.

And . . . they had their asses handed to them like last time. But Kasey got a two base hit, and Abby caught a fly ball, and Pru got two base hits.

And once again, Finn had the time of his life.

Afterward, they all made their way back to O'Riley's. Sean immediately pulled him aside.

"Your girlfriend's wearing your name on her breast. Nicely done. You're faster than I gave you credit for, Grandpa."

"The entire team is wearing our logo, not just Pru," Finn said.

"Interesting."

"What?"

"You didn't deny the girlfriend thing," Sean noted.

Finn didn't take the bait and Sean sighed. "Yeah, yeah, you're still pissed off at me. Newsflash, I'm pissed off too."

"I didn't do shit to you."

"I know," Sean said. "I meant I was pissed off at me. For disappointing you."

Finn stilled and then shook his head. "I know you didn't mean to disappoint me."

"But I did. And not only that, I let you down. I let *us* down." Sean paused. "Earlier today, I handled the liquor license problem with Pru's help."

And then Sean told him the entire story of how Pru had been waiting for him and had smoothed the way with ease.

While Finn was still processing that, marveling over the lengths that she'd gone to help without mentioning it or wanting any credit for it, Sean went on.

"After that I went to pay the property taxes. I was there at their offices when they opened at ten."

"Wow," Finn said. "I didn't know you've even seen ten a.m."

Sean shoved his hands into his pocket and looked a little sheepish. "Yeah, I know. It was a first, and believe me it wasn't pretty. And it was worse than having to go to the damn DMV office, too. Got there right on time and had to take a number. Sixty-nine." He flashed a small smile. "I held up my ticket but no one else in the place was amused. The old lady who had number seventy flipped me the bird. She looked like this sweet little old granny and there she was, telling me I'm number one, can you believe it?"

In spite of himself, Finn laughed. "It's true. You are number one."

Sean's smile faded. "I know."

Regret slashed through Finn. "I didn't mean it like that."

"Yeah, you did," Sean said. "And I deserve it. I'm a fuckup, right?"

"Okay, I'm officially taking that back."

For a beat, Sean's expression went unguarded and filled with relief, making Finn feel even worse. There were times, lots of them, when he wanted nothing more than to wrap his hands around Sean's neck and squeeze.

But more than that, he wanted to never be like his dad. Ever. "So . . . how much were the late fees and penalties on the tax bill?"

Sean grimaced. "You remember Jacklyn?"

"The stripper you dated for a whole weekend last year?" Finn asked.

"Exotic dancer. And she doesn't do that anymore."

Oh shit. "Sean, tell me she doesn't now work at the property tax office."

Another grimace. "Well I could tell you that, but it'd be a lie."

Sean had done his charm-the-panties-off-the-girl and then pulled his also usual I'm-moving-to-Iceland. Or maybe it'd been it's-not-you-it's-me. Either way, he'd dumped her. The only reason Finn even remembered was because Jacklyn had then pulled the crazy card.

She'd stalked Sean. It hadn't been all that hard either, Sean had no sense of secret and always put himself out there, one hundred percent. It probably hadn't taken any effort at all for her to find out about the pub.

She'd come in and had climbed on top of one of the tables, stripping and crying at the same time, telling everyone what a scumbag Sean was.

It'd been a spectacle of massive proportions.

"What happened?" Finn asked. "She refused to let you pay up?"

"Not exactly," Sean said.

"Then what exactly?"

Sean looked . . . embarrassed? Impossible, he never got embarrassed. "She said I could renew on one condition," he said. "If I got up on her counter and did a striptease like she'd done at *my* place of work."

"Well, you gotta hand it to her," Finn said. "It's ingenious."

"Diabolical, you mean," Sean said.

"Whatever, but your next sentence better be 'so I totally got up on that counter and did a striptease for her.'"

"Did I mention the place was full?" Sean asked. "And that there were old ladies in there? *Old ladies*, Finn. I took one look at them and things . . . shriveled."

"And?" Finn asked.

"And . . . I didn't want to take my clothes off with shrinkage going on!"

Finn pressed the heels of his hands into his eye sockets, but it didn't work. His brain was still leaking out. Slowly and painfully. "Fine, I'll go down there and talk to her and straighten things out."

"Because that's what you do," Sean said. "You straighten things out. I fuck it all and you come along and clean it back up again, right?"

"Sean—"

"No. I'm done with that shit, Finn," Sean said. "I'm done being the idiot baby brother who needs saving. For once, for fucking once, I want to do the right thing. I want to save you." He shook his head. "No, I didn't get up on the counter. But I apologized to her for being a dick. And then I paid the penalties and late fees, all from my personal account. Our property taxes are current and will stay that way, and it won't happen again."

"Wow," Finn said. "That's great. And thanks." He paused. "From your personal account, huh?"

"Yeah and that hurt, man." Sean rubbed his chest like he was physically pained. "It hurt bad."

Finn smiled. "Also good."

"Now about your girlfriend," Sean said.

Finn raised a brow. He knew Sean was fishing. He had baited the hook and was going to keep saying "girlfriend" until he got a rise out of Finn.

Not going to happen.

"I like her," Sean said quietly.

Again, not what Finn had expected. He'd do just about anything for Sean, and had. But he didn't think he could walk away from Pru.

Not even for his brother.

Sean shook his head. "No, man, I mean I like her for *you*."

The scary part was that they'd finally agreed on something because Finn liked Pru for him too. So much so that at the end of the night—which was really three in the morning, he found himself outside her front door. Not wanting to scare her to death with the late hour, he texted her.

You up?

It took her less than a minute to respond.

Is this a booty call?

He stared down at the words and felt like the biggest kind of asshole on the planet. He was in the middle of texting back an apology when she texted him again.

Cuz I want it to be . . .

He was still smiling when her next text came in:

There's a key hidden on the top of the doorjamb.

He let himself in, crawled into bed with her and pulled her warm, sleeping form in close.

"Finn?" she murmured sleepily, not opening her eyes.

Well, who the hell else? "Shh," he said, brushing his mouth over her temple. "Go back to sleep."

"But there's a man in my bed." She still hadn't opened her eyes, but she did wind her arms around him tight, pressing her deliciously soft curves up against his body, sliding one of her legs in between his. "Mmm," she said. "A *hard* man . . ."

And quickly getting harder. "I didn't mean for this to be a booty call—"

"Finn?"

"Yeah?"

"Shut up." And she rocked against him so that his thigh rasped over the damp heat between hers, taking what she wanted from him.

He loved that she'd figured out that her confidence and belief in herself was as sexy to him as her gorgeous body.

"Mm," she hummed in pleasure, rocking against him, making him even harder. "I wonder what to do about this . . ." she mused.

He rolled, tucking her beneath him, and buried himself deep. "Let me show you."

Chapter 19

#JustLikeThat

Typically as summer progressed and more tourists poured into San Francisco, Pru got buried in work. This summer was no different. She worked long days, during which time she dedicated most of her daydreams to one certain sexy Finn O'Riley and what he looked like in her bed.

And what he did to her in it . . .

"What are you thinking about?" Jake asked her at the end of a shift while she was doing paperwork. "You keep sighing."

"Um . . ." She struggled to come up with something not X-rated. "I'm thinking about how much of a slave driver you are."

"Uh huh," he said, not fooled. "You tell Finn yet?"

"I'm getting there," she said, her stomach tightening in panic and anxiety at the thought.

"Pru—"

"I know, I know!" She blew out a breath. "You don't have to say it. I'm stalling. Big time."

His voice was quiet, almost gentle. "You're really into him."

She closed her eyes and nodded.

His hand slipped into hers and he squeezed her fingers. "You want a chance with him."

She nodded again.

"Chica, to have that chance, you've got to tell him before your window of opportunity closes and things go too far." He waited until she looked at him. "Before you sleep with him or—"

Oh boy.

"—I've got this," she said. "I know what I'm doing."

But they both knew she had *no* idea what she was doing.

That night, Elle and Willa dragged Pru out for "ladies'" night.

They surprised her when they ended up at a lovely spa, snacking on cute little sandwiches and tea before deciding on their individual treatments.

Pru stared at the spa's menu, a little panicked over the luxury that she couldn't really afford.

"It's my treat," Elle said, covering the prices with her hand. "This was my idea. I owe Willa a birthday present."

Willa smiled. "Cuz I can't afford it either."

"But it's not my birthday," Pru said.

"Pretend," Elle said. "I want a mani/pedi and a Brazilian, and I don't like to primp alone."

Which is how Pru ended up with a mani/pedi and her very first Brazilian.

The next day it rained all day long. Pru joked to Jake that after eight long hours on the water—in the rain—she felt like Noah.

Jake felt no mercy at all. "Make the money now, chica. Come wintertime you'll be whining like Thor does for that mini chow across the street, the one who's got fifty pounds on him and would squash him like a grape if given the chance."

So she worked.

At the end of another crazy day, she changed out of her uniform into a sundress and left Pier 39. She was Thor-less. After a stunt where he'd rolled in pigeon poo for some mysterious reason that only made sense to himself, Jake had once again taken him to the South Bark Mutt Shop for grooming.

All Pru wanted to do was to go home and crawl into her bed. For once she was too tired to even dream about having Finn in that bed with her. She wouldn't be able to lift a finger. Or a tongue.

Not that she'd mind if he insisted on doing all the work . . .

But that fantasy would have to wait. She had an errand to run before getting home, hence the sundress. She wanted to look nice for her weekly visit.

She walked up the steps to the home where her grandpa lived and signed in to see him.

Michelle, the front desk receptionist waved at her. Michelle had worked there forever, so they were old friends.

"How is he today?" Pru asked her.

Michelle's easy smile faded. "Not gonna lie, it's a rough one, honey. He's agitated. He didn't like his lunch, he didn't like the weather, he didn't like wearing pants, the list goes on. He's feeling mean as a snake. You want to come back another day?"

But they both knew that the bad days far outweighed the good ones now, so there was no use in waiting or she might never see him. "I'll be fine."

Michelle nodded, eyes warm, mouth a little worried. "Holler if you need anything."

Pru took a deep breath, waved at Paul the orderly in the hallway, and entered her grandpa's room.

He was watching *Jeopardy!* and yelling at the TV. "Who is Queen Victoria, you jackass!" He picked up his cane and waved that too. "Who is Queen Victoria!"

"Hi, grandpa," Pru said.

"No one ever listens to me," he went on, dropping his cane to shake his fist at the TV. "No one ever listens."

Pru moved into his line of sight and picked up the cane for him, wondering if he would know her today. "It's me, Pru—"

"*You,*" he snapped, narrowing his eyes on her, snatching the cane from her hands. "You've got some nerve coming here, Missy, into my home."

"It's good to see you, Grandpa. You sound good, your cold's gone from last week, huh? How are you feeling?"

"I'm not telling you shit. You were a terrible influence on my son. You encouraged him to be a good time, to party, when you knew—" He jabbed the cane at her for emphasis. "It's your fault he's dead. You should be ashamed of yourself."

This hit her hard but she did her best to ignore the hurtful words. "Grandpa, it's Prudence." She purposely kept her voice low and calm so that maybe he would do the same.

No go.

"Oh I knew who you are. I knew you for what you were the first day I saw you," he said, "when Steven first brought you home. He said 'this is Vicky and I love her,' and I took one look into your laughing eyes and I knew. All you wanted to do was have fun and you didn't care what fell by the wayside. Well, I'll tell you what, our business fell by the wayside because he wanted to spend time with you, not that you even noticed. Our business went into the ground because of you, because you didn't care if he had to work—"

"Dad worked," Pru said. "He worked a lot. Mom just tried to get him to enjoy life when she could because he did work so hard—"

"You were trouble with a capital T, that's what you were," he snapped out. "And you still are. Told you that then and I'll tell you again. You're Trouble to the very bone."

She'd frozen to the spot. She'd had no idea that her grandpa had called her mom Trouble, that he thought she'd been a bad influence on her dad simply because she'd wanted him to have a life outside of work.

The irony of this was not lost on her.

What *was* lost on her was how long she must have stood there, mouth open, gaping, letting old wounds reopen and fester because her grandpa grabbed something from the tray by his bed and chucked it at her.

She ducked and a fork skidded across the floor.

"Okay," she said, raising her hands. "That wasn't nice. Grandpa, I'm not my mom. I'm not Vicky. I'm your granddaughter Pru—"

"I don't have a granddaughter!" A piece of toast came hurtling her way, which she also dodged. "You killed him, Vicky. You killed him dead, so go rot in hell."

The words spilled from him, cruel and harsh and this stopped her cold so that she didn't duck quickly enough the next time.

His mug caught her on the cheek.

"Ouch, dammit!" she said straightening, holding her face. "You've got to listen to me—I'm not Vicky!" She went hands on hips. "Grandpa, you are not two years old, you need to stop with the temper tantrums!"

"That's right," he yelled. "I'm not two, I'm a *million* and two. I'm old and alone, and it's all your fault!"

Up until that very moment she'd somehow managed to separate herself from what he was saying, but suddenly she couldn't. Suddenly she wasn't feeling strong and in charge and on top of her life. She was just a girl who'd lost her parents, who had a grandpa whose elevator didn't go to the top floor. She was doing the best she could with what she had, but it wasn't adequate.

She wasn't adequate, as proven by her track record of no one loving her enough to stay with her, and the terrifying thing was, she didn't know how to be more.

"Get out!" he bellowed at her.

Paul appeared in the doorway, looking startled. "What's going on, Marvin?"

"What's going on is you let her in!" And in case there

was any doubt of the "her" in question, her grandpa stabbed a spoon in Pru's direction.

"Okay, now let's just take it down a notch," Paul said, doing his orderly thing, moving between Pru and her grandpa. "Put that utensil down, Marvin. We don't throw stuff here, remember?"

But Marvin couldn't be deterred. "It's her fault! Get out," he yelled at Pru. "Get out and don't come back, you tramp! You son-stealer! You *good for nothing free-loading hussy*!"

Michelle poked her head in, her eyes wide. "Paul, you need help?"

"We're good," Paul said evenly. "Aren't we, Marvin?"

"No, I'm not good! Can't you see her? She's standing right behind you like a coward. Get out!" he bellowed at Pru. "*Get out and stay out!*"

Michelle slipped into the room and put her hand in Pru's. "Come on, honey. Let's give him some alone time."

Pru let herself be led out of the room, heart aching, feeling more alone than she ever had. Her grandpa had never been the best of company but he'd at least been someone who shared her blood, her history . . . and now he wasn't remembering any of that and all she did by visiting him was upset him. She might have to stop coming entirely and then she'd be completely alone.

You already are . . .

She walked home slowly even though it was misting and she was wearing just the sundress and sandals. Her heart hurt. Rubbing it didn't assuage the deep ache that went behind the bone to her wounded soul. She missed her mom. She missed her dad. And dammit, she'd missed feeling whole.

She missed feeling needed. Wanted. Like she was crucial, critical to someone's life. A piece of their puzzle.

Instead she was a tumbleweed in the wind, never anchored. Never belonging to anyone.

With her head down and her thoughts even lower, she nearly ran right into someone on the street. Two someone's, locked in an embrace, kissing as if they were never going to see each other again. The man's arms were locked around the woman, an expression of love and longing on his face as he pulled back, still holding the woman's hands.

Had anyone ever looked at Pru like that? If so, she'd forgotten it, and she didn't think one could ever forget true love. All she wanted, all she'd ever wanted since the day she'd lost her parents, was for someone to care enough to come into her life and stay there.

Her chest tightened and her throat burned, but she refused to give into that. Crying wouldn't help. Crying never helped. All crying did was make the day a waste of mascara. And since she'd splurged on an expensive one this time in a useless effort to give her lashes some volume, she wasn't about to waste it. *Get it together*, she ordered herself. *Get it together and keep it together. You're okay. You're always okay . . .*

But the pep talk didn't work. The lonely still crawled up her throat and choked her.

The man smiled down at the woman in front of him, his gaze full of the love that Pru secretly dreamed of. He took his girl's hand and off they went into the rain, shoulders bumping, bodies in sync.

It broke her heart more than it should have. They were complete strangers, for God's sake. But watching them made her feel a little cold. Empty.

A crack of lightning lit the sky. She startled and then jumped again at the nearly immediate boom of thunder, sharp and way too close. Skipping the wrought-iron entrance to the courtyard, she instead ran directly into the pub.

She stood just inside, her eyes immediately straying to the bar.

Finn stood behind it with Sean, who was addressing everyone in the place, and all eyes were on him.

Except for Pru, who was watching Finn. He stood at Sean's side, his blank face on. Though Pru knew him now, or was coming to anyway, and she could tell by his tight mouth and hooded eyes that he wasn't feeling blank at all.

"So raise your glasses," Sean concluded, lifting his. "Because today's the day, folks, our first anniversary of O'Riley's, which we modeled after our dear departed Da's own pub, the original O'Riley's. He'd have loved this place." Sean clasped a hand to his heart. "If he were still with us—God bless his soul—he'd be sitting right here at the bar with us every night."

The mention of this loss would normally have made Pru's heart clutch because of her family's part in their loss, and there was certainly some of that, but she hadn't taken her eyes off Finn. He wasn't sad. He was pissed. And she thought maybe she knew why.

His dad hadn't been anything like hers. He hadn't cuddled his sons when they'd skinned a knee. He hadn't shown them love and adoration. He hadn't carried them around on his shoulders, showing them off every chance he had.

But for whatever reason, Sean was telling a different story. She had no idea why, but Finn's feelings on the matter were clear.

He hated this toast.

"We miss him every single day," Sean went on and finished up with a "*Slainte!*"

"*Slainte!*" everyone in the place repeated and tossed back their drinks.

Sean grinned and turned toward Finn. He said something to him but Finn didn't respond because he'd turned his head, and as if he'd felt Pru come in, he'd leveled his gaze right on her.

If she'd thought the oncoming storm outside was crazy, it was nothing compared to what happened between her and Finn every time they so much as looked at each other.

You're trouble with a capital T.

Her grandpa's words floated around in her brain, messing with her head, her heart.

One look into your laughing eyes and I knew. All you wanted to do was have fun and you didn't care what fell by the wayside.

She couldn't do this. She'd thought she was doing the right thing by helping Finn find some fun and adventure in his life but now she knew she wasn't. Worse, she felt too fragile, way too close to a complete meltdown to be here. And yet at the same time, she was drawn, so terribly, achingly drawn to the strength in Finn's gaze, the warmth in his eyes. She knew if he so much as touched her right now, she'd lose the tenuous grip she had on her emotions.

Go. Leave.

It was the only clear thought in her head as she whirled to do just that but Finn's warm, strong arms slid around her, turning her to face him.

He'd caught her.

"I'm all wet," she whispered inanely.

His eyes never left her face. "I see that."

"I'm—" *A mess*, she nearly said but the ball of emotion blocked her throat, preventing her from talking. Horrified to feel her eyes well up, she shook her head and tried to pull free.

"Pru," he said softly, his hand at the nape of her neck, threading through her drenched hair. There were tangles in it but he was apparently undeterred by the rat's nest. Pulling her in slowly but inexorably, his lips brushed her forehead. She could feel his mouth at her hairline as he whispered soothing words she couldn't quite make out.

She melted against him. No other words for it really. He was real. He was solid and whole. He was everything she wanted and couldn't have, no matter how badly she ached for him. She'd already wandered way off the track she'd set for herself, a fact that was now coming back to bite her hard because . . .

Because she was falling for him.

And what made it even worse; her day, her life, this situation . . . was that she not only wanted him in her life, she was desperately afraid and increasingly certain that she *needed* him as well.

She almost cracked at that. Almost but not quite.

But God, she couldn't seem to let him go.

Finn tightened his arms on her, pressing his cheek to the top of her head. "It's okay," he whispered. "Whatever it is, it's going to be okay."

But it wasn't. And she didn't know if she'd ever feel okay again so she pressed her face into his throat and let herself take another minute. Or two.

Or whatever he'd give.

Chapter 20

#HowYouDoin

Finn cuddled Pru into him, alarmed by her pallor, by the way she trembled in his arms, the tiny little quivers that said she was fighting her emotions and losing. Her dress had plastered itself to her delicious curves, her long damp hair was clinging to her face and shoulders.

Pulling back, he took her hand and led her to the bar so he could grab a fresh towel. He started to dry off her wet face and realized it was tears, not rain. "Pru."

"No, it's nothing, really," she said quietly, head down, his fearless fun whisperer . . .

"It's not nothing," he said.

"I just . . . I need to go."

Yeah, not going to happen. At least not alone. Finn turned and jerked his chin at Sean, wordlessly telling him he was in charge of the bar.

Sean nodded and Fin took Pru's hand, leading her down the hallway, not in the least bit sorry for leaving

Sean in the lurch. After that stunt toast Sean had just given, Finn was saving his brother's life by leaving now.

"Finn, really," Pru said. "Really, I'm fine. Really."

"And maybe if you say really one more time, I'll believe you."

She sighed. "But I am fine."

She wasn't but she would be. He'd damn well see to it. He took her to his office.

Thor leapt off the couch where he'd been snoozing, immediately launching into his imitation of a bunny. Bounce, bounce, bounce while bark, bark, barking at a pitch designed to shatter eardrums. "Thor," he said. "Shut it."

Thor promptly shut it and sat on his little butt, which shook back and forth with every tail wag that was faster than the speed of light. The result was that he looked like a battery-operated toy dog.

On steroids.

Pru choked out a laugh and scooped him up. "Why are you here, baby?"

"He got done at the beauty salon and Willa had to go before Jake could pick him up, so I said I'd take him for you."

"It's not a beauty salon," she said, face pressed into Thor's fur, doing a bang-up job at keeping up the pretense of being fine.

"Babe, it's totally a beauty salon," he said. "When I walked in to pick him up, Willa was presiding over a wedding between two giant poodles, one white, one black. The black one was wearing a wedding dress made of silk and crystals."

She slid him a look. No more tears, thank God, but

her eyes were haunted even though she did her best to smile. "Wow," she said.

"Impressed by the lengths Willa's shop goes to make money?" he asked.

"No, I'm impressed that you can recognize silk and crystals."

"Hey, I'm secure in my manhood." He took Thor from her and tucked the dog under an arm. The other he slipped around her waist. "Let's go."

"Where?"

"I'm taking you home. You look about done in."

"I passed done in about an hour ago," she admitted.

They didn't speak again as they crossed the courtyard. But Thor did. He started barking at a pair of pigeons and when Finn gave him a long look, the dog switched to a low-in-the-throat growl.

"They outweigh you," Finn told him. "Pick your battles, man."

The dog was silent in the elevator but that was only because Max, who worked on the second floor in Archer's office, was in it. With his Doberman pinscher Carl.

When Max and Carl got off the elevator, Thor let out a long sigh that sounded like relief, which under better circumstances would've made Finn laugh. "You know your particular breed of mutt was bred to kill Dobermans, right?" he asked the dog.

Thor blinked up at him.

"It's true," Finn said. "They get stuck right here—" He pointed to his throat.

Pru choked out a laugh. "Finn, that's a horrible story!"

He smiled and tugged lightly on a strand of her hair. "But you laughed," he said.

"I laughed because it was a *horrible* story," she said, but was still smiling.

And because she was, he leaned in and kissed her. Softly. "Hey," he said.

"Hey," she whispered back.

He wasn't sure what was going on with her, but it'd only taken one look at her open, expressive face to know she'd somehow been devastated today.

And, given the cut on her cheekbone, also hurt.

Both infuriated him.

The elevator opened and he took Thor's leash in one hand and used the other to guide Pru off. They were in the hallway in front of her door when Mrs. Winslow's door opened.

"Another special delivery?" Pru asked her.

"Not for me," Mrs. Winslow answered. "It's for you."

"Um, I don't eat a lot of special brownies," she said. "No offense."

Mrs. Winslow smiled. "Oh, none taken, honey. I'm just passing the word that there's a little something in the dumbwaiter for you."

"For me? Why?"

"For your bad day," Mrs. Winslow said.

Pru blinked. "How do you know I had a bad day?"

"Let's just say a little birdie looks after all of us," Mrs. Winslow said. "And he let me know to let you know that you're not alone."

"He who?" Pru asked.

But Mrs. Winslow had vanished back into her apartment.

Finn and Pru walked into hers. Finn crouched down and freed Thor from his leash and the dog immediately trotted to his food bowl.

Pru dumped a cup of dry food into it, patted the dog on his head and then went straight to the dumbwaiter.

Finn went to her freezer. He didn't see an ice pack but she did have a small bag of frozen corn. Good enough.

At her gasp, Finn turned to her. She'd pulled out a basket of muffins from the coffee shop. Tina's muffins, the best on the planet.

Finn wrapped the bag of corn in a kitchen towel and gently set the makeshift ice pack to her cheek and then brought her hand up to it. "Hold it here a few minutes," he said.

While she did that, he carried the basket to the kitchen table and they dove into the muffins right then and there.

"Good to have friends in high places," he said instead of asking her about her face, and when she visibly relaxed he knew he'd done the right thing.

Didn't mean he didn't want to kick someone's ass, because he did. Badly.

"It'd be better to know who those friends are," she said, clearly not reading his murderous thoughts. She met his gaze. "Do you know?"

He had an idea but didn't know for certain so he shook his head.

She took another muffin, chocolate chip by the looks of it. "Sean's toast at the pub upset you," she said.

Sitting across from her at her table, with Thor in his lap while he worked his way through a most excellent blueberry/banana muffin, he didn't want to get into Sean's toast. He much preferred to get into whatever had happened to *her*. But he knew that she wasn't going to open up.

Unless he did.

Problem was, he hated opening up. To anyone.

"I'm sorry your dad never got to see the bar and what a success you made of it," she said quietly.

He put his muffin down. "My dad couldn't have cared less what we did with ourselves when we were kids. He wouldn't care what we do now either."

"But Sean said—"

"Sean's so full of shit that his eyes are brown," he said. "My dad never had a pub. Hell, he never even acknowledged he was Irish. My brother perpetuates the lie because he thinks Irish pubs do well and he isn't wrong. We *have* done well but it isn't because we're Irish, it's because we work our asses off."

"You mean you work *your* ass off," she said.

He met her knowing gaze. "I just hate the fraud."

"It's not a fraud if it's true, even a little bit." Reaching across the table, she covered her hand with his. "Stop feeling guilty about something that isn't your fault and isn't hurting anyone. Let it go and enjoy the success you've made of the place, in spite of your father."

He stared at her. "How is it that you're cute, sexy as hell, *and* smarter than anyone I know?"

She gave him a small smile. "It's a gift."

Leaning over the table, he wrapped his fingers around her wrist and pulled the bag of corn from her face. Gently he touched her cheekbone. "You okay?"

"I will be."

Her resilience made him smile. "Yeah?" he asked. "And how's that?"

She shrugged a shoulder. "Well, it's raining, and I love the rain. Someone sent me a basket of muffins, and I love muffins. Thor is actually clean and going to stay that way for at least the next few minutes. I don't have to work until midday tomorrow. And I have company." She smiled. "The good kind." She lifted a shoulder. "It's all good."

She was aiming for light and she'd succeeded. It was how she dealt, he got that. And he was getting something else too—that he could learn a hell of a lot from her.

She rose from her chair and came around the table. She lifted Thor from his lap and set the dog down. Then she climbed into Finn's lap herself and cupped his face.

His arms closed around her and one thought settled into his brain. This feels right.

She feels right.

Chapter 21

#UpShitCreekWithoutAPaddle

Pru lifted her gaze to Finn's, startled by the sudden intensity in his gaze. It said she wasn't alone, that she mattered, a lot.

At least you're not the only one falling . . .

This thought was a cool tall drink of relief immediately followed by a chaser of anxiety.

Because she hadn't meant for this to happen. She hadn't meant for *any* of it; his attention, his affection, his emotional bond . . . and all of it was a secret dream come true for her.

Just as all of it was now a nightmare as well, because how was she supposed to give it up? Give *him* up?

Although the tough truth was, she wouldn't have to. Telling him the truth would accomplish that because *he* would give *her* up once she did.

She'd known they'd be getting to this. She hadn't

missed him looking at her cheek, or the temper that flashed in his eyes whenever he did. "It's—"

"Not nothing. Don't even think about saying it's nothing." His voice was gentle but inexorable steel.

"My grandfather's in a senior home," she said. "Has been for years. I visit him every week but he doesn't always recognize me."

"He hit you?" he asked, his voice still calm, his gaze anything but.

"No." She shook her head. "Well, not exactly."

"Then what exactly?"

"He was trying to get me to leave," she said. "He threw the stuff on his lunch tray at me."

His brow furrowed. "What the fuck?"

"It's that sometimes he thinks I'm my mom," she said. "He didn't like her."

Finn's fingers slid into her hair, soothing, protective, and she felt herself relax a little into his touch.

"Why not?" he asked quietly.

"She . . ." Pru closed her eyes and pressed her face to his throat. "She was a good-time girl. She loved to have fun. My dad loved to give her that fun. We spent a lot of time out on the water and at Giants games, his two favorite things."

He smiled. "And you're still out on the water."

She nodded. "It makes me feel close to them. I used to tell my dad I was going to captain a ship someday, which must have sounded ridiculous but he told me I could do anything I wanted." She paused. "I loved them, very much, but in some ways my grandpa was right. My mom encouraged my dad. The truth is they were partyers, and big social drinkers . . ."

"Is that why you never drink?"

"A big part of it," she admitted for the first time in her life. "Is that weird for you, being with someone who doesn't drink?"

He palmed her neck and waited until she looked at him. "Not even a little bit," he said.

She smiled. "My dad used to say my mom was the light to his dark. He loved that about her. He loved her," she said, her chest tight at the memory of her mom making him laugh. "They loved each other."

There was empathy in Finn's eyes and in his touch. Empathy, and affection, and a grim understanding. He'd had losses too. Far too many.

"I'm glad you have those memories of your mom and dad together," he said. "I know it sucks having them gone, but at least when you think of them, you smile."

Mostly. But not always. Not, for instance, when she thought of how they'd died.

And who'd they'd taken with them . . .

"I'm sorry you don't have those memories," she said quietly.

"Don't be. Because I don't know what I'm missing." He met her gaze. "You had it worse. Your life was a complete one-eighty from mine. You know exactly what you're missing."

And there went the stab to her gut again. "Finn—"

"It's not your fault, Pru. Any of it. Forget it."

As if she could.

He tightened his grip on her. "No more going into your grandfather's room alone. You take an orderly with you, or anyone. Me," he said. "I'll go with you. Or whoever you want, but I don't want you in there with him alone again."

"He's not always that bad—"

"Promise me," he said, cupping her face, taking care with her cheek. "There's only honesty between us, right? We have no reason for anything but. So look me in the eyes and promise me, Pru."

She inhaled deeply, feeling like the biggest fraud on the planet. "I promise," she whispered, hating herself a little bit. "Finn?"

"Yeah?"

Eyes on his, she leaned in close. "Do you remember when you kissed away my hurts?"

"After the first softball game," he said and smiled. "Yeah, I remember. It was a highlight for me." His eyes went smoldering. "Want me to do it again?"

"No, it's your turn," she said. "I'm going to kiss away *your* hurts."

He stilled. "You are?"

"Yes." *Please want me to, please need me to . . .*

A rough sound escaped him then, regret and empathy, making her realize she'd spoken out loud. Closing her eyes, she tried to turn away but his arms tightened around her, his voice low and rough. "I do," he said fiercely. "I'm going to show you just how much I need you. All night long, in fact."

She stared into his eyes, letting the strength in the words, in his body, in his gaze convince her he meant every single word. "The whole night," she repeated, needing the clarification.

"For as long as you need."

Since that was too much to think about, she had to set it aside in her head. Instead she slid her fingers into his hair as his hands caught her, rocking her against her very favorite body part of his. She oscillated her hips, thrilling to the way he groaned at the contact.

No slouch, Finn stroked up her arms, encouraging the spaghetti straps of her sundress to slip from her shoulders. The bodice was stretchy and lightweight and still damp from the rain, which meant it took very little effort for him to tug it to her waist so that her breasts spilled out.

A rough, very male sound of appreciation rumbled up from deep in his throat and his hands went under her dress to cup her ass, pulling her in tighter to him, putting his mouth right at tease-her-nipples level.

He captured one in his mouth and her brain ceased working. Just completely stopped. Probably for the best since she was about to do things with him that she'd told herself she wouldn't do again. "Finn—"

Finn groaned again, a near growl. "Love the sound of my name on your lips," he said and sucked hard, his hands pushing her dress up her thighs as he did.

"Oh no," she said, and right then, with his teeth gently biting down on her nipple and his hands up her dress, he froze.

"No?" he repeated.

"No, as in I'm not going to be the first one naked this time," she clarified. "Why am I always the first one naked?"

"Because you look amazing naked. Here, let me show you—"

"Now just hold on," she said with a low laugh, feeling

dizzy with lust. "Good God, you're potent." She shoved his shirt up his chest and hummed in thrilled delight at the sight of his exposed torso. "Off," she demanded.

He took a hand off her thigh, fisted it in his shirt between his shoulder blades and yanked it over his head, never taking his eyes from hers, immediately going back to the business of driving her right out of her ever-loving mind.

Her hands slid down his bare chest over his abs, which were rigid and taut enough that even though he was sitting, there was no fat ripple. If she didn't want him so badly, she'd hate him for it. She popped open his button-fly jeans and a most impressive erection sprang free into her hands.

He was commando.

"Laundry day," he said.

She stared at him and then laughed. She had him full and hard in her hands, and she was hot and achy and already wet for him, and she was laughing.

"It's not nice to laugh at a naked man," he said, smiling at her, not insulted in the least, the cocky bastard, and it only made her laugh harder.

"I'm sorry," she managed on a snort.

Straightening up, causing those delicious ab muscles to crunch, he nipped her jaw. "You don't look sorry."

She stroked his hard length and her body practically vibrated for him. "I'll work on that," she managed as he pushed up the hem of her sundress.

Her amusement backed up in her throat.

Air brushed over her upper thighs now. Her panties were tiny, enough that when Finn reached his hands around to her ass, there was bare cheek groping.

"Mmm," rumbled approvingly from his throat. His fingers dug in a little, cupping, squeezing, and then slipped beneath the lace, making her quiver.

"Hold this," he said.

She automatically took hold of her own dress at her waist. She felt hot. Achy. *Desperate*. She was already straddling him but his big hands adjusted her legs so that the two of them fit together like two pieces of a puzzle.

"Yeah," he said. "Like that." And then he scraped aside her little scrap of panties and stilled as he got a good look at what he'd exposed.

And that's when she remembered the Brazilian. "It's Elle's fault," she blurted out.

"Oh Christ, Pru." He stroked a reverent finger across her exposed flesh.

Her exposed, *bare* flesh. "She took me and Willa to the spa and—"

The pad of Finn's finger came away wet and he groaned.

"—the next thing I knew . . ." she trailed off when, holding her gaze, he sucked his finger into his mouth. "So . . . you like?" she whispered.

"Love." His hands went to her hips and he lifted her up to the table, plopping her on the wood surface. Then, calm as you please, he scooted his chair in close, draped her legs over his shoulders, lowered his head and . . .

Oh. *Oh*. Her last coherent thought was that maybe Elle had been onto something . . .

"Missed the taste of you," Finn murmured a few minutes later, when he'd rendered her boneless. And not very many minutes either. He shifted back, and afraid he was going away, she made a small whisper of protest and clutched at him.

Flashing her a smile, he reached behind him, pulling his wallet from his back pocket.

"It's a little late to exchange business cards, isn't it?" she asked, trying to make light of their compromising situation because as was already established, her mouth never knew when to stay zipped.

He pulled out a condom.

"Right," she said. Damn, she should have thought of that. Problem was, at the moment, with her dress basically a belt around her waist, exposing all her goodies, she was incapable of thought.

"You take my breath," he said, eyes on her as he tore the packet open with his teeth and then rolled the condom down his length.

She'd never seen anything so sexy in her entire life.

With what looked like effortless strength, he scooped her from the table and lowered her over the top of him, in total control of how fast she sank onto him—which was to say not fast at all. Seemed Finn liked the slow, drive-her-insane grind, and she let out a sound of impatience that made him flash her another smile.

"You think this is funny?" she managed.

"You panting my name, whimpering for more, and trembling for me?" He brushed his stubbled jaw very gently across her nipple and gave her an entire body shiver. "Try sexy as hell."

She was no longer surprised to realize that she felt it. Sexy as hell. It was an utterly new experience for her and she didn't quite know how to rein herself in. So she didn't even try. Instead she went after every inch of him that she could reach, following each touch of her fingers with her mouth. His shoulders, collarbone, his throat . . . God, she loved his throat. But what she loved even more? The rough, extremely erotic sounds she coaxed from him.

"Lift up," he whispered hotly in her ear, and then rather than wait for her to comply, he guided her with his hands on her hips, showing her how to raise up on her knees until he nearly slipped out of her, and then to sink back down, once again taking him fully inside her.

They both gasped as she began to move like that, urged on by his hands, all while their mouths remained fused, kissing hot and deep. When they ran out of air, he wound his fist in her hair and forced her head back, sucking on her exposed throat, his other hand possessive on her ass.

Then that hand shifted to the groove between her hip and thigh, his fingers spread wide so that his thumb could rasp over the current center of her universe. She gripped his wrist and held his hand in place.

"You like?" he asked hotly against her ear.

"Just don't stop." Ever . . .

He didn't. He swirled that roughly callused thumb in a very purposeful circle that was exactly the rhythm she needed, making her cry out his name as she came hard.

When she opened her eyes, his were hot and triumphant, and she wrapped her arms tight around his neck. "It was your turn to go first."

"Always you first," he said and melted her heart.

"I'm not sure that's fair."

He smiled. "Hell yeah, it is. I love watching you come for me." He nipped her chin. "You say my name all breathy and you dig your nails into me. So fucking sexy, Pru."

With a low laugh, she buried her face in his neck.

"That shouldn't embarrass you," he said. "Watching you come makes my world go around."

At the thought, her body clenched around him and he groaned.

"Your turn now," she whispered, and did it again.

"Yeah?"

"Yeah." Empowered, she gave him a little push until he leaned back in the chair. "You just sit there and look pretty," she said. "Let me do the work now."

He flashed her a sexy grin that almost made her come again before he leaned back, clearly one hundred percent good with giving her the reins and letting her have her wicked way with him.

She gave him everything she had, and in the end when he banded his arms around her, his head back, his face a mask of stark pleasure as he shuddered up into her, she felt herself go over again. With him. Into him . . .

It shocked her. A co-orgasm. An *effortless* co-orgasm. She didn't realize it was a real thing. She'd honestly thought it was a myth, like unicorns and good credit ratings.

When she caught her breath and her world stopped spinning out of control she looked at him. Sprawled beneath her, head back, eyes closed, he had a smile on his face.

"Damn," he said. "That just gets better and better."

Dazed, she stood on shaky legs and began to re-arrange her dress. "This isn't anything like what I expected."

He gave a sexy laugh. "Liar."

She froze and looked at him.

"Admit it," he said. "You've wanted me since day one. I sure as hell have wanted you since then."

Laughing at her expression, he pulled her back onto his lap, cuddling her, kissing the top of her head. "You think too much, Pru."

That was definitely also true. She rested her head against his chest and listened to his heartbeat, strong and steady.

"I've got something to say," he murmured, his hands sliding down to palm and then squeeze her ass.

She wriggled a little bit, just to hear that low growl and feel his fingers tighten on her. But while his body was giving her one message, his words gave another.

"You helped Sean out and that means a lot to me," he said.

She froze and lifted her head to look at him. "He told you? He didn't have to do that."

"I'm glad he did. I already knew you're warm and sexy, funny and smart, but what you did, Pru, having his back like that—and by extension, my back as well—that told me everything I need to know about you."

She shook her head. "Anyone would have—"

"No," he said. "They wouldn't. I've got my brother and a select core group of friends that would do anything for me, and that's been it. But now I've got you too. Means a lot to me, Pru. You mean a lot to me."

Oh God. "I feel the same," she whispered. "But Finn, you don't know everything about me."

"I know what I need to."

If only that was true. "Finn—" But before she could finish that statement, the one where she told him the truth, the one that would surely change everything and erase their friendship and trust and . . . *everything*, someone knocked on her door.

"Ignore it," Finn said.

"Pru," came a deep male voice from the other side of her door.

Jake.

Oh, God. *Jake.*

This was bad. Very, very bad. If Jake found Finn here with *that* look on his face, there'd be no holding back the storm. Jake had told her to tell Finn before things went too far, and when Jake told someone to do something, they did it.

But she hadn't.

And things had gone far with Finn. Just about as *far* as a man and a woman could get . . .

She was in trouble. Big trouble. One of the problems with having a wounded warrior as a BFF is that he saw everything as a conflict to fix. She had no doubt he'd take one glimpse at them and very possibly butt his big nosy nose in and enlighten Finn himself.

And that would be bad. Very, very bad. She jumped up and straightened her dress before whirling to Finn. He'd pulled up his jeans, but hadn't fastened them. Nor had he put on his shirt, which meant he sat there in nothing but Levi's, literally, his hair completely tousled from her fingers—bad fingers!—an unmistakable just-got-laid sated expression all over his face.

Not moving.

She waved her hands at him. "What are you doing? Get dressed!"

"Working on it." He stretched lazily, slowly, like he had all the fricking time in the fracking world.

Jake knocked again, annoyance reverberating through the wood. Jake had many good qualities but patience wasn't one of them. "Pru, what the hell are you doing in there—and it'd better not be Finn," he said.

She'd just sent her hands on Finn's chest to give him a little hurry-up nudge, so she had a front-row view of his brows shooting up.

Well, crap.

Then, from outside her door, came the unmistakable sounds of keys rattling, which reminded her of the unfortunate time on moving day when she'd given Jake her damn key. *What had she been thinking?* "You've got to hide!" she whispered frantically to Finn.

"What the hell for?"

With a sound of exasperation she whirled around and eyeballed potential hiding places.

She had little to no furniture.

"Dammit!" Then she focused on the dumbwaiter. Perfect. "Here," she said, opening it and then pushing him toward it. "I need you to get in here for just a minute—"

Finn, solid and steady, didn't move when she'd pushed him. What was it with her and big, badass alphas who only could be budged when they wanted to be budged?

He looked down into her face and seemed to take in her clear panic because he gave a slight head shake. "You've lost it."

"Yes, now you fully understand! I've completely lost it, but to be honest, I lost it a long time ago!"

"I meant me, babe," he said. "I've lost it to even be melted by those eyes of yours, enough that I'll do just about anything for you."

"Good," she said quickly. "Go with that. Please, I can't explain right now, but I need you to hide, for just a minute, I promise."

He shook his head again, muttered some more, something that sounded like "you're a complete dumbass, O'Riley," but then God bless him, he folded up his rangy form in the dumbwaiter.

"Just for a minute," she repeated and slammed the door shut on his gorgeous but annoyed face and turned back to the kitchen—where Finn's shirt and shoes were lying scattered on the floor. *Shit!* She snagged everything up, ran back to the dumbwaiter, opened the door and shoved them at Finn and then slammed the door.

Just as Jake rolled into her kitchen.

Finn sat there in the dumbwaiter, somewhere between pissed off and bemused. And maybe a little turned on, which showed just how messed up in the head he really was.

No one handled him. Ever. And yet Pru just had, like a pro.

Which meant he sat here squished into the dumb-waiter in only his unbuttoned jeans, his shirt in one hand, his shoes in his other, wondering—What. The. Fuck.

He tried to come up with a single reason why, if Pru and Jake were not a thing, that he had to be a dirty little secret. But he couldn't.

And his amusement faded.

Because that's exactly what he was at the moment. Pru's dirty little secret, and while the thought of that might have appealed in fantasy, it absolutely did not hold up in reality.

Not even close.

Leaning in, he tried to catch whatever was going on in Pru's kitchen.

"Why are you breathing like a lunatic?" Jake asked. "And you're all flushed. You sick?"

Try as he might, Finn couldn't catch Pru's response.

But he had no problem catching Jake's next line. "Why is there a pair of men's socks on your floor?"

And that's when the dumbwaiter jerked and went on the move, taking Finn southward.

Chapter 22

#SillyRabbit

"Shit!" Finn had no choice but to hold on as the dumb-waiter began to move, taking him past the second floor, and then the first . . . all the way to the basement. It was a bad flashback to the last time this had happened.

Before he could catch his breath, the dumbwaiter door opened, and yep, he was in the basement. He had an audience too. Luis the janitor, Trudy the head of building cleaning services, Old Guy Eddie, Elle, Spence, and Spence's two buddies Joe and Caleb all sat around a poker table smoking cigars and playing what looked like five-card stud.

They stared at Finn—still in only his jeans, still holding his shirt and shoes—with various degrees of surprise and shock.

Luis didn't even blink, but then again the guy had lost a leg in Vietnam so not much rattled him. He just shook his head. "Some people never learn."

Trudy had been married to Luis—three times. They'd recently celebrated their third divorce, which meant they were already sleeping together again and probably thinking about their fourth wedding. Trudy took in Finn's state of dress—or in this case undress— and her cigar fell out of her mouth.

"Hot damn," she said in a been-smoking-for-three-decades voice. "I didn't even know they made real men that look like that!"

Joe, the youngest one here at twenty-four, who'd MMA-ed his way through college for cash, lifted up his shirt to look down at his eight-pack. "Hey, I'm made like that too."

Spence snorted.

"You're drooling," Elle told Trudy and tossed some money into the pot without giving Finn a second glance.

Finn didn't take this personally. Everyone knew Elle had a thing for Archer. Well, except for Elle herself. And also Archer . . .

Eddie looked at Finn and then pulled the cigar out of his mouth. "You got your wallet on ya somewhere, kid?"

"Yeah," Finn said. Minus his emergency condom . . .

"Well then get over here," Eddie said. "We'll deal ya in on the next round."

Finn looked down at himself. He thought about the night he'd had, how it had started out about as amazing as a night could get, how it'd ended up going south.

Literally.

"I'm raising thirty," Elle said, mind on the game. Not much distracted Elle from her poker game.

"You sure?" Spence asked her.

She narrowed her eyes. "Why wouldn't I be sure?"

Spence just looked at her. He didn't like to waste words but as one of the smartest guys Finn had ever met, he didn't often need them.

Caleb didn't mind using *his* words. "Do you remember the last time we played?"

Elle sighed. "Yeah, yeah, the last time I raised, I ended up signing over my firstborn to Spence. Good thing I'm not planning on having kids." She blew out a breath and folded. "You're right."

"What?" Spence asked, a hand curved around his ear.

"I said you're right!" Elle snapped.

Spence gave a slow smile. "I heard you. I just wanted to hear it again. Can I get it in writing for posterity?"

Elle flipped him off.

This only made Spence grin. "Sticks and stones . . ."

"How about a big, fat loss," Elle griped. "Will that hurt you?" She looked around. "What the hell does a girl have to do to get a drink refill and to keep the game moving?"

Joe scrambled to pour her a drink, infatuation in his gaze. Elle absently patted him on the head and went back to her cards. "You coming or not?" she demanded of Finn.

That was Elle, always on a schedule. With a shrug, he tossed aside his shirt and shoes. What the hell. "Deal me in."

It was three in the morning before Finn staggered home and into bed, where he lay staring at the ceiling.

He'd lost his ass in poker—damn Elle, she had

balls of steel—and afterward he'd dragged himself to the pub to check in and help close. It'd been a busy night, too busy to keep one eye on the door for a certain brown-eyed beauty.

Not that she'd shown up.

Neither had Jake.

Which meant that Finn had ground his back teeth into powder wondering if he'd been played. Or if he was overreacting. Or if he was a complete idiot . . .

It's just that he couldn't stop thinking about how he'd felt buried deep inside Pru, so deep that he couldn't feel regret or pain. Could feel nothing but her soft body wrapped around him, her wet heat milking him dry, her mouth clinging to his like she'd never had anyone like him, ever.

"Shit," he muttered and flopped over, forcing his eyes closed. So she'd wanted to hide what they'd done. So what. He'd had a hell of an incredible time with her and that had been all he'd needed.

Now it was back to the real world.

He'd halfway convinced himself that he believed it when someone knocked on his door.

In Finn's experience, a middle-of-the-night knock on the door never equaled anything good. In the past, it'd meant his dad was dead. Or Sean needed bail money. Or there was a kitchen fire at the pub.

Kicking off his covers, he shoved himself into the jeans he'd left on the floor. As he padded to the door, he shrugged into a shirt, looking out the peephole to brace himself.

It wasn't what he expected.

Instead of a cop, it was a woman. The one woman who had the ability to turn him upside down and inside out. She was in jeans and a tee now, looking unsettled and anxious. Dammit. He pulled back and stared at the door.

"Don't make me beg," Pru said through the wood.

Resisting the urge to thunk his head against the door, he unlocked and opened up.

Pru stared up at him, squinting through the long bangs that hadn't been contained and were in her face. "You left," she said.

"You shoved me in the dumbwaiter."

"You left," she repeated.

He crossed his arms over his chest and refused to repeat himself. She'd stuffed him into the dumbwaiter so she didn't have to reveal to Jake what they'd been up to on her kitchen table. He'd talked himself into filing that away in his head, in a file drawer labeled STUFF THAT SUCKS. He'd thrown away the key.

But apparently he'd forgotten to lock it.

She closed her eyes. "Can I come in?"

"For?"

She opened her eyes and leveled him with those warm brown eyes. "I wanted to apologize."

"Okay. Anything else?"

"Yes." She sighed. "I know this looks bad, Finn, but it's not what you think."

He leaned against the doorjamb. "And what do I think, Pru?"

She put her hands to his chest and gave a little push. A complete sucker, he let her squeeze in past him, taking some sick delight in the fact that she smelled like him.

She strode straight into his bedroom and he followed because he was Pavlov's dog at this point.

She checked out his room, the unmade bed, the moonlight slanting in through his window, casting his mattress in grays and blues. When he came in behind her, she turned to face him and kicked off her shoes.

"We both know what you thought," she said. "But Jake and I aren't a thing. I wasn't hiding you, at least not like that."

"Then like what?"

She held his gaze for a long beat. "I don't always act with my brain. Sometimes I act with my heart, without thinking about the consequences. Jake is my boss and my friend, and he looks out for me."

"He thinks I'd hurt you?"

"No," she said and looked away. "Actually, he thinks *I'll* hurt *you*. And he's probably right."

"You going to break my heart, Pru?" he asked softly, only half joking because what he knew—and she didn't—was that she could absolutely do it if she wanted. She could slay him.

"Actually," she said very quietly. "I'm pretty sure it's going to be the other way around." She reached for him and pushed his still unbuttoned shirt off his shoulders, assisting it back to the floor.

"What are you doing?" he asked.

"What does it look like?" Her fingers drifted down his chest and abs to play with the top button on his jeans.

"You're trying to get me naked."

"Yes," she said. "You going to help?"

Good question. First things first though. He gathered her hands in one of his and cupped her face with the other, tilting it up to his. "You and Jake are—"

"No," she said without hesitation, eyes clear.

He might regret this later but he believed her. "No more hiding, Pru. I won't be anyone's dirty secret, not even yours."

"I know," she said and freed her hands to caress his chest. "We weren't done with each other."

"No?"

She gave a small head shake and let her fingers drift southbound. "Unless . . . you were done with me?"

Not by a long shot. "You're wearing too many clothes," he said and then proceeded to get her out of them. He tugged her T-shirt from the waistband of her jeans and yanked it over her head. Her bra followed the same path and her breasts spilled into his hand, warm and soft, tugging a groan from the back of his throat.

Her hands and mouth were just as busy, landing on whatever they could reach, which at the moment meant she was nibbling at his collarbone, her fingers unbuttoning his Levi's.

Quickly losing control, he crouched in front of her, taking her jeans and panties down with one hard tug. With his face level with one of his favorite parts of hers, he clasped her hips in his hands and tugged her a step closer.

"Oh," she gasped, off balance, sliding her fingers into his hair to steady herself.

But he had her. He had her and he wasn't going to let her fall. He'd had no such luck for himself. He'd already fallen and hard. And feeling his heart squeeze at the thought, he leaned in and put his mouth on her.

Another gasp escaped her lips and his fingers tightened on his hair. "Finn—"

He licked. He nuzzled. He sucked. All while her soft pants and helpless moans and wordless entreaties wormed their way in his ears and through his veins until he didn't know where he ended and she began.

When she came, she came hard and with his name on her tongue. Satisfaction and triumph surged through him at that. When her knees buckled, he rose and scooped her up at the same time, feeling like a superhero as he tossed her down to his bed.

She bounced once and then he was on her. Maybe a little rougher than she expected because she blinked up at him in surprise as he pinned her to the mattress.

"What are you doing?" she asked, her voice a little hoarse, for which he took full credit.

"Giving you what you showed up here for."

"What if *I* wanted to be in the driver's seat?" she asked.

"Dumbwaiter," he said.

"So . . . this is payback?"

He gathered both of her wandering hands and pinned them to the pillow on either side of her head. "Yes." He nudged her thighs open with one of his and made himself at home between them. "But you can do whatever you want to me in return. Later." He bowed his head and licked his way down her neck. Christ, she tasted good. "Much later."

He'd planned on going slow and savoring all the naked skin against him but as she softened beneath him, wrapping her legs around his waist, he suddenly wasn't interested in slow. He could feel her, hot and wet and ready, and when he slid in deep, they both gasped and instantly combusted with his first hard thrust.

Chapter 23

#CaffeineRequired

That day at work, Pru was going over the schedule for the day when Nick poked his head in from the docks. "Hey," he said. "Got a minute?"

She'd gotten him the job here working for Jake, but they were both always so busy, they didn't often get a chance to talk. "I've got exactly a minute," she said, glancing at the clock and then smiling at Nick. "What's up? How's your mom? How's Tim? I talked to him about a week or so ago."

"Mom's fine," Nick said. "And Tim got that apartment." He smiled. "Thanks to you. Does Jake know he has a saint working for him?"

"Believe me," she said on an uncomfortable laugh. "I'm no saint. And Jake doesn't need to be told otherwise."

"Why? Maybe he'd give you a raise."

"For being a saint? No. Now if I figured out how to clone myself," she said. "He might be so inclined."

Nick gave her a quick, hard hug.

"What's that for?" she asked.

"Everything."

When he'd left, she got a text from Elle that had her staring at her phone, mouth open.

I don't know how or why, but thanks for sending last night's comic relief to poker night.

She stared at the text, horrified. She still couldn't believe she'd done that to Finn.

And that's not the only thing you've done to him . . .

She'd let her emotions get the better of her. That was a mistake, but oh God, what a delicious, sexy, heart-stopping wonderful mistake.

She responded back to Elle with a ? on the off chance she was jumping to conclusions, and Elle was all too happy to explain in her next text:

Biweekly poker night in the basement turned into a peep show when Finn showed up in the dumbwaiter half nekkid. Lucy, you've got some 'splainin' to do.

Her stomach hurt. Her plan to bring Finn a little fun, a little adventure while waiting on the fountain to bring him love, had seemed so simple. Fun and adventure, and maybe even a little walk on the wild side. She honestly hadn't meant to do that in bed.

Or on her kitchen table.

Or in her shower . . .

Oh, God. This whole thing was bad. Very, very bad. And yet it'd all been so heart-stopping good at the same time that she found herself just standing in place at odd moments, her brain glazed over as it ran through erotic, sensual memories like a slide show behind her eyelids. Finn bending her over the end of the bed, his mouth at her ear whispering hot little sexy nothings as he'd teased and cajoled her right out of her inhibitions, his body hard against her.

In her . . .

She blew out a shaky breath. Dangerous thoughts. Because it was her being selfish, and she wasn't going to do that again.

Absolutely not.

Or, you know, as much as she could.

Ugh. She slapped herself in the forehead. *Go back to your plan*, she ordered herself, not giving her inner smart-ass a chance to chime in. No more sexy times, no matter how deliciously demanding he was in bed. And this time, she meant it. One hundred percent. Or at the very least, seventy-five percent.

Certainly no less than fifty percent . . .

Luckily, work was crazy busy and helped keep her mind off all things Finn-related. The weather was warm, which meant that everyone and their mama wanted to get outside. They wanted to be on the water, see Alcatraz, Treasure Island, the Pier 39 sea lions . . .

She was on her second tour of the day when a guy tried to propose to his girlfriend. Unfortunately for him, he apparently hadn't checked out her Pinterest page where she'd pinned pictures of acceptable rings. The proposal went fine until she opened the little black box. It didn't end well, especially since he'd done it in the first five minutes of the two-hour tour, and then had to endure the rest of the ride in frosty silence.

On her last tour, Pru had a bunch of frat boys who kept making jokes, wanting to know if she'd be their captain below deck as well, nudge, nudge, wink, wink, if she'd ever played pirates with her passengers, because they wouldn't mind pillaging and plundering. At that she'd pulled out the baseball bat she kept beneath her captain's chair and asked if anyone needed their balls rearranged or if they wanted to sit down and shut up for the rest of the tour.

They'd gone with sitting down and shutting up.

She'd gotten a call from Jake the second the last of her passengers debarked.

"You have problems with passengers, you let me kick their ass, you don't need to do it," he said. "You're not alone out there, I'm always in your ear."

Literally. They were in constant communication when she was on the water via comms. "Maybe sometimes I want to do my own ass kicking," she said.

"My point is that you don't have to."

"It's a good stress reliever," she said.

"Uh huh. As good as sleeping with the guy you haven't been honest with and then shoving him bare-ass naked into your dumbwaiter to avoid your ex, your boss, and your best friend?"

The air left her lungs in one big whoosh. "Who told you?"

"Eddie would snitch on his mama for food or cash, you know that."

"And how did Eddie know?" she demanded. "I didn't tell anyone!"

"Didn't have to. Eddie was in the basement at a very intense poker game with a select few when the dumbwaiter opened and out stumbled your boy, pants in hand."

"Shirt!" she yelled. "He had his *shirt* in hand. He was *wearing* his pants!"

"Just tell me you told him."

"I'm working on that."

"Dammit, Pru, it's like you *want* to self-implode your own happiness. Promise me you won't do anything that stupid again until you tell him."

She closed her eyes, knowing he was right. Hating that he was right.

"Pru—"

"—I hear you," she said.

"Promise me. I know you would never break a promise, so right here and now, promise me that—"

"I promise," she said. "I've always intended to tell him and I will. I get that it's been two weeks but I'm working up to it, okay? I'm going to tell him soon as the time is right."

"Just don't miss your window of opportunity, chica, that's all I'm saying."

"I hear you."

They disconnected and Pru closed her eyes. Hard to pretend something hadn't happened when everyone in the free world knew.

She didn't linger after work like she usually did.

Instead she hightailed it out of there. Needing to clear her head, she and Thor walked. Well, *she* walked. Thor got tired about halfway and stopped. He planted his little butt on the sidewalk and steadfastly refused to walk another step.

"You're going to get fat," she told him.

Thor turned his head away from her.

"Come on," she cajoled. "I want to walk out the Aquatic Park Pier and watch the sky change colors as the sun sets."

Thor sneezed and she could have sworn she heard "bullshit" in the sound. And the sad thing was that her dog had more brain cells than she did because he was right.

She was stalling going home. It was just that she'd come to count on Finn's company so much. Too much. He made her smile. He made her ache. He made her want things, things she'd been afraid to want. He made her feel . . . way too much.

Thor hadn't budged so she scooped him up and carried him out to the end of the long, curved pier. She watched the water and thought maybe this wasn't so bad. Yes, she'd made a mistake. She'd been with Finn a few times.

So what.

Other people, normal people, slept with people all the time and she didn't see anyone else angsting over it. For all she knew Finn hadn't given it a second thought, and in fact would laugh off her worries.

But you've slept with him now, as in actually *slept*, snuggled in his arms all night long . . . And that was more intimate than anything else and it changed things for her. "Maybe I'm just being silly," she said hopefully to Thor.

Thor, lazy but utterly loyal, licked her chin.

She hugged him close. "I always have you," she murmured. "You'll never leave me—"

But he was squirming to get down so desperately she did just that. "What's gotten into you?" She stopped when he bounced over to a fellow dog a few feet away.

A small, dainty, perfectly groomed Shih Tzu. The dog stilled at Thor's approach and allowed him to sniff her butt, and then returned the favor while Pru glanced apologetically at the dog's owner.

The woman was in her thirties, wearing running tights and a tiny little running bra, the brand of which Pru couldn't even afford to look through their catalogue.

"Baby," the woman said. "What have I told you? You're a purebred not a disgusting mutt."

"Hey, he's not disgusting, he's just—" But Pru broke off when Thor lifted his leg and peed on Baby.

By the time Pru got to her building, Thor had fallen asleep in her arms, which were nearly dead. Seemed nothing stopped him from catching his beauty sleep, not snooty little dogs with snooty little owners, and certainly not the squealing of said snooty little dogs' owners about the cost of dog grooming and how Pru had let her heathen ruin her "baby."

A low-lying fog rolled in to join dusk as she entered through the courtyard, staying close to the back wall, not wanting to be seen by anyone.

The temps had dropped so she wasn't surprised to

see the wood fire pit lit. She was surprised to see Eddie manning the pit. He waved her over.

Halfway there she realized the entire courtyard smelled like skunk. When she got to Eddie, she pulled the uneaten half of her sushi lunch pack from her bag and gave it to him.

"Thanks, dudette." Pocketing the sushi in his sweat-shirt, he poked at the fire with a long stick.

"It's going out," she said.

"I know. I burned it hot on purpose, I had some stuff to get rid of."

"Stuff? Stuff related to the skunk smell?"

He just smiled.

A few minutes went by and Pru realized she was still standing there, now with a wide grin on her face. "I'm starving."

"Me too," Willa said from right next to Pru.

Pru blinked. "When did you get here?"

"A while ago." Willa looked into her face and grinned too. "You're high as a kite."

"What? Of course I'm not," Pru said.

"It's a contact high." Willa looked at Eddie, who had the decency to look sheepish.

"I had some dead seedlings I had to get rid of," Eddie said. "It's fastest to just burn them."

"You can't just burn them out here!" Willa said. "Right, Pru?"

But Pru was feeling distracted. "I need food," she said. "Chips, cookies, cakes, and pies."

"And pizza," Willa said. "And chips."

"I already said chips."

"Double the chips!" Willa yelled to the courtyard

like she was placing an order with an invisible waitress.

Pru laughed at her. "I'm not high as a kite. *You* are."

"No, *you* are."

"No," Pru said, poking Willa in the arm. "*You* are."

"You both are." This was from Archer, who'd appeared in front of them.

"Whoa," Willa said. "The police are here. Run!"

Archer reached out and snagged her hand to keep her at his side. Frowning down at her, he then turned and eyeballed Pru.

She did her best to look innocent even though she felt very guilty. Why, she had no idea.

"Shit," he said in disgust to Eddie. "You got them both stoned out of their minds. What the hell did I tell you an hour ago?"

"You said you'd arrest me if I didn't put out the fire. I'm working on it. It's almost out, dude."

A muscle in Archer's jaw bunched. Willa set her head on his shoulder and looked up at him with a dreamy smile. "Elle's right," she murmured, batting her lashes. "You do look really hot when you're all worked up."

"I'm not worked up—" He broke off and slid her a speculative look. "Elle thinks I'm hot?"

"When you're worked up. When you're not, she thinks you're a stick in the mud."

Archer shook his head and pulled out his phone. "Elle, your girls need you in the courtyard. Now." He slid both Pru and Willa a long look and added, "You're going to want to feed them. Oh, and Elle? Remind me that we have something to discuss."

Willa smacked him. "You can't tell her that I told you that she thinks you're hot!" she hissed.

Archer lifted a finger in her direction and listened to something Elle said. He let out a rare smile. "Yes, that was Willa."

Willa smacked her own forehead. "She's gonna kill me."

Archer disconnected with Elle and pointed at them. "Don't either of you move until she comes and gets you. You hear me?"

"Hear you," Pru said, eyes locked on the pub. The doors were open to the street and the courtyard. The place was full and spilling out sounds of music and laughter.

Behind the bar, Sean and Finn were elbow to elbow, working hard. Finn was shaking a mixer and laughing at something a woman at the bar was saying to him.

Elle appeared in a siren red sheath dress that screamed serious business. Her black heels echoed the statement. "What's going on?" she demanded, hands on hips. "Archer pulled me out of a meeting with the building's board—"

"Was the owner there?" Willa asked. She looked at Pru. "None of us have ever met the owner. He's exclusive."

"*Elusive*," Elle corrected, narrowing her eyes on each of them, and then Eddie.

Who unlike when he'd been dealing with Archer, actually sunk in on himself a little, seemingly sheepish. "I didn't realize," he said.

"Oh for God's sake." Elle took a deep breath and looked a little less uptight. She took another and sighed. "I need pizza."

"Right?" Willa said, grinning.

"Count me in." This was Haley, who arrived from the elevator in her white doctor's coat, looking quite official.

"You're still doctoring," Willa said.

"Nope," Haley said, pulling off her lab coat. "The smoke and commotion drew me down here but I'm done for the day, thankfully. It was a busy one."

"Spence come in for glasses yet?" Elle asked.

Haley bit her lower lip. "I saw him, yes."

"And?" Elle asked. "His eyesight is bad, right?"

"I'm sorry, I can't say," Haley said. "Or HIPAA would drag me away in chains. He'll have to tell you himself."

Elle stared into her eyes and then smiled. "Yeah, he got glasses."

"Damn," Haley said. "I hate when you do that."

"She reads minds," Willa told Pru.

"Like magic?" Pru asked, awed.

"Not magic," Elle said. "You all just wear your every single thought on your sleeves."

"Oh, look at you, dear," Mrs. Winslow said to Pru, coming up to her with a wide smile. "You look amazing."

"Uh . . ." Pru looked down at herself. She was still in her usual work uniform of a stretchy white button-down and navy trousers and boots. "Thanks?"

"Must be all the sexual activity with Finn," the older woman said. "Intercourse does wonders for your skin."

Looking shocked, Willa nearly swallowed her tongue. She turned to Elle, who shrugged.

"You *knew*?" Willa asked.

"When are you going to get it? I *always* know," Elle said.

Pru admired a woman who always had the answers. She really hoped Elle shared some of them because she could really use a few right about now.

"Burgers and hot dogs!" a guy yelled walking through the courtyard. It was Jay. He owned the food truck that usually sat out front, but now he had a tray strapped on him and was making sales left and right like he was going up and down the rows at a baseball stadium. "I've got beef burgers and six inches of prime sausages here! Get 'em while they're hot!"

"Six inches would do me just right," Mrs. Winslow said wistfully. "I wouldn't know what to do with seven or eight."

Try nine, Pru thought and clapped a hand over her mouth to keep from saying it out loud.

"Something you want to share with the class?" Haley asked.

Most definitely not, but the vultures had the scent of roadkill and were circling.

"Oh, she'll talk," Elle said, staring into Pru's eyes. "She'll talk over a loaded pie and a bottle of wine. Girls, let's hit it."

And she walked off.

"She's so badass," Willa whispered, staring after her. "I mean look at that dress. She's badass, kickass, *and* she has a great ass. It's really not fair."

"I can hear you," Elle called out over her shoulder without looking back. She snapped her fingers. "Put it in gear."

And Pru, Haley, and Willa followed after her like puppies on a leash.

Chapter 24

#SuitUp

Pru had no idea how Elle did it, but by the time they got to the street, there was an Uber ride waiting on them.

"Lefty's Pizza," Elle said to the driver.

"I thought you were on a diet," Haley said, climbing into the car.

"Some days you eat salads and go to the gym," Elle said. "And some days you eat pizza and wear yoga pants. It's called balance."

"I always eat pizza and wear yoga pants," Willa said. She gasped. "Does that make me unbalanced?"

"No, actually, it makes you smarter than me," Elle said with a small smile.

Willa sighed. "Or maybe I've just given up on men."

"That's only because you dated a few frogs," Elle said.

"That's an extremely nice way of saying that I'm a

loser magnet. And I couldn't get rid of that one frog either. I still owe Archer for stepping in and pretending to be my boyfriend so he'd back off."

"That's not why he backed off," Elle said. "He backed off because Archer threatened to castrate him if he contacted you again."

Willa gaped. "He did? I was wondering at how easy he made it look."

"And you can make it look easy too," Elle told her. "Next time you want to lose a guy, just tell them 'I love you, I want to marry you, and I want children right away.' They'll run so fast they'll leave skid marks."

Willa snorted. "I'll keep that in mind."

Thirty minutes later they were in a booth, one bottle of wine down, another ready to go, and a large pizza on its way to being demolished. Pru's stomach hurt, but that hadn't slowed her down any.

Willa pulled a book from her purse. "Have either of you been to that new used bookstore down the street from our building?"

"I download my books right to my phone," Elle said. "That way I can read while pretending to listen in on meetings."

"Your boss doesn't mind?" Pru asked.

"My boss knows everything," Elle said. "And one of the things he also knows is that me doing my thing allows him to do his thing."

Made sense.

"Plus, I know where the bodies are hidden," she said.

Probably she was kidding.

"Well, I like the feel of a book in my hand," Willa said and looked at Pru.

"I go both ways," Pru said and then blushed when they all laughed. "You know what I mean."

"I do," Willa said and handed her the book. "Which is why I bought this for you."

Pru eyed the title and choked on a bite of pizza. Willa had to pound her on the back while Pru sucked a bunch of wine down to try and appease her burning throat. No go. "*Orgasms For One*?" she finally managed.

Willa nodded.

"Um . . . thank you?"

"I bought it after you told us that you hadn't dated in a while but before I heard about the dumbwaiter, so . . ."

Pru sighed. "So everyone knows about the dumbwaiter."

"Little bit," Haley said. "What we don't know are the deets."

Elle pointed at Pru. "You. Finn. Go."

"It's . . . a long story."

"I love long stories," Willa said.

Elle just arched a brow. She didn't like to be kept waiting.

"Might as well start talking," Haley told Pru. "She'll get her way eventually, she always does. I've found it's best to give in earlier than later. Besides, I'm tired." She accompanied this statement with a wide yawn.

Pru rubbed her aching stomach. She was starting to feel sick. "Maybe we should postpone this for another day. When I haven't eaten my weight in pizza."

Elle didn't break eye contact with her. She didn't budge a muscle, not even to blink.

Pru sighed. "Fine. Maybe something's happened

between me and Finn, but it's not going to keep happening."

Willa grinned. "So you *did* sleep with him."

"Past tense," Pru said, her gaze still held prisoner by Elle's. "Even if I wish it wasn't." Dammit. "Where did you get this super power?" she demanded. "I need it."

Elle smiled. "I'd tell you but—"

"—But she'd have to kill you," Willa finished on a laugh. "Love it when you say that."

"Except you never let me say it," Elle pointed out.

Pru's stomach turned over yet again and she put a hand on it. "I really don't feel so good."

"Because you're holding back on your new BFFs," Willa said.

"I like you for Finn," Elle said to Pru. "He hasn't chosen anyone in a long time. I'm glad it's you."

"Oh, no. That's the thing," she said. "It's not me. I mean, it was great. He was great. And when I was with him, I felt . . ." She closed her eyes, the memories washing over her. "*Really* great." She could still hear his low, sexy voice in her ear telling her what he was going to do to her, and then his even sexier body doing it, taking hers to places it hadn't been in so long she'd nearly forgotten what it was like to be in a man's arms and lose herself.

"So why is it over then?" Haley asked. "Do you realize how rare 'really great' is? I haven't had 'really great' in so long I don't even know if I'll recognize it."

"You'll recognize it," Elle said, looking at Pru, waiting on her answer.

But Pru didn't answer. Couldn't. Because she hated the reason why. "It's . . . complicated."

"Honey," Elle said with surprising vulnerability and wistfulness in her voice. "The best things always are." She paused. "You'd be really good for him."

Elle wasn't a woman to say such a thing unless she meant it so Pru felt herself warm a little at that. Even if it wasn't true. She wasn't good for Finn. And when he found out the truth about her and who she was, she'd in fact be very bad for him.

"He hasn't dated since Mellie," Willa said thoughtfully. "And she turned out to be—"

"Willa," Elle said quietly. Warningly.

"I'm sorry," she said, not sounding sorry at all. "But I hated her for what she did to him. To him *and* Sean."

"It was a long time ago," Elle said firmly.

"A year. He liked her, a lot. And he got hurt," Willa said. "And you hated her for it too, admit it."

Elle gave a slight head nod. "I would have liked to kill her," she said casually in the way most people would comment on the weather.

"And it changed him," Willa said. She turned to Pru. "Mellie had the dressy boutique here in the building for a while before she sold it. She was wild and fun and gregarious, and she was good for Finn. At first. Until—"

"Willa." Elle gave her a long look. "You're telling tales. He's going to kill you."

"Only if you tattle," Willa said. "Pru needs to know what she's up against."

"What am I up against?" Pru whispered in spite of herself, needing to know.

"Mellie and Sean got drunk one night. And they . . ." She grimaced.

Pru gasped. "No," she breathed. "She slept with his brother?"

"Well, apparently when Finn walked in on them they hadn't quite gotten to home plate but it was close enough."

"Finn walked in on them?" Pru asked, horrified, trying to imagine. She didn't have a sibling, but in her fantasies, if she'd had a sister or brother, they would stand at her back, always. "How awful."

Willa nodded. "It caused a big fight, but they've always fought. Sean had had way too much to drink that night, he was really out of it, and later he kept saying he'd never have made a move on her if he'd been in his right mind. But Mellie wasn't drunk. She knew exactly what she was doing."

"But why would she do that to Finn?" Pru asked.

"Because she'd been after him for a commitment. At that time, he was still finishing up his business degree. She hated that he went to classes early in the morning, studied after that, then handled the business side of O'Riley's, and then often had to work the pub all night on top of that. When he wasn't working his ass off on any of those things, he was dead asleep. He was giving everything one hundred percent, even her, but it wasn't enough. She was bored and lonely, two things that didn't agree with her."

Elle slid Willa a look. "You think he's going to thank you for airing his dirty laundry when he finds out?"

"No, I think he'll put out a hit on me," Willa said. "But he's not going to find out. I'm doing our girl a service here, explaining some things about her man that he's certainly not going to explain to her."

"He's not my man," Pru said.

"He's not going to explain," Willa said to Elle as if Pru hadn't spoken, "because he thinks the past should stay in the past."

"He's not my man," Pru repeated, holding her stomach, which was killing her now.

"The past should *absolutely* stay in the past," Elle said to Willa, something in her voice saying she believed that to the depths of her very soul.

Willa closed her eyes briefly and covered Elle's hand with her own, the two of them sharing a moment that Pru didn't understood. They had history. She got that. They were close friends, and clearly there was a lot about them that she didn't know. Such as what had happened to Elle to make her want her past to stay buried.

Pru didn't have many people in her life. Her own fault. She didn't let many in. It didn't take a shrink to get why. She'd lost her parents early. Her only other living relative often mistook her for devil spawn. There were some school friends she kept in occasional contact with, and she had her coworkers. And Jake.

But it would be really nice to have Willa and Elle as well.

Her stomach cramped painfully again, which she ignored when Willa took her hand.

"I'm trusting you with this, Pru," she said. "Do you know why?"

Unable to imagine, Pru shook her head.

"Because you're one of us now," she said and looked at Elle. "Right?"

Elle turned her head and met Pru's gaze, studying her solemnly for a long beat before slowly nodding.

Willa smiled. "Look at that." She looked at Pru again. "Here's something you might not know. Elle doesn't like very many people."

Elle snorted.

"It's because she's scary as shit," Haley said, drinking the last of her wine.

"Sitting right here," Elle said calmly, glancing at her nails.

Which were, of course, perfect.

Not appearing scared in the slightest, Willa just smiled. "But one thing about her, she never says anything she doesn't mean. And once you're a friend, you're a friend for life." She paused and glanced at Elle, brow raised.

Elle shrugged.

Willa gave her a long look.

Elle rolled her eyes but she did smile. "Friends for life," she said. "Or until you piss me off. Don't piss me off."

A new warmth filled Pru and her throat tightened. "Thanks," she whispered.

Elle narrowed her eyes. "You're not going to cry, are you? There's no crying on pizza night."

"Just got something in my eye," Pru said with a sniff and swiped under her eyes.

Elle sighed and handed her a napkin. "Look, I know I'm a cold-hearted bitch, but Willa's right, you're one of ours now. And we're yours. This is why we're trusting you with Finn. Because he's also one of ours and he means a lot to us."

"Oh no, you can't trust me with him," she said. "I mean—" She shook her head. "It's just that I'm not—we're not a real thing."

"It's cute you think that." Willa patted her hand. "But I've seen you two together."

Pru opened her mouth to protest but the dessert they'd ordered arrived—a pan-size homemade cookie topped with ice cream, and then there was no speaking as they stuffed their faces.

When Pru was done, it came up on her suddenly. Her stomach rolled again and this time a queasiness rose up her throat with it.

Uh oh.

The good news was that she recognized the problem. The bad news was that she was about to be sick. She searched her brain for what she might have eaten and gasped.

Sushi for lunch.

Which meant she'd made Eddie sick too. "I've got to go," she said abruptly. The last time she'd had food poisoning she'd laid on her bathroom floor for two straight days. Privacy was required for such things, serious privacy. Standing on wobbly legs, she pulled some money from her purse and dropped it on the table. "I'm sorry—" She clapped a hand to her gurgling stomach and shook her head. "Later."

She got a cab, but the traffic and the ensuing stop/start of navigating said traffic just about killed her. She bailed a block early and moved as fast as she could. When she cut through the courtyard of her building, she slid a quick, anxious look at the pub. *Please don't be there, please don't be there . . .*

But fate or destiny or karma, whoever was in charge of such things as looking out for her humility, had taken a break because all the pub doors were still open to the night. Finn stood near the courtyard entrance talking to some customers. And like a beacon in the night, he turned right to her.

She kept moving, her hand over her mouth, as if that would keep her from throwing up in public. If she could have sold her soul to the devil right then to ensure it, she totally would have.

But not even the devil himself had enough power to alter her course in history. She was dying at this point, sharp, shooting pains through her gut combined with an all-over body ache that had her whimpering to herself with each step. Holding back from losing her dinner had her sweating in rivulets.

"Pru," came Finn's unbearably familiar voice— from right behind her.

"I'm sorry," she managed, not slowing down. "I can't—"

"We need to talk."

Yep, the only four words in the English language destined to spark terror within her heart. Talk? He wanted to talk? Maybe when she died. And given the pain stabbing through her with the force of a thousand needles, it wouldn't be long now. Still, just in case, she moved faster.

"Pru."

She wanted to say *look, I'm about to throw up half a loaded pizza and possibly my intestines, and I like you, I like you enough that if you see me throw up that half a loaded pizza, I'll have to kill myself.*

Which, actually, wouldn't be necessary seeing as she was about to die anyway.

"Pru, slow down." He caught her hand.

But the more she put off the now inevitable, the worse it would be. "Not feeling good," she said, twisting free. "I've gotta go."

"What's wrong?" His voice immediately changed from playful to serious. "What do you need?"

What she needed was the privacy of her own bathroom. She opened her mouth to say so but the only thing that came out was a miserable moan.

"Do you need a doctor?" he asked.

Yes, she needed a doctor. For a lobotomy.

With sweat slicking her skin, she ran directly for the elevator, praying that it would be on the ground floor and no one else would want to get on it with her.

Of course it wasn't on the ground floor.

With another miserable moan she headed for the stairwell, taking them as fast as she could with her stomach sending fireballs to her brain and her legs weakened by the need to upchuck.

And oh lucky her, Finn kept pace with her, right at her side.

Which made her panic all the more because seriously, she was on a countdown at this point, T minus sixty seconds tops, and there would be no stopping or averting liftoff. "I'm fine!" she said weakly. "Please, just leave me alone!" She threw her hand out at him to push him away so she could have room in case she spontaneously imploded.

A very real possibility.

But the man who was more tuned into her body than she was had apparently not yet mastered mind reading. "I'm not leaving you alone like this," he said.

She pushed him again from a well of reserved

strength born of sheer terror because she was about to become her own horror show and didn't want witnesses. "You have to go!" she said, maybe yelled, as they *finally* got to the third floor.

Mrs. Winslow stuck her head out her door and gave Pru a disapproving look. "You might be getting some but you're not going to keep getting some if you talk to your man like that. Especially after shoving him into the dumbwaiter the other night."

Oh for God's sake!

How did everyone know about that?

Not that she could ask.

Hell, no. Instead, she stopped and pawed through her purse for her keys before dropping it to scratch and claw at the door like she was being kidnapped and tortured.

Finn crouched down at her feet to pick up her purse and scoop the contests back in. He had a tampon in one hand and Willa's book—*Orgasms For One*—in the other. He should've looked utterly ridiculous. Instead he looked utterly perfect.

"Pru, can you tell me what's wrong?"

"I think she's having a seizure," Mrs. Winslow said helpfully. "Honey, you look a little bit constipated. I suggest a good fart. That always works for me."

Pru didn't know how to tell her she was about to let loose but it wouldn't be nearly as neat as a fart. By some miracle, she made it inside. She was sweating through her clothes by the time she stumbled along without even taking her keys out of the lock, racing to the bathroom, slamming the door behind her.

She had barely hit her knees before she got sick.

From what felt like a narrow, long tunnel, through the thick fog in her head and her own misery, she heard him.

"Pru," he said, his voice low with worry.

From right.

Outside.

Her.

Bathroom.

Door.

"I'm coming in," he said and she couldn't stop throwing up to tell him to run, to save himself.

Chapter 25

#BadDayAtTheOffice

Pru felt one of Finn's hands pull her hair back and hold it for her, the other encircling her, fingers spread wide on her stomach. He was kneeling behind her, his big body supporting hers.

"I've got you," he said.

No one had ever said such a thing to her before and she would have loved to absorb that and maybe obsess over why it meant so much, but her stomach had other ideas. So she closed her eyes and pretended she was alone on a deserted island with her charged Kindle. And maybe Netflix. When she could catch her breath, she brought a shaky hand to her head, which was pounding like the devil himself was in there operating a jackhammer, whittling away at what was left of her brains.

Finn kept her from sliding to the floor by wrapping both arms around her and bringing her gently back, propping her up against him.

"I'm sorry," she managed, horrified that she'd thrown up in front of the hottest man she'd ever had the privilege of sleeping with by accident.

"Breathe, Pru. It's going to be okay."

"Please just leave me here to die," she croaked out when she could, pulling free. "Just walk out of this room and pretend it never happened. We'll never speak of it again."

And then, giving up trying to be strong, she slid bonelessly to the bathroom floor. Her body was hot and she was slick with perspiration. Unable to garner the energy to hold herself up anymore, she pressed her hot cheek to the cool tile and closed her eyes.

She heard water running and squeezed her eyes tight, but that only made her all the dizzier. A deliciously cool, wet washcloth was pressed to her forehead. She cracked an eye and found Finn. "Dammit, you never listen."

"I always listen," he said. "I just don't always agree."

His hand was rubbing her back in soothing circles and she thought she might never move again if he kept on doing that until the end of time. "Why won't you go away?"

When he didn't say anything, she again opened an eye. He was still looking at her with concern but not like she was at death's door. Except if she wasn't dying, that meant she was going to have to live with this, with him seeing her flat on the floor looking like roadkill.

"Do you think you can move?" he asked.

"Negative." She wasn't moving. *Ever.* She heard him on his phone, telling someone he needed something liquid with electrolytes in it.

"Not drinking anything either," she warned him, her stomach turning over at the thought.

He got up and left her, and she was grateful. When he came back in a moment later, she was back to worshipping the porcelain god, trying to catch her breath.

"Any better?" he asked when she was done.

She couldn't speak. She couldn't anything.

He peeled her away from the seat and gathered her in his lap. He laid her head against his shoulder and wrapped his arms around her. "Take a few deep breaths. Slowly."

She tried but she was shaking so hard she thought maybe her teeth were going to rattle right out of her head. Finn wiped the sweat-matted hair from her face and then pressed the cool washcloth to the back of her neck.

It was heaven.

He cracked a bottle of lime-flavored water with electrolytes.

"Where did you get that?" she asked.

"Willa. She has it in her shop. Says she gives it to the nervous dogs after they throw up."

"You told Willa I was throwing up?"

"She's in the kitchen making you soup for tomorrow when you feel better. Elle's bringing her a few ingredients she didn't have."

Pru managed a moan. "I don't want anyone to see me like this."

"You do realize that friends don't actually care what you look like," he said. "Take a sip, Pru."

She shook her head. She couldn't possibly swallow anything.

"Just a sip. Trust me, it'll help."

She did trust him. But drinking anything was going to be a disaster of major proportions.

He was moving her, using his shoulder to hold her head forward. It was take a sip or drown.

She took a sip.

"Good girl," he whispered and let her settle back against him. They sat there, silent, for what seemed like days. Her stomach slowly stopped doing backflips.

"How do you feel?" he asked after a while.

She had no idea.

When she didn't enlighten him, he took the washcloth from her neck, refolded it, and put it against her forehead.

"Eddie," she croaked. "He might be sick too—"

"I've got him covered. Spence is with him but the old guy's got a stomach of iron and doesn't appear to be affected.

She managed a nod, eyes still closed. She must have drifted off then because when she opened her eyes again the light was different in the bathroom, like some time had gone by.

Finn was still on the floor with her, only he was shirtless now, wearing just his jeans.

Oh yeah. She remembered now. She'd thrown up a bunch more times. She had her hands curled around his neck, clutching him like he was her only lifeline.

And he was. She stared at his chest. She couldn't stop herself. No matter how many times she saw his stomach, she wanted to lick it each time.

Not that she wanted to stop there either.

Nope, she wanted to lick upward to his neck and

then trail back down. She wanted to drop to her knees and slowly ease his jeans over his hips and—

"You okay?" he asked. "You just moaned."

Huh. Maybe she really was going to live. She dragged her back to his. His hair was tousled, his jaw beyond a five o'clock shadow, but he still looked hot.

She hated him. "You should go," she said knowing he either had to work or sleep.

He shook his head and brushed his lips over her forehead at the hairline. "It's been a couple of hours since you last got sick," he said. "Sip some more water."

Her stomach was much calmer now, but her head was beating to its own drum. She could feel it pulsating.

"You're dehydrated," he said. "You need the water to get rid of the fever and headache."

Too achy to argue, she nodded. She managed to take a few sips and then her body took over, demanding more.

"Careful," Finn warned, pulling it away when she started to gulp it. "Let's see how that settles first."

"Thor?"

"He's right here, sleeping on my feet. You want him?"

Yes. But she was in bad enough shape to hug him too tight and the last time she'd done that, he'd gotten scared and bit her. She'd stick with just Finn for now. She was pretty sure Finn only bit when naked. Or on really special occasions.

She fell asleep on him again and woke up much later in her own bed. Willa was helping her change.

"That man is gone over you," Willa murmured, tucking Pru into bed.

"It's the damn fountain." Pru had to hold her head

on, keeping her eyes shut even when Willa had paused.

"Fountain?" she asked.

Maybe if Pru hadn't been dying, she wouldn't have answered. "I wished," she said. "I wished for Finn to find love, but the fountain got it all wrong and gave *me* love instead. Stupid fountain. He's the one who deserves it."

"Honey," Willa said softly. "We all deserve love."

Pru wanted that to be true. God, how she wanted that . . .

"And how do you know the fountain didn't get it right?" Willa asked. "Maybe *you're* his true love."

Pru drifted off on that terrifying thought.

"You're going to want to sip some of this."

It was Elle. She sat on the bed at Pru's hip and offered a mug.

"What is it?" Pru asked.

"Only the best tea on the planet. Try it."

"I'm not thirsty—"

"Try it," Elle said again finally. "You're nearly translucent, you need fluids."

So Pru sipped.

"Now," Ella said calmly. "What's this I hear about the fountain and some wish going astray?"

Pru choked on her sip.

Elle rolled her eyes, leaned forward, and pounded Pru on the back.

"Willa told you," Pru said on a sigh.

"Yeah. She's cute but she can't keep a secret. She doesn't mean any harm, I promise. She doesn't have a mean bone in her body. Mostly she's worried about you and thought I could beat some sense into you."

Pru blinked.

"Metaphorically," Elle said. "And plus she wanted to borrow some change so she could go make a wish, seeing how it worked out so good for you."

"The wish was for Finn!"

"Uh huh."

"It was!"

"Well then, I'd say you got a two-fer."

Chapter 26

#WaxOnWaxOff

The next time Pru opened her eyes, the hallway light allowed her to see that someone was sprawled in the chair by her bed. That someone rose when she stirred and sat at her hip.

"How you doing?" Finn asked.

She blinked at the crack of dawn's early light creeping in through the slats of her blinds, casting everything in a hazy gold glow. From outside the window came the early chatter of birds, obnoxiously loud and chipper. She moaned. "I've never figured out if they're happy that it's morning or objecting to its arrival."

Finn smiled. "I vote for objecting."

Her too. He'd changed, she couldn't help but notice. Different jeans, a rumpled black T-shirt. Hair still tousled. Jaw still stubbled. Eyes heavy-lidded. He was without a doubt the sexiest thing she'd ever seen. Which told her one thing at least.

She hadn't died.

He propped her up in her bed, tied her crazy-ass hair back and brought her toast. Cut diagonally. She just stared up at him. Was he a fevered dream? "Tell me the truth," she murmured, her voice rough and haggard. "You're a fevered mirage, right?"

He frowned and leaned over her, one hand planted on the mattress, the other going to her forehead. His frown deepened and he leaned in even closer so that she caught a whiff of him.

He smelled like heaven on earth.

She did *not* smell like heaven on earth, and worse, she felt like roadkill. Like roadkill that had been run over, back upped on, and run over again. Twice.

But not Finn. She pressed in close and plastered her face to his throat at the same moment he pressed his mouth to her forehead.

"You don't feel fevered," he muttered.

"No, that's what happens when things are a mirage. In fact, last night never even really happened."

Pulling back, he met her gaze. "So I suppose you remember nothing."

"Nothing," she agreed quickly. "How could I? Nothing happened."

His lips twitched. "Nicely done."

"Thank you."

He smiled. And then dropped the bomb. "Tell me about the fountain."

"On second thought," she said. "Maybe I actually died. I'm gone and buried . . ."

"Try again."

She looked into his eyes, trying to decide if he knew

the truth about her wish—in which case she might have to strangle Willa and Elle—or if he was just fishing. "Well," she said lightly. "It was built back in the days when Cow Hollow was filled with cows. And—"

"Not the fountain's history, smartass," he said. "I mean why you were muttering about it in your feverish haze."

Huh. So maybe Elle and Willa didn't have to be strangled after all. "I was feverish and delusional," she said. "You need to forget everything you heard. And saw," she added.

"You wished for love on the fountain?" he asked with a whisper of disbelief.

"What does it matter, you don't believe in the myth anyway, remember?"

"That's not an answer," he said.

"I don't believe in the myth either," she said, and he fell quiet, letting her get away with that.

Instead of pushing, he nudged the toast her way. "Eat. And drink. You need to hydrate."

"You sound like a mom."

"Just don't call me grandpa." He got up to go, but she caught his hand.

"Hey," she said. "You went over and above last night. You didn't have to do that."

"I know."

It was hard to hold his gaze. "Thanks for taking care of me."

He just looked at her for a long beat. "Anytime."

By the next day, Pru was completely over the food poisoning and back to work, which was a good thing for several reasons. One, Jake desperately needed her.

And two, she needed to get over throwing up in front of Finn, and short of a memory scrub, working her ass off was the only way to do it. So she buried herself, banning thoughts of Finn, needing to build up her immunity to his sexy charisma.

This worked for two days but then her efforts to lay low failed when he showed up at the warehouse.

He was waiting for her between two tours, propping up a pillar in the holding area where passengers hung out before and after boarding the ships.

"What are you doing here?" she asked, surprised.

"Need a minute with you." He took her hand and pulled her outside. He was in low-slung jeans and a dark green henley the exact color of his eyes. His hair had been finger combed at best and he hadn't shaved, leaving a day's worth of scruff on his square jaw that she knew personally would feel like sex on a stick against her skin.

"You've been avoiding me," he said.

"No, I—"

He put a finger on her lips, his body so close now that she could feel the heat of him, which made her body shift in closer.

Bad body.

"Careful," he said quietly, dipping his head so that his mouth hovered near hers. "You're about to fib, and once you do, things change."

She absorbed that a moment, and wrapping her fingers around his wrist, pulled his finger away from her mouth. "What things?"

His eyes never left hers. "Feelings."

Any lingering amusement faded away because she

knew what he was saying. He didn't believe in lying. Or in half-truths. Or fibs . . . And if he thought she was the kind of woman who did, then his feelings about her would change.

She'd known this going in, of course. What she hadn't known was how strongly it would affect their relationship.

Because he didn't know one important fact.

She'd been lying to him about something since the very beginning. She'd weaved the web, she'd built the brick wall, *she'd* created this nightmare of a problem and she had no idea what to do about it.

"Okay, so I've been avoiding you a little," she admitted, starting with the one thing she did know what to do about.

"Why?"

She stared at him. The truth shot out of her heart and landed on the tip of her tongue. She wanted to tell him. She wanted it out in the open in the worst way. Holding it in was giving her guilt gut aches. But they'd only known each other a few short weeks. She just needed a little bit more time. To charm him. To somehow get him to do what no one else ever had—fall hard enough for her to want to keep her.

No matter that she'd made a huge mistake. She needed to work him into that, slowly. "I'm not good with this stuff," she said quietly. Hello, understatement of the year.

"Going to need you to be more specific."

"I'm not good with . . . the after thing." And so much more . . .

"The after thing," he repeated. "You mean after food poisoning? Pru, who *is* good at that?"

"No. I mean yes, and I don't know. But I was talking about the after sleeping with someone thing."

He looked more than a little baffled, and also somewhat amused. "So having sex isn't the problem, it's that we've actually slept together," he said.

Knowing it sounded ridiculous, she nodded.

She expected him to try and joke that away but he didn't. Instead, he wrapped his big hand up in hers and gave her a crooked smile. "I guess that makes us the blind leading the blind then. I don't do a lot of sleepovers, Pru."

"But you've been in a long relationship before," she said. "With Mellie."

He paused. "Someone's been telling tales."

"It's true though, right?" she asked.

"What is it that you're asking me, Pru?"

Okay, so he clearly didn't want to discuss Mellie. Got it. Understood it. Hell, she had plenty of things she didn't want to discuss either. "I'm trying to say that not only am I not good at sleepovers, I . . . haven't really had any." She bit her lip. Dammit. That made her sound pathetic. She tried again. "It's more that you're my one and only—" Nope, now she was just making it worse. "Okay, you know what? Never mind." She started to walk off. "I'm going back to work."

He caught her and turned her to face him. "Wait a minute."

"Can't," she said. 'I've gotten—"

"Pru," he said with terrifying tenderness as he

bulldozed right over her with his dogged determination, cupping her face. "Are you saying you've never—"

"No, of course I have." She closed her eyes. "It's just been awhile since Jake—and he wasn't a one-night stand. Or even a two-night stand. He was a week-long stand—" She covered her mouth. "Oh my God," she said around her fingers. "Please tell me to stop talking!"

He gently pulled her hand from her mouth. "You and Jake were together only a week?"

"Yes."

"And before that, you'd not been with anyone else?"

"I had a boyfriend in high school," she said defensively.

"But . . ."

"But he dumped me after my parents died," she admitted. "I was a complete wreck, and—"

"That shouldn't have happened to you," he said quietly, stroking her upper arms, his warm hands somehow reaching deep inside her and warming a spot she hadn't even realized was chilled. "That shouldn't have happened to anyone," he said very gently. "So other than your high school asshole boyfriend and one week with Jake, there's been no one else?"

If she'd ever felt more vulnerable or exposed, she couldn't remember it. It was horribly embarrassing, having her sexual history—or lack thereof—laid out, and with it came an avalanche of insecurities. She shook her head and stared at his throat instead of in his eyes, which was easier. Because he had a very sexy throat and—

"Pru. Babe, look at me."

She reluctantly lifted her gaze to his.

"I think I'm starting to understand more about what's going on," he said.

Oh good. Maybe he could explain it to her. That would be supremely helpful.

"What happened between us," he said, "it never occurred to me that you thought it was a one-night stand."

She stared at him, confused. "No?"

"Hell, no," he said. "Not with our chemistry. I knew from the beginning that one night wasn't going to be enough. Or two. Or ten. I thought you knew it too."

She swallowed hard. She did know it. That wasn't the problem. No, the problem was that the time they'd already spent together . . . it had to be enough. It was all she would, could, allow herself. "I didn't allow myself to think that far. Finn—"

"Look, I know we've done things ass-backwards, but I want to fix that." He smiled at her. "Go out with me tonight."

She stared at him. "Like . . . a date?"

"Exactly like a date."

"But—"

His mouth brushed along her jaw to her ear, his words whispered hot against her. "Say 'yes, Finn.'"

"Yes, Finn," escaped her before she could stop herself. Damn. Her mouth really needed to meet her brain sometime. But the truth was, she needed this, needed him. She wanted this moment and she wanted to enjoy it. Selfish as it was, she was going to think about herself for once, just for tonight. Besides, thinking was overrated. "You make it hard to think," she said.

She felt him smile knowingly against her skin. "Pru, I'm going to be so good to you tonight that there'll be no thinking required.

It's a good thing that thinking was overrated.

He picked her up at six. She was nervous as hell, which was silly. It was Finn. And it was just a date.

At a red light, he glanced over at her and flashed a grin. "You look pretty."

She was in a simple sundress and flats. Hair down. "You've seen this dress," she said.

His eyes heated. Clearly he was remembering that it was the dress he'd made her hold at her waist while he'd had his merry way with her. "I know," he murmured. "I love that dress."

She blushed and he laughed softly.

"Where are we going?" she asked, needing a subject change.

"Nervous?"

Yes. "No."

He slid her a knowing glance. "It's a surprise."

That had her worried. But where they ended up made her smile wide and stare at him. "A Giants game?"

"Yeah." He parked at the stadium and pulled her from the car with a smacking kiss. "Okay with you?"

Was he kidding? For a beat, her troubles fell away and she grinned at him. "Very okay."

He brought her hand to his mouth and smiled over their entwined fingers.

She melted.

He fed her whatever she wanted, which was hotdogs

and beer, and they both yelled and cheered the game on to their heart's content.

They sat next to a couple of serious Giants fans who were wearing only shorts—although the girl also wore a bikini top—and their every inch of exposed skin painted Giants orange.

The guy proposed between innings two and three, and it was nothing like the proposal on her ship. When these two hugged and kissed, there was love in every touch—although their carefully painted Giants logo smeared. The orange and white paint mixed into a pale color that actually resembled pink, making them look like a walking advertisement for Pepto-Bismol.

At the bottom of the fourth, the KISS cam panned the crowd and everyone went wild. It stopped on an older couple, who sweetly pecked. Next it stopped on two men who flashed their wedding rings with wide grins before giving the audience a kiss.

Everyone was still cheering when the KISS cam stopped on Pru and Finn. Pru turned to him, laughing, and he hauled her in and laid one on her that made her brain turn to mush and an entire inning went by before her brain reset itself and began processing again.

It was possibly the most fun date she'd been on since . . .

Ever.

After the game, Finn walked Pru to her door. She was a little tipsy so he held her hand, smiling as he listened to her singing to some song in her head that only she could hear.

She had a smudge of orange paint down her entire right side from the woman at the game. It'd drizzled for a few minutes in the eighth inning and her hair had rioted into a frizzy mass of waves.

He wanted to sink his fingers into it, press her back against her door and kiss her senseless. Then he wanted to pick her up so that she'd wrap her long legs around him.

He wanted her. Hard and fast. Slow and sweet. On the couch. In the shower. Her bed.

Anywhere he could get her.

And it wasn't just physical either. He'd told her he didn't think love was for him, but he'd been wrong. At least going off the way his heart rolled over and exposed its tender underbelly every time she so much as looked at him. He wanted to claim her, wanted to leave his mark on her. On the inside. On her heart and in her soul.

But she wasn't ready. She was way behind him in this and he knew that. What they had between them scared her, and more than a little. She needed time, and he could give her that. *Would* give her that.

Even if it meant walking away from her tonight when she was smiling up at him, her eyes shining, her cheeks flushed, happy. Warm.

Willing.

"'Night," he said softly. "Lock up tight."

"Wait." She blinked once, slow as an owl. A tipsy owl. "You're . . . leaving?"

"Yes."

"But . . ." She stepped into him, running her hands up his chest. "Aren't we going to . . ."

He went brows up, forcing her to be specific.

"I thought you'd come in and we'd . . . you know," she whispered, her fingers dancing over his jaw.

Catching her hand, he brought it to his mouth and brushed a kiss over her palm. "No," he said gently. "Not tonight."

"But . . . when?"

"When you're ready to fill in 'you know' with the words," he said.

She stood there, mouth open a little, a furrow between her brows, looking bewildered, aroused, and more than a little off center.

Maybe she wasn't so far behind him after all.

"'Night," he said, cupping her face for a soft kiss. Walking away was one of the hardest things he'd ever done.

When Pru's door closed, another opened and Mrs. Winslow poked her head out. "You sure you know what you're doing?" she asked him.

Hell no, he didn't know what he was doing.

She shook her head at him. "You sure don't know much about women, do you. You can't leave them alone to think about whether they need you, and do you know why?"

He shook his head.

"Because it's only in the moment that a woman will act impulsively. It's all the testosterone and pheromones that pour off you males, you see. Without you right in front of her, that magic stuff wears off and she'll easily remember that she doesn't need you in her life."

"I'm going to hope that's not true," he said.

"You can hope all you want, but you'll be hoping alone in an empty bed."

Chapter 27

#SmarterThanTheAverageBear

Late the next afternoon, Pru was at work wishing she was anywhere but. She was in the middle of an argument with a guy who'd paid for a tour for him and his son the week before, but they hadn't shown up. Now he wanted a refund.

She'd only stepped behind the ticket counter as a favor to one of the ticket clerks who'd had to leave early. This guy was the last person she had to deal with before going home. She'd paused, looking for a credit option on the computer, when he decided she was dicking him around.

"Listen," he bit out. "I'm not going to deal with some homicidal, hormonal, PMS-y, minimum-wage chick who doesn't give a shit. I want the supervisor. Get him for me."

"Actually," she said. "You've got a supervisor right

here. And no worries. I was homicidal hormonal last week. This week I'm good. Even nice, if I say so myself."

He didn't smile. He was hands on hips. "I want my money back."

Pru's gaze slid to the person who'd just come in behind him. Finn. He stood there quietly but not passively, watching. Pru turned back to Pissy Man and pointed to the large sign above her head.

No refunds.

The guy leaned in way too close. "Do you have any idea who I am?"

An asshole? A thought she kept to herself because she was busy noticing that Finn shifted too, until he was standing just off to her left, body language signaling that while he was at ease, he was also ready to kick some ass if needed.

She'd thought of him today. A lot. Last night after he'd left, she'd nearly called him a dozen times. He wanted words and she had them. She wanted to say "please come back and make love to me."

Because if she knew one thing, it was that what they'd done together wasn't just sex.

Dammit.

For now, her cranky customer was still standing there with a fight in his eyes. "I'm in charge of the budget for the city's promo and advertising department," he told her. "We make sure that your entire industry is listed in all the Things to Do in San Francisco guides. Without me, you'd be cleaning toilets."

Okay, now that was a bit of a stretch. "Listen, it

wouldn't matter if you were POTUS. There are no refunds. I can get you a credit for another tour but you have to be patient with me while I figure out—

He slammed a hand down on the counter, but she didn't jump. She'd dealt with far bigger assholes than this one. Before she could suggest he leave, Finn was there.

He'd moved so quickly she never even saw him coming as he stepped in between her and the guy. "She said no refunds and offered you a credit," Finn said. "Take it or leave it."

"Leave it," the guy snapped.

"Your choice," Finn said. "But unless there's something else you'd like to say, and fair warning, it'd better be 'have a nice day,' you need to go."

The guy stared down Finn for the briefest of seconds before possibly deciding he liked his face in the condition it was in because he strode out without another word.

"Seriously?" Pru asked Finn.

He shoved his hands into his pockets. "What?"

"I had that handled."

He slid her a look. "You're welcome."

She let out a short laugh. "I was handling myself just fine." Always did, always would. Having been on her own for so long, she really didn't know any other way.

And yet he'd been there for her. When she'd been lonely. When she'd been sad. When she'd been sicker than a dog.

Whenever she'd needed.

"Pru," he said, "that guy was a walking fight. Where the hell's Jake?"

"Off today, and I didn't need him. It's not like he

was going to take a swing at me. The only thing he was swinging was a poor vocabulary and a small dick."

His mouth twitched. "Okay, I stand corrected."

"And?"

"And what?" he asked.

"And you're sorry for stepping in and handling my fight for me?"

He just looked at her.

Nope, he wasn't sorry for that. Good to know. She took a longer look at his face and realized that not only wasn't he sorry, he looked a little tall, dark, and 'tude ridden. She'd seen him mad several times now so she recognized the stormy eyes, tight mouth, and tense body language. "So how's your day?"

He lifted a shoulder.

Okay. She reached out and put a hand on a very tense forearm. "Are you okay?" she asked quietly. "Because it doesn't feel like you are."

"I'm fine."

She gave him an arched brow.

He shrugged. "I just hate pushy assholes who think they can push someone around to get what they want."

She stared up at him, once again reminded that she wasn't the only one in this relationship-that-wasn't-happening with demons. "Because of your dad?"

"Maybe," he admitted. "Or maybe because I spent a good portion of my youth protecting Sean. He was a small, sickly kid with a big, fat mouth. It wasn't easy to watch his back and keep him safe because he attracted assholes and bullies." He scrubbed a hand down his face. "I guess I still get worked up about that. I saw that guy being aggressive with you and I wanted . . ."

"To protect me," she said softly.

"Yeah." He gave her a half grimace, half smile. "Not that you can't do it yourself, but emotions aren't always rational."

With her hands still fisted in his shirt, she gave a gentle tug until he bent enough that she could kiss him softly. And then not so softly. "I know," she whispered. She kissed him again.

"What was that for?" he asked when she pulled free, his voice sexy low and gruff now.

"For being the kind of guy who can admit he has emotions."

He cupped her face. "We don't have to tell anyone, right?"

She smiled. "It'll be our secret." But then her smile faded because she wasn't good at secrets.

Or maybe she was too good at them . . . "I'm not helpless," she said. "I want you to know that."

"I do know it." He paused, looking a little irritated again. "Mostly."

"Good," she said. "Now that's settled, you should know, the caveman thing you just pulled . . . it turned me on a little bit."

He slid her a look. "Yeah?"

"Yeah."

Looking a little less like he was spoiling for a fight, his hands went to her hips and he pulled her in tighter.

What the hell was she doing? Clearly, she wasn't equipped to stay strong, and who could? The guy was just too damn potent. Too visceral. Testosterone and pheromones leaked off of him. She dropped her head to his chest. "Ugh. You're being . . . you."

"Was that in English?"

"This is all your fault."

"Nope. Definitely not English."

"You're being all hot and sexy, dammit," she said. She banged her head on his chest a few times. "And I can't seem to . . . not notice said hotness and sexiness."

He smiled. "You want me again."

Again. *Still . . .* She tossed up her hands. "You wear your stupid sexiness on your sleeve and you don't even know it."

His smile widened. "All you have to do is say the word, babe. Or preferably words. Dirty ones are encouraged."

When she blew out a sigh, he laughed.

"You really can't say the words, can you," he said, sounding way too amused about that, the ass. He flung an arm around her. "Cute."

Cute? She had mixed feelings about that. On the one hand, she'd rather he found her unbearably sexy. But on the other hand, he was already more than she could handle. Maybe cute was just right.

She gave him a push and strode around, locking up.

He followed, still looking pretty damn smug, waiting patiently.

"Where do you want to go?" he asked.

"Who says I'm going anywhere with you?"

"Your body."

She realized she'd plastered herself to his front again. "You're not working tonight?"

"Later. I worked all day and have a full crew on now. They'll be fine for a few hours on their own."

Oh God. How was she going to resist? "Are you

going to take me out on another date and then dump me at the door?"

"Depends."

"On?" she asked.

He just smiled mysteriously as he slid his fingers into her hair, letting his thumb stroke once over her lower lip so that it tingled for a kiss.

His kiss.

He wanted her to say the words and she knew what words too. *Make love to me . . .*

"You've got choices," he said. "You can pick a place, or let me surprise you."

His bed. She picked his bed.

She retrieved Thor from his nap spot in Jake's office and then Finn drove them out of there, his hands as sure on the wheel as they always were on her body.

Stop looking at his hands!

He took her for drinks at a cute place in the Marina, where they sat at a small table on the sidewalk with Thor happily at their feet watching the world go by.

Finn paid. He always paid. And he was sneaky about it too. She never even saw the check before he had it handled.

After, they headed to Lands End, a park near the windswept shoreline at the mouth of the Golden Gate Bridge.

The three of them followed a trail along a former rail bed to the rocky cliffs that revealed a heart-stopping, stunning three-hundred-and-sixty-degree vista of the bay. The wild blue ocean below was dotted with white-caps thanks to the heavy surf of the early evening.

"Wow," she whispered. "Makes you realize that the

whole world isn't centered around your own hopes and dreams."

He looked out at the view. "What are your hopes and dreams?"

She glanced at him, startled.

"I know you love being a boat captain," he said. "But what else do you want for yourself? To own your own charter business? To have a family?"

He was serious, so she answered truthfully. "I do love my job but I don't want to run an empire or anything. I'm happy doing what I do. And . . ." Her heart was suddenly pounding. "I do want a family." Because his eyes felt like mirrors into her own soul, she turned to the water again. "Someday," she whispered.

His hand slipped into hers, warm and strong.

She held on and breathed for a moment. "And you?"

"I love my job too," he said. "And I want to keep the pub for as long as it works. But I don't want to live in the city forever. I want a family too, and I'd rather have a yard and a street where they can ride their bikes and have other kids nearby . . ."

She smiled. "You want a white picket fence, Finn?"

"It doesn't have to be white," he said and made her laugh.

And yearn . . .

Thor enjoyed himself thoroughly, chasing after squirrels until one of them turned on him and chased him right back into Pru's arms.

Finn shook his head. "He's missing something."

"He doesn't have the killer gene," she admitted, giving the mutt a squeeze.

"I was thinking balls . . ." But he took Thor and

carried him for her, letting the dog nuzzle at the crook of his neck.

Pru rolled her eyes, but inside, secretly, she wanted to nuzzle there too.

"Look," Finn said, grabbing her hand with his free one, pointing with their joined fingers to the hillside below of cypress and wildflowers every color under the sun.

"Wow," she whispered. "Gorgeous."

"Yeah," he said, looking at her.

She laughed. "That's cheesy."

He grinned. "You liked it."

"No, I didn't."

He peered at her over his dark sunglasses, letting his gaze slip past her face.

She followed his line of sight and realized that her nipples were pressing eagerly against the thin white cotton of her shirt. "That's because I'm cold," she said and crossed her arms over her chest.

He laughed. "It's seventy-five degrees."

"Downright chilly," she said, nose in the air.

Grinning, he reeled her in, and with Thor protesting between them, he kissed the living daylights out of her.

Then he tugged her down the trail, heading for the epic ruins of Sutro Baths.

She'd never been here before. Even better, they were alone. Pru had no idea why, maybe because it was the middle of the week, or just late enough in the day, but they had the place to themselves.

They walked through the ruins and Finn showed her a small, rocky cave. It was cool inside. Quiet.

Finn brought her over to a small opening that allowed

her to see out to the rocky beach. Standing inside the cave, surrounded by the cavernous rock and way-too-sexy man, she could not only see the water but feel it in the cool mist that blew into the cave and stirred the hair at her temple.

Thor wriggled to be freed and Finn set him down, where he immediately scampered to a pile of rocks to explore.

This left Finn's hands free to tug Pru into him. "I should probably admit," he said, his mouth at her ear, "being alone in here is giving me ideas."

She bit her lower lip. Her too!

Laughing quietly at her expression, he fisted one hand in her hair. The other slid down and squeezed her ass. "You too?"

Okay, yes, so maybe she had a secret fantasy about doing it somewhere that they could maybe get caught, but she wasn't about to tell him so. Absolutely not. "I have a secret fantasy about doing it somewhere where we could maybe get caught," she said. *Dammit, mouth!*

His grin was fast and wicked, assuring her he was absolutely up for the challenge. She laughed again, nervously now. "But I'm pretty sure it's just a fantasy," she said quickly, putting her hands on his chest to keep him at arm's length.

Or to keep him close. She hadn't quite decided.

The hand on her ass shifted up a little and then back down, slipping inside the back of her pants. "How sure is pretty sure?" he asked, his fingers stroking the line of her thong, but before they could slip beneath, she laughed again and pulled free.

"Pretty, *pretty* sure," she said shakily.

His gaze slid down her body. "I suppose you're cold again."

Well aware that her greedy nipples were still threatening to make a break right through the material of her shirt, she scooped up Thor and clutched him to her chest.

Thor seemed to give her a long look like *please don't make me wait while you two do disgusting things to each other.* "Don't worry," she muttered to the dog. "I've got a handle on things now."

"I've got something you could get a handle on," Finn said.

She rolled her eyes. "Weak."

"It's not weak."

She laughed. "I remember."

"So if we're not making fantasies come true, how about dinner?" he asked.

Dilemma. She couldn't take him home, she'd sleep with him again. "Pizza," she said, thinking a crowded Italian joint should be safe enough.

"Sold," Finn said.

They left the cave and walked along the rocky beach for a few minutes. The tide was out, the water receded a hundred yards or more it seemed. Pru managed to trip over a rock and then her own two feet, dropping Thor's leash to catch herself. So naturally Thor took off directly toward the waves at the speed of light, barking the whole way.

"Thor!" she yelled. "He can't swim," she told Finn. "Sinks like a stone."

"Trust me, he'll swim if he has to."

But she couldn't be so calm. Her baby was racing

right for the waves. She started after him much slower, having to be careful on the rocks.

"Don't worry," Finn said. "He'll be back as soon as his paws get wet."

But Thor hit the water and kept going, right into a wave. And then the worst possible thing happened.

He vanished.

"Oh my God." Pru took off running down the rocky beach, heading directly for the spot where Thor had vanished. She kicked off her sandals and dove in.

The next wave crashed over her head and smashed her face into the sand. Gasping, she pushed upright, swiping the sand from her face to find . . .

Thor sitting on the shore staring at her, his tail whipping back and forth, his mouth smiling wide, proud of himself. Dripping wet, he barked twice and she'd have sworn he said, "Fun, right?"

Finn laughed and picked the dog up. Thor wriggled to get free but Finn just tucked the dripping wet, very-proud-of-himself dog beneath one arm and reached for Pru with the other, a wide smile on his face.

Pru went hands on wet hips. "Are you laughing at me? You'd better not be laughing at me."

"I wouldn't dream of it."

She narrowed her eyes.

Finn did his best to squelch his smile and failed. "I told you he'd be fine."

"Uh huh."

His laugh drifted over her. "I'm guessing that this time you really are cold instead of just pretending to be."

She looked down at her shirt. Yep, plastered to her

torso and gone sheer to boot, making her look more naked than she would be without a stitch of clothing. She narrowed her eyes at him but he just kept smiling. So she took a step toward him with the intention of wrapping her very wet self around him until he was just as wet as she.

But he dodged her and held up a hand. "Now let's not get crazy—"

She flung herself at him. Just took a running step and a flying leap.

He was a smart enough man to catch her, and in spite of the fact that it meant she drenched him with seawater, he hauled her in and held her close.

"Got you," he said, and melted away her irritation in a single heartbeat. Because he always did seem to have her, whether it was soothing her after *she'd* hit *him* with a dart, or when she'd been upset about her grandpa, or sick with food poisoning . . . He had her. Always.

It was as simple and terrifying as that.

Chapter 28

#SliceOfHumblePie

Finn bundled both the wet dog and the even wetter woman into his car. He pulled a blanket from his emergency kit and tucked it around them.

"I'm f-fine," Pru said, teeth chattering, lips blue.

Uh huh. In other words, "back off, Finn." Not likely. But he wasn't surprised at the attempt. Every time they got too close she seemingly regretted their time together.

He regretted nothing. Not the way she'd felt in his arms and not the way he'd felt in hers. From the beginning, there'd been a shocking sense of intimacy between them, one that had momentarily stunned him, but he'd gotten over it quickly.

He wanted even more but he was smart enough to know a reticent woman when he saw one. She was still unsure. She needed more time.

And he'd already made the decision to give it to her.

"Your teeth are going to rattle right out of your head," he said, cranking up the heat, aiming the vents at her.

Clearly freezing, she didn't utter a word of complaint. Instead she seemed much more concerned that he would skip the afore-promised pizza. "It takes calories to keep yourself warm," she said. "Pepperoni and cheese calories. A lot of them."

"I'll call it in and have it delivered while you shower," he assured her.

"No!" She paused, clearly searching for a reason to ditch him. "Lefty's won't deliver."

"Then we can call Mozza's," he said.

She managed a derisive snort in between shivers. "Mozza's isn't real pizza."

"Okay." He pulled into the back lot of Lefty's. "Stay here, I'll just run in and get it real quick."

But she was right behind him, emergency Mylar blanket wrapped around her and all.

Waiting in line, he slid her a look. "You didn't trust me to pick the right pizza."

"Not even a little bit."

Lefty was taking orders himself, he loved people. Smiling broadly at Pru, he said, "Hey there, cutie pie. What happened, you get pitched overboard? Not a good day for a swim, it's kinda brisk."

"Don't I know it," she muttered. "I had to save Thor. Life or death situation."

Finn grinned and Pru turned a long look his way, daring him to contradict her story.

Finn lifted his hands in surrender and Lefty went brows up. "Sensing a good story here. Someone start talking."

"Would love to," Pru said. "But you've got a long line waiting, so—"

"They'll wait." Lefty set his elbows on the counter and leaned in. "Is it as good as you trying to kill our boy here with a dart?"

She whirled on Finn. "You know that was an accident! You've been telling people I tried to kill you?"

Lefty laughed. "Nah, he didn't say a word. Never does. Willa told me. Oh and Archer's guys too, Max and the scary-looking one with the tattoo on his skull."

Pru smacked her forehead. "How is it possible that the people in our building gossip more than a bunch of guys in a firehouse?"

"Don't you mean a bunch of girls in junior high?" Lefty asked.

"No," she said, glowering. "Girls have got nothing on guys when it comes to gossip." She sent a long look at Finn, daring him to disagree.

"One hundred percent true," he said and paid for their food. And then because she seemed skittish about going back to her place, he brought her and Thor to his.

As they got out of the car, Pru muttered something that sounded an awful lot like "just keep your clothes on and you'll be fine."

Finn hid his grin. "Problem?" he asked her.

She scowled. "Just hungry."

He let them inside. His phone buzzed an incoming call from Sean and he turned to Pru. "Help yourself to my shower to get warmed up."

When she'd shut herself in his bathroom, he answered his phone.

"We're filled to capacity," Sean said.

"Great. And?"

"And," Sean said, sounding irritated. "We need you."

"You're fully staffed. The pub doesn't need me."

There was a silence, during which Finn could hear Sean gnashing his teeth together. "Okay, I need you," he finally said, not sounding all that happy about the admission. "There's a bachelorette party here and the bridesmaids are *insane*, man. They've pinched my ass twice. I've also got a birthday party for some guy who's like a hundred and he's got a bunch of old geezers with him and they're doing shots. What if one of them ups and croaks on us? And then there's the fact that Rosa's sick and says she has to go home early. Code for her boyfriend doesn't have to work tonight and she wants to go see him."

Finn heard the shower go on down the hall. He hadn't had a woman here in this house . . . ever. Not once. The relationships in his life had all been short-lived ones, all existing away from home. He tended to keep his personal life out of his sex life.

And his personal life hadn't been a priority, in any sense of the word. His brother and the pub had been his entire world for a damn long time, which meant that Pru had been right when she'd told him that first night in the bar that he hadn't been living his life. It had been living him.

He wanted to change that. He wanted what he'd been missing out on. He wanted a relationship.

And he wanted it with Pru.

"Are you even listening to me?" Sean asked, clearly pissy now. "I need you to get your ass down here and help me with this shit."

"No," Finn said. "You're in charge."

"But—"

"Figure it out, Sean," Finn said and disconnected. He filled a bowl of water for Thor, and since the little guy was looking a little waterlogged, he wrapped him up in a blanket and made him comfortable on the couch.

Thor licked Finn's chin and closed his eyes, and was snoring in thirty seconds flat.

"If only your owner was as easy to please," Finn said.

Thor smiled in his sleep and then farted.

Pru stood under Finn's heavenly shower until she'd thawed. Then she wrapped herself up in one of his large, fluffy towels and went looking for him, hoping he had a pair of sweats she could wear while her clothes dried.

She found Thor asleep in the middle of Finn's comfy-looking couch. The sliding glass door was open so she left the dog to his nap and poked her head out. The deck there was small and cozy and completely secluded by the two stucco walls on either side.

There was a tiny table, two chairs, and an incredible view of Cow Hollow, and beyond it, the Golden Gate Bridge and the bay.

Finn came out. She heard him set the pizza and drinks on the table and then he came up behind her where she stood hands on the railing staring out at the view. His hands covered hers. She could feel the warmth of his big body seeping into her. And something else. Hunger. Need. He always invoked those emotions in her, and if she was being honest, far more too. "I was hoping to borrow some of your clothes," she managed.

"Anything."

He had her caged in and she liked it. When he lowered his head to nuzzle the side of her throat, she nearly turned into a happy little kitten and began to purr.

"I like you like this," he said huskily. "Just warm, soft, delicious, naked woman in my towel."

"How do you know I'm naked under here?" she heard herself ask daringly.

Taking the challenge, he slid a hand up her thigh, letting out a low, sexy, knowing laugh when she squeaked.

"*Clothes*," she demanded.

"Sure." But instead of backing off, he lifted a hand to point to Fisherman's Wharf, where if she squinted, she could just make out Jake's building. "Sometimes I stand right here and look for you," he said.

She closed her eyes and let her body follow its wishes, which meant she rested her head back against his chest.

Finn brushed the hair from the nape of her neck and slid his mouth across the sensitive skin there, giving her a full body shiver of the very best kind.

"You always smell so damn good," he murmured against her skin, his mouth at her jaw now while his hands slid over her body, revving her engines, firing up all her cylinders. "And now you smell like me. Love that. You make me hungry, Pru."

"Good thing we have pizza," she said breathlessly.

"It's not pizza I'm hungry for." His hands skimmed over her towel-covered breasts, skipping her nipples which were dying for his attention.

She made a little whimper of protest and felt him smile against her neck.

"You're teasing me," she accused.

"No, if I was teasing you, I'd do something like this . . ." And he dragged hot, openmouthed kisses down her throat, his hands continuing to tease until she whimpered in frustration. "*Finn*."

"Tell me."

Stay strong, Pru. "I need you," she whispered. "I need you so much."

"Right back at you, Pru." And then he whipped her around and lifted her up onto the rail. "Hold on tight," he said against her throat.

Not having a death wish, she threw her arms around his neck. This had the towel loosening on her. But left with the choice of holding onto it or Finn, she did what any red-blooded, sex-starved woman would do—she let the towel fall.

Finn kissed her and then pulled back just enough to take a good, long look at her, letting out a rough groan. "You take my breath, Pru. Every fucking time. You're so beautiful."

She opened her mouth to tell him ditto but his mouth covered hers before she could speak as his hands began a full assault on her now naked body. It took him only a few beats to have her writhing under his ministrations, straining for more, and his hot gaze swept over her, heating her up from the inside out. "You're not cold?"

He was really asking this time and she managed to shake her head. "Not even a little."

With a smile, his mouth worked its way south-ward. As for Pru, she kept a monkey-like grip on him, her head falling back. "Oh my God," she whispered. "We're *outside*."

His mouth curved against her bare shoulder. "Do you want me to stop?"

"Don't you dare—" She broke off and sucked in a breath as he gently captured her nipple with his teeth.

Mindless now, she rocked up into him. "Please don't let go of me."

"Never." He sucked her into his hot mouth making her moan and clutch at him. He had one arm tight to her back while his free hand danced its way up the inside of her thighs. The flat of the railing that she was balanced on wasn't quite as wide as her ass but he had her, and in spite of joking that she didn't trust him to pick the pizza, she did.

Truth was, she trusted him one hundred percent, with her pizza, with her body, and if she was being honest, with her heart too.

It was a shocking thought but she didn't have the brain power to lend to it at the moment. She was far too busy being taken apart by Finn's fingers as they stroked knowingly over her. But in the vague recesses of her mind, she was aware that if she trusted him one hundred percent, she needed to trust him with the facts of who she was.

And she would. It was just that things between them had heated up so quickly and unexpectedly in their short time together, and had become so unexpectedly complicated. She wanted to tell him everything, and soon. But it hadn't really been all that long—only been two weeks—and she needed a little more time to figure it all out first.

The early evening's breeze floated over her bare skin, along with Finn's heated gaze. Every inch of her was crying out for his touch, needing him more than she'd ever needed anything in her life. *"Finn."*

"Don't let go of me," he said and tugged a gasp from her when his fingers went from teasing to driving her right to the edge, moving in beat with her heart. Suddenly she no longer cared if she was in danger of plummeting to her death because she was too busy coming apart.

When she could hear past the roar of her own blood in her ears, she hoped like hell that his neighbors hadn't been able to hear her cries. "Were we loud?" she whispered.

He grinned. "We?" he asked, laughing when she smacked him in the chest.

He caught her hand, kissed her palm, and then tore open a condom packet. Protecting them both, he plunged into her as his mouth claimed hers again.

Good God. She wasn't going to die from a fall. She was going to die of pleasure, right here . . .

Chapter 29

#HoustonWeHaveAProblem

The week went by in a blur for Pru. It was a rare blue moon–two full moons in the same calendar month—so SF Tours held a special moonlit cruise week.

Which meant that Pru and the other boat captains worked during the day, crashed for a few hours on whatever horizontal surface they could find in the building, and then went back out at night on the water.

This went on for three days.

On the fourth day, she crawled home and into bed right after grabbing dinner—Frosted Flakes. But she came awake some time later in her dark bedroom to find someone in it with her. Then that someone pulled his shirt over his head and shucked his jeans.

She'd recognize that leanly muscled bod anywhere and swallowed hard at the gorgeous outline of him bathed in nothing but moonlight. It didn't matter how many times she saw him in the buff, he never failed to steal her breath. With her still blinking through the dark trying to see his every sexy inch, he slipped beneath the covers with her.

Naked.

"Chris Pratt?" she asked. "Is that you?"

"You don't need Chris Pratt," Finn said as he pulled her into a heated embrace.

He was damp and chilled. "Hey!" she complained.

"It's raining sideways," he explained, wrapping himself around her. "Nasty storm. Your bed was closer than mine. And mine was missing something."

"What?"

"You."

Aw. Dammit. "How did you get in?" she asked. "I mean, your hands are magic but not *that* magic."

"Your hidden key." His magical hands began stroking her, while at the same time he pressed hot kisses against the back of her neck. "Do you mind?"

She loved being in the circle of his arms. Loved the way he touched her so knowingly and sure, and since he was actually licking her now, she couldn't concentrate on anything beyond his tongue. Did she mind? "Only if you stop."

His hands were hypnotic, his palms a little rough with calluses, his long talented fingers tracing over her breasts, teasing her nipples.

One thing she'd come to know about him, he was incredibly physical. Whenever they were together like this, he wanted to touch and taste and see . . . everything. There was no hiding, not that she could remember to. He was an incredibly demanding lover, but also endlessly patient and creative. She never knew exactly what to expect from him but he always left her panting for more. "Aren't you tired?" she asked.

"I can sleep when I'm dead." He slipped his fingers inside her panties to cup and squeeze her ass, and then wriggled them to her thighs.

And she was a goner.

"Missed this," he murmured in her ear.

She'd been hoping for sleep. Now she hoped for this to never end. "It hasn't been all that long," she managed. "A few days."

"Four. Too long." Her T-shirt and panties vanished and then his hand was back to its serious business of driving her out of her mind. In less than a minute she was thrusting against his fingers. And in the next, she came so fast her head was spinning.

"God, I love watching you come," he said, and then proceeded to show her what a true force of nature could accomplish.

Mother Nature had nothing on him.

Later Pru lay in Finn's arms, her head on his shoulder, her face pressed into his throat, knowing by the way he was breathing that he was out cold, dead asleep. Poor baby, being a sex fiend was exhausting.

He'd left work and had come here, to her. And there in the dark, she smiled, her body sated, her heart so full she almost didn't know what to do with herself.

Had she ever felt like this? Like she just wanted to climb into the man next to her and stay there?

Being with Jake had been good. She'd had no

complaints, but she wasn't for him. When they'd split, he'd moved on with shocking ease.

And in truth, so had she.

But it'd left her feeling just a little bit . . . broken, and more than a little bit unsure about love in general.

But then Finn O'Riley had come into her life. She knew that she had no business feeling anything for him at all. But apparently, some things—like matters of the heart—not only happened in a blink but were also out of her control.

She felt her heart swell at just the thought and before she could stop herself, she mouthed the words against his throat. "I love you, Finn."

She immediately stilled in shock because she hadn't just mouthed the words, she'd actually said them.

Out loud.

She remained perfectly frozen another beat, but Finn didn't so much as twitch.

It took a while but eventually she relaxed into him again, and there in the dark, told herself it was okay. He didn't know.

He didn't know a lot of things . . .

The panic that was never far away these days hit her hard. She'd been telling herself that she'd waited to tell him the truth in the hopes he'd understand better once he knew her. But deep down, she wasn't sure she'd done the right thing. Telling him now was going to be harder, not easier.

And the outcome felt more uncertain than ever.

As always, Pru woke up just before her alarm was due to go off at the shockingly early hour of oh-dark-annoying-thirty. But this time it wasn't thoughts of the day ahead that woke her. Or the knot of anxiety wrapped in and around her chest.

It was the fact that she was wrapped around a big, strong, warm body.

Finn had one hand tangled in her hair and the other possessively cupping her bare ass, and when she shifted to try and disentangle herself without waking him, he tightened his grip and let out a low growl.

Torn between laughing and getting unbearably aroused—seriously, that growl!—she lifted her head.

And discovered she wasn't the only one wrapped around Finn like a pretzel.

Thor was on the other side of him, his head on Finn's shoulder, eyes slitted at her.

And she did laugh then because it'd been Thor who growled, not Finn. "Are you kidding me?" she whispered to her dog. "He's *mine*."

But no he's not, a little voice deep inside her whispered. *He doesn't yet know it but you wrecked this— long before it'd even begun.*

Pru told the little voice to *shut up* and concentrated on Thor. "I found him first," she whispered.

Thor growled again.

Thor didn't look impressed in the least. She opened her mouth to further argue but Finn spoke, his voice low and morning gruff. "There's plenty of me to go around."

Pru felt the pink tinge hit her cheeks and she shifted her focus from Thor to Finn.

Yep. He was wide awake and watching and, if she had to guess, more than a little amused that she'd been willing to fight her own dog for him.

"He's mine?" Finn repeated.

"It's a figure of speech." She grimaced at the lameness of that but he smiled.

"I like it," he said. "I like this. But mostly, I like where we're going."

If she could think straight, she'd echo that thought, but she couldn't think straight because every moment of every single day she was painfully aware she'd built this glass house that couldn't possibly withstand the coming storm . . .

"Pretty sure I just lost you for a few beats," Finn said quietly, eyes serious now, dark and warm and intense as he ran a finger along her jaw. "Was it what I said about liking where we're going thing?"

She tried to play this off with her customary self-deprecatory humor. "Since where we're going is always straight to bed, I can't do much complaining about that, can I," she said in a teasing voice, desperately hoping to steer the conversation to lighter waters, because one thing she couldn't do was have the talk with him while naked in his arms.

But she should have known better. Finn couldn't be steered, ever.

"This is more than that," he said, voice low but sure, so sure she wished for even an ounce of his easy confidence. "A lot more."

His gaze held hers prisoner, daring her to contradict him, and she swallowed hard. "It's only been a few weeks," she said softly.

"Three," he said.

"It just seems like we're moving so fast."

"Too fast?" he asked.

She gnawed on her lower lip, unsure how to answer that. The truth was, she'd already acknowledged to herself how she felt about him. And another truth—she wouldn't mind moving along even faster. She wanted to leap into his arms, press her face into his neck, and breathe him in and claim him as hers.

For always.

But she'd gone about this all wrong, and because of that she didn't have the right to him. Not even a little.

His fingers were gentle as they traced the line of her temple. "Babe, you're thinking too hard."

She nodded at the truth of this statement.

"You're scared," he said.

Terrified, thank you very much. She nodded again.

"Of me?"

"No. *No*," she said again, firmly, cupping his face. "It's more than I'm scared of what you make me feel."

He didn't seem annoyed or impatient at her reticence. Instead he kept his hands on her, his voice quiet. "I'm not saying I know where this is going," he said. "Because I don't. But what I do know is that what we've got here between us is good, really good."

She nodded her agreement of that but then slowly shook her head. "Good can go bad. Fast." As she knew all too well.

"Life's a crap shoot and we both know it," he said. "More than most. But whatever this is, I can't stop thinking about it. I can't stop wanting more. I think we've got a real shot, and that doesn't come around every day, Pru. We both know that too." He paused. "I want us to go for it."

Heart tight, she closed her eyes.

He was quiet a moment, but she could feel him studying her. "Pru, look at me."

She lifted her gaze and found his still warm, but very focused. "Say the word," he said seriously. "Tell me that this isn't your thing, that you're not feeling it, and I'll back off."

She opened her mouth.

And then closed it.

His fingers on her jaw, his thumb slid over her lower lip. "You're the self-proclaimed Fun Whisperer," he said. "You're the one preaching about getting out there and living life. So why are you all talk and no go, Pru? What am I missing?"

She choked out a laugh at his sharpness and dropped his head to his chest.

"Tell me what you're afraid of," he said.

Her words came out muffled. "It's hard to put words to it."

He wasn't buying it and slid his hands into her hair and lifted her face. "Fight through that," he said simply. "Fight for me."

Of course he'd say that. It was his MO. Want something? Get it. Make it yours. Go for it, one hundred percent.

Which brought home one hard-hitting point—she needed to adopt that philosophy and do what he'd said, fight for what she wanted. Fight for him.

She'd left her cell on the kitchen counter the night before and from down the hall, it rang. She ignored it but once it stopped, it immediately started up again. Not a good sign so she slid out of bed. Realizing she was very, very naked, she bent to pick something from the pile of discarded clothes and heard a choked sound from the bed.

She turned and found Finn watching her every move, eyes heavy-lidded but not with sleepiness.

He crooked his finger at her.

"Oh no," she said, pointing her finger back at him. "Don't even think about waving your magic wand and—" Shit. "I didn't mean *wand* as in . . ." Her gaze slid down past his chest and washboard abs to the part of him that never failed to be happy to see her. "You know."

He burst out laughing. "Babe, if my 'wand' really was magic, then you'd be on it right now."

She felt herself blush to the roots, which only seemed to amuse him all the more. She actually took a step toward him when her phone rang yet a third time. With a sigh, she slipped his shirt over her head and padded out of the room.

Three missed calls, all from Jake. She tapped on the voicemail he'd just left, hitting speaker so she could make some desperately needed coffee as she listened.

"You're either still sleeping or hell, maybe you're out playing fairy godmother before work," he said, sounding disgruntled. "I heard from a little birdie that you got Tim a place to live."

Damn. Not a little birdie at all. Nick had spilled the beans on her. Again.

"I don't know how long you intend to go around fixing wrongs that aren't yours to fix," Jake said. "But at some point you're going to have to let go. You know that, right? You can't go on keeping track of everyone from the accident and righting their worlds. The seed money for what's-her-name—"

"Shelby," she said, as if Jake could hear her.

"Then there was the place to live for Tim. The job for Nick. And how about what you did for F—"

At the sound behind her, Pru hit delete at the speed of light.

Because she knew the rest of Jake's sentence.

The beep of Jake's message being deleted echoed in the room as she turned to face Finn, wearing only his jeans, unbuttoned.

"What was that about?" he asked.

"Oh . . ." She waved her hand. "You know Jake, sticking his nose into everything."

"Sounds like he thinks you're the one sticking your nose into everything."

She took a deep breath. *Be careful. Be very careful unless you're ready to give up the fantasy right here, right now.* It needed to be done. She knew that now more than ever. She'd do it tonight after work, when they had time to talk about it. *And after you figure out how to make him realize you'd only meant to help.*

Even if in her heart she knew that was no way to make him understand. He was smart and resourceful and sharp, and he was standing there steady as a rock.

Her rock.

Waiting for answers.

"I do tend to stick my nose into things," she said as lightly as she could. "I've got to get to work . . ."

"Or you need to change the subject."

Her smile faded. "Or that."

"You know . . ." He stepped into her, slid his hands to her hips and ducked his head to meet her gaze. "You once told me I needed to let stuff go."

She choked out a low laugh and stared at his Adam's apple. "Haven't you heard, swallowing your own medicine is the hardest thing to do?"

He wrapped her ponytail around his fist and gently tugged until she looked up at him. "What's going on, Pru?"

"What's going on is that I need to get ready for work—"

"In here." He slid his free hand up and tapped a finger over her temple.

She managed another smile. "You'd be surprised by how little's going on in there—"

"Don't," he said quietly. "If you don't want to do this, you only have to say so."

She hesitated and he took a step back. "Wow," he said, looking like she'd sucker punched him.

"No," she said. "I—"

He'd already turned and headed into her bedroom. She started to follow, but he came back out again, holding his shoes. Still no shirt, since she was wearing it. "Finn."

He headed to the door.

"Finn."

He stopped and turned to her, eyes hooded.

"Can we talk about this tonight?"

"Sure. Whatever." He started to leave but stopped and muttered something to himself. He then came at her, hauled her into his arms and kissed her. When his tongue stroked possessively over hers, her knees wobbled, but far before she was ready, he let her go.

He stared down at her for a beat and then he turned and left, shutting the door quietly behind him.

She moved to the door and put her hands on it, like she could bring him back.

But it was far too late for that.

Chapter 30

#JustTheFactsMa'am

Outside Pru's front door, Finn stopped and shook his head. She was holding back on him, big time. But he knew something else too.

So was he.

Because as long as she wasn't one hundred percent in, it felt . . . safe. The crazy thing was that he wanted her to be one hundred percent in. He wanted to do the same.

But he wasn't going to beg her. He wanted her to come to him on her own terms. Until she did, he could hold back that last piece of his heart and soul and keep it safe from complete annihilation.

He was good at that.

He dropped his shoes to the floor and shoved his feet into them. He'd just bent over to tie them when Mrs. Winslow opened her door.

"Whoa, good thing my ovaries are shriveled," she

said. "Or you'd have just made me pregnant from that view alone."

Finn straightened and gave her a look that made her laugh.

"Sorry, boy," she said. "But you don't scare me."

With as much dignity as he could, he hunkered down and went back to tying his shoes, attempting to keep his ass tucked in while doing it.

When he'd finished, he stood up to his full height to find her still watching. "You're a nice package and all," she said, "but I like 'em more seasoned. Men are no good until they're at least forty-five."

"Good to know," he muttered and started down the hall.

"Because until then," she said to his back. "They don't know nothing about the important things. Like forgiveness. And understanding."

He blew out a breath and turned to face her. "You're trying to tell me something again."

"Now you're thinking, genius," she said. "If you were forty-five or older, you'd have already picked up on it."

He went hands on hips. "Got a busy day ahead of me, Mrs. Winslow. Maybe you could come right out and tell me what it is you want me to know."

"Well, that would be far too easy," she said and vanished inside, shutting her door on him.

Finn divided a look between her door and Pru's before tossing up his hands and deciding he knew nothing about women.

Finn strode into the bar. His morning crew cleaners Marie, Rosa, and Felipe all lifted their heads from their various tasks of mopping and scrubbing and blinked.

Shit. He forgot that he was making the morning walk of shame.

Shirtless.

It was Felipe who finally recovered first and gave a soft wolf whistle. "Nice," he said with an eyelash flutter and a hand fanning the air in front of his face.

Finn rolled his eyes in tune to their laughter. Whatever. He strode to his office and—as a bonus annoyance—found Sean asleep on his damn couch.

In Finn's damn spare shirt.

He kicked his brother's feet and watched with grim satisfaction as Sean grunted, jerked awake, and rolled off the couch, hitting the floor with a bone-sounding crunch.

"What the fuck, man?" Sean asked with a wide yawn.

"I need my shirt."

"I'm in it," Sean said. Captain Obvious.

Fine. Whatever. Finn slapped his pockets for his keys. He'd just drive home real quick and—

His keys weren't in his pockets. Probably, given his luck, they were on the floor of Pru's bedroom. He walked out of his office and strode through the pub.

"Just as nice from the rear," Felipe called out.

Finn flipped him off, ignored the hoots of laughter, and hit the stairs, knocking on Pru's door.

From behind him he heard a soft gasp and a wheeze. Craning his head, he found Mrs. Winslow once again in her doorway, this time with two other ladies, mouths agog.

"You were right," one of them whispered to Mrs.

Winslow, staring at Finn. She was hooked up to a portable oxygen tank, hence the Darth Vadar–like breathing.

"I haven't seen hipbones cut like that in sixty years," the other said in the same stage whisper as her friend.

"You realize I can hear you, right?" Finn asked.

The women all jumped in tandem, snapping their gazes up to his. "Oh my god, he's *real*," the woman with the oxygen tank said—wheezed—in awe.

Mrs. Winslow snorted. "You'll have to excuse them," she said to Finn. "They probably need their hormone doses checked."

Finn decided the hell with waiting on Pru to answer her door. He'd slept with her. He'd tasted every inch of her body. She'd done the same for him. So he checked the handle, and when it turned easily in his palm, he took that as a sign that the day had to improve from here.

When Finn had left, Pru stood there in the kitchen, shaken. She grabbed her phone because she needed advice. Since she was still wearing only Finn's shirt, she propped her phone against the cereal box on the counter so that when the FaceTime call went through to Jake, he'd only see her from the shoulders up.

No need to set off any murder sprees this morning.

When he answered, he just looked at her.

"Hi," she said.

"Hi yourself. You think I don't know your thoroughly fucked face?"

She did her best to keep eye contact. "Hey, I don't point it out to you when *you* get lucky."

"Yes you do. You march your ass into my office, pull out your pocketknife, and make a notch on the corner of my wood desk."

"That's to make a point," she said.

"Which is?"

"You get lucky a lot."

He arched a brow. "And the problem?"

Well, he had her there. "I need your advice."

"Why now?"

"Okay, I deserve that," she said. "But remember when you were worried that Finn was the one who would get hurt?" She felt her eyes fill. "You were off a little."

"Ah, hell, Pru," he said, voice softer now. "You never did know how to follow directions worth shit."

She choked out a laugh. "I know this is a mess of my own making, I totally get that." She closed her eyes. And I've got no excuse for not finding a way over the past few weeks to tell Finn sooner." Well, she did sort of have one—that being she was deathly afraid to lose him when she'd only just found him.

Not that Finn would take any comfort from that.

Jake sighed. "Chica, the mistake's been made. Shit happens. Just tell him. Tell him who you are and who your parents were. Get past it. Stop hiding. You'll feel better."

No, she wouldn't. Because she knew what came next.

Finn would be hurt.

She'd been so taken aback by the speed of events between the two of them, at how fast things had gotten out of her control, that she was scared. Terrified, really.

Because hurting him had been the last thing she'd ever wanted. She opened her mouth to say so but at the sound of footsteps coming toward the kitchen, not hurried or rushed or trying to be stealthy, she whirled around, already knowing who she'd be facing.

Finn, of course. Still shirtless, face carefully blank, he strode to the table and picked up his forgotten keys.

Shit.

God knew how long he'd been there or how much he'd heard. It was impossible to tell by his expression since he was purposely giving nothing away.

Which really was her answer.

He'd heard everything.

"Finn," Jake said, taking in his shirtless state with a slight brow raise.

"Jake," Finn said, either not noticing the unspoken question from Jake or ignoring it completely.

Then they both looked at Pru, to their credit both doing so with a mix of affection and concern. With good reason, as it turned out, because she suddenly felt like she was going to be sick.

Go time, she thought.

"Pru," Finn said quietly. Not a question really but a statement. He wanted to know what was going on.

Oh God, this was going to suck. And the worst part was she'd started all of this with the best intentions. All she'd ever wanted was to fix a wrong that had been done to him, a terrible wrong that she regretted and had carried around until she'd been able to do something about it.

And she'd righted wrongs before, successfully too. But she'd crossed the line this time and she knew it.

And now she had to face it head on.

"Trust him, chica," Jake said from her phone. "He deserves to know and you deserve to be free of this once and for all. If he's who you think, it'll be okay."

And then the rat fink bastard disconnected.

"Pru?" Finn brought up his free hand and slid his fingers along her jaw, letting them sink into her hair. His expression was wary now, but that didn't stop him from standing in her space like they were a couple. An intimate one.

Her heart tightened. It'd been everything she'd ever wanted.

Only a few moments ago he'd been looking morning gruff and deeply satisfied. Now there was something much more to his body language and—Oh good Lord. He had a bite mark just to the side of his left nipple. She felt the heat rise up her cheeks.

"I have another on my ass," he said, his tone not its usual amused or heated when discussing their sex life. "We'll circle back to that. Talk to me, Pru."

Her heart was pounding, her blood surging hard and fast through her veins, panic making her limbs weak. She looked at her phone but Jake was long gone and in the reflection of the screen she could see herself.

She hadn't gotten away from last night unscathed either. There was a visible whisker burn on her throat and she knew she had a matching mark on her breasts.

And between her thighs.

Finn had brought her pleasure such as she'd never known, both in bed and out.

And now it was over . . . "I'm so sorry," she said. "I've kept something from you."

"What?" There was some wariness to his tone now, though he still spoke quietly. Willing to hear whatever she had to say.

She immediately felt her blood pressure shoot through the stratosphere.

"Just tell me, Pru."

Well, if he was going to be all calm and logical about this . . . She inhaled a deep breath. "It's about my parents. And their accident."

His eyes softened with sympathy, which she didn't deserve. "You never say much about how it happened," he said. "I haven't wanted to push. You don't push me on my dad's shit and I appreciate that, so—"

"It was a car wreck." She licked her suddenly dry lips. "They . . . caused other injuries." She paused. "Life-altering injuries."

His eyes never left hers. "And?"

"And I . . . got involved."

"You've been . . . helping them?"

"Yes, but only in the smallest of ways compared to the damage my parents caused."

He looked at her for a long moment. "That's got to be painful for you."

"No, actually, it's healing."

He looked skeptical.

"I had to," she said softly. "Finn, my parents are the ones in the car who killed your dad."

His brow furrowed. "What are you talking about? The man driving the car that hit him was some guy by the name of Steven Dalman."

"My dad," she said quietly. "My mom never took his last name. Her family was against the match every bit as much as his. She gave me her name, not his . . ." She trailed off when Finn abruptly turned from her.

He shoved his fingers into his hair and didn't say a word. She wasn't even sure if he was breathing, but she couldn't take her eyes off him. Off the sleek, leanly muscled lines of his bare back. The inch of paler skin low on his waist where his jeans had slipped.

The tension now in every line of his body.

She tried to explain. "I just wanted . . ."

Finn whipped back around. "Want what? To satiate your curiosity? See if Sean and I were as devastated as you? What exactly did you want, Pru?"

"To make it better," she said, throat tight. "That's all I've ever wanted, was to make it better. For both of you, for everyone who my dad . . ." She covered her mouth.

Destroyed.

"I see," he said quietly. "So that's what I was to you, another pet project like the others you collected and fixed their broken lives."

"No, I—"

"Truth, Pru," he said, voice vibrating with fury. "You owe me that."

"Okay, yes, I needed to help everyone however I could. I needed to make things right," she reiterated, swallowing a sob when he shook his head. She was losing him. "So I did what I could."

"I didn't need saving," he bit out. "Sean and I had each other and we were fine—" He stilled and his eyes cut to hers, sharp as a blade. "It was you. You got us that money that was supposedly from a community fundraiser. Jesus, how did I not guess this before?" His gaze narrowed. "Where did that money come from?

Is that why you sold your childhood home? To give it to us?"

"No, the money from the house went to the others. For you and Sean, I used my parents' life insurance policy."

He stared at her. "Fuck," he said roughly and turned to go.

She managed to slide between him and the door. "Finn, please—"

"Please what?" he asked coldly. "Understand how you very purposely and calculatedly came into my life? Moved into this building? Sat in my pub? Became my friend and then my lover? All under the pretense of wanting me, while really you were just trying to assuage some misguided sense of guilt." He stopped and closed his eyes for a beat. "Jesus, Pru. I never even saw you coming."

Having her crimes against him listed out loud made her feel sick to her soul. "It wasn't like that," she said.

"No? You sought me out, decided I needed fixing, slept with me, probably had a good laugh over me telling you how much you meant to me . . . all without telling me why you were really here—to ease your damn conscience." He shook his head. "Hope you got everything in that you wanted because we're done here."

"No, Finn. I—"

"Done," he repeated with a terrifying finality. "I don't want to see you again, Pru."

And then he walked out, breaking the heart she hadn't even realized she had inside her to break.

Chapter 31

#MissedItByThatMuch

Weighted down by so many emotions that she couldn't name them all, Pru called in sick, letting Jake think she'd gotten her period and had debilitating cramps.

Since she'd never used such an excuse before, had in fact never missed work at all, she didn't feel in the least bit sorry.

Her ovaries had to be good for something, right?

She marathoned *Game of Thrones* and never left the couch. Every time her mind wandered to Finn, her heart did a slow somersault in her chest, her lungs stopped working, and her stomach hurt, so she did what anyone would do in the throes of a bad breakup.

She ate.

The next morning she was jerked out of her stupor when someone knocked on her door. She blinked and looked around. She was still dressed, still on her couch, surrounded by empty wrappings of candy bars and other varieties of junk food—the evidence of a pity party for one. She grabbed her phone but there were no missed calls, texts, or emails from Finn.

And why would there be? He'd been pretty clear.

He didn't want to see her again.

The knock came again, less patient now. She got to her feet and looked out the peephole.

Willa, Elle, and Haley.

Elle was front and center, her eyes on the peephole.

"I'm not feeling very sociable," Pru said. "In fact, I'm feeling pretty damn negative and toxic so—"

"Okay, listen, honey," Elle said. "Life sucks sometimes. The trick is not letting negative and toxic feelings rent space in your head. Raise the rent and kick them the hell out. And I've brought help in that regard." She lifted a bag.

Tina's muffins.

Pru opened the door.

Elle handed her the bag.

Haley handed over a very large coffee.

Willa smiled. "My job is to be supportive and get you to talk."

"Way to be subtle," Elle said.

Ignoring that, Willa hugged Pru. "Okay, so I missed the subtle gene," she said. "But you should know, we are unbelievably supportive."

"Even if I screwed up?"

"Even if," Willa said.

"I'm not going to talk about it," Pru warned, barely able to talk past the lump in her throat. "Not now. Maybe not ever."

Seemingly unconcerned by this, they all moved into Pru's apartment and eyed the scene of the crime.

Willa picked up an empty bag of maple bacon potato chips. "They make bacon chips?" She looked into the empty bag sadly. "Damn, I bet they were amazing."

"How did you know something was wrong?" Pru asked with what she thought was a calm voice.

"Because you missed Eighties Karaoke and didn't answer any of our calls last night," Elle said. "And you'd told me you wouldn't miss it unless Chris Evans came knocking at your door." She looked Pru over, her rumpled sweats and what was undoubtedly a bad case of bedhead hair. "And I think it's safe to say that didn't happen."

"It could have," Pru muttered and set the coffee down to dive into the bag of muffins. She started with a chocolate chocolate-chip.

Haley reached to put her hand in the bag and Pru clutched it to her chest with a growl that rivaled Thor's.

Haley lifted her hands. "Okay, not sharing. Got it." She turned to Elle and Willa. "I think we've verified the breakup rumor."

Pru froze. "There's a breakup rumor?"

Willa lifted her hand, her first finger and thumb about an inch apart. "Little bit."

Pru sank to the couch, still clutching her muffins. "I'd like to be alone now."

"Sure," Elle said. "We understand." And then she sat on one end of the couch and picked up the remote to turn the volume up. "Season three, right? Love this show."

Eyes on the screen, already enraptured, Haley sat on the other end.

Pru opened her mouth to complain but Willa took the floor, leaning back on the couch, leaving a spot right in the middle for Pru.

She blew out a breath and in the respectful silence that she appreciated more than she could say, she wasn't alone at all.

Two days later Pru walked to work. In the rain. She knew she was bad off when Thor didn't complain once. He did however, keep looking up at her, wondering what their mood should be.

Devastated. That was the current mood. But she didn't want to scare him. "We're going to be okay."

Thor cocked his head, his one stand-up ear quivering a little bit.

He didn't believe her.

And for good reason. She hadn't slept. She'd called in sick again and Jake had let her get away with that.

Until this morning. He'd called her at the crack of dawn and said, "I don't care if your uterus is falling out of your body, take some Midol and get your ass into work. Today."

She wasn't surprised. And to be honest, she was ready to get back to it after a two-day pity party involving more ice cream than she'd eaten in her twenty-six years total. She'd run out of self-pity stamina. Turned out it was hard to maintain that level of despair.

So with it now at a dull roar, she'd showered and dressed and headed to work. "I just feel . . . stupid," she told Thor. "This is all my fault, you know."

"Honey," a woman said, passing her on the sidewalk. "Never admit that it's all your fault." She was wearing the smallest, tightest red dress Pru had ever seen, and the five-inch stilettos were impressive.

"But this time it really is," Pru told her.

"No, you're misunderstanding me. Never admit it's your fault, *especially* when it is."

The woman walked on but Thor stopped and put his front paws on Pru's leg.

She picked him up and he licked her chin.

Her throat tightened. "You love me anyway." She hugged him, apparently squeezing too tight because he suffered it for about two seconds and then growled.

With a half laugh and half sob, she loosened her grip. When she got to work, she walked straight through the warehouse to the offices. She passed those by too and headed back to the area where Jake lived.

He was lifting weights, the music blaring so loud the windows rattled. She turned off the music and turned to face him.

"You okay?" he asked, dropping the weights, turning his chair to face her, his face creased in worry.

She'd planned what she would say to him. Something like *I know, you told me so, blah blah blah, so let's not talk about it, let's just move on.* And she opened her mouth to say just that but nothing came out.

"What's going on?"

She burst into tears.

Looking pained, he stared at her. "Did you forget the Midol? Because I bought some, it's in my bathroom. I've had it for over a year, I've just never figured out how to give it to you without getting my head bit clean off."

She threw her purse at him. "I didn't get my damn period!"

"Oh shit," he said, blanching. "Oh fuck. Okay, first I'll kill him and then—"

"No!" She actually laughed through her tears. "I'm not pregnant."

He let out a long breath. "Well, Jesus, lead with that next time."

Pru shook her head and turned to go, but he was faster than her even in his chair. He got in front of her and blocked the door.

"Talk to me, chica," he said.

"You done being a stupid guy?"

"I'll try to be." He said this quite earnestly, his gaze on hers. "You did tell him then."

She nodded.

"And . . . it went to hell?" he guessed.

"In a hand basket," she agreed.

"I'm sorry."

She shook her head. "Don't be. I was a dumbass. I should have told him from the get-go like you said a million times."

Jake let out a rare sigh. "Look, chica, yeah, you made a mistake. But everything you did was for the right reasons. You should feel good about that. You set out to help everyone from the accident and now you can say you did that. In a big way. In a much bigger way than anyone else I know would have."

She thought about it and realized she did feel good about that part. "So it's mission accomplished," she said softly.

"Yeah." He smiled. "Proud of you."

The words were a balm on her broken heart. The ache didn't go away and she wasn't sure if it ever would.

Loss was loss, and Finn no longer being in her life was a hard pill to swallow. But she'd survived worse and she'd come back from rock bottom.

She could do it again.

Well . . . next time maybe tell him who she was before sexy times and getting hearts involved . . .

The first two days were a complete blur to Finn. On day three, he stood in his shower contemplating the level of suckage his life had become until the hot water ran out. He stood there as it turned cold and then icy, completely forgetting that they were on a water watch and he'd pay a penalty if he went over his allowed usage for the month.

He was sitting on his couch staring at the still-off TV when Sean called. "I'm taking tonight off," Finn said.

"Oh, hell no you're not," Sean said. "Three fucking nights in a row? I can't do this by myself, Finn. This is a damn partnership and you need to start acting like it."

Finn dropped his head, closed his eyes, and fought the laugh. "Are you throwing my words back in my face?"

"Hell yes." Sean paused. "Is it working?"

"I think you owe me more than a few nights."

Sean blew out a breath. "Yeah." He paused again, this one a beat longer. "What's wrong?"

"Nothing."

"Bullshit," Sean said. "You take time off never. Let me guess. You're . . . running away from home? No, it's worse than that. Shit. Just tell me quick, like ripping off a Band-Aid. You're dying?"

"I'm not dying. Jesus, you're such a drama queen."

"Right, then what?" Sean demanded. "Are you dumping me, is that it?"

Finn pinched the bridge of his nose. Sean's greatest fear was being dumped, and to be fair, he'd earned that particular anxiety the hard way from their parents. Pulling his head out of his own ass was hard but Finn managed for a second to do just that. "I can't dump you," he said, "you're my brother."

"People dump their family all the time," Sean said, and then paused. "Or they just walk away."

Finn softened and let out a sigh. "Okay, so yeah, I suppose I *could* dump you. And don't get me wrong, there are entire days where I'd like to at least strangle you slowly. But listen to me very carefully, Sean. I've honestly never, not once, wanted to dump you from my life."

There was a long silence. When Sean finally spoke, his voice was thick. "Yeah?"

"Yeah. I'd do anything for you. And I'll never walk away from you." And up until a few days ago, he'd have given Pru that very same promise.

And yet he had walked away from her.

At that thought, the first shadow of doubt crept in, icy tendrils as relentless as the afternoon fog.

"Are you going to tell me what's up?" Sean asked. "If it's not me and the pub's okay, then what? You mess up with Pru or something?"

"Why would you say that?" Finn demanded.

"Whoa, man, chill. It's a matter of elimination. Other than work, there's nothing else that could get to you like this. So what happened?"

"I don't want to talk about it."

Sean was quiet a second. "Because of Mellie? I apologized for that like a thousand times but I'll do it again. I was an asshole and an idiot. And drunk off my ass that night. And it was a long time ago. I'd never—"

"This has nothing to do with Mellie," Finn said.

"Then what? Because Pru's pretty damn perfect."

Finn sighed. Not perfect. But perfect for him . . . "Why does it have to be anyone's fault?"

Sean laughed wryly. "It's just the way of the world. Men screw up. Women forgive—or don't, as the case often goes."

Finn blew out a breath. "I walked away. I had my reasons but I'm not sure I did the right thing." It was a hell of an admission considering he rarely second-guessed himself.

"If I've learned one thing from you," Sean said, "it's to suck it up and always do the *right* thing. Not the easy thing, the right thing."

Finn managed a short laugh. "Listen to you, all logical and shit."

"I know, go figure, right? So . . . you going to do it? The right thing?"

Finn sighed. "Who are you and what have you done with my brother?"

"Just hurry up and handle it and get your ass back to work."

"There he is."

Chapter 32

#TakeMeToYourLeader

When Finn finally made his way to the pub that night, he stood in the middle of the bar as music played around him. His friends and customers were all there having fun, laughing, dancing, drinking . . .

The pub was a huge success, beyond his wildest imagination. He'd never really taken the time to notice it. But he was noticing now that his heart had been ripped out of his chest by a gorgeous dynamo of a woman with eyes that sucked him in and held him, a sweet yet mischievous smile that had taken him places he'd never been . . . then there was how he'd felt in her arms.

Like Superman.

And he'd dumped her. Roughly. Cruelly. And her crime? Nothing more than trying to make sure he was okay after a tragedy that hadn't even been her fault. Not in the slightest.

Hating himself for that, he stopped right in the middle of the place. He wasn't in the mood for this. He needed to think, needed to figure out what the hell to do to alleviate this pain in his chest and the certainty that he'd walked away from the best thing that had ever happened to him.

But everyone was at the bar, waving at him. Bracing himself for the inquisition, he headed that way.

"Rumor is that you've been a dumbass," Archer said.

Finn stared at him. "How the hell did you know—"

"The girls and I stopped by Pru's place," Willa said. "Is she okay?"

"She looks and sounds like her heart's been ripped out." Willa met his gaze. "She'd clearly been crying."

Shit.

Elle squeezed his hand. "Whatever you did, it's not completely your fault. You're a penis-carrying human being, after all. You're hard-wired to be a dumbass."

"Sit." Spence kicked out a barstool for him and poured him a beer from the pitcher in front of them.

Finn took a second look at him. "You're wearing glasses."

Haley grinned proudly. "Do you like them? I picked them out for him."

"No, you didn't," Spence said. "I did."

Haley patted him like he was a puppy. "You were impatient as always and grabbed the first pair off the display you could. It took you less than two seconds. I waited until you'd left and put them back and picked you out a better pair that would better suit your face."

Spence pulled his glasses off and stared at them. "I liked the other pair better."

"Yeah?" Haley asked. "What color were they?"

Spence paused. "Glasses color."

Haley rolled her eyes. "Just like a man," she said to Will and Elle, who nodded.

Archer shook his head at Spence. "This is why you're single."

"You're single too," Spence said.

"Because I want to be."

Spence closed his eyes. "We were going to rag on Finn, not me. Let's stick with the plan."

"Right," Archer said and looked at Finn. "Tell us all how you messed up so we can point and laugh."

"And then fix," Willa said, giving the others a dirty look as she patted the empty seat. "Come on now, don't be shy. Tell us everything."

"Yes," Ella said. "I want to hear it all, because that girl? She's not just yours, Finn. She's ours now too."

"She's not mine," Finn said.

Everyone gaped at him.

Elle narrowed her gaze. "Does this have anything to do with that wish she made for you on that damn fountain? You know about that, right?"

Finn blinked. "She wished for *me*?"

"Have you ever heard of being gentle?" Archer asked Elle. "Even once?"

Elle sighed. "Okay, so he didn't know. Sue me." She shot Archer a dirty look. "And like you know the first thing about being gentle."

"Didn't know what exactly?" Finn demanded, refusing to let them go off on some tangent. "Someone needs to start making sense or I swear to God—"

"She made a wish for you to find true love," Willa

said. "I was never clear on why she wished for you and not for herself. Probably because that's who she is, down to the bone."

Spence sucked in a breath. "I've been by that fountain a million times. It never once occurred to me to make a wish for someone else. That's . . ."

"Selfless," Willa said. "Utterly selfless. And, by the way, it's also something that *none* of us would've thought to do. So it's not just Spence here who's an insensitive ass."

"Thanks, Willa," Spence said dryly.

She turned expectantly to Finn. "So? What happened?"

A terrible knot in his chest twisting, Finn snatched Spence's beer and knocked back the rest of the glass, not that it helped.

"Sure, help yourself," Spence muttered.

Everyone was looking at Finn, waiting.

He shook his head. "I can't. It's . . . private. What happened between us stays between us."

"Hey, this isn't Vegas," Spence said, and earned himself a slap upside the back of his head by Elle.

"Do you love her?" Willa demanded of Finn.

At the question, that knot in his chest tightened painfully. "That's not the problem. She . . . kept something from me."

"That sucks," Archer said, as Finn knew, understanding all too well the power of secrets and how they could destroy lives.

"No," Elle said, glaring at Archer. "No, you don't get to blindly side against her. She maybe had her reasons. Good ones," she said very seriously.

Something they knew that Elle understood *all* too well. She had secrets too, secrets they kept for her.

Archer met Elle's gaze and something passed between them. The fight might have ratcheted up a notch but Willa, always the peacemaker, spoke up. "Do you love her?" she repeated to Finn firmly.

Finn's mind scrolled through the images he had. Pru coming into the pub drenched and still smiling. Pru dragging him away from work to a softball game. Comforting him after a fight with Sean. Clutching a photo of her dead parents and still finding a smile over their memory. She'd brought a sense of balance to his life that had been sorely missing. It didn't matter whether she was standing behind the controls of a huge boat in charge of hundreds of people's safety or diving into a wave to save her dog, she never failed to make him feel . . . alive.

Just a single one of her smiles could make his whole day. The sound of her laugh did the same. And then there was the feel of her beneath him, her body locked around his when he was buried so deep that he couldn't imagine being intimate with anyone else ever again . . .

"Yes," he said quietly, not having to speak loud because the entire group had gone silent waiting on his answer. "I love her."

"Have you told her?" Willa asked.

"No."

"Why not?"

"Because . . ." Yeah, genius, why not? "And exactly how many people have *you* told that to?" he asked.

"Good one, going on the defensive," Elle said, not looking impressed.

Willa agreed with an eyeroll. "I mean I get that when you're playing sports or bragging to the guys and you need a six-foot-long dick," she said. "But this is Pru we're talking about."

"Six-foot-long dick?" Spence asked, grinning.

Willa waved him off and spoke straight to Finn. "Whatever she kept to herself, you did the same, Finn. You always do, even with us. You held back. You think she didn't feel that? Pru keeps it real and she's tough as nails, but she lost her family," she said, unknowingly touching on the very subject of the breakup. "She lost them when she was only eighteen and it left her alone in the world. And as you, more than anyone else knows all too damn well, it changes a person, Finn. It makes it hard to put yourself out there. But that's exactly what she does every single day without complaint, she puts herself out there."

I love you . . . Pru had whispered those words to him when he'd been drifting off to sleep that last night, and he'd told himself it was a dream. But he knew the truth. He'd always known.

She had more courage than he'd ever had.

"So presumably there was a fight," Elle said. "And then what? She walked?"

"And you let her?" Willa asked in disbelief. "Oh, Finn."

"You can fix it," Haley said softly. "You just go to her and tell her you were wrong."

Archer, eyes on Finn, put his hand on Haley's, stopping her. "I have a feeling we've got things backwards," he said.

"Ohhhh," Willa said, staring at Finn. "*You* walked."

Finn nodded. He'd walked. And she'd let him go without a fight.

Not that he'd given her any choice with the *I don't want to see you again* thing . . . *Fuck*. Willa was right. He'd been wielding around a six-foot dick, which made *him* the six-foot dick.

Willa looked greatly disappointed. "I don't understand."

Finn shook his head. "I know. But I'm not going to tell you more." He might have turned his back on Pru, but he wouldn't have these guys doing the same. She deserved their friendship. She deserved a lot more than that, but he was still so angry and . . . *shit*. Hurt. He pushed away from the table. "I've gotta go."

He hoped to be alone but Sean followed him back to his office. "What aren't you telling me?" he asked. "What is it she did that was so bad?"

Finn shook his head.

"Just tell me," Sean pushed. "So I can tell you that you're being an idiot and then you can go make it right."

Finn stared at him. "What makes you believe that this can be made right?"

Sean lifted a shoulder. "Because you taught me that love and family is where you make it, with who you make it. And even in this short amount of time, Pru's become both your love and your family."

That this was true felt like a knife slicing through him. "Sean, her parents were the ones in the car that killed dad. Her dad was the drunk driver."

Sean stared at him. "Are you shitting me?"

"I couldn't have made that up if I'd tried."

Sean sank to the couch. "Holy shit."

"Yeah. Listen, this stays right here in this room, yeah?"

Sean lifted his gaze and pierced Finn. "You're protecting her."

"I just don't want to hurt her," he said. At least not more than he already had . . .

"No, you're protecting her." Sean stood again. "The way I bet she was trying to protect you when she didn't tell you who she was."

Finn shook his head. "What are you saying?"

"That *you're* the dumbass, not her." Sean shook his head. "Look, I've got to get back out there. One of us has to have their head in the game, and trust me, no one's more surprised that it's me." He stopped at the door and turned back. "Listen, I get that you're too close to see this clearly, but take it from someone who lost as much as you did in that accident . . . we didn't lose shit compared to what Pru lost. She doesn't deserve this, not from you. Not from anyone."

And then he let himself out and Finn was alone. He went to his desk and pushed some paper around for half an hour, but it was useless. He was useless. He'd just decided to bail when Archer walked right in. "Ever hear of knocking?"

Archer paced the length of the office and then came to him, hands on hips.

"*What*?" Finn asked.

"I'm going to tell you something," Archer said. "And I don't want you to take a swing at me for it. I'm feeling pissed off and wouldn't mind a fight, but I don't want it with you."

Shit. "What did you do?" Finn asked wearily.

Archer grimaced. "Something I once promised you I wouldn't."

Finn stared at his oldest and most trusted friend in the world and then turned to his desk and poured them both some whiskey.

Archer lifted his glass, touched it to Finn's, and then they both tossed back.

Archer blew out a breath, set the glass down and met Finn's gaze. "I looked into her."

Archer had programs that rivaled entire government computer systems. When he said he'd looked into someone, he meant he looked *into* them. Inside and out. Upside down and right-side up. When Archer looked into someone, he could find out how old they were when they got their first cavity, what their high school P.E. teacher had said about them, what their parents had earned in a cash-under-the-table job four decades prior.

Archer didn't take this power lightly. He had a high moral code of conduct that didn't always line up with the rest of the world, but he'd never—at least not to Finn's knowledge—looked into his friends' pasts or breached their privacy.

He had, however, looked into Willa's last boyfriend, but that had been for a good reason.

"When?" Finn asked.

Archer gave him a surprised look. "Shouldn't the question be *what*? As in what did I find out?"

"You know who she is."

"Yes," Archer said. "Do *you*?"

"Why the fuck do you think I'm standing here by myself?" Finn asked.

Archer looked away for a beat and then brought his gaze back. "There's stuff you might not know."

"Like?"

"Like the fact that she's spent her life since the accident trying to right that wrong to everyone who was affected. That she, anonymously through an attorney, gave every penny she was awarded in life insurance to the victims of that accident, including you and Sean. She not only kept zero for herself, she sold the house she was raised in and used that money to help as well. She kept nothing, instead dedicated the following years to making sure everyone else was taken care of, whatever it took. She helped them find jobs, stay in college, find a place to live, everything and anything that was needed."

Finn nodded.

"You know?" Archer asked in disbelief. "So what happened between you two? She came clean and . . ."

"I got mad that she lied to me."

"You mean omitted, right? Because not telling you something isn't lying."

Finn swore roughly but whether that was because he was pissed or because Archer was right, he wasn't sure. "It was more than that. She had plenty of opportunities to tell me. If not when we first met, then certainly after we—"

Archer let that hang there a moment. "I'm thinking she had her reasons," he said quietly. "And it wasn't all that long. What, three weeks? Maybe she was working her way up to it."

Finn shook his head.

"Look, I'm not excusing what she did," Archer said. "She should've told you. We both know that. But we also both know that it's never that easy. She had a lot working against her, Finn. She's alone, for one. And she's got the biggest guilt complex going that I've ever seen."

Finn swore again and shoved his fingers in his hair. "She shouldn't feel guilty. The accident wasn't her fault."

"No," Archer said. "It wasn't. So I'm going to hope like hell you didn't let her think it was, no matter how badly she stepped on your ego."

"That's completely bullshit. This isn't about my ego."

"Your stupid pride then," Archer said. "I was with you when your dad died, don't forget. I know how your life changed. And I realize we're talking about a soul here and I don't like to speak ill of the dead, but you and I both know the truth. Yours and Sean's life changed for the better when your father was dead and buried."

Finn let his head fall back and he stared at the ceiling.

"You know what I think happened?"

"No," Finn said tiredly, "but I bet you're about to tell me."

Archer smiled grimly, and true to his nature, didn't hold back. "I think you fell and fell hard, and then you got scared. You needed an out and she gave it to you. Hell, she handed it to you on a silver platter. Well, congrats, man, you got what you wanted."

At his silence, Archer shook his head and headed for the door. "Hope you enjoy it."

Finn sat there stewing in his own frustration, both bad temper and regrets choking him. Enjoy it? He couldn't imagine enjoying anything, ever again. He looked around him. In the past, this place had been his home away from home.

But that feeling had migrated to Pru's place two floors up.

Just as his emotions had migrated to the same place, over softball, darts, hikes, and long conversations about what they wanted out of their hopes and dreams, often chased by the best sex he'd ever had.

He hadn't realized just how far gone he was when it came to her. Or how lost in her he'd allowed himself to become.

But he was. Completely lost in her, and lost without her.

He hadn't seen that coming. He'd assumed they'd continue doing what they'd been doing. Being together. Hell, it'd been so easy it'd snuck up on him.

And he'd fallen, hard.

That wasn't the surprise. No, that honor went to the fact that in spite of what she'd done, he was *still* in love with her.

And, he suspected, always would be.

Chapter 33

#LifeIsABowlOfCrazy

Pru was up on the roof with Thor, watching the fog roll in when she felt someone watching her. "I'm not going to jump, if that's what you're worried about," she said.

Archer stepped into her line of sight and crouched at her side. "Of course you're not, you're stronger than that."

She felt a ghost of a smile cross her lips. "You sure about that?"

"Very."

She turned her head and met his gaze, and saw that he knew everything. She sighed. "For what it's worth, I realize that I should've told him from day one, but I thought if he knew, he wouldn't give me the time of day and I wanted to help him."

"He doesn't like help."

"No kidding."

Archer smiled. "Finn's got the world in black or white. Like . . . the Giants or Dodgers. Home grown or imported. Us or them. For me, and for you too, I suspect, it's not so simple. He's a smart guy, though, Pru. He figures things out. He always does, in his own time."

She shook her head, kissed the top of Thor's, and rose. "That's sweet of you to say, but he won't. And I don't expect him to. I made a mistake, a really big one. And sometimes we don't get second chances."

"You should," Archer said.

"He's right." This was from Willa, who appeared from the fire escape and came over to them. "Everyone deserves a second chance."

"Where's Elle?" Archer asked.

"She couldn't climb the fire escape in her heels and she refused to leave them behind. She's taking the elevator."

Spence showed up next. He came from the fire escape like Willa and held Pru's gaze for a long beat before nodding and stepping out of the way, making room for the person hitting the rooftop right behind him.

Finn.

He climbed over with agility and ease and dropped down, coming straight for Pru without a glance at any of his closest friends.

Pru's heart stopped. Everything stopped including her ability to think. She took a step back, needing out of here. She wasn't ready to face him and pretend to be okay with the fact that they were nothing to each other now.

"Wait," Finn said, reaching for her hand. "Don't go."

God, that voice. She'd missed him so very much. Feeling lost, she looked at the others, who'd backed off to the other side of the rooftop to give them some privacy. "I need to go," she whispered to Finn.

"Can I say something first?" he asked quietly. "Please?"

When she nodded, he gently squeezed her hand in his. "You told me you made a mistake and that you wanted to explain," he said. "And I didn't let you. That was my mistake, Pru. I was wrong. We each made mistakes, not just you. And I get that we can't pretend that the mistakes didn't happen, but maybe we can use them to cancel each other out."

Her heart was a jackhammer behind her ribs, pounding too fast for her veins to keep up with the increased blood flow. "What are you saying?"

"I'm saying that I forgive you, Pru. And in fact, there was never anything to forgive. Can you forgive me?"

The jackhammer had turned into a solid lump, blocking her air passage. "It's . . ." She shook her head and tried desperately to keep hope from running away with her goose sense. "It can't be that easy," she whispered.

"Why not?" He reached for her other hand, taking advantage of her being stunned into immobility to tug her into him. Toe to toe now, he cupped her jaw. "Our last night together, you said something to me when I was drifting off." His gaze warmed. "You said it and then I felt your sheer panic, so I let it go. Or that's what I told myself. But the truth is that I was just being a coward."

She had to close her eyes at his gentle touch because just the callused pads of his fingers on her felt so right she wanted to cry.

"I love you, Pru," he said quietly but with utter steel.

Her eyes flew open and her breath snagged in her lungs. She hadn't realized how badly she'd needed to hear those words but . . . "Love doesn't fix everything," she said on a hitched breath. "There are rules and expectations in a relationship. And there are some things you can't take back. What I did was one of those things."

He shook his head. "Life doesn't follow rules or expectations. It's messy and unpredictable. And it turns out love is a lot like life—it doesn't follow rules or expectations either."

"Yes, but—"

"Did you mean what you said?" he asked. "Do you love me, Pru?"

She stared up at him and swallowed hard, but her heart remained in her throat, stuck there with that burgeoning hope she hadn't been successful at beating back. "Yes," she whispered. "I love you. But—"

"But nothing," he said fiercely, eyes lit with relief, affection. *Love.* "Nothing else matters compared to the fact that I managed to get the most amazing woman I've ever met to fall in love with me."

She slowly shook her head. "I'm not sure you're taking my concerns seriously."

"On the contrary," he said. "I'm taking you and your concerns *very* seriously. What you did was try to bring something to the life of two guys you didn't even know. You set aside your own happiness out of guilt and regret, when you had nothing to feel guilt and regret for. You lost a lot that day too, Pru. You lost more than anyone else. And there was no one to help you. No one to try to make things better for you."

Her throat closed. Just snapped shut. "Don't," she managed to whisper. "We can't go back."

"Not back, then. Forward." He gently squeezed her fingers in his. "I was wrong to walk away, so fucking wrong, Pru. What we had was exactly right and I'm sorry I ever made you doubt it."

Eyes still closed, she shook her head, afraid to hope. Afraid to breathe. He brought their entwined hands to his heart so that she could feel its strong, steady beat, as if he was willing his calm confidence about his feelings for her to soak in.

She let it, along with his warmth, appreciating more than she could say what his words meant to her. She hadn't realized how much she'd needed to hear him say he didn't blame her, that she had nothing to feel guilty for . . . It was as if he'd swept up all her broken pieces and painstakingly glued them back together, making her whole again. "Finn—"

"Can you live without me?" he asked.

Her eyes flew open. "What?"

"It's a simple question," he said. "Can you live without me?"

She stared past him at the others. Elle had arrived and maybe they were on the other side of the rooftop, but they were making absolutely zero attempt to hide the fact that they were hanging on every word.

"Pru," he said quietly.

She met his gaze again, chewing on her lower lip.

"Not talking?" he asked. "Fair enough. I'll go first. I can't live without you. Hell, I can't even breathe when I think about you not being in my life."

"You can't?"

"No." He gently squeezed her. "I live pretty simply, always have. I've got these interfering idiots—" He gestured to his friends behind them.

"Hey," Spence said.

"He's right," Willa said. "Now shh, I think we're getting to the good stuff."

Finn shook his head and turned back to Pru. "I thought they were all I needed and I felt lucky to have them. But then you came into my life and suddenly I had something I didn't even realize was missing. Do you know what that was?"

She shook her head.

"It's you, Pru. And I want you back. I want to be with you. I want you to be mine, because I'm absolutely yours. Have been since you first walked into my life and became my fun whisperer. And you can't tell me it's too soon for a relationship because we've been in one since the moment we met. We're together, we're *supposed* to be together. Like peanut butter and jelly. Like French fries and ketchup. Like peaches and cream."

"Like titties and beer," Spence offered.

Archer wrapped his arm around Spence's neck and covered the guy's mouth with his hand.

"No," Pru said.

Finn stared at her. "What?"

"No, titties and beer don't go together," she said. "But also no, I can't live without you either."

Finn stared at her for a beat, his eyes dark and serious and full of so much emotion she didn't know how to process it all. And then suddenly he smiled the most beautiful smile she'd ever seen. He took her hand, brought it to his mouth and brushed a kiss over her fingers before hauling her up against him.

"You ready for this?" His voice was rough, telling her how important this was. How important *she* was.

"For you?" she whispered against his jaw. "Always."

Epilogue

Two months later . . .

Finn let out a long breath as he parked. Santa Cruz was south of San Francisco and thanks to traffic, it'd taken them over an hour to get here. He got out of the car and came around for Pru.

"Keep the blindfold on," he said, as he'd been saying the entire drive.

Her fingers brushed over the makeshift blindfold—a silk handkerchief that they'd played with in bed the night before—and smiled. "I'm hoping we're heading toward a big cake."

"I told you to aim higher for your birthday."

"Okay," she said. "A nice dinner first and *then* a big cake."

"Higher," he said.

She let their bodies bump and she rubbed her hips suggestively to his. "Dinner, cake, and . . . that weekend away you promised me?" she asked hopefully.

"Getting warmer." He gripped her hips, holding her close enough that she could feel exactly what she did to him.

She smiled warmly, sexily, gorgeous . . . his everything. "Can I peek yet?"

His gut tightened as he turned her so that she faced the small Santa Cruz beach cottage in front of them. "Okay," he said. "You can look."

Pru tore off the blindfold and blinked open her big eyes, which immediately widened as she gasped. She stared at the place in front of her and then turned her head and stared at him for a beat before swiveling back to the house. "Oh my God," she breathed and put a hand to her chest. "This is—was—my parents' house. Where I grew up."

"I know," he said quietly.

Pru stared at the tiny place like it was a sight for sore eyes, like it was Christmas and Easter and every other holiday all in one. "I haven't been here in so long . . ." She looked at him again. "It's ours for the weekend?"

He took both of her hands in his so that she faced him. "The owners had it in a beach rental program." He slipped a key into her right hand.

"You rented it for me?" she breathed.

"Yes." He paused. "Except I didn't rent it. I bought it. It's in your name now, Pru."

Her mouth fell open. "What?"

"The owners live on the other side of the country. They instructed the management program to sell it if the opportunity arose." His heart was pounding and he hoped like hell he'd done the right thing here, that she would take it in the spirit he intended. "The opportunity arose."

Looking shaky, she took the few steps and unlocked the front door. Then she stepped inside. He followed, slowly, wanting to give her time if she needed it.

The place was furnished. Shabby beach chic. Tiny kitchen, two tiny bedrooms, one bathroom. He already knew this from his previous visit to scope everything out, but he followed as Pru walked through, quiet, eyes shuttered.

The postage-stamp-size living room made up for its tininess with the view of the Pacific Ocean about three hundred feet down a grassy bluff.

Pru walked to the floor-to-ceiling windows and looked out.

Finn waited, willing to give her all the time she needed. He was prepared for her to be mad at him for overstepping, but when she turned to him, her eyes didn't hold temper.

They held emotion, overfilling, spilling down her cheeks.

"Pru." He stepped toward her but she held up a hand.

"Finn, I can't accept this. We're just dating, it's not right—"

"Yeah, about that just dating thing." He tugged her into him—where he liked her best. Cupping her jaw, he tilted her face to his. "I don't want to just date anymore."

She blinked. "You bought me a house and now you're dumping me?"

"I bought you a house and now I'm asking you to take us to the next level."

She just stared into his eyes in shock and he realized something with his own shock. "You expected me to change my mind about you," he said.

She shook her head. "More that I'm afraid to want more from you. I don't want to be greedy."

Finn cupped her face, keeping her chin tilted so that she had to look at him. He needed her to see how serious he was. "Pru, don't you get it yet? I'm yours until the end of time."

She relaxed against him with a small smile. "Okay, that's good," she said a little shakily. "Seeing as I want whatever of you that you're willing to give me."

He let out a low laugh. "Everything. I want to give you everything, Pru."

Her eyes shined brilliantly. "You already have," she whispered and tugged his mouth to hers, kissing him with all the love he'd ever dreamed of and more. So much more.

When they broke for air, her eyes were still a little damp but also full of affection and heat. Lots of heat. "Did you really mean *everything*?" she asked.

"Everything and anything." To prove it, he pulled a small black box from his pocket where it'd been sitting for a week and flipped it open.

With shaking fingers, she took out the diamond ring. "Oh my God."

"Is that 'oh my God yes I'll marry you, Finn O'Riley?'" he asked.

She both laughed and cried. "Did you doubt it?"

"Well, I still haven't heard 'yes, Finn.'"

With a laugh, she leapt into his arms and spread kisses over his jaw to his mouth. "Yes, Finn!"

Grinning, he slid the diamond ring onto her finger.

She admired her hand. "So how pushy would it be of me to ask for something else right now?"

"Name it," he said.

She put her mouth to his ear. "I'd like some more of what you gave me last night. Right here, right now."

Remembering every single hot second of last night, he smiled. "Yeah?"

"Yeah." She bit her lower lip again, which didn't hide her smile. "Please?"

"Babe, anything you want, always, and you don't even have to say please."

#TheFirstCutIsTheDeepest

She hadn't even had breakfast yet and Willa Davis found herself elbow deep in puppies and poo. As owner of the South Bark Mutt Shop, she spent much of her day scrubbing, cajoling, primping, hoisting—and more cajoling. And she wasn't above bribing either.

To that end, she had a pet treat in every pocket of her cargos, which meant she smelled irresistible to any and all four-legged creatures within scent range.

Too bad there wasn't a biscuit guaranteed to make two-legged male creatures roll around at one's feet, begging for a kiss.

But then again, she'd been the one to put herself on a Man-Time-Out so she had no one to blame but herself for that.

"Wuff!"

This from one of the pups she was bathing. He wobbled in close and licked her chin.

"That's not going to butter me up," she said but it

totally did and unable to resist that face, she returned the kiss on the top of his cute little nose.

Stace, one of her regular grooming clients, had brought in her eight-week-old heathens—er, golden retriever puppies.

Six of them.

It was over an hour before her nine a.m. opening time but Stace had called in a panic because the pups had rolled in horse poo. God knew where they'd found horse poo in the Cow Hollow district of San Francisco. Maybe a policeman's horse had left an undignified pile in the street.

Two puppies, even three, were manageable, but six was bordering on insanity. "Okay, listen up," she said to the squirming, happily panting puppies in the large tub in her grooming room. "Sit."

One and Two sat. Three climbed up on top of both of them and shook, drenching Willa in the process. In the meantime, Four, Five, and Six made a break for it, paws pumping, ears flopping over their eyes, tails wagging wildly as they scrabbled, climbing all over each other like circus tumblers to get out of the tub.

"You little ingrates," she said, unable to keep from laughing at their antics. "Rory!" she called out. "Could use another set of hands." Or three . . .

No answer from her employee. Either the twenty-one-year-old had her headphones cranked up to make-me-deaf-please or she was on Instagram and didn't want to lose her place. "Rory!"

The girl finally poked her head around the corner, the tips of her ears red with embarrassment.

Yep. Instagram.

"Holy crap," Rory said, eyes wide at the sight of Willa, prompting her to look down at herself. Yep, her cargo pants splattered with suds and water and a few other questionable stains, at least one of which included cat yak from an earlier incident.

It didn't take a mirror to tell her that her short strawberry blonde hair had rioted and probably resembled an explosion in a mattress factory. "Give me a hand here?"

Rory dug right in, not shying from getting wet or dirty. She took on half of the wayward pups, and in a few minutes they had all of them out of the tub, dried, and back in their baby pen.

One through Five had fallen into the instant slumber that only babies and the very drunk could achieve. Six stayed stubbornly awake, climbing over his siblings trying to get back into Willa's arms.

Laughing, Willa scooped up the little man. His legs bicycled in the air, tail wagging faster than the speed of light, taking his entire hind end with it.

"Not sleepy, huh?" Willa asked.

He tried to lick her face.

"Oh no you don't," she said. "Don't think I don't know where that tongue's been." She carried him out front to the retail portion of her shop and set him into a baby pen with some puppy toys. "Now sit there and look pretty and bring in some customers, would you?"

The puppy pounced on a toy and got busy playing.

Willa shook her head and moved around, flipping on the lights out here. As she did, the shop came to life, mostly thanks to the insane amount of holiday decorations she'd put up the day before.

"It's only the first week in December and it looks like Christmas threw up in here," Rory said, coming into the room behind her.

Willa looked around at the shop that was an absolute dream come true for her. "But in a classy way, right?"

Rory sucked on her lower lip as she eyed the myriad of strings of lights and more boughs of holly than the North Pole could ever have. "Um . . . right."

Willa ignored the doubtful sarcasm. One, Rory hadn't grown up in a stable home. And two, neither had she. For both of them, Christmas had been a luxury that, like three squares and a roof, had usually been out of their realm of possibility. They'd each dealt with that differently.

Rory didn't need the pomp and circumstance of the holidays.

Willa did, desperately. So now at the ripe old age of twenty-seven, when after five years she finally had her shop in the black—well, mostly in the black—she went just a tad bit overboard for the holidays.

"Ohmigod," Rory said, staring at their newest cash register display. "Is that a rack of penis headbands?"

"No!" Willa said on a laugh. "It's reindeer antler headbands for cats and small dogs."

Rory stared at her.

Willa grimaced. "Okay, so maybe I went a little crazy—"

"A *little*?"

"Haha," Willa said, picking up a reindeer antler headband. It didn't look like a penis to her, but then again it'd been awhile since she'd seen one up close and personal. "These are going to sell like hotcakes, mark my words."

"What are you doing—don't put it on," Rory said in sheer horror as Willa did just that.

"It's called marketing," Willa said, rolling her eyes upward to take in the antlers jutting up above her head. Huh. "Do they really look like penises?" She paused. "Or is it peni? What's the plural of penis?"

"Pene?" Rory asked, and they both grinned.

"Clearly I'm in more need of caffeine than I realized," Willa said. "Tina's caffeine."

"I'll get it. I caught sight of her coming through the courtyard at the crack of dawn this morning wearing six-inch wedge sneakers with her hair teased to the North Pole, making her like eight feet tall. Can't wait to get a closer look at the perfection up close."

Tina used to be Tim, and everyone in the five-story, offbeat historical Pacific Heights building had enjoyed Tim—but they *loved* Tina. Tina rocked.

"I'll take one of her It's-Way-Too-Early-For-Life's-Nonsense coffees," Willa said, pulling cash from her pocket. Puppy treats bounced on the floor.

"And to think, you can't get a date," Rory said.

"I can get a date, I just pick the wrong ones. Hence the man-embargo. You know what? Tell Tina to make mine a double, I'm bonking already and the day hasn't even started."

Nodding, Rory headed toward the back door, where she'd run through the courtyard to Tina's coffee shop.

"Oh, and grab us each one of her muffins too." Willa paused. Tina made the best muffins on the planet. "Wait, make it two each. Or *three*. No. Shit, that's like the entire day's calories. *One*," she said firmly. "And make mine blueberry so it counts as a serving of fruit."

Rory was grinning. "So a coffee and a blueberry muffin to go, and a straitjacket on the side then?"

"You'd be in it right alongside of me, babe," Willa responded and Rory laughed in agreement.

When she left, Willa's smile faded. Each of her four employees were between the ages of eighteen and twenty-two, and they all had one thing in common.

The foster system had churned them up and spit them out, leaving them alone in the world.

Since Willa had been one of those lost girls herself, she collected them. She gave them jobs and advice that they only listened to about half the time.

She figured fifty percent was better than zero percent.

Rory had been with her the longest. The girl put up a good front of being wry and stoic, but she was struggling. She still had the faded markings of a bruise on the right side of her jaw where her ex-boyfriend had knocked her into a doorjamb.

Willa clenched her fists. Sometimes at night she dreamed about what she'd like to do to the guy. Castrating him was high on the list. She had a deal with one of the local vets so she could afford it too.

In any case, Rory deserved better. The girl was tough as nails on the outside but a tender marshmallow on the inside, and she'd do anything for Willa.

It was sweet but also a huge responsibility because Rory looked to Willa for her normal.

A daunting prospect on the best of days.

She checked on Six and found him asleep sprawled on his back, feet spread wide to show the world his most prized possessions.

Just like a man for you.

Next she checked on his siblings and found them asleep as well. Feeling like the mother of sextuplets, she tiptoed back out to the front and opened her laptop, planning to inventory the new boxes of supplies she'd received late the night before.

She was knee-deep in four different twenty-five-pound sacks of bird feed—she still couldn't believe how many people in San Francisco had birds—when someone knocked on the front glass door.

Damn. She glanced at the clock on the wall. It was only a quarter after eight but it went against the grain to turn away a paying customer so she straightened, swiped her hands on her thighs, and turned to the front.

A guy stood on her doorstep, mouth grim, expression dialed to Tall, Dark, and 'Tude-ridden, and unbelievably, her nipples stood up and took notice. This annoyed the crap out of her because her brain and body weren't in agreement on the no-man thing.

But damn, he was something, all gorgeous and broody and . . . she paused. There was something familiar about him. She headed to the door and froze as she got a closer look, her heart just about skidding to a stop as she realized . . . *she did know him.* "Keane Winters," she murmured. The only man on the planet who could make her feel good about her decision to give up men.

And in fact, if she'd only given them up sooner, say back on the day of the Sadie Hawkins dance in her sophomore year of high school when he'd stood her up, she'd have saved herself a lot of heartache in the years since.

On the other side of the door, Keane shoved his dark sunglasses to the top of his head, revealing dark chocolate eyes that she knew could melt when he was amused or aroused, or turn to ice when he was so inclined.

They were ice now. Catching her gaze, he lifted a cat carrier. A bright pink bedazzled carrier.

He had a cat. Her body wanted to soften at this knowledge because that meant on some level at least he had to be a good guy, right?

Luckily her brain clicked on, remembering everything, every little detail of that long-ago night. Like how she'd had to borrow a dress for the dance from a neighbor girl in her class who'd gleefully lorded it over her, how she'd had to beg her foster mother to let her go, how she'd stolen a Top Ramen from the locked pantry and eaten it dry in the bathroom so she wouldn't have to buy both her dinner and his, as was custom for the "backwards" dance.

"We're closed," she said through the glass, knowing he'd be able to hear her just fine.

Not a word escaped his lips. He simply raised the cat carrier another inch, like he was God's gift.

And he had been. At least in high school.

Wishing she'd gotten some caffeine before dealing with this, she blew out a breath and stepped closer, her eyes apparently caught in some sort of spinning vortex because they couldn't be torn away from his as she unlocked and then opened the door. "Morning," she said, determined to be polite. Yep, he was just another customer . . .

But when his face showed no sign of recognition at all, she found something even more annoying than finding this man on her doorstep.

He didn't remember her.

"I'm closed until nine," she said in her most pleasant voice, although a little bit of fuck-you *might* have escaped.

"I've got to be at work by then," he said. "I needed to be there fifteen minutes ago. I want to board a cat for the day."

Keane had always been big and intimidating. It was what had made him such an effective jock. He'd ruled on the football field, the basketball court, and the baseball diamond. The perfect trifecta. The perfect all-around package.

Every girl in the entire school—and also a good amount of the teachers—had spent an indecent amount of time eyeballing that package.

But just as Willa had given up men, she'd even longer ago given up thinking about that time, inarguably the worst years of her life. While Keane had been off breaking records and winning hearts, she'd been drowning under the pressures of school and work and basic survival.

It wasn't his fault that the memories were horrific. Nor was it his fault that just looking at him brought them all back to her. But emotions weren't logical. "I'm sorry," she said, "but I'm all full up today."

A muscle in his jaw clenched. Probably he wasn't used to being turned down. "I'll pay double."

He had a voice like fine whiskey. Not that she ever drank fine whiskey. Even the cheap stuff was a treat. And maybe it was just her imagination, but she was having a hard time getting past the fact that he was both the same and yet had changed. He was still tall, of course, and built sexy as hell, damn him. Broad shoulders, lean hips, biceps straining his T-shirt as he held up the cat carrier.

His T-shirt invited her to BITE ME.

She wasn't going to lie to herself, she kind of wanted to. *Hard.*

He wore faded ripped jeans on his long legs and scuffed work boots. His T-shirt only enhanced all those ripped muscles and every move he made exuded raw, sexual power and energy—not that she was noticing. Nor was she taking in his big, hard, toned body and expression that said maybe he'd already had a bad day.

Well, he could join her club.

At the thought, she mentally smacked herself in the forehead. No! There would be *no* club joining. She'd set boundaries for herself. She was Switzerland. Neutral. No importing or exporting of anything including sexy smoldering glances, hot body parts, *nothing.*

Period.

Especially not with Keane Winters, thank you very much. Which would make this easy because she didn't board animals for the general public anyway. Yes, she sometimes boarded as special favors for clients, a service she called "fur-babysitting" because her capacity here was too small for official boarding. If she agreed to "babysit" overnight as a favor, she had to take her boarders home with her, so she was extremely selective.

And handsome men who'd once been terribly mean boys who ditched painfully shy girls after she'd summoned up every ounce of her courage to ask them out to a dance did not fit her criteria. "I don't board—" she started, only to be interrupted by an unholy howl from inside the cat carrier.

It was automatic for her to reach for it, which Keane readily released with what looked to be comic-like relief.

Turning her back on him, Willa carried the carrier to the counter, incredibly aware of Keane following her through her shop, of the way he moved with an unusually easy grace for such a big guy.

The cat was continuously howling now so she quickly unzipped it, expecting the animal inside to be dying, given the level of unhappiness it had displayed.

The ear-splitting noise immediately stopped and a huge Siamese cat blinked vivid blue eyes owlishly up at her. She had a pale, creamy coat with a darker facial mask that matched her black ears, legs, and paws.

"Well, aren't you beautiful," Willa said and slipped her hands into the box.

The cat immediately allowed herself to be lifted, pressing her face into Willa's throat for a cuddle.

"Aw," Willa said softly, involuntarily. "It's all right now, I've got you. You just hated that box, isn't that right?"

"What the ever-loving hell," Keane said, hands on hips now as he glared at the cat. "Are you kidding me?"

"What?"

He scowled. "My great-aunt dropped her off with me last night. Sally's sick and can't care for the cat right now, so I'm up."

Okay, so that was a pretty nice thing he was doing but she refused to let that soften her any further.

"The minute my aunt left," Keane said, "this thing went gonzo."

Willa looked down at the cat, who gazed back at her, quiet, serene, positively angelic. "What did she do?"

Keane snorted. "What *didn't* she do would be the better question. She hid under my bed and tore up my mattress. Then she helped herself to everything on the counters, knocking stuff to the floor, destroying my laptop and tablet and phone all in one fell swoop. And then she . . ." He trailed off and appeared to chomp on his back teeth.

"She . . . ?" Willa prompted.

"Took a dump in my favorite running shoes."

Willa did her best not to laugh out loud and say "good girl." "She's just upset to be away from home and probably missing your aunt. Cats are creatures of habit. They don't like change." She spoke to him without taking her gaze off the cat, not wanting to look into those eyes that didn't recognize her because she might be tempted to pick one of the tiaras displayed on her counter and hit him over the head with it. "Will your aunt be taking her back soon?"

"Tonight if there's a God," he said.

"What's her name?" she asked.

"Petunia, but I'm going with Pita. Pain in the ass."

Willa stroked along the cat's back and Petunia pressed into her hand for more. Then she began to purr, the sound low and rumbly, her eyes slitted with pleasure as Willa continued to pet her.

Keane let out a breath as the purring filled the room. "Unbelievable. Tell me the truth, you're wearing catnip as perfume, right?" he asked.

She raised an eyebrow. "Is that the only reason you think she'd like me?"

"When it comes to that antichrist?" he asked. "Yes."

Okay then. Willa opened her mouth to end this little game and tell him that she was too busy today to board anything, but she looked into Petunia's deep-as-the-ocean blue eyes and felt her heart stir. Crap. "Fine," she heard herself say. "If you can provide proof of rabies and FVRCP vaccinations, I'll take her for today only."

"Thank you," he said with such genuine feeling, she glanced up at him.

A mistake.

His dark eyes had warmed considerably. "Do you always wear X-rated headbands?" he asked, gesturing to her head.

She'd completely forgotten she was wearing it. "It's not what you think," she informed him and resisted the urge to yank it off and throw it at him. "It's reindeer antlers."

"Whatever you say." He was smiling now, the rat fink bastard. At her expense, of course.

"My name's Keane," he said. "Keane Winters."

He waited, clearly expecting her to tell him her name but she hesitated. If she told him and he suddenly recognized her, he'd also remember exactly how pathetic she'd once been. And if he *didn't* recognize her then that meant she was even more forgettable than she'd thought and she would have to throw the penis head-band at him after all.

"And you are . . . ?" he asked, rich voice filled with amusement at her pause.

You know what? What the hell. "Willa Davis," she said and watched him very carefully.

But there was no change in his expression whatsoever. Forgettable then—and she grinded on her back teeth.

"I appreciate you doing this for me," he said.

Uh huh. She had to consciously unclench her teeth to speak. "I'm not doing it for you. I'm doing it for Petunia," she said, wanting to be crystal clear. "And you'll need to be back to pick her up before closing."

Five extremely long minutes later he'd filled out the required form, provided the information she needed after a quick call to his aunt, and—with one last amused look at her reindeer antlers, aka penis-headband—walked out the door.

Willa watched him go.

"Are you looking at his ass?" Rory asked, coming to stand next to her, casually sipping her coffee as she handed over Willa's.

Yes, she was looking at his ass. To her eternal annoyance, it was a pretty great one too. How unfair was that? The least he could have done was get pudgy. "Absolutely not."

"Well then, you're missing out," Rory said.

"He's too old for you."

"He's twenty-nine. What," she said at Willa's raised brow. "So I looked at his driver's license and did the match, that's not a crime. And anyway, you're right, he's old."

"Hey. I'm only a few years behind him you know."

"Yeah well, you're old too," Rory said and flashed a grin.

The equivalent to a declaration of love.

"And anyway," the girl went on. "For the record, I was noticing his ass for *you*."

"I gave up men, remember? It's who I am right now."

"Who you are right now is a woman imitating a chicken, but hey, if you want to let your past bad judgment calls rule your world and live like a nun, you'll get no argument from me."

"Gee," Willa said dryly. "Thanks."

"But I reserve the right to question your IQ. I hear you lose IQ points when you get old. Maybe you should start taking that Centrum Silver or something."

Willa threw the penis headband at her but she, being a youngster and all, ducked in time.

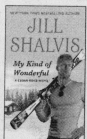
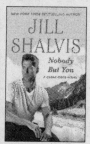